SECOND SKIN

Praise for *The Lizard*

'A terrific, atmospheric thriller. Taut, compelling, masterfully constructed. Outstanding' William Boyd

'Intrigue, action and excitement...a terrific debut' Charles Cumming

'Bruce Lockhart ramps up the tension and the result is a read-at-a-sitting page-turner' Best Recent Crime Thrillers, *Guardian*

'This impressive debut is written with huge verve, the story twists and turns like a malign serpent' *Daily Mail*

'You'll be swept up in the hedonistic pursuits and the sun-drenched world of sex and drugs, compelling you to finish this book in one go' *Marie Claire*

'Impressive .... this riotous chase through the glories of the Greek Islands is entertaining'

Best Recent Thrillers, *Observer*

'Wicked, dramatic and dripping in the intensity of summer heat' *Women's Weekly*

'This novel is horrible, atmospheric and gripping' *Literary Review*

'The heady cocktail of kaleidoscopic plot twists and slick writing make this a sure-fire winner for fans of fast-paced thrillers' *LoveReading*

'Reminiscent of Alex Garland's *The Beach* this is pitch perfect escapism to effortlessly take you away from it all' *Living Magazine*

'An incredibly gripping tale, awakened by Bruce-Lockhart's vivid imagination' *The Field*

SECOND SKIN

Dugald Bruce-Lockhart

MUSWELL
PRESS

First published by Muswell Press in 2024
Copyright © Dugald Bruce-Lockhart 2024
This edition published 2025

Typeset in Bembo by M Rules
Printed by CPI Group (UK) Ltd

Dugald Bruce-Lockhart has asserted his right
to be identified as the author of this work in accordance
with under the Copyright, Designs and Patents Act, 1988

A CIP catalogue record for this book
is available from the British Library

ISBN: 9781068684456
eISBN: 9781739123888

Our authorised representative in the EU for product safety is Easy
Access System Europe, Mustamäe tee 50, 10621 Tallinn, Estonia
gpsr.requests@easproject.com

Muswell Press
London N6 5HQ
www.muswell-press.co.uk

For Penny

Prologue

The last time I travelled to Greece, I ended up in jail.

So I made a promise to myself – well, two, in fact.

Firstly, I'd never let love get the better of me again. It was an addiction, an affliction – a compulsion to define myself through the eyes of someone else; and it had led me a merry, bloody dance. Secondly, I wouldn't return to the country for many, many years. To set foot again in a land where I almost lost my life – when even the mere hint of jasmine, pine trees, or thyme conjured a crippling flashback of slit throats, twisted limbs and vomit – was a dragon I had no need to slay. My therapist agreed. I was only twenty-one; everything in good time.

Willpower and judgement, however, are fickle friends.

When I accept forbidden fruit, is it because I have no will to resist, or an unshakeable compulsion to partake?

Does judgement ever stand a chance in the face of obsession?

If the mind is but the sum of electrical stimuli, governed by chemical stimuli, dependent on the moment-to-moment accumulation of random information dating back to the nanosecond we left the womb – perhaps, even before – then, in one sense, our response to any given situation is pre-ordained.

Begging the question: are we ever truly in charge?

Five years after my release from the Athens penitentiary, I reneged on both of my well-intentioned promises; and for that, I accept full responsibility. No one forced me. I had a choice – or, so I'd like to think.

As for the ensuing consequences: the lies, the violence and the slaughter – were they also on me?

The jury is out.

Not that it matters.

I wash my hands. I still see the blood.

1

July, 1994

A month away from my 26th birthday, I was temping for a lifestyle magazine in a fifth-floor office overlooking London's Drury Lane; an airless, claustrophobic environment at the best of times, with its Formica desks, fax-machines and phones sprawling beneath a stratum of cigarette smoke. Terry, my esteemed colleague from Kent had been moved to my workstation to help improve my telesales technique, but the oppressive heat was taking its toll on even our most experienced players and charitable thoughts were thin on the ground.

'You're too nice,' he muttered, stubbing out his cigarette and leaning back in his swivel-chair. 'Gotta be more of an arsehole.'

'Sure,' I replied, wondering if Terry 'Top Gun' Keeley, had a life beyond Millpool Publications' nicotine-stained walls.

'Treat 'em like the enemy,' he added, flicking the fake Rolex on his wrist. 'Get inside their head and fuck 'em over. Like a game of chess.'

'Right.'

It was best to stick to one word answers with Terry.

'You're not here to make friends,' he continued, toying with his Zippo lighter, as the room darkened. 'You're here because you wanna make some dosh.'

A sudden gust of wind rattled the window, heralding the imminent arrival of a summer storm.

'Yup,' I replied, nodding enthusiastically; resisting the urge to inform him the only reason I was undertaking such soulless work was because my contract teaching English in Japan had been pushed back to September, leaving me in the lurch over the summer. Stupidly, I'd fallen for the 'no experience necessary' blurb, along with the promise of 'huge commission potential', rather than opt for honest graft on a building site, or a bar job. Too late now, I'd committed.

'Just chess, man,' he sneered. 'Start using your queen and stop pissing around with the foot-soldiers. Pawns are there to be sacrificed, yeah?' He stuffed the cigarette into the corner of his mouth and, picking up his phone – his 'Walther PPK' – placed another call.

Truth was, chess was something I was good at. Chess, I could do. But I'd been fingering my metaphorical kings and queens for three weeks straight and had failed to make a single solid move. Telesales was simply not my thing.

Then all of a sudden, the telephone rang.

I stared at it in disbelief. Red flashing light, rhythmic vibration on the desk . . .

Thomas Cook?

Condé Nast?

'Want me to take it?' Terry offered, sucking on his cigarette. 'Split the commission.' As he reached forward for my phone, I batted away his hand, grabbed the receiver and sucked in a lungful of smoky air.

'Millpool Leisure Publications,' I rasped, trying not to cough. 'Alistair Haston.'

'Good morning,' came the reply.

Male. Middle-Eastern? A slight echo suggested international.

'Hi,' I countered.

Pawn to king four.

'Mister Haston,' exclaimed the caller, in a tone that was neither interrogative nor statement.

The Ruy Lopez opening. Predictable. Safe.

'Hit me.' I snapped, cutting to the chase.

Terry nodded enthusiastically.

Encouraged, I stuck a foot up on the desk, swivelled away towards the window, where a pigeon sought shelter from the first fat drops of rain.

'You want to review your options,' I continued, wedging the receiver between my shoulder and ear as I reached behind me for the stack of magazines. 'Front cover's gone. Back cover under offer ... centre-page spread?'

'This is mister Manolis,' the caller replied.

Manolis? Had to be Greek.

Waiting for him to continue (Terry's rule was never to speak unless you had to – 'let 'em hang themselves'), I swivelled back to my desk, wondering when I'd placed a call to Greece, and to whom. Olympic Airways? Club Med?

'Just trying to recall when we last spoke,' I said, giving in and shuffling a stack of paper, as if searching through a copious Rolodex. 'If I'm not mistaken, it was, er ...'

'This is the first time we are speaking.'

'Of course.'

Whoever I had called previously – some underling – I was now talking to a key player; someone who had the power to change company policy, if only I could persuade him.

'How can I turn things around for you today?' I'd heard Terry use that one.

Nothing but static.

Stalemate.

As a flicker of lightning drew my attention to the window, I wondered if I'd be better off admitting defeat and coming clean, but then, out of the corner of my eye, I noticed Terry watching me, a lopsided grin plastered across his pointy features. When I spun around to face him, he dropped his head, scratched the back of his ear and began to dial.

Unless . . .

'I'm still here, mister Manolis,' I exclaimed, peering around the office, noticing several heads were turned in my direction. 'What's on your mind?'

Humiliate-the-rookie-day, was it?

'I am calling on behalf of my daughter,' Manolis said, finally.

'And how the devil is she?' I jeered, scanning the room for the culprit.

'She is not well.'

'I AM sorry to hear that, mister Manolis.'

'Kristos.'

'Kris-Kross? Of course,' I replied, stifling a laugh as I spun back to the window, noticing that the pigeon now had company. 'Well, Kris-Kross, I hate to break this to you, but, shit happens.' Over at a table by the door, several more of my illustrious colleagues were studying me with an air of smug amusement.

'Amara cannot talk,' he said finally. 'Because of her injuries.'

At which point, I saw my boss returning from the toilets, heading in my direction. Time to wrap it up: 'It's been a pleasure, Kris-Kross, but I'd better get back to washing my hair.' And then, to cut to the chase: 'Wanker.'

I turned, ready to slam down the phone, but at the last moment stopped, receiver hovering in mid-air. 'Did you say Amara?'

'My daughter.'

Hovering briefly at my side, my boss patted me on the shoulder then passed on by, while behind him on the windowsill the pigeons shuffled to a corner and began to copulate.

Amara . . .

I'd only ever known one person by that name: the actress I met in the Greek islands, summer of '88 . . .

'You're calling from Naxos?' I asked, tentatively.

Amara's father had a restaurant in Naxos. I'd been there — before she and I . . .

'Athens,' he grunted.

I hung suspended in a curtain of cigarette smoke as an image presented itself: Amara, standing at the docks, shielding her eyes from the setting sun as the police-launch pulled away from its moorings and transported me captive towards Paros. In another life . . .

'Mister Haston?'

A life I'd all but erased from memory.

'She has been in an accident.'

Across from me, Terry held his thumb held out horizontally like a Roman Emperor waiting to give his verdict.

I shook my head and turned away. 'Forgive me Mister Manolis, is she okay?'

I just called her father a wanker.

He proceeded to recount how Amara, her husband and their son had been on holiday south of the capital. Amara had taken the child to the beach, and on returning, she had skidded and driven the car off the road. Both she and her son were found unconscious and had to be cut free by a fire and rescue team. They were now recovering in hospital in Athens.

'I'm so sorry,' I replied, finally. 'That's — awful.'

'It is a difficult time,' he said flatly.

'I see,' I replied, not seeing at all, wondering also how he had managed to find me.

'When accidents like this happen,' he continued, 'there is always an investigation.'

Then again, Amara knew I'd been to St Andrews Uni. They'd have passed on my home contact details — got my work number off the answerphone.

'What I am trying to say,' he continued, 'is that they can

be very thorough. And it is only a matter of time before they contact you directly.'

A distant rumble of thunder was followed by a spatter of rain against the windowpane.

'Who, sorry?'

'The police.'

Baffled, I turned in time to see the pigeons untangle themselves and shuffle to opposite ends of the window sill.

'Mister Haston, you must understand ...' he continued, breaking off to cough into the mouthpiece. 'Amara's husband is not the father of the boy.'

The heavens opened, and the birds took wing.

'You are.'

Unable to think straight, I feigned illness to my boss and, taking leave of the grimy publications office, walked five miles home to Putney in sheeting rain. I hoped the elemental weather might help me work out what the fuck I was supposed to do with such information, and, more to the point, whether I might be facing financial or legal responsibility for the child.

At Battersea bridge, none the wiser, I ducked out of the storm into a phone box and put in a call to the to the Citizens Advice Bureau. The bored official informed me I wouldn't have any parental or financial responsibilities unless my name was on the birth certificate. For my name to be on the certificate, I would have had to have been there, in person, to sign it. Which, of course, I wasn't – I'd been in St Andrews finishing off my finals.

So, that was that – legally speaking.

Still clueless as to what, if anything, I should do next, I continued my sodden journey along the Thames path, replaying the conversation I'd had with Amara's father over in my head, wondering if, in fact, there was absolutely nothing to be done. He'd made it clear that any input or participation on my behalf was neither expected, nor welcome. After dropping the bombshell, he had simply given me his address and telephone number in Athens, saying that any attempt at communication was to be made through him, and him only – after which he'd promptly hung up. It seemed to have been a kind of bizarre courtesy call; the family making contact in light of an impending police investigation – to save embarrassment, perhaps, on both sides, in the event of me finding out via a third party.

As I reached Barnes, the rain backed off, and patches of blue sky broke through the cloud cover.

Stopping at the railings on the riverbank, I gazed dumbly down into the swollen flood waters of the Thames and, following the meandering path of flotsam spiralling in the current, noticed a twig caught up in a backwater eddy. Every time it swung out towards the main flow of the river, it was pulled back towards the bank, before being sent spinning back around again – stuck in an endless, fruitless circuit.

After several minutes of bobbing and weaving, however, the twig was struck by a floating coconut shell, knocking it off its path and pushing it into the main current, where it promptly shot off downstream, free at last.

Which was when it hit me:

That phone call . . . the accident – what if it had been a sign?

What if it was it the universe telling me my one-night stand with Amara had not been an end, but a beginning? A chance to rewind the clock and resume a love story that had been squashed before it had ever had the chance to blossom?

Was it possible Amara was the one?

She was the mother of my child, after all.

Turning away from the river with a fluttering heart, I pushed my way back through the steaming undergrowth and, quickening my pace, set off again along the tow path in the direction of Putney, in search of a second opinion.

*

'You're gonna drop everything and fuck off to Greece?'

Flipping the steaks in the frying pan, my flatmate, Vince, began to jig along to Crowded House's 'Italian Plastic'.

'I'm getting a sense of déjà vu,' he added.

'Last thing you need is me crashing the party,' I murmured, regretting having broached the subject. 'I'll get out of your hair.'

Vince had listened attentively enough to begin with, but it was becoming apparent my oldest friend and confidant wasn't best placed for a heart-to-heart. After a 'working lunch' with several of his well-heeled colleagues from his father's PR firm in Kensington, he'd taken the rest of the day off and persuaded his latest accessory, Kate, to join him first for drinks in Mayfair, then dinner at home. Very much the third wheel, I was cramping his style.

'Bollocks, have some wine,' he objected. 'It's a South African Pinot Noir.'

In a show of support, Kate drew herself up from behind the table and took a fresh glass from the counter. 'I think you should,' she said, fingering her black turtle-neck. 'Sounds like you need it.' Without waiting for my answer, she stretched cat-like over the table and filled my glass half way, her dark brown locks falling forwards to hide her fine features.

A blue-eyed Audrey Hepburn with long hair – except, taller.

'To help you out,' I conceded, noting her boozy slurring had the effect of giving her a slight accent – a transatlantic twang.

'Here's the thing,' Vince continued, testing the peppercorn sauce. 'Amara never planned on telling you. And there's every chance the police won't get in touch. Why should they? It's not like you were there, or had anything to do with the accident. Leave it. Not your concern.'

'I'm the father of her child,' I protested.

This was the line I'd decided to take with Vince: that my intended departure was to clear up the issue of paternity and make sure I had no legal responsibilities to the boy. He didn't

10

need to know the real reason. When it came to matters of the heart, Vince was a philistine.

'You don't know that for sure.'

'Why would she lie?'

Vince took another sip of the sauce and licked his lips. 'I mean, it could be the other guy's—'

Kate waited a moment for Vince to elaborate, then turned to me. 'Who's the other guy?'

Vince threw me a look of apology.

'It's not Ricky's,' I replied. 'The minute he returned to Naxos he was arrested. Before that, he and Amara hadn't seen each other for days – weeks, even.'

Vince pulled a face. 'Or so she told you.'

'I can go into the garden if – well . . . you'd rather,' said Kate, taking a pull on her wine and drawing in her chair, suggesting it was the last thing she intended.

'No need,' I replied. 'It's all out in the open.'

As he topped up my glass, I brought Kate up to speed; a story I'd told countless times over the last five years. How I ended up spending six months in an Athens penitentiary; how a charismatic Australian called Ricky had offered me work on the island of Paros and, with the help of a few dodgy individuals in the local police, framed me for murder; how, with the help of Amara, Ricky's on-off girlfriend, we'd tried to capture him on Naxos, but failed. And how I ended up killing him in self-defence while protecting my ex-girlfriend, Ellie.

As always, I held back on the finer details of the nature of Ricky's murders – that his victims had been killed on camera, usually in the act of sex, in what was known as 'snuff films'. The trick, according to my therapist, was to come up with a conclusive summary which would both satisfy curious well-wishers and shut them up at the same time.

'Shit,' said Kate, eventually.

'Shit, indeed,' echoed Vince, serving up the steaks onto two plates. 'Anyway, my point is: you don't know for sure the baby isn't Ricky's. And if she really was as bohemian as you always made her out to be, there could be other contenders.'

Kate coughed a mouthful of wine back into her glass. 'I think a woman knows whose baby she's carrying.'

'What I meant, was—'

'Her father telephoned Alistair because the police might get nosey,' she said, cutting him off. 'She's not going to lie to the police. Not with DNA testing.'

Picking up a plate in each hand, Vince turned and faced Kate.

'This isn't about the boy,' he began, a grin spreading across his face. 'He's after Amara.'

From the stereo, the chorus of 'How Will You Go?' rolled through the sitting room.

Vince was spot on, of course. But no way was I going to admit it.

'Am I right?' he added, setting down the plates.

'We had a connection,' I ventured, twisting sideways in my seat. 'No doubt about it.'

'Bollocks – he thinks he's in love.'

'She's just reaching out to him, Vince,' Kate said, frowning at her boyfriend. 'He should do the right thing – go out and show some support.'

'Not true,' Vince objected. 'Her father's phone call was a formality – you said it yourself, Haston.'

'I owe her,' I replied, catching Kate's eye. 'If it weren't for her help that summer, who knows what might have happened.'

'Spin it how you like,' said Vince, sitting down and taking a sip of his drink. 'You're just looking for a project.'

'A project?'

Kate turned to me. 'Is he always this rude?'

'Soon as you get yourself a proper career and sort your act out,' Vince continued, carving into the meat, 'trust me, the right woman will come running.'

'A proper career?' I objected.

'Really, Vince?' Kate snapped. 'Is that how it works?'

'For a start, the woman has a husband,' Vince declared, forking a chunk of blood-oozing steak into his mouth. 'You don't think he'll have something to say about it?

'Alistair's just found out he has a son,' said Kate, incredulous. 'If I was him, I'd sure as hell want to go over and sort it out.'

'Sort what out?'

'Clarify . . . confirm it.'

'Then ask her to send confirmation,' said Vince, with his mouth full. 'Seriously, I can't believe we're even having this conversation.'

Kate pushed back her chair.

'Personally, Alistair, I think you should go,' she muttered, before knocking back her wine. 'If nothing else, to get away from your prick of a flatmate.'

'What's bitten you?' came Vince's riposte, as Kate stood up and made her way across the sitting room.

At the doorway into the corridor, she turned again and glared at her boyfriend.

'I came running?'

Contrite at last, Vince leaped to his feet.

But Kate had gone.

While Vince joined Kate in the bathroom with the hope of salvaging the rest of their evening, I sat out in the garden with a can of beer and, breaking a two-year abstinence, chain-smoked my way through a pack of Vince's Silk Cuts, staring up at the airliners on their final approach to Heathrow.

My best friend's caustic behaviour was nothing unusual. After a few drinks, he would often resort to trying to fix me and sort my life out with lashings of one-sided advice. He didn't like the idea of me working from job to job, free at any moment to set off around the world while he remained chained to his desk in nine-to-five purgatory. Strong-armed into his dad's family business straight after uni, he had all the trappings of success: a high-salaried job, his own house, a Porsche convertible . . . but no life experience to go with it.

He was jealous – plain and simple.

But he also cared about me. He'd been there to pick up the pieces when I'd returned from Athens after my release from prison; he insisted on me paying him only a modicum of rent. He was merely being protective, in the way an older brother might.

On paper, his arguments against me returning to Greece made sense. But that was Vince. He was all about toeing the line, risk aversion and spread sheets.

Yes, Amara had a husband – but the marriage had almost certainly been one of convenience. A single mum, at the age of not even twenty? Of course she was going to settle for security; a pair of safe hands. Her controlling father had most likely hastened on the union. He'd interfered elsewhere in her life – stopped her from seeing me after I went to prison; put an end to her dreams of becoming a professional actress by not allowing her to go to drama school.

A low-flying Jumbo passed overhead, its silhouette a blinking triangular behemoth sliding westwards over the neighbouring rooftops.

Stubbing out my cigarette in the empty beer can, I hauled myself to my feet and turned to face the house.

For all I knew, Amara was thinking the same as me: that fate had offered us a second chance. An opportunity to pick up where we left off and continue what should have been.

If I was back in two days, chastened and humiliated – so be it. If I was to remain the estranged father to a boy who wanted nothing to do with me – so be it.

But was I prepared not even to investigate?

Sorry Vince, but – fuck you.

14

2

The Olympic Airways 737 resumed its cruising altitude and cabin crew returned to their duties, serving up much-needed refreshments. Skies had been clear over France, but conditions deteriorated rapidly crossing the Alps when we flew through a succession of thunderstorms, forcing the shaking aircraft ever higher in order to avoid wind shear. Now fairer conditions had returned, passengers seized the opportunity to ease their jitters with a helping hand from the drinks trolley.

Flicking on the overhead light, I dug out my copy of *Let's Go Greece* and leafed through the extensive section on Athens in an attempt to locate Amara's father's address – 102 Ion Street – but without success. I did establish the relevant district, however. Kallithea was a residential area in the southern part of Athens, just to the east of the port, Piraeus. I made note of several cheap hotels and a youth hostel in the vicinity of three of the larger hospitals listed, pinpointed two police stations, and found the location of The Royal Bank of Scotland – in case I needed an injection of emergency cash.

Quite how Amara's father would react when I knocked on his door, I had no idea.

I'd tried to give him the heads up. Before leaving for

Heathrow to join the queue for the standby flights, I rang his home in Athens and connected with an elderly woman who had an incomprehensibly thick accent and spoke no English whatsoever. Hashing together the little Greek I could remember, I explained I was a friend of Amara's, coming over from England to see her. *Did she have a telephone number for the hospital?* At which point she became excitable again, repeating the word *'apopse'* ('tonight') over and over, before hanging up. Baffled by her fervour, I came away confident there'd at least be someone home when I arrived, if not Amara's father himself.

I buried the *Let's Go Greece* back in my rucksack and turned to the window.

The sky above was a deep cobalt blue, melting into a streaking blood orange towards the horizon. Below us, the air had thickened with the onset of evening. No tell-tale city lights. A uniform slate-grey. Must have been over the Adriatic, somewhere off the Dalmatian coast.

Catching my eye in the reflection of the window, my thoughts returned to Amara and our candlelit dinner beneath the stars, on the rooftop of her father's house in Naxos:

Legs touching in the shadows of the flickering yellow light; fingers brushing as we shared a humble plate of olives ... discussing Shakespeare, Yeats, and the nature of obsession ... And in the morning, her lying naked in the four-poster bed, sheets down below her breasts; hair tumbling over the pillows ... the aroma of honeysuckle drifting in on the night air, mingling with the scent of sex ...

Before it had all been taken away.

By Ricky.

Turning away from the window, I switched off the overhead light and gazed down the aircraft cabin.

I hadn't thought of the Australian in over two years, let alone spoken his name out loud. He'd been banished, extinguished from my mind – thanks to the help of my therapist. He'd visited

16

me, of course, in the early days – and nights. Once I'd returned to university; once normal life had resumed and everyone else had forgotten my ordeal. The nightmares had increased tenfold after I'd found the Greek postcard waiting for me in my cubby hole at St Salvator's Hall. No postage stamp, and bearing only two words: 'Missing You'. Signed 'Rx'. For weeks, I deluded myself that Ricky was still alive, that he was coming for me. That he might at any moment crawl out from under my bed and finish what he'd started. Of course, he never materialised. My mind was the adversary, not Ricky. Ricky was dead. No one could have survived those injuries. I knew it. The world at large knew it. The postcard had evidently been delivered to my room by mistake. Post was always getting mixed up in the antiquated postal system in the lobby; such were the foibles of a uni that prided itself on immutable tradition.

Just then, a flight attendant came into view down the aisle on her return journey with the trolley. Catching her eye, I ordered another drink.

She smiled and gave me two.

We touched down at Athens International Airport just after 9 p.m.

Not having any luggage to collect, I bypassed Baggage Reclaim and joined the queue at customs, wondering if they'd pull me over.

Before long, impatience gave way to a fretful restlessness, and I found myself scanning the hall for signs of police activity.

Had my arrival been clocked?

Was that why it was taking so long?

I'd been proved innocent of all charges from the fateful summer of '88, and my name cleared, but who knew what details remained on the police database? Computers were prone to error ... humans were prone to error. And if the police investigation was already aware of me being father to Amara's injured child, it was even more likely my name would surface on their radar. Then what? I'd be questioned at the very least. Detained . . . searched . . .

With each shuffling step closer to Border Control, the paranoia grew. I began to recognise faces in the queue. People were whispering about me . . . pointing, laughing. The officer in the booth: despite his Ray Ban sunglasses, I was convinced I'd seen him before . . . Leo, from the campsite on Paros? Same set of the shoulders . . . the shaggy mane of hair. No! he was more like the guard from the Paros police station – the man who attacked me in my cell . . .

But that was impossible, he'd been executed.

Knifed to death in the caves off Antiparos . . .

As I would have been, had I not murdered the murderer.

It wasn't murder – it was self-defence . . .

A hand on my back snapped me out of my stupor and I whipped around, ready to smash the owner in the face.

An elderly lady.

A kind, elderly lady.

'Are you alright, dear?' she croaked, recoiling at my twisted face.

It took me an eternity to find the words, but then I apologised and assured her I was just a little tired. When she offered me a packet of Aspirin, I muttered my profuse thanks and, crimson with embarrassment, turned back to face the front of the queue.

How fucking embarrassing.

When I eventually handed over my passport, the burly official barely looked at me.

It was the same going through customs: no one could be less interested in Alistair Haston, graduate of St Andrews University, sporting a second-class degree in German and Moral Philosophy, ex-inmate of the Athens state penitentiary. Indeed, why should they be? I was just another tourist, visiting Athens on a weekend break.

18

Hoisting my rucksack higher on my sodden shoulders, I set out with a spring in my step across the arrivals hall in the direction of the EXIT sign, then came to a stop in the middle of the concourse.

The heat . . .

Dry oven heat. Not a drop of moisture on the air. Traditional bouzouki music from Duty Free clashing with R.E.M. blaring from a tinny radio in the arrivals café; the heady cocktail of coffee and cigarette smoke floating above the hubbub of human traffic. And then, weaving my way to the threshold of the open doors of the terminal, the sweet scent of night-blossoming jasmine drifting on the faint breeze; a row of cypresses silhouetted against a low-slung crescent moon. The solicitous chirrup of crickets from the shadows.

Greece.

I'd forgotten what it was like: the lure of the Mediterranean that lay beyond the asphalt of the airport. Endless blue horizons and cut-glass azure ocean . . .

The promise of romance.

I set off once more and crossed the threshold of the terminal building to join a queue for the taxis that was already twenty-deep. But the moment I stepped out into the night air, I was shoved sideways by a young woman struggling with an enormous suitcase.

I was about to object, but she looked up and smiled apologetically, then tripped and fell backwards, dropping the suitcase on the ground, which burst open, strewing its contents onto the pavement.

Instinctively, I bent down to offer a helping hand.

She was already on her feet, cursing in Greek and kicking the suitcase in anger. '*Panagia mou,*' she muttered, sweeping her hair from her eyes. 'I am sorry – I did not mean to hit you.'

'*Den pirazee,*' I said – *no problem.* Then began to scoop up various items of clothing off the ground.

'*Efkaristo*,' she said, stuffing some underwear deep into the case.

Then she stood up, brushing invisible dirt from her dress while I took over trying to fasten the bulging suitcase. Sitting on it to keep it closed, I eventually fastened the clasps, and then, hauling the thing upright, lugged it behind me, following her to the kerb where a Volkswagen estate had pulled up.

'Well, better get going,' I said, eyeing a group of German tourists barrelling towards the taxi rank. 'Good luck with the suitcase.'

As I turned to go, she reached out and put a hand on my arm. 'You need a taxi? Please – we can share.' Her tone was serious. More instruction that invitation.

'Well, I'm erm ... going to the Kallithea district, near the port,' I replied, brushing a mosquito off my cheek.

'It will be the morning before you arrive,' she said, thrusting her chin in the direction of the taxi queue. 'I am getting off in Glyfada, but the driver will take you wherever you need. Come.'

Fifteen minutes later, we were on a busy dual carriageway heading downtown through the suburbs towards the city centre.

Having given Mr Manolis's address to our driver, my companion fell quiet and began to apply make-up from a small compact mirror, while I stared out at the rows of billboards advertising Coca Cola, Pampers and Canon bubble-jet printers, recalling the last time I had made the same journey. That 4 a.m. arrival; the rickety tourist bus that had threatened to break down any moment; my obsession with my ex-girlfriend, Ellie ...

'Your first time to Greece?' she asked finally, breaking the silence.

'No, actually,' I replied. 'Travelled to Paros a few years ago. Spent the summer there.'

'Ah yes. Paros. You have the party and the beaches,' she murmured, snapping shut her mirror. 'Best of both.' She turned and looked across at me, smiling. 'You have friends in Athens?'

I couldn't work out how old she was – maybe thirty. Strong cheekbones, yet sensitive eyes. A thick cascade of black hair brushing her shoulders. Her lips a deep blood red.

'Yes,' I replied. 'A chance to catch up and see a few sights before work starts.'

There was no need to give her the real reason.

She stopped listening anyway. Adjusting her dress, she called out to the driver to pull up.

'I am getting out here,' she announced, as the car rolled to a stop. 'He will take you where you need.'

She paid up, then the driver re-set the clock on the dashboard before hopping out to fetch her suitcase. 'Have a good trip,' she yelled from behind the open boot.

Before I had a chance to thank her, she disappeared across the road into the entrance of the high-rise, dragging her unwieldy suitcase behind her, while my driver turned the car around and we set off once more along the main road.

After ten minutes, we entered a residential area that had a distinct air of prosperity about it. Tall spreading cedars and palm trees; Pampas grass, lush lawns, and swathes of jasmine climbing over expansive whitewashed walls; the glimpse of a swimming pool here and there through wrought-iron fences.

Made sense. I knew that Amara's father had done well in the food trade.

'*Endaxi*,' said my driver, pulling up behind a Domino's Pizza Van that was parked outside a building resembling an old colonial out-house. '*Afto, einai*,' he grunted. *We're here.*

I paid him eight hundred Drachma and told him to keep the change. Then, inhaling a lungful of honeysuckle, I followed the pavement up to a short flight of steps that led to an expansive set of doors flanked by a pair of Doric columns. The number 102 was imprinted on a brass plate underneath a frond of bougainvillea.

I pressed the bell.

For a while nothing happened, just dogs barking in the distance. The sound of a helicopter circling overhead; the crickets in the oleander shrubs . . .

I buzzed again. Almost immediately, the door flew open and a wizened old woman dressed in traditional black beckoned me in with a jabbing finger, without waiting for me to speak. '*Ella. Ella etho! Grigora, grigora!*'

Evidently the person I'd spoken with on the phone.

'Hello,' I began, '*Emai Alistair Haston, sto Anglia. Ti kaneis – Kala?*'

'*Ti Kaneis, ti kaneis,*' she echoed, and then disappeared into the hallway, chattering to herself – or to me – I wasn't sure.

Gingerly, I took a step onto the expansive marble flooring, expecting to meet Amara's imposing father. But there was no sign.

Waiting for her return, I hung back in the vast open-plan sitting room, noting the Turkish carpets, the opulent chandeliers and a pair of Rothko copies on the wall, the abundance of framed black-and-white photographs . . .

I let my rucksack slide to the floor and wandered over to what appeared to be a family portrait, hoping for a glimpse of Amara, her father – and, of course, the boy. But before I was close enough to make out any detail, a voice came from behind me.

'Good evening.'

I spun around and came face to face with a square-jawed man in a pinstriped suit; slick haircut, early thirties.

Where the hell had he come from?

Had I walked right past him?

'My name is Alistair Haston,' I said, scratching at the mosquito bite on my right cheek which had already begun to itch. 'I have come to see Amara's father. You must be . . .'

'Takis,' he replied. 'His son.'

I stared at him, uncomprehending.

'Is there a problem?'

'No, it's just – Amara never mentioned she had a brother.'

'Ah, yes,' he smiled. 'Strictly speaking – half-brother. Same father. Different mother.' He thrust his hands amiably into his pockets. 'How can I help you?'

'I've come to see Amara and her boy,' I explained. 'Your father told me of the accident. I came as soon as I possibly could.'

'You spoke to my father?'

'He called me in London.'

Behind his head, a gecko shot out from behind a Rothko and scuttled up to the ceiling.

'I see,' replied Takis, stroking an earlobe, before shrugging off his suit jacket and tossing it on the sofa. 'I'm afraid there must be some mistake. Amara is not in Athens. She left for Zakynthos yesterday morning.'

I stood immobile for a moment, wondering if I'd misheard.

'They're out of hospital?'

'They are on holiday,' he replied, knitting his thick eyebrows.

'But, your father called me, the day before yesterday,' I protested. 'He told me about the accident – that they were in hospital, here, in Athens.'

Despite the air-conditioning, I suddenly felt unbearably hot.

'I am sorry to disappoint you, Mr Haston,' he replied, 'but this is not possible.' Casting his gaze to his feet, he kicked away an imaginary pebble, before looking up at me once more, his smile fading. 'My father died two years ago.'

Dumbfounded, I remained rooted to the floor as Takis poured two large glasses of Scotch and expounded on the subject of his family: explaining first that his father had died of bone cancer after a seven-year battle with the disease, and second that, being Amara's half-brother from his father's first marriage (along with the fact he was eleven years her senior), they'd never been close – rarely spoke, even.

'We see each other very occasionally,' he added, passing me

a drink. 'At Christmas, or Easter. When she and Xander got married, three years ago ... But not since my father's funeral.'

He took a packet of cigarettes out of his jacket pocket and lit up, apparently expecting me to make some form of comment. But I was so blown away by his earlier revelation I was unable to utter a word.

'I can assure you she is not in Athens,' he continued, easing himself into the leather sofa. 'When my father died, I took over his financial affairs, including the management of the family villa. Usually it is for the tourists, but for some weeks in the year it is reserved for family. Amara is there now, with Max and her husband.'

He gestured for me to sit, but I remained standing. I had the sickening feeling that the whole affair had been a prank; that someone, somewhere – for reasons best known to themselves – had played an unholy trick on me. Who, though? And why? Why on earth would anyone go to such lengths?

I could almost hear Vince's scornful laughter.

'I'm sorry for your loss,' I said finally, struggling to find the words. 'And for taking up your time. But the person who pretended to be your father and lied about the accident also told me Max was my son.'

Takis held my gaze, unblinking; the slightest frown creasing his heavy brow.

Above him, the foraging gecko returned to his lair behind the painting, a moth twitching between his translucent jaws.

'My father was a proud man,' Takis eventually replied. 'Always protective of his daughter.'

'That's not an answer,' I said, as politely as I could.

I felt a droplet of sweat slide down my spine.

'There were ... rumours, of course,' he added. 'But, as I say, we were forbidden to talk about it.'

'Forbidden?'

Takis didn't respond.

Why was he being so evasive?

I knew I'd been persona non-grata as far as Amara's father had been concerned – he hadn't wanted his daughter to be associated with a murder suspect. But the father was dead. I'd been proved innocent.

'You have a photograph?' I asked, scanning the pictures on the walls.

'Of Amara?' he replied, puzzled.

'Of her family – of Max.'

'Yes, of course,' he said, tipping back the rest of his Scotch. 'Please – help yourself to another whisky.' Then he disappeared off down the corridor into the kitchen, where I heard him rummaging around in a drawer.

Utterly baffled, I returned to the first photo-frame I'd seen, only to discover it wasn't a family portrait at all. It looked like a graduation ceremony: Takis in a robe and decorative hat, standing with three other men – they appeared to be clutching their diplomas, or something of that ilk. I quickly roamed the room and found all the other photographs to be of Takis, taken sometime between his early to mid-twenties. In one of them he was with a woman – blonde, elegant and pale skinned – but in all the rest he was with one or two men of his own age, and of similar Mediterranean complexion. On the beach, in cafés ... on a ski lift.

Other than the Rothkos, the only other non-photograph was an oil painting hanging above the archway into the kitchen. At first glance, it had the appearance of an amateur work – by Takis himself, perhaps? It was of a naked man wrapped in a bed sheet; again, Mediterranean? Impossible to say.

'Sorry you are waiting,' Takis announced, emerging from the corridor with a fistful of photographs. 'Loula is too good at her job. You can never find anything.' He handed me the photos then wandered back to the drinks cabinet and poured another Scotch, before extending the offer to me.

25

I declined with a shake of the head and addressed the photographs, wiping the sweat first from my eyes, and then off the celluloid.

My heart leaped.

The top photo was of Amara on the beach in a bikini, unchanged in appearance since I had seen her last, except that she had cut her waist-length hair into a bob. She was as exquisite as I had remembered: thick raven locks framing a button nose and fathomless doe eyes, that lithe, supple physique . . . the hint of mischief playing about her parted lips.

My eyes reluctantly shifted left . . .

Sitting half-buried in sand next to her was a fair-haired boy of maybe three or four years, holding a bucket and spade above his head and apparently shouting, eyes screwed shut.

No way of knowing from that shot. But . . . *fair hair?*

I turned to the next photograph. Amara sat, legs crossed, at a restaurant table, holding hands with a good-looking man considerably older than herself; swarthy, athletic and looking decidedly pleased with himself. He wore a gold chain around his wrist, and a medallion nestling in his hairy chest.

'This is Amara's husband – Xander,' grunted Takis disapprovingly, sucking on his cigarette as he peered over my shoulder. 'He is a musician, from Crete. A playboy.'

A playboy?

'When did they meet?' I asked.

'A few months before they got married.' He stubbed out his cigarette in the ashtray on the drinks cabinet and thrust his hands back in his pockets. 'Amara is impulsive. She doesn't think.'

I'd been wrong. Amara hadn't married a safe pair of hands at all; she'd done the precise opposite. To piss off her father. To get revenge upon the man who had interfered with her life . . . and prevented her from reaching out to me.

I flipped over the final photograph:

Max. Standing in his pyjamas in front of a Christmas-tree,

clutching a toy aeroplane. Unruly locks of blond hair framing his elfin face, head tilted to the left, chin thrust forward, gap tooth-grin glinting in the flashlight ...

I sensed Takis move away. Heard the tinkle of ice cubes.

'This is at the villa,' he said, topping up his drink. 'Last Christmas.'

I could only stare in wonder.

The resemblance to my five-year-old self was astounding. 'I have a similar photograph,' I murmured, enthralled. 'Taken at my grandparents' house in Norfolk. They gave me a toy Spitfire ...'

A truck rattled past the front of the house, then all was still.

I threw another glance around the siting room.

Amara had a husband and a son – that much was true. And that photograph of Max, along with Takis's reluctance to talk of Max's paternity, left no doubt in my mind that I was indeed the father.

But what of the fictional car crash? The person claiming to be Amara's father?

'Do you know who telephoned me?' I asked finally, meeting his gaze.

'I have no idea,' he replied, unblinking.

He was lying.

Indeed, the three shots of whisky he'd poured in the space of less than five minutes suggested he was far from comfortable in my presence.

As I continued to study him, however, it dawned on me.

How could I have missed it?

'It was Amara,' I exclaimed, taking an involuntary step backwards. 'She had someone call me on her behalf ...'

Takis remained implacable.

'Was it you?' I added, heart thumping at my rib cage.

Averting his gaze, Takis checked his watch and placed his glass decisively down on the table. 'The villa overlooks Gerakas beach on the west of Zakynthos,' he declared slowly, dropping his arms to his sides. 'Villa Aphrodite.'

That was as good as a confession.

Amara had enlisted the services of her half-brother in a ruse to bring me over to Greece.

To rescue her from her no-good husband.

'I'm very grateful,' I replied slowly, handing him the photographs. 'Sorry again for the intrusion.' No point pressuring Takis any further. He'd done his bit. Now he was washing his hands of the matter.

'I wish you luck,' he said, sweeping open the front door and letting in the muggy heat of the night. 'Any friend of Amara's is a friend of mine.'

He couldn't have made it any clearer.

Admitting – without admitting.

'The name of that beach again?' I said, reaching for my rucksack and heading for the door.

'Gerakas,' he replied, avoiding my eyes. 'It is famous for its sea turtles.'

'Villa Aphrodite?'

'Exactly.' He gave a curt nod and clicked his heels together.

I shook his hand and stepped out into the night.

3

Hovering by the roadside, I took a moment to get my bearings, then headed downhill towards the city centre.

Next step – a bed for the night.

In the morning, I'd book the first available flight to Zakynthos.

And rescue Amara.

But as I started to cross the road in front of the Domino's Pizza van, an engine fired up off to my right, followed by a flash of headlights.

Shading my eyes against the glare, I found myself staring at the same Volkswagen taxi that had delivered me an hour or so earlier.

'Boss!' called out the driver, hanging his head out of the window. 'You need taxi?'

Approaching the vehicle, I spotted an abundance of cigarette butts in the central ashtray, along with fast-food cartons and a crushed can of Coke.

'You are looking for something?' he asked, stepping out onto the road and hitching up his jeans. 'Food? Bar? Girls?'

I told him I wanted to head towards the port – anywhere I could find a cheap hotel.

'*Endaxi*,' he replied, coming around to open the rear passenger door. 'Hotel, no problem. Please.'

Seconds later, we shot off downhill, the city lights of downtown Athens blinking in the distance.

Seizing the opportunity, I asked if he knew about flights to Zakynthos.

'Every day, there are two,' he grumbled, turning down Oasis's 'Rock 'n' Roll Star' on the radio. 'One in the morning – the other ... I don't know. Night time, maybe.'

He then asked if I was a football fan.

'Rugby,' I replied. 'Or cricket – sometimes.'

I caught his disapproving frown in the rear-view mirror just as we pulled up at a crossroads, where we stopped, engine idling. After a minute or so, when it became clear there was no traffic in either direction, I asked the driver if there was a problem.

'One moment, please,' he said, fiddling with the rear-view mirror.

As I swung around to see what he was looking at, the passenger door opened and a heavily-set man in a linen suit and Hawaiian shirt slid into to the seat beside me.

Before I could protest, the taxi kicked into gear and we did a U-Turn, speeding off and taking a small side road west.

I fumbled for the door-handle, but my intruder was a step ahead.

'Apologies for the intrusion, Alistair,' he said, in a cut-glass English accent. 'Just wanted a quick chat.'

'Who the fuck are you?' I spat, swivelling around, fists clenched.

'Gerald Alexander,' he replied, dabbing his thick neck with a handkerchief. 'A friend.'

We took off in the direction of downtown Athens, winding our way through the back streets towards the waterfront. All the while, my intruder sat next to me, erect, hands folded in his lap like an attentive school-boy.

He'd given nothing away. Other than handing me a business card, he'd held a finger to his lips, recommending we wait until we were 'better situated to talk openly', before banally asking if I'd had a pleasant flight. I assured him I had. After that, conversation ceased. Despite his deliberate air of mystery, however, I was under no illusion as to why he was there. My arrival into the country had been clocked; eyebrows raised as to why the individual who had caused so much embarrassment to the Cyclades police in '88 was back.

Less than five minutes later, the taxi pulled up outside Hotel Euphoria; a 1970s high-rise situated in a small square, two blocks back from Piraeus harbour. From the stifling entrance hall at reception, I was led up seven flights of stairs – the lift was 'unreliable' – to the roof bar, where we took up position at an isolated table, away from the clusters of tourists and businessmen gathered at the edges of a shabby ten-metre pool.

'Fewer mosquitoes out here,' Gerald declared, folding his suit jacket over the back of his chair and placing a bottle of Amstel down in front of me. 'Nasty little buggers, particularly at this time of year. Grab the breeze while you can, that's what I say.' Tugging at his ill-fitting shirt, he lowered himself into his seat and once again produced a handkerchief to wipe the sweat from his bulging neckline.

I scanned the terrace and made a mental note of my exit route.

'You can start by telling me what your plan B was, if I hadn't got into the taxi with that woman at the airport,' I said, tossing his business card onto the table. 'What are you, MI5, or something?'

Corpulent and sweaty-faced in his flowery shirt, Gerald Alexander slotted perfectly into the role of bumbling expat. But his demeanour, like his job title, rang false. Aside from the fact it was now obvious my encounter with the woman at the airport had been a set-up, the idea that the 'Head of Translation for the British Council' had cause to jump into the back of my taxi, unannounced, in the middle of the night was preposterous.

He looked up from his beer and smiled. 'No flies on you,' he said, his attention drawn by a couple dancing at the edge of the pool. 'But MI5 is homeland security, strictly speaking . . .'

'Secret service, MI6 – whatever,' I said, interrupting him. 'I don't see why I have to explain anything. And I certainly don't appreciate having the shit scared out of me by a complete stranger hijacking my taxi.'

'I can only apologise again for the abrupt introduction,' he replied, with a frown. 'Unfortunately, it was a necessary precaution.'

For a man of supposed authority, he seemed oddly nervous. As for myself, the earlier paranoia and anxiety I'd felt at the airport had gone. Now the tap on the shoulder had come, I felt only a growing sense of indignation.

'Feel free to get to the point, Gerald,' I snapped. 'It's been a long day.'

'Of course, absolutely,' he replied, nodding his head vigorously. 'The thing is, Alistair, we know of your past troubles. And I need to know why you've come back.'

From the streets below, the wail of a siren cut through the music and chatter.

'Why the hell shouldn't I come back?' I retorted. 'I don't see what business it is of yours or anyone else's.'

He took a long pull on his beer. 'It's of paramount importance, for the sake of everyone concerned, that you tell me why you are here. Otherwise, things could get . . . tricky.'

Tricky?

I could feel the artery in my neck pulsing against the skin.

'What if I drop by the Embassy – see what they have to say about it?'

'You could,' he replied genially, glancing over at the swimming pool. 'They'd tell you to return in the morning. At about

32

9.45 we'd have the same conversation again. With an audience. But I don't think you'll get that far.'

I grabbed my rucksack off the ground. 'This is bullshit.'

Gerald grunted and ran a hand through his thinning hair. 'Your call. But don't say I didn't warn you. The Greeks will be eager to get stuck in once they get the nod. Kidnapping is a serious offence.'

He turned casually towards the bar, produced a pipe from his shirt pocket and began to tap out the charred remains on the side of his chair.

I froze, my rucksack slung over one shoulder.

Kidnapping?

I felt the outbreak of sweat across the back of my neck. 'What the . . .?'

'You paid a visit to Takis Manolis,' he snapped, cutting me off. 'Why?'

I continued to stare, uncomprehending.

'Don't test me, Alistair,' he said quietly, all trace of the goofy Englishman dissolving in an instant. 'Unless you get off your high horse and tell me, right now, exactly what you are doing here, things will become complicated. And I assure you, the Greeks will be far less understanding.'

I remained rooted by stupor, my brain capsizing.

This was insane.

I'd done nothing wrong. I didn't owe Gerald, or MI6, or the Greeks anything.

'Who the hell am I supposed to have kidnapped?' I stammered, rising to my feet. 'I've only just arrived in the bloody country.'

'Sit down Alistair,' hissed Gerald through gritted teeth, nodding to dismiss the nearby couple who had turned to see what the fuss was about. 'And tell me what you are doing here. Now.'

For a moment, the music died on the PA system and a strange quiet befell the roof terrace. Above the chatter, I heard the distinctive rhythmic chant of a lone cicada, somewhere in the vine

33

trellis on the far side of the pool – it must have been confused by the lights.

All at once, I was back in the Parikia jail: moths and flies buzzing around the flickering bulb; dead hornets hanging from spider webs in the paint-cracked corners. The stench of shit and piss wafting in through the barred, windowless, square hole that served as a window. The sickening fear that I had been discarded, forgotten, left to rot . . .

Music struck up once more from the speakers and the flashback passed as quickly as it had materialised. Gerald was still watching and waiting – his eyes catching the fluorescent light of the fly traps, cracking and popping on the walls as they dispatched their winged victims.

He rose to his feet and placed his hands on his hips. 'Alistair?'

He was about to blow the whistle.

Experience had taught me it was vital to be straight up with the authorities from the off. Bravura had its place, but it was an unpredictable grenade that could detonate if one held on too tight. I'd made that error in Paros, and it had nearly cost me my life.

Resuming my seat, I hastily explained everything that had happened from the moment my phone rang on my desk at the telesales office, to my leaving Takis's house and being picked up by the taxi. I told him how the man on the phone claimed to be Amara's father; how he'd informed me of a car accident involving herself, her husband and her boy, and that I'd soon be hearing from the police investigating the accident, on account of the fact the boy was my progeny. I described how Takis had claimed to know nothing about the phone call; how he'd refused to either confirm or deny that Max was my son – alluding that his father had sworn the family to secrecy. And how, when asked as to whether the phone call had possibly been Amara's doing – again, Takis didn't deny or confirm it. He'd simply told me that any friend of hers was a friend of his, before hurrying me out of the house.

34

'It's the God's honest truth,' I said, breathless, wiping the sweat from my neck. 'So, if you're trying to catch me out, don't bother. My story won't change.

I reached for my beer and downed it in one.

'Whatever Takis has done,' I continued, 'I have nothing to do with it. I'd never heard of the guy until I met him. I'm here to meet my supposed son, Max. For the first time. Ever. That's it. Ask anyone I've ever met. Ask my friends and family . . . check my bank statements and phone records.'

It wasn't the whole truth, of course. I'd omitted the key factor – my yearning to be reunited with the woman whom fate had brought back into my life. But I knew it would carry no water with the likes of Gerald.

And in any case, it was none of his fucking business.

Gerald lit his pipe and extinguished the match between forefinger and thumb. 'You've come to meet your son . . .'

'I came to take a DNA test,' I said, in a bid to strengthen my case. 'You'd do the same.'

He nodded. 'I sense you're holding something back.'

'I've told you everything,' I snapped. 'Your turn now.'

'Fire away,' he said, cracking a smile.

'For a start, who do the Greeks claim I've kidnapped?' I retorted, simultaneously aware how absurd it sounded to speak such words out loud.

'No one. Yet,' said Gerald, eyeing me steadily. 'It's what's about to happen that they are worried about.'

'Well who, for Christ's sake? I mean – they must have someone in mind.'

The words hadn't even left my lips, before the penny dropped. And with it, the whole sequence of events took on a violent clarity.

'Max?'

Gerald didn't budge a muscle.

The sentiment was so utterly beyond comprehension, that I

had to fight the urge to burst out laughing. 'You can't seriously believe ...'

But he cut me off: 'Not us – the Greeks.'

I struggled to find the words to continue. Where the hell did one start to counter a proposition that was so far beyond the realms of reality?

'I mean – how?' I stammered. 'Who ... am I supposed to be planning this – *thing* – with?'

I'd only met one person so far.

'Takis?'

'The whole family are under surveillance,' Gerald replied.

'You believe me, though – right?' I exclaimed. 'You understand that I have absolutely nothing to do with this?'

'I do,' he replied, pulling at his jowls. 'The Greeks may need a little more persuading.'

'Somebody phones me up out of the blue and tells me the son I never knew I had was hurt in a car crash. What was I supposed to do, just sit at home and wait? Of course I'm going to come and investigate. But from that, they've concluded that I'm here to abduct my own child? A child that – I'll say it again – I never even knew existed?'

Gerald leaned back in his chair and smoothed down his linen trousers.

'Amara's husband Xander is planning the kidnap,' he announced, gazing over my shoulder to the swimming pool. 'Takis is possibly also involved. The Greeks think you too may be in on it.'

I stared at him, jaw hanging.

Gerald shrugged. 'You're Max's natural father. You've been denied access to your son. You're angry. Amara's family are very wealthy.'

'I never knew Max existed until that phone call,' I protested again, pushing back from the table. 'Xander – less than an hour ago. How could I *possibly* be a suspect?'

'Which is why you're sitting opposite me, not the Greek police,' Gerald replied, tugging at the sweat-stained under arm of his Hawaiian shirt. 'It's a delicate situation and we're working together. But when your name appeared on the passenger list of the flight from Heathrow, action had to be taken. Luckily for you, they let us handle it.'

I swept his business card off the table and studied it.

'It says you're a translator for the British Council. What are you doing working for MI6?'

Gerald cocked his head and smiled. 'It's not a complete lie. I head up translation services for the British Council and the Embassy. I also teach English at the University of Athens – been doing it for fifteen years now. But for MI6 and Interpol, my appeal is of a slightly different nature. I happen to be an expert in Mediterranean organised crime.'

'The Mafia?'

'In essence – yes.'

Scraping back my chair, I stumbled to my feet.

'I think we've wasted enough of each other's time.'

'Alistair – wait,' he urged, also rising from the table.

'Leave me the fuck alone!'

But then he lunged forward and seized me by the arm.

'The telephone call you received in London had nothing to do with Amara,' he hissed, levelling me with his puffy, bloodshot eyes.

Sliding the rucksack off my shoulder, I slowly prized his hand off me.

'Touch me again, Gerald, and I swear . . .'

He stepped back and let his arms fall limp by his sides.

'Xander is trying to frame you,' he said simply, his gaze unwavering. 'For the kidnapping.'

For fifteen mind-bending minutes, Gerald recounted how Amara's playboy husband, Xander – the ex-front-man of an almost famous pop group – had got himself into debt over a gambling and drugs addiction, and had ended up courting a couple of hoods from an Athens Mafia cartel in a bid to find a way of replenishing his funds. After a series of meetings in a lap-dancing bar, they'd drawn the attention of the security services, who, in turn, recorded a handful of their conversations, one of which was centred around extortion tactics – kidnapping, in particular; how much money Xander might expect to make from such a venture, as well as how to action it.

'In April, however, they break off contact and the trail goes cold,' continued Gerald, studying me over the top of his pipe. 'Greek Intel figures Xander has had second thoughts, or found another source of revenue. But his bank account remains unaltered – so, they watch and wait. Six weeks later, in mid-May, one of their undercover agents working as a driver within the cartel learns of an operation to kidnap Xander's five-year old stepson and ransom him for Amara's sizeable inheritance fund. The driver also hears that the boy's real father will have a part to play in it.' He paused to clear his throat. 'Greek Intelligence accesses Max's birth certificate, discover you're the natural father, then contact British Intelligence to give us the heads up and work out how to proceed.'

In the distance, another siren echoed off the walls of the surrounding tower blocks.

He gave me a thin smile. 'With me so far?'

I nodded and gripped the chair arms tighter, hit by another dizzy spell.

Breathe, Haston.

It'll pass.

It always passes.

'Having spoken with you,' Gerald continued, 'it's quite clear you're innocent. Takis too. It seems you have both been played.'

He produced his box of matches and relit his pipe.

'Xander, or whichever of his entourage telephoned you, sent

you to Takis's house knowing that, being an honourable sort of chap, he would honour his late father's wish for secrecy and simply instruct you as to where to find Amara and her family on Zakynthos – effectively using Takis as an unwitting go-between to bring you out to Greece without implicating himself in the paper trail, as it were. In preparation for the kidnap.'

A waiter appeared, asking if we wanted more drinks.

Gerald ordered two more Amstels, then waved him away.

'You can see why the Greeks feel Takis might be a part of it, though,' he added.

He went on to explain how Takis had been made executor of Amara's inheritance, but that he himself wasn't a beneficiary. It was possible Xander might have approached Takis and offered him the chance to get his hands on the money.

'Takis controls the purse strings, after all,' Gerald continued, tapping the pipe stem against his teeth. 'Much easier for Xander if he has the exchequer onside. Between them, they use a portion of the inheritance funds to pay off the Mafia, then pocket the rest. Amara is none the wiser. She presumes the whole funds have been used to pay off the kidnappers.'

'Why would Amara's own brother do such a thing?'

'Half-brother.'

'But . . . he's family.'

'So is the husband,' he countered. 'I've no idea why people do such things – greed, I presume. Whatever Takis's involvement – and, as I said, I believe that he, like you, is innocent – it's this same line of thinking that led the Greeks to believe you were coordinating the operation as a third party to Xander and the Mafia . . . for financial gain.'

My brain had begun to capsize.

And yet, utterly bewildering though it was to hear such an outlandish suggestion, I was struggling to come to terms with an entirely different matter:

The phone call had had nothing to with Amara.

She was oblivious of me.

No thoughts of winding back the clocks ... starting over again with the man who had sired her child ...

'Alistair?' said Gerald, leaning in.

Instead, I was facing a return to banality; to a string of meaningless temping work, plagued by dreams of what might have been.

Vince would have a field day.

'The question now, old boy,' Gerald murmured, glancing at his watch, 'is what we do next.'

I stared at him blankly, my vision blurring from a sudden overwhelming tiredness.

'Do you have somewhere to stay?'

I told him I didn't. I'd been heading into the port to find a cheap hotel when he'd jumped in my taxi.

'Stay here,' he said genially. 'I'll put it on our tab – it's the least we can do. Only a twenty-minute cab ride back to the airport. Half an hour, in rush hour, perhaps. I can help change your ticket and get you on a lunchtime flight.'

I stared at him, head spinning.

'I'm supposed to just head back to the UK?'

Gerald pursed his lips. 'Afraid so, old chap. Go home, let the dust settle. In a couple of months, pick up the trail where you left off. Make contact again with the family and let Amara know you have been made aware you're the father of her boy. Take it from there.'

'But ... what about the kidnapping?'

'Your no-show will alert Xander and the Mafia that you've got wind of something,' he continued breezily. 'The abduction will be called off, and that'll be that. Of course, we'll keep eyes on the family while they're still on Zakynthos, just to be sure. But no – that'll pretty much be the end of it.'

That'll pretty much be the end of it ...

I cast a glance around the terrace, at the partygoers. One

couple had stripped down to their underwear and were kissing in the shallows. Others looked on admiringly, debating whether to follow suit.

So that was that – it was all over before it had even started.

Gerald caught my eye.

'It's a little seedy this place,' he said. 'But it's a good place to chat without drawing attention to yourself.'

As I stared at him, lounging back in his seat, it dawned on me that, for a man who had just called the night to an end, he was busy not going anywhere.

'What's my other option?' I asked, studying him.

'I'm sorry?'

'You don't seem to be in a hurry to leave.'

Gerald broke into a grin.

'They said you were a sharp cookie,' he murmured, sipping his drink. 'Good for you.'

Maintaining eye contact, I waited for him to continue.

'I'd be lying if I said there wasn't an alternative,' he said finally, shuffling forwards in his seat and resting his elbows on the table. 'But I don't want to twist your arm.'

'I'm still listening,' I said, gazing at the vein pulsing at the side of his neck.

'The other option,' he eventually continued, puffing out his fleshy cheeks, 'is that you stay here and work with us.'

He broke off, awaiting my response, but I remained silent.

'You're in a unique position,' he added lightly. 'We could use your help.'

I leaned back in my chair and eyeballed him.

'My help?'

'The Mafia believe they're one step ahead,' Gerald continued, casting a look across the terrace. 'As long as they keep thinking that, we have the advantage. You just have to show up and play along. When the moment comes, we will move in.'

A sudden cheer broke out by the pool. More guests had

stripped down to their underwear and were now play-fighting in the water, egged on by waiting staff.

Gerald chuckled and turned back to face me.

'Been there – done that,' he said with a wink.

'You were saying,' I shot back.

He cleared his throat. 'We stand to score a considerable blow against Mediterranean organised crime. You have proved in the past to be resilient and resourceful. You've got guts and you can take care of yourself . . .'

He tapped his pipe and stuck it in his shirt pocket.

'Not that you will need any of those attributes here, I hasten to add. As I said, all you have to do is turn up and do what you came here to do – find out if Max is your son. Let it play out.' Again, he looked me in the eye and smiled. 'But yes, I'd like to make you an offer.'

In that moment, I realised his entire interrogation, all the threats and posturing had been an act of smoke and mirrors while he steered me towards his end-game.

He was here precisely to twist my arm.

'You'll pay me?' I said finally, studying him closely.

He nodded. 'If that's what it takes – of course.'

With that, his gaze drifted over to the eastern terrace wall where a young couple were glued by the lips, gyrating and thrusting to the music, oblivious to the crowd around them; watched over by the Acropolis, lit up on the hillside.

The woman was wearing a see-through white dress . . . scarlet high-heeled shoes.

Just like Amara had worn on the night I first met her.

'Alistair?'

I turned and faced him.

'Sleep on it,' said Gerald, wiping his forehead with a handker-chief. 'I'll meet you back here in the morning, once I've had a chance to talk to my Greek counterparts. Assuming they agree, you can give me your answer.'

He smiled, raised his bottle in a toast and took a lengthy swig.

'But seriously, no pressure,' he added. 'You can simply walk away and go home. All we'd ask is that you refrain from contacting Amara's family until you get the nod. Someone from our office will call or write to you to let you know.'

But I'd stopped listening.

Go home?

To Vince's 'I told you so'?

To my dead-end telesales job and my empty bed?

'Alistair?'

Go home? When I was in a position to rescue Amara from her twisted, drug-addicted husband? When I had the chance to sweep her off her feet and reinstate myself firmly in her life . . . to reunite the family that fate had brought into being?

I took a long pull on my beer then slapped it down on the table.

'I don't need to sleep on it, Gerald,' I murmured, gazing over his shoulder at the distant lights of Piraeus harbour. 'I'm in.'

4

The following morning, I was back on the hotel roof terrace, washing away the oily aftertaste of a fried breakfast with an iced coffee.

I checked my watch: approaching 10 a.m.

Draining the granules of sugar from the bottom of my glass, I left the shady side of the terrace with its view north up to the iconic Acropolis and began to retrace my steps back to the swimming pool, when a familiar voice cut through the morning air.

'Post prandial swim?'

Through the sliding glass doors on the far side of the bar, a sweating Gerald emerged, dressed in a suit and tie, accompanied by a tall, suave-looking Greek man in his forties, equally formally attired, holding a black briefcase.

'How was breakfast?' Gerald continued, barrelling his way towards me.

'Great – thank you,' I replied, studying the man beside him. 'For the room, too.'

'Don't thank me, thank Stelios,' he replied, edging his way around the pool.

Stelios approached, drew up short and eyeballed me.

'Your reputation proceeds you,' he grunted, before I'd had a chance to thank him.

As we shook hands, I glanced back at Gerald.

My reputation?

'Stelios works for the National Central Bureau in Athens – Interpol,' said Gerald, still smiling. 'Although you put the wind up some of our friends in the government in '88, there are a few that are grateful for what you uncovered in the Cyclades. Stelios is one of them.'

He pulled back some chairs at one of the tables, gestured for me and Stelios to sit, then waved at a waitress who'd popped her head through the sliding doors.

'We are grateful for your – how can I say? – resilience,' said Stelios, cracking a smile and then his knuckles. 'I must apologise for your time in the prison.'

'No hard feelings,' I replied. 'You can read a lot of books in six months.'

Except, I'd been allowed no books. None that weren't in Greek.

Stelios frowned. 'You are a teacher?'

How had he come to that conclusion?

I nodded. 'English as a foreign language.'

Gerald must have told him.

'But, this is not your ambition, no?'

But then, how did Gerald know? It hadn't come up in conversation.

'Erm, no, I suppose not ...'

Because he's MI6, he knows everything.

Stelios took out a packet of Karelia Lights and offered it to me. I accepted.

'You speak German, Greek ...' he continued, leaning forwards to light my cigarette. 'You have proven yourself to be a natural detective. There are other careers for you, perhaps.'

Then he smiled and turned to Gerald. 'You could use a man like this, no?'

Gerald chuckled and folded his hands behind his head. 'I'm not sure he'd have us.'

Their flattery was superfluous.

'I don't need persuading,' I interjected, smiling at Stelios. 'Just tell me what to do.'

The flight to Zakynthos departed shortly after three o'clock.

With the rugged Peloponnese to port and starboard, our hundred and fifty-seater propeller plane hit cruising altitude, then bounced its way west for half an hour, before dropping down over the shimmering Ionian Sea towards the southern end of Zakynthos, where the eponymous capital lay.

Along with my original packing, I was now in possession of three additional items, courtesy of Gerald and Interpol: an envelope containing a hundred and eighty thousand drachmas in cash – around five hundred pounds; a detailed army map of Zakynthos, showing the position of the Manolis villa (a half-kilometre back from the crescent-shaped Gerakas beach on the south-eastern peninsular of the island); and finally, two original copies of Max's birth certificate – both signed and dated 28th September 1989, but one with no name under the section: 'father', and the other with my name written in, along with a signature that definitely wasn't mine.

Thanks to Stelios, I'd learned that the amended document bearing my name had been the work of Mister Manolis himself, who, being a proud man with old-fashioned values, was at odds with having his grandson go through life unable to utter his father's name. Detectives pinned down the associate who'd accepted a cash bribe directly from Mr Manolis in exchange for accepting a paternity consent form two years after Max's birth – apparently signed by a Mr Alistair Haston, in absentia.

I found it odd that Gerald, who would have been aware of this, hadn't offered up the information the previous night, and I was keen to talk more with Stelios. But the latter had apologised, explaining he was only dropping by and had to head back to the NCB for a meeting. He wanted to do something to make amends for my wrongful imprisonment – hence the gifts: paying for the room at the hotel, the detailed army map and shedding light on Max's birth certificates. It wasn't much, he admitted, but he was grateful for the opportunity to stop and shake a hand. Two cigarettes and an espresso later, he wished me luck, picked up his briefcase and left.

After that, Gerald was quick to move things along.

His instructions were simple enough: do exactly as I would, as if I had no knowledge of the kidnapping plot. I had to act naturally and not anticipate anything, or look for trouble. It was likely I'd be followed from Zakynthos airport, and my every move would be scrutinised.

The only piece of information he gave me was the name of the hotel I was to use as a base – the Porto Roma – explaining, also, that I'd have to hire a car at the airport. As it was a large island, taxis couldn't be relied upon, and I'd need to preserve my autonomy.

When I asked him how and where I'd make contact with his team, he told me they'd make themselves known.

'They'll be with you every step of the way,' he'd assured me. 'In the background mostly, but they'll be there. Your job is simply to connect with Amara, initiate the discussions about your paternity and let it play out.'

I asked him how long he thought I'd have to wait, but he couldn't say. He explained that the Mafia would take time to scope me out before setting their trap.

Ultimately, I had to proceed as if Gerald and I had never met. Yes – I now had the birth certificates, but I still had to push for the DNA test. Firstly, it was the only guaranteed proof that Max was my son, but more importantly, as far as Gerald was concerned, it would buy the time needed for the operation to mature.

'A DNA test is a simple enough procedure,' he'd explained. 'Done with a swab of saliva from the cheek, usually. But it takes about three days to get the results back from hospital. Insist on it – Xander will be counting on your doing so.'

Then he took down my bank account details, saying he would have a thousand pounds transferred immediately, and another thousand when the job was complete.

Finally, handing me an envelope of cash 'to help tide things over', he'd instructed me to memorise his phone number and call him twice daily for updates.

I asked him how long they'd been following me in London.

'A month or so,' he'd replied, smiling amiably. 'Low-level stuff. No phone tapping or anything of that sort – takes a lot of paperwork to put that through. We just kept track of your movements here and there, checked on your finances now and then. Nothing sinister.'

I waited for more, but that was all he was offering.

'"Need to know,"' I'd said, scanning the lobby.

He clapped me on the shoulder and told me that Stelios was right – I was a natural.

The flight terminated in a heavy crosswind at Zakynthos's seaside airstrip; a hair-raising aerobatic endeavour which drew spontaneous applause from the entire cabin as the wheels hit the asphalt.

Once through arrivals, I bought a pack of cigarettes, loaded up on water bottles and booked a car at the Hertz Rentals, following my assistant out into the blinding sunshine of the parking lot, where, after a flash of signature on the paperwork, followed by a cursory look around the five-door Nissan Micra for scratches, I was dismissed.

Four thirty p.m.

After consulting first the short entry on Zakynthos in *Let's Go Greece* and then Stelios's army map, I exited the carpark,

48

crossed the airport perimeter and soon found myself driving north across a wide, dry plain; past isolated hotels and abandoned building sites, tucked away behind copses of poplars and bamboo. All the while, a shadowy range of hills loomed in the rear-view mirror; an austere hinterland, which, as I also understood from the map, was largely unpopulated, due, in part, to the difficulty of access.

As I drove with the sun behind me, I found myself grinning from ear to ear – happier than I had been in months, if not years. I had a job, a mission – for which I was getting paid handsomely, no less. Nothing so pedestrian as selling marketing and PR campaigns to city corporations – sorry Vince. I was in the employment of the secret service, helping the authorities in their war against the Mafia. Doing something useful, meaningful – with real human impact.

Above all, I was on my way to meet Amara.

To fall in love again.

And start a new life.

I understood, of course, that I had to keep my overtures temporarily on the back burner until I'd helped foil the kidnapping – which was all grist to the mill. Once Xander was behind bars and no longer an impediment, I'd be free to claim Amara for myself – along with Max, of course.

Ignoring a flicker of anxiety about how I'd cope with fatherhood, I focussed on the road ahead, continuing alongside an undulating field of head-high sunflowers for about a kilometre, before passing the first of several turnoffs to Laganas; an 18–30s clubbing mecca known for its all-night cocktail bars, crowded beaches and water sports. A further two kilometres later, I entered Zakynthos town, following a dry canal lined with Eucalyptus and cypresses, which led, in turn, to the marina and the town centre – a micropolis of cobbled streets and tiny alleyways, bustling with restaurants and tourist shops, all happily ignoring the traditional siesta.

49

No sign of any tail.

Pulling up in the marina carpark, I sat in the car, smoking, wondering if at any moment another car might park up next to me and initiate contact; but after twenty minutes and several half-smoked cigarettes, nothing had changed. There were no signs of activity, either human or vehicular, that made me believe I was being followed or watched.

Performing a final circuit of the square for good measure, I left the yachts in the marina and took the winding coastal road south, passing through the tourist resort of Argassi, then on through a series of sprawling fishing villages, in the direction of Agios Nikolaos on the south-east peninsular.

Eventually, at a sandy crossroads in the all-but-deserted Vassilikos, I headed downhill towards the furrowed sea glinting ahead in the sunlight. A few hundred metres more, the road became a pitted rocky track, snaking its way through an ever-encroaching maze of vineyards and lemon trees, until I crested a hillock and narrowly avoided colliding with a dilapidated tractor, skidding to a stop in the dusty forecourt of a bijoux terracotta-roofed hotel perched high on a cliff above a narrow inlet – the Porto Roma.

Killing the engine, I sat for a moment, listening to the rhythmic thrum of cicadas in the farmland behind me. I had a view straight through the restaurant terrace, overlooking the choppy water, some eighty feet below. No one was sat at the tables – no sign of staff or any hotel guests; it was that dead hour, when everyone was either asleep or down at the beach, cooling off in the afternoon heat.

Apart from a single quad bike, the place appeared deserted.

Exiting the car, I shouldered my rucksack and made my way through the dusty rear courtyard, accompanied by a posse of scrawny cats mewing and skittering around my feet. Trying first the bell and then knocking, I waited as the cats snaked their way in and out of my legs. Eventually, a bejewelled, bright-eyed woman in her late thirties with dyed blonde hair and thick mascara answered the door with a subdued grunt.

I explained I needed a room for a few nights – how many, I couldn't be sure.

She announced that she'd need to see ID, and that they didn't take American Express.

Producing my passport, I told her I'd be paying in cash.

After flicking briefly through the passport pages, she cast an eye over my rucksack, then led me up two flights of stairs to an airy twin-room directly overlooking the harbour below. 'Best view in the hotel,' she declared, blowing a frond of hair off her face as she motioned me into the room. Then she leant against the door frame and began filing her nails.

Agreeing I'd pay three nights up front and then play it by ear, I handed over the cash, upon which she disappeared to photocopy my passport.

As soon as I was alone, I investigated the drawers and cupboards, in case I'd been left a clandestine message somewhere, but found nothing apart from a Gideon's Bible. I then made a second tour of the room, looking for listening devices – attempting even to unscrew the phone by the bed, along with the various light fittings. But again, I came up empty handed.

Approaching the window, I studied the fishing boats moored at a pontoon thrusting out into a crescent cove below. No sign of life. Equally, the little café built into the cliffs at the bottom of a steep track to the north end of the bay was closed up, devoid of people.

Then my hostess reappeared and returned my passport, informing me that the phone in the room was for incoming calls only. All outgoing calls, long-distance or otherwise, had to be made from the reception office. I thanked her for the heads up and stood by the bed waiting for her to leave.

'If you want to see the turtles, you must go very early in the morning,' she declared, calling back as she headed down the stairs. 'They are shy. I have only seen them one time, myself.'

Alone again, I surveyed my lodgings once more.

What the hell was I supposed to do – sit and wait for someone to make contact?

I checked my watch again: 5 p.m.

Beachgoers would soon be returning to shower and freshen up . . .

Stashing my passport, cash, and the two birth certificates under the mattress, I locked up, then made a quick turn of the hotel grounds in case someone was lying in wait for me, looking to establish a connection out of view of the management.

But there wasn't a soul to be seen. Even the quad bike had gone.

Making my way back to the Nissan, I gave Stelios's map the once over, then set off, turning south in the direction of Gerakas beach and the villa.

MI6 would have to play catch-up.

I had to see Amara.

Following the broken track around the rocky headland, I passed between thick banks of windswept myrtle as I negotiated one perilous hairpin bend after another, wondering what my first words would be when Amara opened the door. Or would it be Xander who met me first? It might, of course, be Max. What the hell did you say to the five-year-old boy you never knew you had, who was in imminent danger of being abducted by the Mafia?

Other than that, however, my plan of action was simple enough.

I'd give Amara and Xander a portion of the truth – just not the whole truth.

I'd mention the phone call; how I'd been directed to Takis's house – and how, in turn, he'd given nothing away, but simply explained where to find them on Zakynthos. I'd say nothing of Gerald – or Stelios. Nor would I produce the birth certificates; how would I explain my having got hold of them? I had to act according to the narrative that Xander believed he had created, and not do or say anything that might draw suspicion.

As for Amara, it was critical for now to keep my cards close to my chest.

I'd use the time to take the temperature of her relationship with Xander, and evaluate when and how I'd make my intentions known, once Xander was in police custody. Any opportunity to reconnect, however – I'd jump on it. But I'd choose my moments carefully. Xander would be watching my every move.

I lit another cigarette and hung my arm out of the window, the warm flush of adrenaline coursing through my veins.

How good it was to be underway. To have a sense of purpose. *To be alive . . .*

The further I drove, the more rugged the seascape became; a heaving sweep of royal blue, flecked with spindrift-strewn white-caps, rolling in from the channel between Zakynthos and the mainland, just visible on the horizon. And despite the unnerving sensation of being watched, I was quite alone. Just lizards, dust and rocks.

After what felt like an eternity, I came across the first homestead; a solitary bungalow, complete with a fenced-off chicken coop, a rusting dilapidated Ford Escort, and two listless dogs shackled to a single rope, standing sentinel over a huddle of ducks sleeping in the shade of a plum tree. Two hundred yards later, I crested a hill and came to a crossroads, finding myself back in civilisation.

To my right, the road became tarmacked once more, off which three sprawling restaurants vied for business, each with a generous children's play area at the front. To my left, the track continued for ten yards, and, at a junction in the road, by a convenience store selling watermelons and beach attire, forked right, up to a gate signed 'Gerakas Nature Reserve'; while, to the left, it disintegrated into a shrub-lined, pebbled

53

trail, which, according to Stelios's map, was the access route to the Manolis's villa.

I pulled up in the pitted field-cum-car-park alongside a line of dusty jeeps, mopeds and quadbikes, and stepped out into the sea air to survey the restaurants and their clientele. They were all doing a solid trade, serving drinks and ice cream to a mixture of international and home-grown tourists, kicked back in the shade of bamboo and vine trellises while their progeny let off steam on the array of swings and slides.

No sign of Amara and Max.

And still no sign of a tail. Although ... there was a pair of middle-aged men drinking coffee at a corner table of Sunset Cocktail Bar, who, in slacks and button up shirts, seemed a little over-dressed for the beach.

Making a pretence of taking in my surrounds, I leaned up on the car bonnet and watched them for a while out of the corner of my eye, but they appeared oblivious of my presence. One of them, short, stocky flicking his set of keys; the other, lanky, balding, thumbing a set of worry-beads. Vigorously engaged in conversation, they didn't even acknowledge the waitress when she brought over a plate of olives. Two blue-collar locals winding down after a day's business. Zakynthos was only a forty-minute drive away, after all. The heaving tourist resort of Laganas was even closer. Hoteliers, perhaps? Or car rental managers.

Satisfied that I was still alone and unwatched, I locked up and traversed the field, passing through the worn gate and an adjacent wooden hut, advertising itself as 'Zakynthos Turtle Museum', then followed a crumbling path between a row of stunted, windblown tamarisks to the edge of the clifftop, where the path widened and dropped steeply down to a picture-postcard beach: a kilometre-long sickle of dazzling sand, ending in a cascade of boulders at the headland point, and backed along its entire length by clay cliffs that were streaked with diagonal layers of rock-strata. The result of an earthquake, or volcanic

54

eruption that had buckled the earth's crust during its primordial past. Sandwiched between the sand and the foot of the cliffs were towering chalky mounds resembling termite hills, adding to the prehistoric feel.

Turtle sanctuary aside, it was easy to see why the beach was so appealing to families. Isolated and utterly unspoilt, safely sheltered from the northerly sea-breeze by the jutting headland, the water was mirror flat and crystal clear, shelving gently towards the open sea.

But I could also see the appeal for the kidnappers. By night-fall, the entire peninsula would be well-nigh deserted.

Gerald had said the task force was 'in hand' ...

Where, exactly?

I remained on the lookout for another half hour as the sun slowly sunk to the west, until I became convinced that Amara and Max weren't on the beach.

Turning my back on the view, I followed a group of tank-topped garrulous Russian men down to the crossroads, dropped in at the beach shop to buy some water, and checked the restaurants. Then two men had gone from their corner table at the cocktail bar, their place taken by what appeared to be a troupe of Scandinavians; tall, dapper and uniformly blond.

Downing the water, I disposed of the bottle and set off along the shingled trail to the villa. As I strode steadily downhill towards sea-level, the wind dropped and the air became noticeably hotter, thicker. Lizards skittled across the stones to either side of me, while the chant of cicadas urged me onwards.

Dripping with sweat, I eventually rounded a bend in the track and came across a long stone wall, crawling with honey-suckle and hibiscus, behind which I could hear the faint strum of a guitar.

I stopped and waited.

Above the guitar I could just make out a hummed melody – a male voice, not unpleasant.

I crept forwards a further twenty feet until I found a break in the shrubbery and, making out the faded yellow stone of a rambling villa, pulled in closer to the wall.

Not five yards in front of me, straddling a wooden sunbed in a pair of swimming trunks, a guitar balanced on his knee, sat Xander. His hair was pulled back in a ponytail and he had a cigarette hanging out of the corner of his mouth. At his feet, several discarded bottles of local beer spilled the remains of their liquid on the tiles, attracting a long line of foraging ants.

Holding my breath, I listened and watched, waiting for signs of Amara and Max.

Then I heard a woman's voice from inside the villa.

Creeping on tip toes alongside the perimeter wall, I came across a break in the shrubbery where a flight of stone steps led up to a raised porch.

Strike now, while Xander's out the back.

I stepped up and rapped on the door.

For a moment, all I could hear was the mournful plucking of strings and the chorus of cicadas, as, above me, a flock of wheeling swifts plucked insects from the heavy air.

Then the door opened.

It was Max.

My heart jumped.

He stood before me, naked, dried sand on his lower half, ice cream smeared across his cheeks. '*Ti theleis?*' he asked, wiping his face with the back of his arm, spreading the ice cream further along to his ear. *What do you want?*

For a moment, I couldn't speak – I just stared at him.

'*Pou einai i mitera sou?*' I finally asked, feeling my stomach tighten. He looked even more like me than in the photograph: matted blond hair and wide blue eyes – that familiar frown of consternation . . .

'*Ti?*' he asked again, tilting his head to one side and putting his weight on one hip.

'*I mitera sou,*' I tried again. '*Einai etho?*'

I wanted to hug him.

'You wanna see my mommy?' he asked, in an American accent, one hand idly swaying the door back and forth.

'Yes please,' I replied, my voice a low rasp. 'That would be great.'

He wrinkled his nose, then turned and ambled a little way-down the tiled hallway, before shouting out that there was a man at the door. Amara called back in rapid Greek – something I was unable to pick up. But her voice had momentarily increased in volume, and with it came the sound of rushing water. She was taking a shower.

Max turned around and skipped back to the door, smiling. 'She says she doesn't need any food. We have enough groceries.'

Just then, I heard a gruff bark of Greek approaching from the rear of the villa, and at all once, Xander was before me; a fresh bottle of beer in hand, cigarette hovering on his lip.

He was taller than I had reckoned. Six foot-four, built like a brick shithouse.

He stood stock still.

'*Ti symvainei?*'

'My name is Alistair Haston,' I replied, after a moment's hesitation.

Xander frowned and then approached me, his flip flops slapping the tiles.

'Alistair Haston?' he echoed, sizing me up while taking a drag on his cigarette. 'From England?'

I nodded. Forced a smile.

He was playing his part well.

Question now was, what role would he assume – jealous husband, or Mister Nice?

'What do you want?' he finally asked, the faintest hint of suspicion in his voice.

'I'd like to talk to Amara,' I replied.

57

Max turned from me to Xander, and back. '*Ti einai?*' He squeaked. *What's going on?*

Xander ignored him and took a drag on his cigarette.

He was prevaricating, unsure which way to go.

But then he exploded into life, extinguishing his cigarette and thrusting the butt into the beer bottle. '*Nai, endaxi.* Of course, of course,' he grinned, pulling Max out of the way. 'Good to meet you, man. I have heard much about you. But, *Panagia mou*, this is crazy – what a fucking surprise!' He stepped towards me and held his hand out wide; wrist cocked, thumb up – looking for the matey, casual handshake.

'Daddy, we don't say "fucking",' remonstrated Max, punching Xander on the thigh and then turning to flash his gap-toothed grin at me.

'Sorry *Maxi mou*,' said Xander, contrite. 'But, Alistair is from England. A long, long way away.'

He looked up and caught my eye, his hand still hovering in mid-air.

'It's a pleasure to meet you too,' I replied, meeting his cupped hand with mine – the resounding clap echoing in the hallway. 'I heard your guitar playing. Sounded pretty good.'

Still no enquiry as to what the hell I was doing there.

He knew I'd be coming, of course – but he still had an act to keep up.

'Thanks, buddy.'

He reached out beside him and ruffled Max's hair, drawing him in close.

'*Papi, papi, poios einai afto?*' asked Max, jumping up and down and tugging on Xander's trunks.

So, Xander was 'daddy', but did Max know he wasn't his real father?

'A friend of mommy's,' Xander replied in English. '*Ella, ella* – come in, Alistair. Amara is in the bathroom. You wanna beer?'

'My name's Max,' interrupted Max proudly, breaking away from Xander.

He stopped equidistant between us, his skinny arms swinging wildly at his sides.

'Of course,' apologised Xander, rubbing his ear. 'This is my boy.'

Fuck you.

Avoiding meeting Xander's eye, I crouched down to shake Max's hand, but before I could grasp it, Amara materialised in the hallway wrapped from head to toe in bath towels, thick chocolate brown hair cascading over her bare shoulders as she sipped a glass of water.

Leaping to my feet, I let out an involuntary gasp.

A robed Venus de Milo.

Xander pulled Max to one side and addressed his trophy wife.

'A friend to see you,' he announced proudly. 'From London.'

Amara looked up and instantly froze, her sultry eyes wide with astonishment.

Then the glass slipped from her hand, shattering at her feet.

5

Before I could explain myself, Amara grabbed Max and whisked him away to get changed, instructing Xander to clean up the mess. I offered to help, but Xander wouldn't hear of it. Maintaining his faux bonhomie, he instead invited me to help myself to a beer from the fridge and wait out in the garden, saying they'd be through in a few minutes.

I complied and, heart thumping against my rib cage, drank a beer on the patio in the diffused sunlight, roaming the oleander shrubs along the garden perimeter, trying to grasp snippets of the hushed conversation emanating from within, but without success.

Their reaction had left me utterly baffled; why had neither Xander or Amara asked me what I was doing there, or how I'd tracked them down? Xander knew, of course – this was all his doing. But the fact that Amara hadn't enquired suggested only one thing:

Takis had phoned ahead.

And told them what, exactly?

Not for a good half hour later did they all finally appear – the presence of Max acting as a shield against any sensitive discussion.

Dressed in a figure-hugging black dress, and hiding behind Gucci sunglasses, Amara apologised again for her clumsiness and told me how well I looked, before Xander stepped in and declared that we should all head to a local restaurant where Max could play, and where we'd be left alone to have an 'adult chat'.

On the brief walk up to the restaurant, Amara kept her own counsel, while Xander dominated the proceedings, giving me a breezy low-down on the turtle sanctuary which had been in operation since the late seventies, along with a potted history lesson on the famous Shipwreck Beach which lay to the north of Zakynthos; explaining how a merchant vessel had run aground during a storm while trying to deliver contraband to the island in 1980, and had since become a tourist attraction. A must-see, he'd added, that I should count on making if I was planning on 'hanging out'. Amara briefly looked our way at his remark – the only time she paid us any attention during the walk. After that, she quickly resumed her shadowing of Max in his pursuit of grasshoppers flitting back and forth across our path.

Minutes later, we arrived at Nikos Taverna; a wooden construct built a metre or so off the ground – to discourage the insects, I presumed – situated at the end of the row of restaurants along the beach track, at the junction of the crossroads where I'd made my approach from the Porto Roma.

Choosing a corner table looking out over the beach, Xander gave the waitress our drinks order, while Amara led Max off to the play area at the rear of the restaurant.

I scanned the field-cum-carpark, noting there were only a handful of jeeps and quadbikes left – the occupants of which had adjourned to Gerakas Beach Bar, two doors down; getting stuck in to happy hour cocktails, as Radiohead's 'Creep' let rip from the bar's PA system.

It was now 7 p.m. An hour since my arrival at the villa.

Still no sign of Gerald's agents.

'Tried the wine?' barked Xander cheerfully, as Amara

reappeared, accompanied by our waitress. 'Made by a farmer in the next village. Best rosé on the island. He'll sell you it at cost price if you bring him the empty bottles.'

As the waitress promptly delivered a bottle of beer and a plate of olives, along with a carafe of rosé and three glasses to the table, Xander pulled out the chair between Amara and me and dropped into it, sticking a sandaled foot up onto the adjacent stone wall, before flicking his cigarette butt over his shoulder into the road behind.

'Sorry about my husband, he thinks he's a rock star,' said Amara, sliding the ashtray across the table and, for the first time since my arrival, flashing a smile. 'I can't believe you are here, Alistair. It's been so long.'

I smiled, stuck for a reply.

I had forgotten what a contradictory cocktail of vulnerability and world-weariness Amara could summon with just one slow-motion flicker of those eyelashes. A sensuous, slender-hipped siren giving the illusion of needing to be saved, when, in reality she was already a universe out of reach.

Xander was one lucky bastard.

For now.

Out of the corner of my eye, I saw him studying me.

Keep your head in the game, Haston.

'Almost six years,' I replied finally, taking a sip of my beer and shifting my gaze from her lips. 'And to be honest, I never thought our paths would ever cross again . . . until I received a phone call in London from a man pretending to be your father.'

I waited for her to respond but she kept her eyes trained on her son.

'A man who told me you and Max had been in an accident,' I continued, 'and who warned me that the police would be investigating me, because I was the boy's father.'

For a moment, both Amara and her husband remained immobile.

'Is this true?' I asked. 'Is Max my son?'

62

Amara finally lifted her head and turned to me, eyes glistening.

'What were you expecting?' she rasped, her voice catching in her throat. 'To jump back into his life and play father? With no warning – after all this time?'

She drew herself up in her chair and glared at me.

'I was never in his life,' I replied, stunned by her vehemence. 'I would be clueless if it weren't for that phone call.'

This was certainly not how I'd imagined our first conversation to run.

Xander pulled his chair in and put an arm on her shoulder, then, as one, they turned to face me.

'We know who called you,' Xander intoned. 'We have been expecting this for some time.'

Blindsided, I stared at him.

But it was Amara who spoke next.

'Takis,' she announced, before taking a long pull of her wine. 'My brother. He is responsible.'

Takis?

'He hates me,' spat Xander, flicking his ash into the ashtray. 'Just like his father—'

'My father was a good man, a proud man,' said Amara, cutting him off, 'but he was always unfair to Xander. Never gave him a chance.'

'Because I'm a musician,' retorted her husband, pushing back in his chair and tugging at the ribbon in his ponytail. 'Because I don't have a job in a fucking office. Like Takis. I mean, what the—'

Amara held up her hand. Her husband dutifully obeyed.

The waitress popped up out of nowhere, wielding a pencil and pad, but Amara dismissed her with a flick of the wrist.

'My father paid to have your name put on the birth certificate,' she continued, her tone firm. 'Against my wishes. He never saw Xander as a family man. Kept insisting I contact you – tell you about Max so that Xander would be pushed away. But my father was misguided. He was wrong. When he died, Takis told me at his funeral that I deserved better than Xander. That he did not belong in our family, and that he was after my father's money.'

'Takis wants you to break our family apart,' said Xander, rubbing an eye with his thumb, cigarette still in hand. 'Over my dead body.'

Brows knitted in anger, he again reached an arm around his wife and the two fell silent.

Xander's performance was astonishing. More unnerving, though, was the fact Amara was corroborating the narrative. True, both Gerald and Takis had insinuated that Xander was an ill fit for the Manolis family, and I knew from the aftermath of Paros that her father had been a domineering personality – but why was Amara so quick to believe that Takis had made the phone call?

Because she's been expertly manipulated.

'I'm not here to break your family apart,' I began, weighing my words carefully as I tried to keep the facts clear in my head. 'I am here because—'

'Takis told you where to find us?' interrupted Amara, folding her arms about her, suspicion lighting up her eyes.

'Sorry?'

'When did he tell you?' clarified Xander. 'How?'

'He told me in person,' I answered. 'The man who telephoned me in London sent me to Takis's address in Athens. Takis seemed surprised to see me. Claimed to know nothing about the phone call—'

'Lying bastard,' snapped Xander, cutting in. 'It was Takis himself. He was deceiving you.'

'And when I asked about Max,' I continued, shifting my focus to Amara, 'he showed me some photographs, but wouldn't say anything to confirm the fact that I was his father. He told me

64

you'd just left for Zakynthos. Said he was in charge of renting the villa out to tourists, but that it was sometimes used by family. He also mentioned your father. I'm sorry to hear about his passing.'

'Did he say anything about me?' Xander asked, exhaling a stream of smoke.

'Just that you were a musician,' I replied. 'But I sensed you weren't the family favourite.'

'Nothing else?' asked Amara, narrowing her eyes.

Xander too was studying me intently.

Wondering if Takis had given anything away?

'He pretty much kicked me out of the door after that,' I concluded. 'Look, I don't want to get involved in any family politics. I just want proof that I'm Max's father.'

That was Gerald's direction – and right now, I was clinging dearly to it.

Because I sensed Amara was about to send me packing.

'Proof?' she exclaimed. 'Why would I lie?'

'I'm not saying you are lying,' I replied, wishing I could take her to one side and tell her exactly what was going on. 'I just want to formalise it.'

Xander mumbled something in Greek and lit another cigarette. 'You mean a test? One of those, er ...'

'A DNA test,' I said, helping him out.

'Alistair, I beg you,' pleaded Amara suddenly, her eyes welling up again. 'As far as Max is concerned, Xander is his father. We are a family. Why would you want to destroy that? You want to make it official? And then what – go home and leave us to pick up the pieces?'

'There are legal implications for me,' I replied, feeling an overwhelming urge to reach forward and hold her in my arms. 'I need to be sure. After that, I admit ... I don't know what to do about it.'

It was the truth; I had no idea how to progress.

I'd been so wrong – Amara and Xander were solid.

Except that Xander is a lying bastard.

'You don't believe me?' Amara asked, hardening.

'Why did you keep it a secret?' I asked. 'One phone call, all of this could have been avoided.'

Amara glared at me, incredulous. 'You were going to give up your studies, give up your life in England and come over to Greece?' she flared, sweeping a clawed hand through her hair. 'Bullshit!'

'I had a right to know,' I exclaimed.

'A right?' shot back Amara.

'To be part of the decision.'

'You weren't there. It was me. On my own. Alone.'

'You could have called,' I insisted. 'Or sent a letter . . . at the very least.'

'You were in fucking prison!'

'Hey guys!' chipped in Xander, placing an arm on Amara's shoulder.

But Amara pushed him away.

'I don't know, Haston, you tell me,' she continued, incensed. 'I was broken. What happened to you . . . to me . . . it was a mess. My father – he locked me up with my aunts and uncles in the middle of nowhere, keeping me prisoner. Stopped me from going to drama school. When I found out I was pregnant, it seemed like the only good thing left for me. Why didn't I tell you? I don't know. Maybe I was protecting you. From a big fucking disaster.'

As she leaped to her feet, Xander caught her by the hand. 'Baby, Alistair is not here to cause us pain—'

But she wasn't finished. 'And if you are half the man you think you are,' she seethed, turning to her husband, 'you will call Takis tonight and tell him never to contact us ever again.' She then added a flurry of Greek expletives, too rapid for me to catch, before turning on her heels and fleeing across the

66

restaurant floor, her black dress cursing the eyes of all who dared light upon her.

Xander hesitated a moment, scratching at his designer stubble, then kicked his chair back and picked up his wine glass. 'Excuse me,' he said, clapping me on the shoulder. 'I, er . . .'

'Of course.'

Over the next ten minutes, the sun dipped below the bank of cloud on the horizon and dusk began to fall; cicadas giving way to the chirrup of crickets, as the sky bruised purple and orange above the horizon and the first stars pushed through the darkening sky to the east.

Tapping the beer bottle against my teeth, I watched Amara and Xander in muted discussion to one side of the playground, out of Max's earshot. I could only fathom that Xander was still trying to persuade Amara to acquiesce and show some understanding – to undergo the DNA test, sticking to his reasoning that they'd then be rid of me as soon as it was over.

Give him an opening, Gerald had instructed.

Xander was hooked and running.

As for Amara – she appeared to hate me. I was causing her nothing but heartache and distress. But I was now in too deep to pull out. Once on the other side, once she knew the truth, everything would change.

The waitress then appeared for the third time, interrupting my train of thought by pointedly dropping a set of menus on the table. I thanked her, apologised for the delay in ordering and asked her for another bottle of Mythos. As she set off across the restaurant floor, grumbling to herself, I turned back towards the sandpit to find Xander only feet away. Following on behind, some twenty yards and closing, were Amara and Max, hand in hand.

'Hey man, it's gonna be fine,' Xander declared jovially, puffing out his cheeks and reaching for his glass of wine. 'I'm gonna call the hospital in the morning and set up an appointment. We will figure out something to tell Max.'

Just like that?

I nodded and took a swig of beer. 'Amara's okay about it then?'

'Sure thing,' he beamed, draining his glass and immediately refilling it. 'While we wait for the results to come through you can get to know Max. Amara agrees you should come with us to the beach tomorrow. You sail, right? Maybe you can take Max out in a boat.'

'What's that about a boat?' Amara called out, as she picked Max up and set him down in a chair.

'A boat! I wanna go on a sailing boat,' squeaked Max, banging his fist on the table top.

'If you ask Alistair nicely,' said Xander, 'I'm sure he will take you.'

How did he know I could sail?

'Can you take me please, Mister Alistair?' asked Max, waving a sandy hand in my face.

An educated guess, or had Amara told him?

She'd known how much time I'd spent sailing with Ricky, on Paros.

'Of course. I . . .' I began.

'Except we don't have a boat,' said Amara, her smile tightening.

'We can go to Laganas and rent one there, right?' countered Xander, clicking his fingers at the waitress.

A loud revving of an engine from the road directly behind us drowned out Max's overjoyed response, and a cloud of dust billowed across the table.

'*Poustis malakas!*' yelled Xander, craning his neck around to catch sight of the perpetrator on the road below. 'Fucking tourists and their quadbikes.'

'Xander!' coughed Amara, spitting her wine back into her glass.

Through the railings, I caught sight of said tourists walking up towards the cocktail bar, arm in arm, with their backs to us. The man was heavily built with a buzz cut, sporting a tie-dyed t-shirt. His accomplice was tall and lithe, in skin-tight cut-off jeans, with peroxide hair.

'Russians,' scoffed Xander, sliding back into his chair and grinding his cigarette butt into the ashtray. 'Think they own the place.'

Max brought our attention back to the table. '*Papi*, you said "fucking".'

'Max!' snapped Amara, turning to her son and clapping a hand over his mouth, before breaking into a laugh. 'You do not say this word. Ever!'

'*Papi* does,' replied Max, turning to me as he dug into his ear with his straw. 'Alistair, do you say—?'

'Max!' bellowed Xander, wagging a finger. 'Do not disrespect your mommy.'

Just then, the waitress returned, threw me a look of disdain, and sidled flirtatiously up to Xander.

'So, Englishman,' began the latter, wrapping an arm around the waitress's waist, 'you must be hungry, it's getting near your bedtime. Anna here recommends the calamari.' Then turning to Max, he winked and whispered, 'Best on the fucking island!'

By the time we had finished our Calamari and frites – Xander, once again having taken control of the proceedings, ordering on behalf of all four of us – darkness had fallen, the remaining tables taken up by a motley ensemble of sunburnt tourists and their frolicking children.

The tension from our earlier three-way discussion eased as Max commandeered the conversation, asking me what England was like and what kind of animals lived in London, particularly by way of lizards, chameleons and cicadas. I disappointed him by explaining we had none of the latter two in England, let alone London, and that there was only one kind of lizard on the British Isles, found primarily in the south. In return, I quizzed Max about school and what he wanted to be when he grew up. He declared his intent to become an astronaut, then extended a formal invitation to visit their house in Athens, where he and his *papi* had built a spaceship in the garden.

Eventually, Xander dismissed himself from the table and disappeared off once more in the direction of the kitchens.

Up until this point, Xander, Amara and I had barely exchanged a word that wasn't either directly or indirectly related to the chat between Max and me. But the minute Xander was out of sight, Amara let out a sigh and suddenly came to life.

'You like the rosé?' she exclaimed, sweeping her hair back over her shoulders to expose her neck.

Instantly, my heart rate shot up.

Max cocked his head to one side, watching me closely.

'Very nice,' I replied. 'Dry. How it should be. The stuff we have in England is always too sweet.'

'Hmm,' she murmured, biting her lip. 'And what about my husband – you like him too?'

'Sorry?'

'Xander is a little intense, no?'

'He's er . . . full of gusto,' I replied, turning to check Xander's whereabouts. 'What's he doing in the kitchen?'

'He always has business of some sort. A deal here, a deal there.'

'With the chef?'

Laughing, she drew her chair in closer and topped up her wine. 'With Xander, you never know what he is up to. But he has known the boss here for a couple of years – Kostas. Maybe he is trying to arrange a boat for tomorrow?'

'Right.'

'Or maybe Kostas will know somebody who has. Xander will sniff it out.'

I felt a nudge against my thigh. At first, I thought that Max had swung a foot underneath the table. But when I looked down I saw it was Amara's knee.

'Is there a Mrs Haston?' she said, before taking a generous hit of her wine. 'Or, a girlfriend?'

Keeping the wine glass at her lips, she held my gaze.

Aware of a stirring in my groin, I quickly threw a look to Max, as if somehow, he might have picked up on it. But the sleepy boy was now otherwise engaged, drawing a dinosaur on a napkin with a pen borrowed from the waitress, his head propped up on an elbow.

'No girlfriend, no,' I eventually replied, gazing into her eyes. 'Busy with this and that. No time, it seems.'

Tell her, Haston. Tell her the truth!

'Shame,' she said, breaking eye contact. 'There should always be time for this.'

I glanced below the table again as her leg pushed harder against mine, the dress riding up and exposing her tanned thighs.

'Time for what?' came a voice from behind us.

Xander was back, clutching a plastic bag with an octopus inside.

'A gift from the kitchen,' he continued, tossing it onto the table.

'Xander!' remonstrated Amara, gently sliding her chair away from mine. 'Not on the table.'

'So Max can look at it,' he said, nudging the boy.

But Max's head had dropped face-down onto the napkin.

'You were saying there's no time?' Xander continued, adjusting the band on his ponytail.

'For a girlfriend,' said Amara, draining her glass. 'Alistair is too busy.'

'Hey, but this is terrible,' objected Xander. 'You stick around, man. I'll find you a hottie.'

'*Endaxi!*' snapped Amara, rising to her feet. 'Time to go. Max is asleep.'

71

Xander slid over to me and wrapped an arm around my shoulder as I hauled myself to my feet. 'Englishman, come tomorrow, any time after ten o'clock. We take it from there, *nai?*' Then he moved around the table and picked up the comatose Max, cradling him into the crook of his neck. 'A girlfriend, by tomorrow? I can't promise this. But maybe we take a boat from Laganas to Shipwreck Beach? Pick up some ladies along the way?'

Amara grimaced and punched Xander on the shoulder.

'Tomorrow?' I replied, my stomach tightening. 'But ...'

'Yes, of course tomorrow,' he cheered, cutting me off. 'After I have made the call to the hospital, for sure,' he added, raising his eyebrows and turning to his wife. 'We will not take his English "no" for an answer. Tomorrow – Shipwreck Beach.'

Amara acknowledged her husband with a fleeting smile, then reached out and touched my arm. 'It will be nice to spend some time together,' she said, producing a scrunchie and tying her hair back in a ponytail. 'Max likes you.'

I could barely breathe.

Xander threw her a look, that, again, I couldn't decipher.

'I'll be there,' I said, feigning nonchalance. 'I look forward to it.'

'*Endaxi, pame!*' yelled Xander, grabbing Amara by the hand. 'We have a plan.'

Gunning the Nissan as hard as I dared, I raced back towards the Porto Roma, crashing through the potholes in my haste to get back to the hotel.

Gerald had assured me the kidnappers would bide their time to ensure the set up was fool proof, and yet, there was Xander, operating at breakneck speed, proposing an excursion the very next day.

A trip to Shipwreck Beach?

I could hardly refuse. Amara had agreed to the DNA test,

showing willing to let go any resentment and spend some time together. If I were to deny the gesture, Xander would surely smell a rat. And yet, to proceed headlong into a potential trap when there was zero evidence of back up, was unthinkable.

Where the fuck were Gerald's men?

Wiping the sweat from my eyes, I pressed on through the barren moonscape, pulling out of the last of the series of hairpin bends where the track straightened out just yards from the silvering sea and hammered onwards for the final kilometre stretch.

But as for Amara . . .

The minute Xander had left us, she'd dropped the hostility and begun flirting outrageously; the sexual tension, the chemistry between us unmistakeable . . .

I'd been right all along.

She was trapped . . . she needed freeing.

It was meant to be.

Suddenly, I arrived at an unexpected bend in the road, where, distracted by a low-flying owl, I almost missed the turning.

Stamping on the brakes, I veered briefly into the ditch before managing to regain control, swinging sharply to my right and skidding across the forecourt of the hotel. Engine screaming, the car slammed to a halt a few feet from a row of parked cars.

Leaning on the steering wheel, I cursed myself for having drunk so much wine and took a moment to catch my breath.

Up ahead, the restaurant terrace was packed, dinner in full swing. A live band had set up by the northern wall, thrashing out the theme tune from the film *Zorba the Greek* on zithers and mandolins. My inquisitive hostess would be busy helping out on the restaurant floor . . .

Perfect. I could put in a phone call to Gerald without risk of eavesdropping.

Then I noticed the quadbike.

Two o'clock to my right, half illuminated by the headlamps. The occupants were sat smoking, arms draped casually over the sides of the vehicle, engaged in conversation. I immediately recognised them as the Russian couple from earlier – the ones who'd offended Xander with their unnecessary revving of the engine. Not only that, I realised it was the same quadbike I'd seen on my arrival at the Porto Roma earlier that afternoon.

Switching off the engine, I left the lights on, watching as the man flicked a cigarette into the dust, before sliding off the bike and stalking around the side of the terrace to climb the stone steps up to the restaurant. As he went, I had a fleeting glimpse of his profile: firm jawline and heavy brow, with a thick, muscular neck. Early thirties. A fitness freak by all accounts.

Meanwhile, his companion remained straddled on the seat, still smoking.

I was about to get out, when she too disengaged herself from the machine and turned to face my direction. Cigarette in hand, she tugged her t-shirt down over her stomach, while simultaneously hiking up her jeans, then raised a hand in salutation.

I froze rigid in disbelief.

Impossible.

A trick of the light, surely?

But as the rider stepped forwards from the shadows into the full beam of my lights, all doubt vanished in an instant.

Xander was wrong. They weren't Russian – at least, she wasn't.

She'd dyed her hair since I'd last seen her. And I never knew she smoked. But there was no mistaking that cool allure and elegant, film star poise.

It was my flatmate Vince's girlfriend.

Kate.

6

Transfixed, I continued to stare through the windscreen as Kate threw a glance back towards the restaurant, then approached the car.

'Drink?' she said, opening the passenger door and folding herself into the seat. 'Take a right and follow the road to Banana Beach. Bar's open till two.'

Flicking her cigarette into the dust, she pulled the door shut.

Neither of us moved, as I continued to gawp at her.

'Any time now would be good,' she declared, breaking into a smile as she reached for her seat belt. 'We don't have all night.'

Still speechless, I fired the ignition and threw the car into gear, skidding across the courtyard, before pulling out onto the tarmac road and accelerating uphill through the olive grove plantation in the direction of Zakynthos town. Only when the road levelled out and the engine pitch dropped, did I loosen my grip on the wheel.

Averting my eyes from the potholes speeding towards us amid the illuminated moths, I tried briefly to make out Kate's features, but in the scant glow from the dashboard her expression remained inscrutable.

'So, does Vince know you're here?' I asked finally. 'Or is he MI6 too?'

'He thinks I'm in Paris,' Kate replied, craning her neck to check the road behind. 'At a design convention.' Twisting back around, she tugged at the hem of her jeans shorts and leaned forward, peering through the windscreen into the dark.

'Uh, huh,' I said, lacking a comeback.

Vince had told me how Kate was a clothes buyer for high-end department stores. It was how they'd met, at an event Vince's PR firm was hosting. A boring job, she'd claimed, but one that allowed her to travel – *to get air miles*.

'It's about three kilometres,' she said, tucking her hair behind her ears.

Focussing on the road ahead, my thoughts raced along with the wheels as they screeched and ground their way through bend after bend, until finally a sign appeared in the headlights: Banana Beach, 1Km.

'Quite a lie you spun,' I said, swerving to avoid an errant hedgehog as the road bore downhill once more, heading back to the sea. 'To Vince. To me . . .'

'A sharp turn to the right,' she replied, without taking her eyes off the tarmac.

'All in the name of duty, eh?' I added, as we skidded through another hairpin bend.

Why the hell hadn't Gerald given me the heads up?

'If you're looking for the brake,' Kate said, turning to me and cracking another smile, 'it's the one in the middle.'

Banana Beach café was rammed.

Head still reeling, I sat at a shadowy table furthest away from the bar and dance floor, the water hissing on the sand a mere ten feet from my chair, and watched Kate thread her way back through the gyrating partygoers, a Mojito in each hand.

'No idea how this place does such good business,' said Kate with a laugh as she stepped off the concrete dance floor onto the sand. 'Stuck out in the middle of nowhere, you have to drive through half a mile of fir trees and then there's fuck all when you get there except a bloody concrete bandstand. Still, beats having to drive to Zakynthos town, right?'

Dropping into her seat, she tossed a pack of Camel Lights onto the metal table and slid over my drink.

'Didn't know you smoked,' I said, studying her as she sipped her Mojito.

'Holiday habit,' she said, before taking a long drag, inhaling deeply and letting out a plume of smoke into the night air. 'Like you.'

There it was again, the transatlantic twang I'd clocked at the dinner in Putney and had put down to alcohol. Except, it was stronger now.

'Except, neither of us are on holiday.'

She smiled and nudged the pack towards me. 'I won't tell.'

'Is Vince expecting you back from Paris?' I asked. 'Or is he officially dumped?'

She smiled and took another sip of her drink. 'We had a falling out. It won't come as a surprise. You were there – he was being a prick, right?'

Fixing me with her gaze, she took another hit on her cigarette.

'Well, it's nice of someone to show up,' I said lightly, taking a pull on my drink. 'Even if it turns out to be the woman who's been shagging my best mate and lying to us for the last six weeks.'

She smiled and turned towards the bar, as Ace of Bass's 'All That She Wants' drew a cheer from the dance floor.

'Gerald might have warned me,' I added, slapping away a mosquito.

After a sip of her cocktail she turned back from the melee.

'Gerald couldn't possibly know I'm in Zakynthos,' she said slowly, blowing a tuft of peroxide hair from her eyes. 'Because Gerald has no idea who I am, or what I do.'

Drink poised at my lips, I stared at her, uncomprehending.
'You're MI6.'

'I'm here for the same reasons you are,' she said, smiling.

Baffled, I watched as she took a long draw on her cigarette then slowly ground it into the ashtray.

'A year ago,' she began, drawing herself taller in her seat, 'Gerald scored a major coup against the Greek Mafia. Forty million dollars' worth of cocaine, recovered from the panels of a luxury speedboat moored at Piraeus. Quite a feat. "The Seven Stars", as they're known in Athens, are a notorious cartel, not one for sloppy mistakes. And the arrests led to the incarceration of two of the biggest players in the Med. The story was all over the Athens papers and some of the internationals too. Gerald had flown solo initially, and then when everything was in place, he approached MI6 and Greek security services for additional manpower. He couldn't have pulled it off without them. But it was his show. His glory. The public of course had no idea. His name was kept out of the press for obvious reasons. But in certain circles, he became somewhat of a secret celebrity . . .'

She broke off, distracted by a flicker of sheet lightning out to sea.

Waiting for her to go on, I shifted in my seat, peeling a sweaty thigh off the plastic.

Gerald was an egotist, no doubt about it; I'd sensed it from the off. Why hadn't he taken the opportunity to regale me with his exploits at the hotel the previous night?

'It was later discovered,' Kate continued, 'or rather, he admitted, that he'd had been tipped off by a phone call from a rival cartel operating out of Thessaloniki. Unsurprisingly, Gerald never revealed his sources. He'd be a dead man walking. But then it also transpired that, three days after the sting, a hundred thousand dollars showed up in his bank account, traceable to a shell company registered in the Caymans . . .'

She broke off again, eyeballing me, as if awaiting a response.

But as soon as I opened my mouth to speak, she cut me off with a curt wave of her hand.

'Not admitting to the cash doesn't mean, per se, he was complicit, of course,' she said, crossing her legs as she stretched once more for the Camel Lights. 'The payment may have been a bribe, a coercive move to silence him.'

'Or to buy his services for another time,' I added, still trying to get over the fact I'd been sitting across from this woman in the kitchen in Putney only three days ago.

'Indeed. Although, what level of involvement he actually had in the proceedings, other than providing the authorities with a time and location, remains unclear.'

She tapped the packet and pulled out two cigarettes.

I accepted without hesitation.

'There was the usual backlash,' Kate continued, raking a hand through her hair as she lit first my cigarette then hers. 'Certain elements within the authorities kicked up a fuss as to what business a university lecturer had playing at James Bond, doing deals with the Mafia and interfering with police work. But it was quickly smoothed over, no further questions asked.'

She paused to tuck a lock of blonde hair behind her ear.

'Is Gerald a crook? Unlikely. He doesn't have the head for it. Too much of a showman. But he's an opportunist, and a wild-card. In the end, we turned a blind eye to the money to give him the impression he'd got away with it, because we realised it was more expedient to keep him in play.'

Batting away a moth, she took a long hit on her cigarette then sat back in her chair, folding an arm across her chest as a second flicker of lightning lit up the horizon to my right.

'"We?"' I said, picking up my cue.

'Greek Intelligence.'

I sat rigid, my eyes trained on hers.

Kate was *Greek?*

'Turns out, it was the right move,' she continued, her

shoulders dropping as she exhaled a lengthy stream of purple haze into the night. 'Because Gerald is back in business.'

'The kidnapping . . .?' I began, tailing off as soon as the words had left my lips.

Kate nodded. 'An informant from the same Thessaloniki cartel who tipped him off about the drugs haul in Piraeus, also tipped him off about the plot to kidnap Max,' she said, her features hardening. 'Once again, it's the Seven Stars Athens cartel who are responsible.'

I stared at her dumbfounded.

'Gerald talked of the Mafia, but never mentioned anything about any tip-offs, or a cartel called the Seven Stars.'

She nodded. 'Which makes us even more concerned that he will try to take matters even more into his own hands and go off piste. With a five-year-old's life on the line, that's a risk we simply can't afford to take.'

'You're here to call off the sting?'

'We're here to make sure he doesn't fuck it up.'

For the next half hour, as an electrical storm discharged itself over the mainland twenty miles to the east, Kate made me revisit my conversation with Gerald in its entirety, cross-checking every fact he'd given me to ensure we were 'up to speed and on the same page'.

It turned out that for the most part, he'd withheld information rather than lied about it. The chief discrepancies being, his alluding to the idea he was working hand in hand with MI6; the lack of transparency about his relationship of convenience with a Thessaloniki cartel against the Athens Seven Stars; and finally, how he'd come to be involved in the sting in the first place.

'He told me Xander approached the Mafia in a night club and that it was the Greeks who picked up on it first,' I explained, revolving my empty glass in the palm of my hand. 'And that

Greek Intelligence approached MI6 only when they realised I was Max's real father.'

'Implying that Gerald and MI6 were one and the same,' Kate snorted, indignant. 'He's a cheeky bugger but, no, I can assure you, Gerald isn't on the payroll, and what he told you simply isn't true. Ever since October of last year, he's been under close watch. In any case, we know for a fact that someone informed him, because he's already confessed it.'

'To whom?'

'The same man he confided in the first time around,' she replied, stroking an earlobe. 'A contact in Greek Intelligence who he's known since his schooldays.'

'And Gerald is sure it was the same Thessaloniki group who tipped him off this time around?'

She nodded. 'It's an age-old rivalry. As I said, Greece is the gateway from the east to the rest of continental Europe. A prize worth fighting for.'

'So, they have a mole on the inside?'

'Almost certainly.'

I took a pull on my drink. 'But why would they use Gerald as a middle-man when they could just call it in to the police?'

Kate frowned. 'It's a very good question. Which is why his services must amount to more than being a whistle-blower.'

'And you were party to this information?' I asked, eyeing her closely, still digesting the fact Gerald had been resident in Greece since childhood, yet had somehow acquired perfect public schoolboy mannerisms.

'I only found out when my involvement became necessary.'

Kate then confessed that she'd been sent to London to keep an eye on me, as the Greeks thought I might also be involved, due to the events of '88 – just as Gerald, too, had suggested. She was convinced of my innocence, of course – but they had to make sure.

'And that was your sole brief?' I asked. 'To keep an eye on me?'

'Amongst other things, yes.'

She then admitted that part of her job was to make sure I got on the plane to Greece – revealing that the dinner at Vince's wasn't so impromptu after all. It had been of Kate's doing; timed to perfection. She'd sided with me against Vince merely to encourage me on my way.

'Although, I'm sure that the prospect of seeing Amara helped?' she murmured, a smile playing at the corners of her lips.

So they had counted on that, too.

'Gerald said he had surveillance on me in London,' I said, changing tack. 'Was that true?'

Shaking her head, she passed me a fresh cigarette, cupping her hand around mine as she lit it. 'Gerald didn't need eyes on you in London. He knew that we'd take care of that side of things, he was simply waiting for you to arrive in Athens. Once we alerted him of your imminent arrival, all he had to do was catch you at the airport.'

The woman in the taxi; Kate was no doubt privy to that too.

How much did she know about Takis, though? His name had yet to come up.

'So, Gerald has no idea that the entire Greek secret service knows what he's up to?' I asked, deciding to keep shtum about both the taxi ride and the fact I'd been sent to Takis's house. If Kate wanted information, she'd ask for it.

'He knows we're in the loop,' she replied. 'He brought it to us, after all. But he also knows it's in everyone's interest to let him work unhindered. Gerald would never have confided in us if he thought we'd assign a task force. He's counting on us to play ball and step in at the last minute to finish the job. As we did before.'

'He's definitely not aware you guys know about the money he received – the payment, or whatever it was?'

'Correct.'

'And what about MI6?'

82

'They're taking a back seat.'

'Too many cooks.'

She nodded. 'In any case, they'll be happy to keep in the background. Should anything go wrong they can walk away with a clean pair of heels.'

Something didn't sit right. There was an inherent contradiction to her logic.

'If it's agreed Gerald will fly solo until you step in,' I began, eyes trained on the distant lightning, 'what's the concern?'

'Sorry?'

'You're worried he's going to go "off-piste",' I answered, turning back to her. 'But if you already know that's his MO, and you're on board with it, then what's the problem?'

She nodded thoughtfully, breaking eye contact to study the glowing tip of her cigarette. 'He's cutting it too close to the wire. He hasn't told us what kind of outfit he's running here, or the size of his team, and yet we believe the sting to be imminent. Maverick or not, at the time of the Piraeus drug haul we were brought into the picture much earlier. His previous success appears to have gone to his head. He now has – well . . . aspirations, it seems. To be a player.'

She smiled and flicked a speck of ash from her cheek.

I asked if she had been part of the Piraeus sting, but she replied that it had been before her time; she'd joined the service in the autumn.

Less than a year ago. A high-flyer, evidently.

'So, what do I do now?' I asked. 'Gerald's expecting me to report back to him.'

'Proceed exactly as he instructed,' she replied, leaning back in her chair to let a waiter collect our glasses. 'But anything you say to Gerald, any information you give him, you need to brief us first. Any information he gives you, anything he says to you that you feel is relevant in any way – any change of plan, or anything you think may be important – you need to tell us immediately.'

'"Us?"'

'Me,' she said, forcing a smile. 'I'm your point of contact. And the first thing we need to know is who his men on the ground are.'

When I told her I'd seen no sign of any tail or watcher other than Kate herself, she insisted I challenge Gerald on the fact and ask for proof that he had my back.

'I was instructed to trust him,' I objected.

'Tell him it's that or you quit,' she shot back. 'It's completely reasonable – he'll be expecting it. Suggest a rendezvous. Then tell me when and where.'

Announcing her colleague would be returning soon to pick her up, she made me fill her in on my conversations with Xander and Amara. I informed her that they were both adamant Takis had made the phone call in a bid to bring me into the equation to upset the family balance. I also told her I suspected that Takis and Xander might be working together, as Greek Intelligence had also suggested – according to Gerald.

As she listened, Kate gave away nothing, and I couldn't tell if she was hearing these ideas for the first time or whether Greek Intelligence was already ahead of the game. She was quick to conclude, however, just as I had, that Xander had clearly manipulated his wife into the belief Takis had set them up. She also felt this might support the idea of Takis's and Xander's collusion, and said she would look into it further. As for Xander's enthusiastic offer to put in a call to the hospital and arrange the DNA test, Kate surmised, as I too had done, that he was being disingenuous, merely seeking to buy time and keep me in play. Nor was she surprised to hear of Amara's reluctance to proceed with the paternity test – it could potentially destroy the relationship with her son. Finally, she felt Xander's offer to head to Shipwreck Beach the next day was inconsequential. I'd only been on the island for a day; the Seven Stars Mafia would need time to prepare and get organised.

'And Amara?' she asked finally, holding my gaze. 'How's that working out?'

I smiled and told her it was none of her business.

With that, Kate wrapped up the session – reiterating the need to identify Gerald's men – before producing a napkin with a telephone number scribbled on it, instructing me to call her first thing in the morning.

As we made our way through the potted Oleander shrubs surrounding the bar perimeter up the hill into the shadows where I'd parked the Nissan, a quadbike came flying over the top of the hillock in a shower of gravel, skidding up to a halt a few metres from where we were stood at the edge of the pines.

'By the way, I presume you've got a map?' Kate asked, hitching her shorts up on her hips as she made her way over to her companion. 'You'll need to know this island like the back of your hand.'

'Gerald gave me one at the hotel,' I called out, shading my eyes from the glare of the headlights. 'Or rather, his friend Stelios did.'

She stopped and turned. 'Stelios?'

'One of his colleagues who works in BNC,' I replied. 'Or something like that.'

She took two steps towards me. 'NCB? National Central Bureau?'

'That's it.'

Silhouetted by the headlights it was impossible to make out any detail of her expression – other than the fact she had frozen, head tilted to one side.

'Stelios Papadakis?'

'I didn't get a second name,' I replied. 'But Gerald introduced me to him as Stelios from the NCB – Interpol.'

I told her he'd dropped by to thank me for my help in '88, as well as to apologise for my stint in jail. I also mentioned that he'd given me two birth certificates for Max. Both original.

One without a father's name in place – and the second, bearing my name and signature.

Still, Kate's silhouette didn't budge.

There was an impatient beep from the quadbike.

'Why, who's Stelios?' I added.

She tossed her cigarette into the sand and moved out of the light, around to the side of the bike. 'Gerald's friend from high-school,' she murmured. 'My boss.'

'It was at about ten this morning,' I said, following her up to the machine. 'Is there a problem?'

'No problem,' she replied breezily, stepping up to ride pillion. 'Just surprised he didn't tell me.'

Her driver gave a taciturn nod, fired the engine then spun the bike around.

And in a cloud of dust, they were gone.

The telephone box was situated at the bend in the road, on the edge of a cluttered courtyard belonging to a small convenience store, a half kilometre from the Porto Roma. Initially, I passed it by, thinking it was far too late to call Gerald, but then feared I'd stay awake all night trying to work out what to say to him. Tired as I was, I had to get it over with. Shoot from the hip without overthinking it.

He picked up after the first ring.

'A little tardy, Alistair,' came a tired voice on the other end.

I immediately went on the offensive. 'Well, apart from being a long fucking day, Gerald, I'm starting to wonder if I'm all alone out here. No sign of anyone watching, or tailing me. Everything okay?'

There was a burst of static, followed by the rustle of paper.

'We'd hardly be doing our job properly if you spotted us,' he said, his mouth closer to the receiver. 'I told you to just get on with making advances with Xander – don't look for us. We'll find you. Now, what gives your end? How did it go?'

'I'd like proof.'

'Of what?'

'That you have my back,' I shot back. 'Otherwise I'm heading straight to the police and getting the fuck out of here.'

Another burst of static. Longer this time.

'No one twisted your arm, old chap,' exclaimed Gerald, his tone less agreeable. 'It was entirely your choice.'

'Goodbye Gerald.'

I dropped the receiver.

'Wait!' came the tinny voice dangling on the end.

Re-connecting the receiver to my ear, Gerald begrudgingly gave me his word his men would make contact first thing in the morning. When I asked him how I'd spot them, he told me not to worry. They'd approach me.

'No one's showed by 10 a.m. I'm gone, you understand?' I said.

'Just don't be on the lookout,' he replied, his tone lightening. 'Blend in. You're a tourist. Now, give me the low down on Xander.'

I let him hang for a moment, then debriefed him on my evening with Xander and his family.

In each case, his reactions were a carbon copy of Kate's. And crucially, he too opined that the trip to Shipwreck Beach was most probably a dummy run. The important thing, he advised, was to keep nurturing the relationship with Xander and to stay sharp. *It will play itself out.*

'When and where tomorrow morning, Gerald?' I said, cutting to the chase. 'I doubt your boys will be joining me for breakfast on the hotel terrace.'

'Gerakas, nine o'clock sharp,' he grunted. 'On the beach.'

Then the line went dead.

7

At 8.30 a.m. the following morning, I was back on the road heading north, winding my way through the olive groves to the village convenience store and the phone box, in order to check in with Kate and update her on my movements.

The air was utterly still, the landscape silent and unmoving. The only other soul sharing the morning light with me was the lone mule tethered under an olive tree, as it had been the day before; sturdy and immobile, gazing unblinking as I drove by. But then, as I rounded the corner in the road into the village, I met with the first signs of life: a tractor with the engine running; children's voices skittering from within the depth of the olive groves; the distant cry of a bird of prey above the pines on the hill.

Killing the engine, I threaded my way through a trio of circling cats and went straight to the telephone.

My first attempt rang out.

Second time round, a male voice picked up after the second ring.

'*Ebros?*'

'Hi, it's Alistair Haston.'

'*Ti theleis?*'

'Is Kate there?'

'*Oxi.*'

Perhaps I shouldn't have mentioned her by name.

'I'm going to Gerakas.'

'*Now?*'

'Yes. Well – my, erm, meeting is at nine. On the beach.'

Half an hour from now.

'Okay.' Then he hung up.

After a quick round of the cramped aisles to stock up on cigarettes and water, as well as a pair of cheap swimming trunks – I'd need them for the trip to Shipwreck Beach, if not Gerakas – I shooed the cats from under the car, started up the engine and set off back towards the Porto Roma and the coastal route.

As the Nissan rattled through the dust towards the peninsula, I wound down the window and smoked a cigarette, wondering at what point I'd pick up a tail. But there wasn't another vehicle in sight. Just the occasional blur of an unidentifiable bird as it shot skywards from the scrub.

My thoughts returned to last night's conversation with Kate.

One thing had struck me as odd: her surprise at how her boss Stelios had joined Gerald and me at the hotel in Athens, but hadn't told her about it. As far as I could see, there was no reason a manager should feel obliged to confide in his underling about anything, if so inclined. Had her reaction, therefore, been for my benefit, or was it genuine? If it was designed for me in some way, to catch my attention, I couldn't for the life of me think why. If, on the other hand it was a genuine response, it was strange that she should reveal it.

Driving on past the farmstead with the ducks and the plum tree, I pulled out onto the tarmac road by the restaurants, before crossing over onto the parched field to park up. There were already a surprising number of cars, camper vans and jeeps in situ, and a steady trickle of early morning bathers were making their way along the chalky track between the myrtle bushes down to the sea. Which was when I spotted the quadbike.

Switching off the ignition, I remained in my seat.

Kate was already in position?

How had she got there so quickly? No one had passed me.

Unless it wasn't her ride.

Still seated, aware now of the cicadas in full swing, their orchestrated chant reverberating from the cypresses dotted between the restaurants, I twisted around and scanned the area. None of the eateries were open yet. Although, yes – it appeared the beach shop was up and running.

Tracking the progress of a group of tourists en route to the sea, my eyes lighted on a couple tucked in by the hedgerow, next to the turtle museum. They appeared to be limbering up for a jog – or yoga. Well, she was. The man was smoking a cigarette, his free hand down the back of his shorts. But when they simultaneously turned towards the road, they caught the sunlight. Even at a distance, there was no mistaking the peroxide hair and angular physique.

Kate. And she'd brought her sidekick.

They must have arrived via the main road to the north. And from close by, too. Since ending the telephone call and arriving at Gerakas, barely fifteen minutes had passed.

I changed into my trunks in the front seat of the Nissan – realising at the same time that I hadn't brought a towel – and smoked two more cigarettes, debating whether I should try to make contact with Kate before heading down onto the sand. But as every minute passed, yet another car or jeep bounced along the track onto the field and unloaded more beachgoers. My watchers could be anywhere.

I decided I'd let her see me and allow her to take the initiative.

With five minutes to go, I exited the car and, making brief eye contact with Kate as I passed the turtle museum, joined the queue of beachgoers stumbling their way down the crumbling path to the water. Scanning ahead for signs of company, I was amazed at how many people were already on the beach; far more than suggested by the number of cars in the field. Maybe a bus had dropped them off – a turtle tour from Zakynthos town, or Laganas?

Stepping out from the shadow of the cliffs, I strode across the thick sand to the sea, removed my trainers and t-shirt and stood at the waterline, trusting my pale English skin would be sufficiently conspicuous for anyone trying to identify me amongst the bronzed sun worshippers.

A good ten minutes passed. Still nobody seemed the slightest bit interested in my presence. Everyone was too busy fitting their snorkels, applying sun cream and gazing dreamily out over the turquoise sea.

No sign of Kate and her companion. They were evidently well camouflaged.

I glanced at my watch: five past nine.

I commenced a slow walk along the shore towards the northern end of the beach, picking up the occasional shell or stone and tossing it into the shallows, until I reached the point where the sand turned to shingle, then rocks. There, I waited a while, then set off in the opposite direction until I'd reached the limit of the sunbathers on the southern flank – the naked swimming area, apparently. Pausing once more to survey my surroundings, I lobbed a few more pebbles into the water, then turned around, wading out up to my ankles into the bath-warm shallows as I followed the curve of the beach back to the centre, every now and then peering up to the skyline above the clifftop, as if studying the local flora and fauna.

Checking my watch again, I saw it was now half-past.

Where the fuck were Gerald's men?

And then I became aware of a figure jogging along the shore towards me. Female. A relaxed, flowing rhythm to her stride . . .

Kate.

I held my position, wondering if she was going to stop and

talk, but as she closed down the distance she continued to avoid eye contact.

I took a step back so she'd have to pass between me and the water's edge rather than behind me, offering her the chance for a passing comment should she wish, but she jogged by without so much as a blink in my direction.

After half a minute or so, I allowed myself to sneak a look. She was at the southernmost end now, one foot up against a boulder, peering out to sea.

Several more minutes passed, and I began to overheat.

To sweat . . .

And then, the uncanny feeling that I was being watched.

By everyone.

Head throbbing, I decided there was nothing for it but to get in the water and cool off.

Stripping off my watch I wrapped it in my t-shirt and, dumping the bundle on the sand with my shoes, was about to throw myself into the shallows when I became aware of someone standing to my immediate right: a tanned, stocky man in an open white shirt and shorts, sporting sunglasses, with a towel draped over his shoulder.

'When the water is calm you can see for many miles,' he said, without looking at me. 'If you are lucky you will see a dolphin. Not so much in the afternoon. The wind comes and there are too many waves.'

'Is that right?' I answered, steadying myself; exhaling slowly over a count of five.

His English was perfect, a mere trace of an accent.

'Yes. I have been coming here since I was a boy.' He turned to me and pushed his shades higher on his nose. 'It is a famous beach, because of the turtles. But to see them, you must come much earlier. Five, six o'clock in the morning.'

He smiled again and moved his towel from his left shoulder to his right.

'So I have heard,' I replied, flicking a glance to my left to see if Kate was watching.

Something about him seemed familiar.

Or was I still being paranoid?

He kicked at the sand in front of him. 'This is your first time to Gerakas?'

I nodded. 'First time to Zakynthos.'

'Visiting friends?'

He was Greek. Mid-forties maybe.

'Yeah. Hoping to meet up with them later on.'

For a moment he simply nodded, scratching at his chest.

A glance to my left confirmed Kate's presence, drifting slowly in our direction.

'You have everything you need?' he asked suddenly. Still facing out to sea.

'I think so,' I replied, taking half a step towards the water. 'Apart from sun-tan lotion.'

He laughed and edged in closer, lifting his arm and pointing to the far southern end of the cliffs. When he spoke, however, it had nothing to do with whatever he was pointing at.

'If you need anything – money, a weapon – you only have to call our friend in Athens and I will deliver it to you at the hotel. Understand?'

'Got it,' I replied, aware of Kate ten yards away, hovering at the water's edge.

A weapon?

'Okay.' He lowered his sunglasses briefly and rubbed the bridge of his nose. 'Everyone is happy? There is no problem?'

I nodded.

Come on Kate, move in closer, for fuck's sake.

'*Orea*,' he concluded, pursing his lips. 'So, relax. We are watching.'

With that he flashed a smile, then turned and ambled back along the beach, heading for the path to the cliffs.

A moment later, Kate jogged by.

'Good job, Haston,' she muttered under her breath as she brushed past me.

As my contact approached the bottom of the footpath, Kate closing in fast behind him, he took out a set of keys from his pocket and began to flick them back and forth in his hand. Which was when I realised where I'd seen him before: at Nikos Taverna. He was one of the two men sitting drinking coffee the day before. I hadn't recognised him in sunglasses and beach attire.

Gerald hadn't been lying. He had my back after all.

At the car, I changed out of my swimming trunks into my jeans.

Gerald's man was nowhere to be seen. Over by the quadbike at the hedgerow, Kate's accomplice was smoking another cigarette, toying with a camera. As for Kate, I eventually spotted her at the far end of the line of restaurants, leaning up against a dusty blue Volkswagen, poring over a map.

There'd been no further communication between me and her, and I was keen to know what she'd made of my meeting. Had she recognised him? Was he a familiar face in the world of espionage? Or was he an unknown entity? Kate would no doubt brief me later. And I'd be sure to mention the second man who'd accompanied him at the restaurant the day before.

Locking up the Nissan, I set off across the field, passed the tourist shop and turned down onto the rocky track leading to the villa. By the time I arrived at the garden gate, I was already soaked in sweat, my jeans clinging to my thighs.

Cursing my lack of foresight for not having packed the appropriate clothing, I climbed the steps and knocked on the front door.

Almost immediately, it flew open and revealed Xander, dressed in shorts, sandals and a Hawaiian shirt, grinning from ear to ear.

'The punctuality of the Englishman!' he bellowed, opening his arms for an embrace. '*Kalimera. Ti Kaneis? Kala?*'

'All good, thanks,' I said, complying with the hug and clapping him on the back to match his zest. 'You guys?'

'Yeah, cool man,' he shot back. 'All cool.'

He drew up in height, eyeing me as he chewed on his bottom lip.

'So, I brought some trunks,' I ventured, when I realised he wasn't about to say anything else. 'Ready for the beach.'

He sniffed and vigorously rubbed his nose. 'No, my friend, not the beach. The plan – the *plan* is . . . we go to the fucking hospital.'

He took a step back and beamed at me.

'The DNA test?' I replied. 'You got an appointment?'

'Shh!' Xander replied. 'Max is changing in the next room.' He sniffed again and guided me out onto the steps. 'We told him we have to go for a check-up because there has been – how do you say? – a virus in the water, and we may need medication.'

'That's great,' I said, wondering how he'd pulled it off. 'I had the impression it would take a day or two to sort that out.'

'Don't thank me, thank your ex-girlfriend.' He slid an arm around my shoulders. 'When she gets an idea in her head, she won't take "no" for an answer.' Then he turned and yelled into the doorway. '*Ella, Amara, viasou! Erchesai?* Haston is here, we're ready to go! Come on!' Again, he sniffed and wiped his mouth.

Xander seemed particularly hyper this morning.

Edgy, even.

Just then, Max came barrelling out of the front door onto the steps and threw himself at me. 'Mister Alistair!' he yelled, waving a plastic dinosaur at me. '*Papi* says we will go sailing today!'

'Maybe buddy, maybe,' said Xander, puffing out his cheeks as he threw a look around the garden.

'After the hospital, Max,' came a stern voice from the corridor.

Amara emerged from within into the sunlight, wearing a simple white dress and flip flops; Jackie Onassis sunglasses perched on her head.

'Xander has told you the plan?' she said, pushing past without even looking me. 'We're going to the hospital.'

'Shipwreck Beach off the cards, then?' I said, noting how the light from behind exposed the silhouette of her parted thighs.

Amara didn't reply.

'It will be too late by the time we finish in town,' said Xander, jumping in. 'All the boats leave for the beach in the morning from Zakynthos. I have a friend who has a private boat, but he is not returning my calls. *Den pirazee* – tomorrow.'

Max ducked past me and hurried to join Xander and Amara making their way through the garden path to the track.

'We all going in my car?' I called out.

Amara spun around. 'No, take Xander with you. I will bring Max in the jeep.'

'Got it.'

Something had happened. A definite shift in atmosphere compared to the previous night.

'*Endaxi, pame!*' said Amara,' pushing Xander in my direction. 'Meet outside Nikos Taverna.' Then she grabbed Max by the hand and pulled him along the pebbled track in the direction of a Toyota Jeep parked under the tamarisks along the shore.

Perhaps they'd had a fight?

Once again, as much as I wanted to take her to one side and have a heart-to-heart, I knew I had to sit on it. Having set the ball in motion, my success with Amara was entirely dependent on the success of the mission.

Would she forgive me for lying to her?

Once it was all over, for sure. Once she knew the truth.

'Let's go,' I said turning to Xander. 'We can pick up a frappé before we hit the road.'

*

Waiting to be served at the Beach Bar Café, I scanned the car park and checked everyone's position.

Amara's jeep was parked on the opposite side of the road just ten yards away, engine running; Quadbike man had moved closer to the line of restaurants; and as for Kate, she was studying the menu at Nikos Taverna next door, twirling a pair of sunglasses in her hand.

Moments earlier, crossing the road to the café, I'd caught her eye and held her gaze long enough to suggest I wanted to talk. She hadn't wasted time complying.

Once the drinks arrived and Xander had returned from the toilets, I paid up and led the way towards the car via the restaurant next door.

As I approached, Kate stepped back from the menu and turned to walk in the opposite direction towards us. Just as she passed by, she let her sunglasses slip to the ground.

Allowing Xander to continue onwards, I stopped, picked up the glasses and doubled-back to catch up with Kate.

'You forgot these,' I said, tapping her on the shoulder.

'*Ti?*' she replied, spinning round. '*Ti theleis?*'

'Your shades,' I repeated. 'You dropped them.'

In the corner of my eye, I could see Xander turn and stop, slurping on his iced coffee as he waited for me.

'*Efkaristo poli,*' she replied, flashing me a smile. 'Thank you.'

'No problem.'

'Heading to the beach?' she said, running a hand through her hair.

'No such luck,' I replied. 'Off to the hospital.'

'Nothing serious?'

At that point, Xander began to wander back towards us.

I gave Kate a smile. 'No – just you know ... Testing. That kind of thing.'

'Uh, huh.'

There was a honk of a car horn. Amara: telling us to get on with it.

Xander stopped advancing and crossed over to the jeep.

'I think they had an argument,' I said quickly. 'Something's up.'

Kate nodded. Kept smiling.

'Gerald's guy,' I added. 'Recognise him?'

'Never seen him before,' she said. 'Boris took photos.'

Boris was Quadbike man, evidently.

'There's a sidekick,' I added. 'They were drinking coffee together here, yesterday. Same age, roughly. Mediterranean-looking.'

'Hey Englishman!' yelled Xander heading towards us once more. 'Stop flirting. Let's go!'

'Keep your eyes on Max,' I said quickly. 'We're in separate cars.'

'I'll be following.'

'On the quadbike?'

She shook her head. 'The blue Golf at the entrance to the field.'

Then she waved her sunglasses, thanked me in Greek and walked away.

I crossed the road, and flicking a quick look to where her vehicle was parked under an olive tree, led Xander to the Nissan.

'Dude, she was totally checking you out,' he said, tipping back the dregs of his coffee. 'You get her name?'

Fifteen minutes later, Xander and I were following behind Amara along the coastal route to Zakynthos.

If Kate had been concerned about the change of plan, she hadn't shown it. It was possible, of course, I'd overreacted – both Kate and Gerald had been certain the kidnappers would take time to make their preparations – but it was prudent to be cautious. After all, she'd insisted I alert her to the slightest change in the status quo. I was only doing as instructed.

Xander's mood, conversely, had plummeted. Since making his quip about my flirting, he hadn't spoken another word. The

98

hail-fellow-well-met bonhomie had long gone; he sat beside me, shrunken and morose, legs jigging up and down in the footwell.

'Everything okay?' I offered, negotiating the Nissan through a steep hairpin bend as we descended through a pine plantation into the fishing village of Porto Zorro.

Xander didn't reply. Instead, he puffed out his cheeks and shifted in his seat, then continued to bounce his legs. 'They should have air-conditioning in these things,' I added, trying to coax him into conversation. 'I guess fresh air is healthier.'

We continued on in silence for a further two kilometres, while I tried to keep up with Amara's jeep. In the end however, she slipped away from us, and I realised it would be down to Xander to navigate the final leg of the journey to the hospital. As for Kate in the Volkswagen, she'd been following discreetly, leaving one, sometimes two cars between us, but my speeding ahead to keep a visual on Amara had eventually left her behind.

Passing a skewed signpost for the tourist resort of Argassi, Xander finally broke his silence, muttering under his breath as he reached into his pocket and drew out a wallet.

'There is a parking place coming in a few minutes,' he announced, picking at his teeth. 'After the petrol station. When we get there, pull over.' He then produced a triangular wrap of paper from the wallet, cradled it in the palm of his hand and wound his window shut. 'Close your window, man.'

'Sorry?'

'The window.'

I obeyed, and within seconds the car began to cook.

'You want some?' he asked, avoiding eye contact as he opened the wrap to expose a mound of white powder.

I shook my head. 'I'm good, thanks.'

What the fuck?

'Don't tell Amara,' he added. 'She'll kill me.'

'No problem.'

It was a serious fucking problem. What the hell was he doing?

'Okay, here – pull over.'

I complied, and we rolled to a stop at the edge of a steep cliff, with a view over Zakynthos harbour in the distance.

Without further ado, Xander chopped out several lines of cocaine onto the dashboard and dispatched them with a rolled up fifty-Drachma note. Then he sneezed, swore again, and announced he was ready to get going.

Speechless, I pulled back onto the road and slowly wound down my window.

Was he going to explain himself?

And where the hell was Kate's Volkswagen?

Continuing a further kilometre, we passed through the bustling hotel and restaurant strip of Argassi, and then finally, as we approached the southern end of Zakynthos town, Xander leaned over towards me. 'I did something bad, Haston,' he said, rubbing his nose. 'Really fuckin' bad.'

I gave him a blank look.

'It's crazy – I knew it was fucking crazy,' he mumbled. 'But I'm innocent. It wasn't my idea. You gotta believe me, man—'

'Xander, slow down,' I said, interrupting him. 'What are you talking about?'

'It's fucked up,' he urged, twisting around in his seat to look through the rear window before turning back to me. 'But I'm telling you . . . I said I wouldn't do it. I quit, man. I fuckin' quit.'

'Said you wouldn't do what?' I replied, avoiding eye contact.

In the rear-view mirror, I finally spotted Kate's blue Golf rounding the bend in the road, following directly behind at a distance of a couple of hundred yards.

'These guys . . .' Xander said, breaking off to rub some powder into his gums.

'What guys?'

Muttering in Greek, he leaned forward over the dashboard, head in hands.

'Last night at the villa, the phone rang,' he said finally,

100

without looking up. 'Like, three o'clock in the morning. Amara answered. But when she came back to bed she said there was nobody there. Half an hour later, it rings again. So, this time I answer it.' He paused and scratched at the thick curls on the top of his head. 'I recognised the voice immediately. He said "we're ready." Told me to wait for instructions. Then he was gone.'

He began to rock back and forth in his seat.

'Ready for what?'

'*Malakas*,' he said emphatically, thumping the roof of the car. '*Poustis malakas*.'

'What is it?' I urged, swerving to overtake a tractor pulling out in front of us. 'Xander, what the hell's going on?'

Then he flipped.

'They know we're here!' he wailed, inches from my face. 'And there's nothing we can do about it. We're fucked. Totally fucked!'

'Who?' I said, reaching a hand towards him. 'Xander, what the hell are you talking about?'

'The mob, man!' he sobbed, staring at me wild-eyed. 'The fuckin' Mafia. They are here on Zakynthos. And they're going to take my boy.'

Shoulders heaving, he broke down and wept.

8

Crossing the narrow canal bridge into Zakynthos town centre, I swung into the car park overlooking the marina and killed the engine. A strong sea breeze had picked up, whipping up the coastal waters into spindrift-blown waves that crashed up against the harbour walls and sent plumes of spray across the wooden pontoons. In the rear-view mirror, Kate's Golf cruised slowly by the entrance before speeding up and disappearing off into the traffic.

I wound down the window, took a couple of deep breaths of salty air then reached for the cigarettes.

'Smoke?' I said finally, placing a hand on Xander's still-shuddering back.

He didn't reply.

As he continued to weep, I peered out at the tourists eyeing the yachts and gin palaces lurching against their moorings along the quay.

Xander's outburst was tantamount to a confession, and a game-changer for the entire operation. But what was behind it – a crisis of conscience? Or had he sensed that I was onto him? Gerald and Kate had mentioned nothing about any prevarication on Xander's part. As far as they understood, he'd been a committed player from the off.

'You've got to go the police,' I said, by way of an opening gambit.

He shot upright and glared at me with bloodshot eyes.

'No fuckin' way, man,' he growled, wiping snot from his nose. 'I do that, and I'm a dead man.'

'Kidnapping? The Mafia?' I objected. 'This is insane.'

A car pulled in next to us and I found myself staring at a swarthy local glaring at me with unblinking eyes. My Nissan no doubt had 'tourist' written all over it.

I quickly wound the window back up and stubbed out my cigarette.

Once again, the temperature rocketed.

Xander reached again for the wrap of cocaine but I snatched it away. 'Xander, this isn't just about you. It involves the safety of your whole family. Me too, for that matter. If you don't go to the police, then I sure as shit will.'

'*Oxi*, please!' he begged, grasping me by the shoulder as I made a play of reaching for the door handle. 'You don't understand—'

'Tell me what the fuck is going on, Xander,' I said, cutting him off. 'If you don't, I'm going up to the first policeman I see. And I'm taking you with me.'

For a moment, he sat staring at me, his dark eyes wide with panic.

Across the marina, a flock of seagulls cackled and squawked as they dive-bombed a tug boat negotiating its way through the choppy harbour entrance, while in the car next to us, the local eyed us with an air of vague amusement.

'Can I have a smoke?' he asked finally, twisting towards me with a supporting arm on the dashboard.

Unwilling to open the window on account of our prying neighbour, I reluctantly lit it for him and watched him take a couple of puffs, wondering how long it would be till Kate returned. Or would she deem it safer to stick with Amara and Max?

'Okay, man,' said Xander finally, as his smoke filled the car. 'Here's the thing.'

After another pull on his cigarette, he told me how two years ago he'd fallen out of favour with his record label, blowing his advance on drugs and drink while failing to pen a single new song, let alone deliver the album he'd been contracted to write. The record company sacked him then sued him for breach of contract. Too embarrassed to share his predicament with Amara, he'd dug his head in the sand and continued to hit the party circuit, cashing in on favours and borrowing money in the belief some friendly soul would bail him out. In the process, he became hooked on cocaine and ended up doubling his debts, until eventually his drug dealer threatened to send round the heavies. At this point, the bassist in his band approached him and said he had a connection who might be able to help.

'So he took me to this club in downtown Athens,' said Xander, scratching at his stubble. 'The kind of place where you have to be like totally famous to get let in, you know? Sure, I had a hit in the charts when I was nineteen – as a solo artist. But the new band? We were nobody.' He glanced wistfully at the wrap of cocaine in my hand. I promptly stashed it in the glove compartment.

'So the bassist got you into the club?' I said, encouraging him to move on, as I blinked away the sting of cigarette smoke.

Xander nodded. 'Alexei, yeah. I don't know how. But these guys put him on the guest list.'

'They were friends of his?'

'He never told me where he knew them from,' he replied. 'But he said he'd met them at a party one night, and they'd boasted they could help him get our band noticed. Connect us with gigs, publicity, and even pay for recording sessions and stuff.'

'For a cut?'

104

'I don't know, he never said. But yeah, I guess. Anyway, these guys said to get in touch if ever we needed help.'

'Go on.'

For a moment Xander gnawed on his lower lip, staring out across the marina quay where an artist fought against the gusting wind to set up her easel and paints.

'Get on with it, Xander!' I barked, switching to the offensive. 'We need to get to the hospital. I don't like the idea of Amara and Max being alone out there.' Not to mention that Kate would be wondering what the hell had happened to us.

Xander went on to explain how he and Alexei the bassist had partied the night away, and then just before the club closed, a man who went by the name of Yiorgos took Xander to one side and said he could help him.

'He tells me to come back the next night and "talk business",' Xander continued. 'I'm like – fuck, yes. And when I go back, I find I'm a paid-up member of the club. So, for the next two weeks I meet with this guy, hang out with all these famous dudes and hangers-on. There's no more talk of work, or money. I figure he's forgotten about it. But I don't care, man. I'm too fucked up and having too much fun. Then one night – bam! He takes me to a private booth and gives me the talk.'

Extinguishing his cigarette, Xander progressed onto how Yiorgos brought up the idea of a 'friendly kidnap': a ruse to extort cash or assets out of friends and family. There'd be no risk to the victim; they'd simply stay in hiding until the cash was paid and then they'd be anonymously 'released'.

'He made is sound so simple,' Xander murmured, head bowed. 'But, to offer up my boy . . . shit.'

The fact he'd been planning to steal money from his wife was apparently not a concern.

'Hang on,' I said, backtracking. 'I thought they had offered to help the band – get you guys noticed and stuff?'

'We started off talking about our music and the band, but

they said it would take time – like a year, maybe two. I told them I couldn't wait that long. I needed the money now. Which was when they said they had other ways they could help me.'

'You, specifically – not the band?'

'Uh, huh.'

A better return of their investment, in other words. Why wait a couple of years to reap their profits managing a pop band that might or might not turn out to be a success, when they could reap an instant cash reward in one fell swoop?

Xander sniffed, flicking his eyes to me before studying the floor. 'In the end,' he continued, 'Yiorgos convinced me that for Max, it would be like going on a vacation. He'd be treated well. Fuck, he'd even be given a share of the money – like, savings, or something, for when he was older. So finally, I agreed. I was too fucked up to say no. Then Yiorgos asked if there was anyone I knew who could be framed for the kidnap. An old enemy, or someone who was a likely culprit. That's when I told him about you, how you were the father of Amara's boy but didn't even know it. He said it was perfect.'

Xander pressed on, told me how for the next few days he'd helped pass on information about me which he sourced from the unwitting Amara, and how, via my old university, St Andrews, they found out I was living in London.

'When I asked him what he planned to do with you, he told me to relax and let them take care of it.' He turned away and shook his head, cursing under his breath.

So far, everything Xander was telling me matched what I'd learned from Gerald.

'And you didn't confide in anyone else?' I asked, gazing out beyond the harbour to a passenger ferry carving a furrow of white through the windblown channel between Zakynthos and mainland Greece. Not even your bassist, Alexei?'

'No way,' he coughed. 'Alexei knew something was up but he never asked. In the end, he stopped coming out to party with us.

It was then that I started to question what the fuck I was doing. So, finally I tell Yiorgos I want out. He was like, "no problem, man. Come and find us when you're ready."''

'That was it?' I said, wiping away the sweat from the back of my neck. 'You just upped-sticks and walked away?'

He nodded.

'You didn't say anything to Amara?'

'What – that I was planning on trying to steal money from her family? You kidding?' He helped himself to the packet of cigarettes. 'I was panicking, dude. Totally freaked out. Didn't know what the fuck to do. But then three days later the villa on Zakynthos came free and I was like – let's get the hell out of here.'

'Zakynthos was a last-minute decision?' I continued, turning towards the artist on the quay who was now applying the first brushstrokes to her canvas. 'I thought that was part of the plan . . . to come to an island where the kidnap would be easier to carry out?'

That was what Gerald had been led to believe. Or so he told me.

Xander looked at me, puzzled. 'No, it was supposed to take place in Athens – or on the outskirts. Yiorgos told me that, once you were in Athens, I was to set up a situation where you and Max were alone and they would carry out the kidnap. Like, you know – at a fairground, or a waterpark. There's a big one just to the south of Athens. I think he mentioned it as a possible place.'

'So you decided to take some time out. Get away from it all and get your head straight?'

'You got it,' he replied, his face brightening. 'I didn't want anything to do with these guys.'

'Except, they weren't taking "no" for an answer?'

'*Malakas.*'

'And they tracked you down at the villa . . .'

'I'd recognise Yiorgos's voice anywhere,' he said, grimacing. 'Like sandpaper.'

I broke eye contact and, leaning forwards onto the steering wheel in a bid to suck fresh air in from the dashboard vent, asked him if he hadn't suspected something was wrong when I showed up.

He told me he that he'd thought it odd to begin with, but then figured that Yiorgos had already set the ball in motion, luring me to Greece with the telephone call, and hadn't bothered to stop it.

'When you said that you had been given Takis's address,' he continued, scratching at his neck, 'I was certain of it. The plan had always been to send you to his house and not ours. It would have been too obvious. Takis did exactly what we had expected – pass you on to us. So yeah, I convinced myself it was nothing to worry about and managed to persuade you that Takis had been behind the idea, trying to get me out of the family by bringing in Max's real father. Amara and I have talked about this often. It was an easy lie, because it's partly true.'

He looked at me wide-eyed, fingering his shorts like a frightened child.

For a fleeting moment, I wondered if he was playing me; that somehow, I'd been rumbled, and Xander had got spooked. What if he had raised the alarm and the Mafia had instructed him to 'confess' as a tactic – to lure me into a false sense of security and lay ambush to the ambush, as it were?

Except, I couldn't see how that would work. They weren't to know if Xander would panic, or how I or the authorities would react. It could only complicate matters for them. Too much of a risk. Besides, there was something in Xander' desperation that was all too convincing.

'Why would the Mafia want to force you to go ahead with this?' I asked, as the man next to us finally stepped out of the car and lumbered slowly along the boardwalk, shirt flapping in the breeze. 'Against your wishes?'

'I don't know, man,' he said, reaching for the door handle. 'I need some fuckin' air!'

'Wait!' I snapped.

He turned away and banged his head against the window. 'What the fuck are we gonna do?' he exclaimed, his voice breaking. 'We gotta get out of here – back to Athens. Like – tonight.'

'I don't . . . let's just – think,' I said, stalling.

Something still didn't make sense. Why would the Mafia risk Xander's non-cooperation? How did they know Xander wouldn't shop Yiorgos and the other contacts he'd made? Was it ultimately worth their while?

'What figure did you come up with?' I asked, studying him closely.

'Huh?'

'How much money did you promise them?'

Xander hesitated for a moment, nodding to himself as if debating whether or not to answer the question. Then: 'Amara's mother had a publishing company, like, in the seventies,' he murmured, digging his nails into his palms. 'Sold it for nearly ten million dollars. At least, that's what Amara told me. But before she died, she gave it all to her husband. It was supposed to be for Amara and any children she might have, but then when he got cancer, he signed over power of attorney to Takis.'

'Why?'

He cleared his throat. 'I dunno. Shit, man – you ask a lot of fucking questions.'

'The police will ask a whole lot more.'

Sighing, he covered his head with his hands. 'Maybe he didn't trust Amara with the money. Or maybe he wanted to protect her. Stop people like me trying to marry her for money. At least, that's what Takis thinks, right?'

Again, that was in accord with what Gerald had mooted. And Takis himself had pretty much implied the very same.

'But why didn't you confess your problems to Amara in the first place?' I replied. 'She'd have helped you, surely? She could have asked Takis to release the funds.'

'Takis would want to know why.'

'None of his business.'

'You tell Takis that,' Xander exclaimed. 'That's why I was surprised when he called up and offered us the villa. Usually we have to beg him to use it.'

I stared at him for a moment, watching his jaw muscles flex in his cheeks as a volley of sea spray spotted the windscreen.

'Takis proposed it?'

He nodded.

'Out of the blue?'

'Yeah, man – I just told you that,' he snapped.

I reverted to the swaying forest of masts in the marina, as an idea wormed its way into my mind. 'Xander, how do you think the Mafia – Yiorgos – found you?'

'I told you, Alexei introduced me.'

'I mean, did you tell anyone you were going to Zakynthos?'

'No. Alexei knows about the villa, of course. We had talked about recording the album there. But he didn't know we were going. Like I said, it was a last-minute decision.'

Peeling my thighs off the plastic, I swivelled in my seat to face him.

'So, the only people who knew about the trip to Zakynthos were Amara and Takis?'

He looked across at me, knitting his thick eyebrows. 'What are you saying?'

'Did you tell Yiorgos about the villa?'

''Course not.'

'And he had no idea you were leaving Athens?'

'I didn't tell a soul,' Xander objected. 'That was the whole point – to get the fuck out of there without anybody knowing.'

'Jesus Christ!' I exclaimed, cracking the window open a couple of inches now our neighbour had headed further out along the quay. 'Takis phones up three days after you quit your business with Yiorgos, and out of the blue – out of character – offers

110

you the perfect place to hide and recuperate ... And then hey presto! Yiorgos tracks you down at the villa. How could he have known? How could he have found the telephone number, even?'

Xander turned away, dumbstruck, and peered out across the marina.

'Takis?'

'Who else – Amara?'

Xander didn't move a muscle.

'However the Mafia came to you,' I continued, 'you were set up by Takis.'

It was a spur-of-the-moment conclusion, but it held weight. Takis was enlisting the Mafia to steal the ten million dollar proceeds from the sale of Amara's mother's publishing company – using Xander as a patsy. Being the family banker, Takis was perfectly placed to execute such a theft; the Mafia simply had to hold his hand along the way and collect their cheque at the end of it.

'But ... her brother would do this?' he asked, incredulous.

'Half-brother,' I said, correcting him. 'In any case, how's that any different from her husband having a go?'

Xander hung his head.

'But he already has the money,' Xander muttered. 'He's in charge of it.'

'It's not legally his. By using the Mafia, he can effectively launder it.'

Xander stared at me, lost.

'The same principle as it would have been for you,' I explained. 'The Mafia kidnap Max, right? Takis pays a sum of money as a ransom – Amara's inheritance – and then a portion of that money goes to paying off the Mafia – a commission, if you like – while the remainder of the ransom money goes back into Takis's own account.'

For a moment, there was just the frantic metallic clanging of halyards from the yachts at their moorings.

'But the whole thing was my idea, no?' said Xander, scratching furiously at his neck.

'Was it, though?' I replied. 'You were manipulated. You were broke, and drug dependent. The perfect target.'

As for how Takis got in with the Mafia in the first place – well, the banking world was rife with dubious clients and offshore tax havens. Where better to strike up connections with organised crime?

'Shit!' coughed Xander. And as the colour drained from his cheeks, he flung the passenger door open and threw up onto the pavement.

Pushing my door open against the wind, I sidled round the Nissan to join him.

'Easy. Man, easy,' I said, lifting him up by the shoulders and dragging him over the boardwalk towards the water's edge. 'Just breathe.'

'We gotta get to Amara and Max,' he exclaimed, fingering a chunk of vomit from behind his teeth. 'We got to get them and get the fuck to the airport and go home.'

'Xander,' I began, steering him to the nearest yacht. 'Listen carefully – don't react. Just keep your eyes on this boat . . .'

Kate and Gerald would be informed as soon as I had the opportunity, but right now, I was on point, and the onus was on me to make a judgement call. Xander was a liability at the best of times, but a panicking liability was a considerably worse proposition. He needed reassurance. Fast.

So I told him.

Leaving out specifics, I recounted how after meeting Takis at his house in Athens, the British and Greek intelligence services had approached me the same night; and how, after initial questioning as to my own potential involvement, they'd informed me I was being framed for a ransom kidnapping of my son – and that I had the choice of either heading home and keeping quiet, or staying and helping them with their counter operation.

112

'I came to Greece to find out if Max was my son,' I concluded, offering him a cigarette without taking my eyes off the rocking vessel in front of us. 'But now I'm helping the police.'

I could hardly tell him the truth – that my aim was to help get him behind bars so I could have free access to Amara.

Xander, meanwhile, said nothing. He seemed to have stopped breathing.

'I will go to prison, no?' he eventually mumbled, as his legs wobbled underneath him.

'Not necessarily,' I said, getting ready to catch him. 'I believe your story, Xander. And they will too. If you co-operate . . . if you prove your innocence by helping us catch these guys.'

It was a false promise. For all Xander's protestations of innocence, his weakness, stupidity and self-centred blindness were the catalysts of the entire kidnap plot. He was a cowardly would-be thief; at best, his jail term might be mitigated.

And Amara would be free.

He doubled over and began to dry heave. 'I'll do anything man,' he whimpered, peering up at me with puppy dog eyes. 'Just tell me . . . please God, tell me what to do . . .'

As the tears began to flow, I pulled him upright.

'The first thing you have to do is pretend you know nothing,' I hissed. 'Act normally. Because you can count on it that we are being watched.'

And then a shrill voice cut through the whistling in the rigging:

'Hey Mister! You want me to do your picture?'

I spun around to find the artist I'd seen earlier standing between us and her easel, one hand clutching a paintbrush, the other trying to stop her dress riding up around her stomach.

'I give you two for one. Come.' She cocked her head and squinted into the sun, smiling at me as another blast of wind swept across the pontoon, dousing us in a film of salt. 'Your friend – he is okay?'

I nodded and gave her a dismissive wave, at which point, she shifted her attentions to a passing English family, universally sunburnt and weighed down with cool boxes and beach mats, struggling their way to the opposite side of the quay.

I turned back to Xander and began to rub him on the back.

'Right now, you're recovering from a bit of food-poisoning. Something you ate last night. It's fine – just puke. Then laugh it off and follow me back to the car.'

'Okay, okay,' Xander shot back, straightening and forcing a ghoulish smile as his hair blew over his face. 'Then what do we do?'

Good question.

I re-offered the cigarette – which he took this time – and escorted him across the boardwalk back to the Nissan.

First thing I had to do was alert Gerald and Kate; although, not necessarily in that order. From all I'd learned about the former, it was prudent to tell the Greeks first and let them dictate how and when the maverick Gerald should be brought into the picture. Investigations into Takis's involvement would need a delicate touch; one wrong move at this stage in the game could arouse his suspicions and blow the whole operation. How to get a moment to talk to Kate, though? I'd have to engineer an opportunity at the hospital.

Xander didn't need to know any of this, however.

'I need to make a telephone call,' I said, wiping a crust of salt from the back of my neck. 'But first we go to the hospital – they'll be wondering what happened. I do the DNA test. Then we go to the beach. We wait. And when Yiorgos calls you again and gives you the instructions, you agree to it all. You tell me everything. I tell the police. They will make their preparations and set up an ambush. Job done.'

Exactly how and when the Mafia would give Xander his instructions was another matter. I told him we had to let that play out naturally. The key thing, as far as Xander was concerned, was to show confidence. Underneath the veneer of his pop-star personality, Xander was a career turncoat – out for himself at all costs, destined to follow the loudest voice.

'And the next time Yiorgos calls,' I added, 'you need to take him to task.'

'What do you mean?' said Xander, his voice rising in panic.

'Challenge him as to why he's going back on their word, when he said he was happy for you to walk away.'

'You crazy?'

'The Mafia are steamrollering you,' I replied. 'They're counting on the fear factor. But if you don't make some show of protest, they might suspect something.'

'But what do we tell Amara?' he exclaimed, pulling me by the hand and stopping me in my tracks.

'Amara?' I repeated, stalling as I caught sight of a police car kerb-crawling past the entrance to the marina. 'We don't tell her a thing.'

After ten minutes negotiating the narrow streets and one-way systems of Zakynthos town we pulled into the car park of the newly built municipal hospital, perched halfway up a gentle hill, overlooking the coast.

Killing the engine, I stepped out onto the tarmac and, sipping from my warm water bottle, quickly located Kate's blue Volkswagen under a row of swaying cypress trees to the southern end of the carpark by a run-down café. A further scan of the area revealed Amara's jeep parked up close to the entrance of the hospital.

In total, there were twenty or so cars scattered haphazardly across the shimmering asphalt, the shady spots along the perimeter walls already taken. All vehicles were uniformly empty, apart from a dusty brown Peugeot sandwiched between two other cars in the eastern corner. Someone sitting in the driver's seat . . . Hard to make out any physical detail, but the shape of his silhouetted profile gave him away: the guy I met on the beach. Gerald's man. His accomplice was most likely waiting inside, staking out reception.

I opened the driver's door to the Nissan, tossed my empty bottle onto the back seat and made my way around to Xander's side. 'Act natural and be your bright bouncy self,' I said, throwing open the passenger door to let him out. 'Everything's going to be fine.'

9

The DNA test was over in fifteen minutes.

Requiring only a swab of the inside cheek with a cotton bud, Amara and Max had their samples taken together first; the jovial nurse playing her part well, explaining to Max that she was checking for signs of an infection from the water. Nothing serious, easily treatable, but something that could spoil their holiday if left unchecked. Max remained oblivious and entirely unfazed about the whole affair – the promise of ice cream working its magic. Once mother and son left to join Xander in the waiting room, I too slipped in and had my saliva sampled. Foraging around my tonsils, the nurse informed me that the result could be returned within as little as twenty-four hours, but seeing as the nearest laboratory was in Athens, we'd be looking at a two to three day wait. Max's presence wouldn't be obligatory; being a minor, it was our prerogative as to how and when he'd be told. Finally, with a twinkle in her eye, she wished me well and ushered me out.

Reconvening back at the waiting area, a sterile box room with a handful of children's paintings plastered across the walls, we established a plan for the rest of the day, which, as far as Max was concerned, involved finding him a Cornetto, followed by an afternoon at the resort of Laganas, where it was hoped I might take him sailing.

'Sounds good,' I proffered, turning to Xander who was leaning back against the wall, one arm around Amara, the other trying to stop his left leg from bouncing up and down. 'But listen – ice creams are on me. Bound to be something in the café.'

It was my only chance to get to Kate before hitting the road.

Max jumped to his feet. 'Can I come with you, Mister Alistair?' he squeaked, tugging free from his mother. 'I wanna choose.'

'Sure, go ahead, *Maxi mou*,' said Amara, smoothing down her dress as she rose to her feet.

'Hey, you can trust me,' I objected, offering Max the palm of my hand as a target for his swinging fists. 'You want a Cornetto, young man? Then that's what you'll get.'

'But I want to come with you,' he insisted.

What was Xander thinking?

Hard to tell – he was staring out of the window.

'There's a shop in the hospital,' offered Amara. 'We can all go.'

'I need to pick up cigarettes,' I added quickly. 'I'll meet you in the car park.'

'No chocolate,' demanded Max, his brow creasing in consternation. 'Mummy, tell Mister Alistair I don't like chocolate.'

'Point taken,' I said, ruffling his hair and giving Amara a wink, before making my way towards the door. 'See you at the car park in five.'

Gerald's second man still nowhere to be seen, I jogged out of the air-conditioned reception into the heat and made a beeline for the café under the Cypresses, keeping one eye on the brown Peugeot over by the far wall as I passed in front of Kate's Golf.

Pushing through the creaky door, I picked up a pack of Karelia Lights and investigated the ice cream selection in the freezer compartment. Cornettos were in plentiful supply – but only chocolate.

With my hand hovering over the plastic sliding door, debating whether to risk going off-piste with an iced lolly, I became aware of a female figure at my side.

'Xander has confessed,' I said quickly, pulling myself upright and handing Kate a Callipo. 'Told me in the car. He's shitting himself. Got a phone call last night from a man called Yiorgos. Mafia. He says he got cold feet in Athens and tried to walk away from the whole thing, but they're now forcing his hand. Tracked him down at the villa and they're preparing to give him instructions.'

She nodded, brushing her hand across the top of the ice cream compartment.

I continued: 'And get this: it was Takis who offered the villa to Xander out of the blue, just a few days after Xander backed down from the operation. He was the only person who knew Xander had gone to Zakynthos. How else could the Mafia have tracked him down, except via Takis? Xander's just the patsy.'

Still no response.

I paid the owner and checked once more for any sign of the others in the car park.

'And what did you tell Xander?' said Kate finally, bending down and swapping the orange Callipo for strawberry.

'I came clean. Told him I was working alongside MI6 and Greek Intelligence, and that with his help he might be able to get out of this without a prison sentence.'

She frowned and examined the contents label. 'It didn't occur to you to consult me first?'

'There wasn't time,' I whispered. 'He was ready to take his family to the airport.'

She nodded and continued to stare at the label.

'I told him to await instructions from the Mafia – this Yiorgos guy – and then to tell me,' I added. 'I didn't tell him about you, or Gerald. I just said there were people watching us.'

'Again – a good idea, you think?' she murmured, changing the Callipo for a Magnum.

'I had to calm him down for Christ's sake,' I objected, my voice rising to counter the bouzouki music coming from the speaker above the counter. 'He was ready to split.'

'You trust him?'

'He's terrified. He'll do whatever we ask.'

'That doesn't answer the question.' She let out a slow whistle through her teeth. 'Amara?'

'She doesn't know.' I leaned in closer. 'But what do we do about Gerald?'

'You have to tell him,' she said under her breath. 'I'll contact Stelios. Chances are he'll make Gerald take a back seat. But Gerald has to hear it from you first. If he finds out you've been secretly working alongside me, he'll stop trusting you. He might even stop trusting Stelios. That won't be helpful.'

I nodded. 'Don't you think it's time we officially joined forces? I mean – this is it.'

Just then there was the tell-tale creak of the door opening.

Max. Followed by Xander.

'Laganas,' I whispered, as I turned away to face the counter.

Sunglasses in place, Kate pushed past me deeper into the café and made a point of studying the menu board, as Xander and Max sidled up to join me. 'Sorry, only chocolate Cornettos,' I announced, keeping my eyes on the attendant who was leaning on the till. 'We'll find another place.'

'What else have they got?' inquired Max, bouncing over to the ice cream box and thrusting in a fist. 'Did you look properly?'

Just then, Xander turned and noticed Kate.

'Xander,' I called out. 'Help me out here.'

Had he recognised her?

Or was he just admiring her legs?

'Come on, mate,' I exclaimed, pulling him over and pushing

his head down towards the ice creams. 'Do you see any other Cornettos in there?'

I felt a movement of air as Kate exited the shop behind me.

Again, the door creak.

Safe.

Then Amara's voice: 'You're taking your time – *Ella!*'

They must have passed in the doorway.

'Just double checking,' I said, throwing a smile in Amara's direction. 'No joy. But we can get one at the beach – right Max?'

'*Endaxi*,' said Max, nodding furiously as he grabbed my hand and led me to the door. 'Mummy, *papi* – let's go. Let's fucking go!'

Words of admonishment were followed by laughter, and we stepped onto the asphalt just as Kate's Golf pulled away from under the trees.

'That was the woman from the beach,' said Amara, pausing, hands on hips as she watched the car disappear in a cloud of dust.

'Huh?' muttered Xander.

'Alistair was flirting with her outside Nikos Taverna,' she added, turning to me and raising an eyebrow. 'The one who dropped her sunglasses.'

'Really?' I said. 'I didn't see.'

'She certainly saw you,' Amara continued, hitching up her dress as she stepped out towards the jeep. 'Left in quite a hurry.'

'My loss,' I concluded, patting Max on the head. 'Okay. Laganas Beach . . . *pame!*'

I travelled alone this time, Amara insisting Xander accompany her and Max; the plan being for me to pick up whatever I needed from the Porto Roma, then to meet at the villa and go on in the one car – mine – to Laganas for the remainder of the day. Kate followed two cars behind me, having stopped in a lay-by just south of the hospital to wait for us to pass by. Several vehicles behind her, I caught an intermittent glimpse of the brown Peugeot doing its best to keep up.

121

As we headed south back down the coast, I tried to figure out why Kate wouldn't feel this to be the moment to join forces with Gerald. Was he such a liability? He'd proved his worth with the drugs bust in Piraeus last year; he'd brought them the case, even – just as he had the kidnapping plot. True, the Greeks had yet to identify Gerald's men; perhaps they knew he had a penchant for using characters who operated on the shady side of the law. If so, did that matter? The Intelligence services were hardly squeaky clean. Their whole MO was to get the job done. Whatever it took. And as for that moment back at the café, Kate being rec-ognised by Amara – that was sloppy; we needed a better system of communication. Relying on 'bumping into each other' at a moment's notice was hardly a viable long-term solution. Bringing both teams together would make things a hell of a lot easier.

After a forty-minute drive, I left Amara's jeep at the junction to the Porto Roma, then doubled back through the olive groves and drew up by the telephone box outside the convenience store.

It connected on the second ring.

'Yup,' came the cheery greeting as Kate's Golf shot past.

'Xander's spilled the beans,' I said, without preamble. 'Turned out he tried to walk away from the whole thing, but they're not letting him off the hook. A guy called Yiorgos telephoned him at the villa and told him to await instructions.'

Nothing but the hum of static.

As a dangly-legged hornet blundered its way into the booth, I stepped out of the phone box as far as the cord would let me and told Gerald everything I had reported to Kate, reiterating my conclusion about Takis, along with what I'd learned from Xander about Amara's mother's publishing legacy.

'Obviously, we can't do anything yet,' I said by way of con-clusion. 'Don't want to spook Takis. But when the time is right, he's there for the taking.'

'There for the taking . . .' repeated Gerald slowly. 'And what, pray, did you say to Xander?'

So much for his good humour.

'I came clean,' I said, eyeing the hornet as it became part-entangled in a spider's web in the corner of the booth. 'Told him that I had initially come over to find out if I was Max's father, but had got caught up in the operation – partly because I had been deemed a suspect. And that I'd agreed to help MI6 and Greek intelligence with a counter operation.'

The was a long burst of static.

'What makes you think he won't go straight back to the Mafia and tell them?' said Gerald finally, his voice tight.

'Not a chance,' I replied. 'If he does that, he's admitting he's ratted on them. He's out to save himself.'

'You think we're going to protect him?'

'I told him, if he helped us – if he was willing to betray the Mafia – he might stand a chance of avoiding prison.'

More static.

'He was ready to leave the island,' I continued, resisting the urge to let rip. 'He was on the verge of taking his family to the bloody airport.'

'You think so?'

What the hell was wrong with Gerald and Kate? I'd made a massive breakthrough –why the negativity?

'But now he's in,' I added. 'He's on our side. He's going to wait for the instructions and then pass them on to us. Things are looking up.'

The telephone static was drowned out by a furious buzzing of the trapped hornet's wings. A couple of inches away, a generously proportioned spider kept its distance.

'Just stay focussed and watch your back,' replied Gerald. 'I need continual updates from now on.'

'Understood.'

'Tell me you haven't said anything to Amara?' he added.

'Of course not.'

'You'll tell the Greeks, I presume?' I asked.

123

'Unless you're planning to?' came the curt reply.

Static.

What did he mean by that?

'I just feel it's high time we joined forces,' I said by way of recovery.

Realising he was probably smarting from having been upstaged by his protégé, I let it slide and moved quickly on. 'We should check out Takis's accounts. Where he keeps his money, how many accounts he has etc. You can do that kind of thing, I take it?'

The hornet was getting weaker – the last of its lanky legs now ensnared in the web.

'It takes time,' Gerald grunted. 'We'll need a court order. Could take days if not weeks.'

'Can't you pull some strings?' I asked, noting the buzz of pleasure I'd felt at his use of 'we'. I was now part of the inner circle. A decision maker.

'I'll see what I can do,' came the flat reply.

'Great, well – I won't keep you any longer. We're heading to the beach.'

Gerald coughed. 'By the way, what makes you think we're not?'

'Sorry?'

'Working together with the Greeks.'

The struggling hornet fell momentarily quiet.

I decided to go on the offensive. 'Nothing, Gerald. It's just I've seen bugger all sign of anyone out here other than your friend at Gerakas beach. So, a little more evidence of a team effort would be highly appreciated.'

I heard him take an in-breath to speak, but then he held off, as if having changed his mind.

'Any indication from Xander as to when the Mafia will make their move?' he asked finally.

'Not yet. They told him they were "ready" – that was it.'

'They minute he gets the call, you need to tell me.'

'Of course.'

I hung up and exited the phone box as the spider wrapped its lunch into a ball of fizzing silk.

10

An hour later, I turned the Nissan onto the beachside road at the Club Med resort of Laganas and parked up overlooking the bay. There'd been no further sign of a tail since arriving at the Porto Roma. Kate had most likely gone on ahead, having received my heads-up in the hospital car park café. The absence of her opposite number in the brown Peugeot however, not being privy to my destination, suggested he'd either been held up, or taken a wrong turn.

At least the Greeks were on the ball.

As for the beach expedition, we were now down to a party of three. At my instruction, Xander had told Amara he would stay at the villa, claiming the onset of a migraine. This meant the Mafia would have free reign to contact him without having to navigate any eavesdroppers.

But it also gave me the chance for some alone time with Amara.

Piled high with towels and an assortment of buckets and spades – Amara having dispensed with her white dress in favour of a tank top and cut off shorts – we made our way south along the bustling promenade checking out the cafés and bars in search of lunch, and eventually settled on the incongruously named

'Solitude' café opposite the windsurfing and sailing boat rentals. Commandeering a central table under the dappled shade of the overhanging vine trellises, we decamped our kit and promptly ordered three full English breakfasts – at Max's behest.

When our food finally arrived, Max held court, bringing his mother and me up to speed on the precarious sex life of the male praying mantis, as well as how to tell the difference between a skink and a lizard, until, finally, I managed to steer the conversation in a nautical direction. Idly twirling the loose end of a bikini string riding the nape of her neck, Amara watched closely as I explained to Max how the wind powered a boat forwards, when, to his way of thinking, it ought only to blow it sideways.

'All to do with the keel,' I said, through a mouthful of bacon. 'The keel stops any sideways momentum, and all the energy is redirected to pushing the craft forwards. It's simple physics.'

Sucking on his Pepsi, Max contemplated the new information in earnest.

'He's five,' exclaimed Amara with a grin, dabbing at a speck of egg in the corner of her mouth before licking the tip of her finger. 'A genius – of course. But go easy on him.'

There followed a rapid exchange in Greek as Max admonished Amara for interfering, claiming, in the end – in English – that I was the teacher, not mummy.

'Fine, but mummy's the boss,' she said, reaching across the table with a napkin to rub away a smear of ketchup from Max's forehead, inadvertently exposing a silver piercing in her belly button.

'So, we must all obey,' I added with a laugh, unable to tear my eyes away from her flat, tanned stomach.

Once again, I succumbed to another flashback of the night we spent together on Naxos. She hadn't had a piercing then. But I remembered how firm she had felt underneath me; writhing ... entwining ... limbs slipping over each other in sticky, sweet sweat.

'So, how's London treating you, Mister Haston?' came Amara's silvery voice, interrupting the reverie. 'What are you doing with your life?'

A waiter swept by, delivering two fresh bottles of Mythos to our table.

'London's good,' I answered, catching another glimpse of her midriff. 'Waiting for my next teaching gig in September. Off to Japan. Don't think I can carry on teaching English forever, though. So – yeah. I've got a few ideas up my sleeve, but nothing certain. And you guys? I know Xander's in a band ...'

She paused for a moment, as the sound of breaking plates from the kitchens behind us cut through Oasis's 'Cigarettes & Alcohol' from the café speakers.

'I work in a kindergarten,' she finally answered, wrapping her fingers around a lock of hair dangling by her cheek. 'But it pays the bills. Unlike Xander's music.'

Maintaining eye contact, she remained inscrutable for a moment, before the smile slowly faded and she busied herself with the remains of her eggs.

Even the act of eating was a sensual event; her bangled wrists rhythmically working her deftly poised fork, as it impaled willingly self-sacrificed morsels of food from plate to parted lips ...

A sudden cheer from the sports bar two doors down brought me back to the present.

'And what about you?' I asked, inwardly berating myself for becoming distracted. 'Ever had the desire to get back into acting?'

Somehow, I needed to broach the subject of Takis.

'I missed my chance,' she murmured, gazing at me through tumbling locks of hair. 'If I was going to reapply, I should have done it five years ago.'

'I want to get down,' exclaimed Max, kicking his chair back and wandering to the edge of the terrace.

Amara ignored him.

'Your father ...' I began, forcing myself back on point. 'Forgive me – but, he isn't around to stop you anymore.'

She forced a smile. 'No.'

Was that regret, or relief?

'What does Takis think about—'

But she cut me off.

'I have responsibilities. Drama school is out of the question.' Then she turned her attention to Max, who had pushed through the bordering oleander hedge and was perched above the road, admiring a windsurfer doing tricks in the shallows.

'*Maxi, ella makria apo to dromo.*'

Max waved her away, but nonetheless took a step back in compliance.

'I'm sorry about your father,' I said, adjusting my cutlery.

Pursing her lips, she gave a silent nod.

I lifted my gaze from the empty plate and, peering along the dusty beach track in the direction of where we'd parked, scanned the area for any sign of my watchers.

Where the hell had they got to? Had they decided to slacken off now we were waiting for the go-ahead from Xander?

'So, I guess Takis is the head of the family now?' I asked, turning back to the table.

'Of course.' Her gaze drifted over to Max. 'He is the eldest. The sensible one. Not to mention, the only son.'

'A banker, too, I understand. When your father died, he took over your father's estate and the family finances.'

She turned back to me, puzzled.

'Takis told me. At his house in Athens.'

'Yes, it's true,' she replied. 'He manages everything. He's the control freak in the family.'

'Sounds like he's in charge of a fair whack.'

'A fair what?'

'Xander told me your mother sold her publishing company for nearly ten million dollars,' I said, casually sweeping a crumb off the tablecloth. 'Takis is responsible for divvying that up too, right?'

She frowned. 'Xander told you this?'

I nodded. 'In the car, earlier. When we were chatting.'

'What else did he tell you?'

'We were just talking about family history,' I replied, flicking a look out to sea. 'That kind of stuff.'

'My family history, you mean?'

'I guess.'

To back off too quickly would only draw further suspicion, so I decided to press on.

'So what's the plan with the ten million, then?'

She studied me a moment before answering.

'Takis and I think we will maybe use some of it to build a new a restaurant,' she answered finally. 'In memory of our father.'

We?

The money had been left to Amara – not Takis.

'Great idea,' I said. 'Where?'

'We don't know yet.'

Because Takis was stalling – unwilling to deplete his potential windfall.

'But you guys get on okay?' I continued. 'You and Takis?'

'Enough about my silly brother,' she interrupted. 'Max is waiting.'

Rising to her feet, she smoothed down her tank top and called out to Max across the restaurant terrace.

'*Maxi mou, ella etho.* Alistair is ready to go sailing.'

From the selection of available boats, we opted for a Mirror; a sturdy, reliable dinghy that comfortably accommodated two people and was easy to manage with its minimal sail area.

Donning our life jackets, I deposited Max by the masthead then hopped on board at the stern, cheered along by Amara who stood at the water's edge in a bikini, shielding her Gucci shades

130

from the glare of the sun. Serene and statuesque, she had tied a sarong elegantly around her waist; a magazine tucked under one arm; her free hand giving a relaxed, regal wave.

She'd been considerably less flirtatious than yesterday; if anything, she'd become somewhat preoccupied and distant.

And as for making inroads on Takis, I'd failed miserably.

In Amara's eyes, he could do no wrong, despite the fact that – as she understood – he had lured me over to Zakynthos with the express intention of breaking the family apart. How could she perceive that to be anything other than devious, calculating and ill-intentioned?

I'd do better next time.

For now, I'd abandon my theorising and give my undivided attention to Max.

He proved to be an attentive student.

Sat up forwards by the mast, one hand on the jib sheet and one hand firmly gripping the gunwale, Max listened rapt as I demonstrated first how to balance the boat using bodyweight position, followed by how to trim the mainsail by tightening or loosening the ropes – the 'sheets' – depending both on how strong the wind was, and in which direction one was heading in relation to it. Chest puffed out with pride, he eventually gave it a go himself; every now and then swivelling around to offer me a toothy grin; tousled blond locks flitting about his elfin face in the breeze.

And then fifteen minutes into our session, I noticed that the two jet-skis I'd spotted earlier had begun to circle closer and closer to the safety zone. Not only that, but they appeared particularly interested in our Mirror dinghy.

Putting in a tack at the eastern limit of the safety zone, I bore into the wind to see what would happen. And sure enough, they followed us at a distance of fifty yards along the line of buoys towards the western end of the beach.

Both men looked Mediterranean – nothing untoward about that, we were in Greece.

But why were they shadowing us?

I put in a gybe and let the sail out, attempting to head for shore, but my path was blocked by a straggle of learner windsurfers, and I was forced to maintain the higher line.

Sure enough, the jet skis turned and followed me.

Squealing in delight as the spray from the bow covered the two of us, Max urged us on as I tried to find an opening within the crowd.

What the fuck was I doing out in a boat with Max, alone?

Kate and Gerald's man were nowhere to be seen . . .

Exactly the scenario the kidnappers would be looking to exploit.

And then to our right, I heard the peel of laughter: a quartet of women in a pedalo boat, beer cans in hand, waving and cheering Max and me on.

At least, so I thought.

But when I twisted around on the transom, I witnessed the men on the jet-skis returning the salutations, fist-pumping the air, shouting in broken English for the women to come for a ride.

Then a shout further away: another pedalo – two more women; one pedalling while the other attempted to dance on the back with a glass of wine in her hand. Both crafts were the subject of the jet-skier's attention . . .

Which was why they had been careering back and forth between the two.

I was simply in their way.

Letting the sails out again, I luffed into irons, waited for both pedalos to unite upwind of us, then tightened the sheets and tacked back in the opposite direction.

Once my heart rate had subsided and I'd got over the embarrassment of my overreaction, I began to compose an admonitory salvo for Kate, for having left Max and me unguarded. Although, no one had forced me to get in a boat with Max. I should have known better than to take a risk without necessary support in place.

'How do you know my mummy?' asked Max apropos of nothing, as he ducked under the sail and sat next to me.

I let out the mainsheet and made a show of scanning the water for approaching watercraft.

I should have checked with Amara as to what she had already told him.

'A few years ago, now,' I eventually replied. 'On the island of Naxos.'

Still he continued to stare at me.

For a moment, all I could hear was the water running alongside the hull.

'My *pappous* has a restaurant on Naxos,' he said finally.

His grandfather.

'Ah, yes,' I replied. 'I've been there. Manolis Gardens.'

He gave me a slow nod.

'I think I've got that right,' I added.

He was five years old, for heaven's sake. Why did I feel like I was being interrogated?

Max's face clouded over. 'My *pappous* died.'

'Yes, your mummy told me,' I answered. 'I'm very sorry.'

'Mummy told you?'

In fact, Takis had told me.

For a moment I stared at him, wondering if I should correct myself, but then, unwittingly he came to my rescue.

'It's okay,' he said, reaching out a little hand in sympathy and putting it on my knee. 'He is in heaven. One day I will see him again.' He scratched thoughtfully at some dried salt on his cheek. 'Maybe you can see him too?'

'I would like that very much,' I replied, pulling a strand of wet hair away from his eyes. 'I bet he's incredibly proud of you.'

He nodded in agreement, and shuffled closer.

'My mummy said one day we will visit you in England.'

'Really?'

Why would she say that?

'Well, you are welcome – any time,' I replied. 'We could go hunting for hedgehogs.'

'*Kala*,' he exclaimed. '*Poli kala.*'

Had Xander been present?

'Your mummy and daddy were talking about me?' I asked, scanning the shore and catching sight of Amara sunbathing in between a pair of beached catamarans.

'Just mummy,' he said, his brow furrowed in concentration. 'Last night at bed time. *Papi* doesn't like it when she talks about you.'

'Oh?'

'You won't tell him I told you?' Max added, chewing on his thumb.

I smiled. 'Of course not. What happens on the boat, stays on the boat.'

'*Ti?*'

'Nothing. It's an expression. Like ... *etsi-ketsi.*'

Max studied my face for a moment, a finger briefly exploring his right nostril.

'When we go to England, *Papi* can stay at home,' he concluded, nodding to himself.

Damned right. In a cosy Athens penitentiary.

I turned back to the shore in time to catch Amara waving at us and had a sudden vision into the future: Max and me rowing on the Serpentine in Hyde Park, while Amara looked on from under a sun hat on a deckchair, learning lines for a new role she was working on ...

Or, in the Cotswolds, perhaps. The three of us wrapped from head to toe in hats, scarves and gloves, striding across the hills before a warming pint in a local pub.

Then a little fist punched me on the knee.

'Mister Alistair?' Max said, rising to his feet. 'Can you buy me a Cornetto? You promised.'

'Absolutely,' I agreed, leaning down to hand him the loose jib sheet. 'Now, don't forget the boat. We don't want to capsize.'

'Ti?'

'Capsize – tip over. That would be bad, right?'

'Very bad,' he replied, clasping his fingers around the rope. 'What happens on the boat, must stay on the boat.'

The long-awaited strawberry Cornetto was consumed further along Laganas beach to the west, opposite the jetty where the glass-bottomed boats left for Marathonisi, also known as turtle island. Sticky prize in one hand, plastic spade in the other, Max set to building a fortress at the water's edge while Amara and I sat up on dry sand, surrounded by a melee of oiled-up sun worshippers, sipping our iced coffees.

Still not a sign of Kate or the brown Peugeot.

Disposing of our plastic cups, I stripped off my t-shirt and returned to sit next to Amara, who had stretched out on the sand.

It was impossible not to stare at her: semi-supine, her coral ankle bracelet, pink nail polish and flawless mahogany tan contrasting against the pristine white of her towel. One knee pointing skywards, not quite masking the tiny triangle of bikini between her thighs.

There was no point pushing further on the subjects of Takis or Xander. It was clear Amara had no intention of being drawn into any further discussion. As far as she was concerned, the sailing had been a success and it was a chance to enjoy the moment.

There was, however, another subject waiting to be broached.

'We haven't spoken about Ricky,' I began, as Max was joined by a group of Italian children at the water's edge. 'I wondered if—'

'You don't have any sun cream on,' she said, interrupting

me as she reached over and brushed something invisible off my shoulder. 'You'll burn.' And before I could reply, she sat up on her knees and began to massage sun lotion into my shoulders.

As her deft fingers gently worked the muscles on my back, I was rendered momentarily tongue-tied; once again prey to a memory of our night in her father's house . . . one hand on my shoulder, the other, guiding me into her . . .

'English skin,' she murmured, her mouth inches from my ear. 'You have to be careful.'

Eventually, I found my voice. 'How much do you know?' I asked, closing my eyes as I felt the faint brush of her bikini across the small of my back. 'I imagine you've heard mixed reports.'

Ignoring the question, Amara continued to apply the cream. 'Too late, you're already burning,' she said cheerfully. 'Sorry.'

'He was hit by the outboard engine,' I continued, hunching further over my knees in a bid to hide the tumescence in my trunks. 'There was nothing I could do.'

The whine from the jet-skis intensified as a second pair shot across the water from the eastern end of the bay and joined the pedalos in their aquatic revelry.

'Why would you do anything?' Amara said finally, hands sliding down to my waist. 'He was going to kill you.'

Once again, my body flinched involuntarily at her touch.

It would be so easy, I thought . . . to turn around and kiss her.

'I know everything,' she continued, replacing the cap on the sun lotion and sitting beside me on the towel. 'Takis told me.'

'Takis?'

'He wrote to me many times over that period. Sent me newspaper cuttings. I don't know if he did it for me or for him, but I was grateful. Ironic, isn't it? That six months was the most communication I've ever had with my brother.'

It took me a second to catch up.

'I don't understand,' I said, twisting around to face her. 'Why might it have been for Takis's benefit?'

She paused a moment, playing with the bunched-up towel between her legs.

'Takis was in love with Ricky,' she said, without looking up. 'He needed someone with whom he could share his pain.'

For a moment I stared at her, trying to digest what I'd heard.

'He wasn't on the islands the summer I met you,' she continued, reaching again for the sun lotion. 'He came out two years before, to help my father set up the restaurant. We were all there to help. My cousins, my uncle. And it was over that summer that Takis met Ricky.'

'Uh, huh.'

'The same way you and Ricky recruited people for Heinrich. Except, he had no interest in any of the other stuff that went on.'

Starting with her calves, she began to smooth the cream into her legs, working her skin in slow, rhythmic semi-circles; around the knees, up to her thighs . . .

'Right.'

'Takis introduced me to Ricky and – yeah, we started seeing each other,' she said, looking over her shoulder at me, Guccis perched on her head. 'All that time he was infatuated with Ricky. The feeling was not mutual. Ricky flirted with men – maybe he even slept with them, I don't know. But that was part of what he was doing for Heinrich. His job. They became friends, though, for the remainder of that summer. And possibly beyond that, too. In the end, Ricky painted Takis's portrait and gave it to him as a present.'

'I saw it,' I said, as the penny suddenly dropped. 'It's hanging upon the walls of Takis's flat in Athens.'

'It's a good likeness,' Amara added, releasing her oiled legs and snapping the cap back on the bottle. 'But you know, Ricky had no confidence as a painter. He was always in Heinrich's shadow.'

At which point, I was hit by a flashback: Heinrich, bolt upright in his chair by the swimming pool. Eyes wide, as Ricky plunged the kitchen knife into his heart . . . then twisted it . . .

'You said Takis and Ricky had a friendship "possibly beyond" that summer,' I continued,' pulling myself together. 'What kind of relationship, do you think?'

'Seriously? You wanna talk about that now?' she exclaimed, pushing away my knee in exasperation. 'Maybe we should go back to the villa.'

'I just . . . need to know,' I insisted, catching hold of her hand. 'Ricky's friendship with Takis is a whole piece of that puzzle I know nothing about.'

She raised her sunglasses. 'What is it? Why do you give a shit about Takis?'

I managed a smile. 'Indulge me.'

She sighed, took a moment to clean her sunglasses with the edge of her towel and then turned to face me, stretching a leg out across my lap.

'Ricky knew that Takis was helping my father with financing the restaurant. Sorting out the accounts and stuff. After Takis had returned to Athens, Ricky asked me for his telephone number – said he wanted to get some financial advice.'

'Like – a personal banker?'

'I suppose so.'

Running her hands through her hair, Amara fell quiet as her gaze settled on Max, covered in sand, alone, at the shoreline.

'Ricky had made a serious amount of money over the course of several years,' I ventured, determined to dig deeper. 'What do you think happened to it – when he died?'

She threw me a look of incredulity, before lifting her leg off mine and lying back on her towel to face away from me.

'I have absolutely no idea,' she sighed.

We left Laganas just after 6 p.m. and arrived back at the villa to find Xander chain smoking on the patio.

Politely declining an invitation from Amara to dinner – her husband looked distinctly displeased at the suggestion – I nevertheless managed to find a moment to check in on the status quo. It was only a fleeting shake of his leonine head on my walk back to the car, but I understood from the frustrated pop idol that nothing had come through from the Seven Stars.

Racing back to the Porto Roma in the Nissan, I wracked my brains to come up with some kind of connection between Ricky and Takis that would shed light on the kidnapping plot – but to no avail. I couldn't possibly see how the legacy of a dead man, albeit prolific and far-reaching, could be in any way connected. The only possible link was that Takis might still be executor of Ricky's finances and that, along with Amara's inheritance, he was somehow looking to launder Ricky's estate into his own accounts via his dealings with the Mafia.

Ten minutes later, I pulled up at the telephone box to put in a call to Gerald and Kate. Firstly, to chastise them for abandoning me at the beach; and secondly, to update them on what I had discovered from Amara about Takis and Ricky – in case they were be able to think outside the box and come up with something more tangible.

However, when I tried Kate, the call rang out.

Same thing happened when I phoned Gerald.

Squatting under the shade of an olive tree, I chain-smoked three cigarettes then tried both of them again, twice, before finally giving up.

How was I supposed to effect expeditious communication, if Gerald wasn't in to pick up the bloody phone?

Baffled, I drove back to the hotel, parked up, and was about to make my way upstairs to my bedroom when the hotel owner stopped me in the corridor and told me I had a visitor waiting for me on the terrace.

'A woman,' she declared, batting her eyelash extensions.

Thanking her, I headed straight out to the terrace expecting to find Kate, and, pushing through the bougainvillea, discovered I wasn't wrong.

139

Except, she had company. The driver of the brown Peugeot –
Gerald's man. The one I'd met at the beach. They were sitting
opposite each other at a table overlooking the clifftop view, each
nursing a glass of wine, deep in conversation.

Uncomprehending, I made my way over to the table.

As one, they both turned and smiled.

'Ah, Alistair,' said Gerald's man in his cultured Anglo-Greek
accent, rising to his feet. 'I hope you have had a nice day at
Laganas. Please, join us.'

11

Pulling out a chair, I sat down between them with my back to the kitchens and turned to Kate.

'This is cosy.'

'A drink first,' said Peugeot man holding up his hand in mock disapproval. 'Will you have some of the local Retsina? Not too dry.'

'I'm okay,' I answered, keeping my eyes on Kate.

Kate smiled broadly. 'You must be thirsty. Have a drink.'

I returned the grin. 'No thank you.'

'It will look odd.'

I let a few bars of the traditional music play out from the terrace speakers, before turning to catch the eye of the waiter and signalling for another glass.

'So tell me,' I said, producing my pack of Karelia Lights and tossing them onto the table. 'When did you become friends?'

Peugeot man went to speak, but Kate got in there first.

'The decision was taken today for us all to work together,' she said, one hand pinning her glass to the table. 'In light of what you discovered, it seemed the right thing to do.'

'Absolutely,' said her counterpart.

'You never told me your name,' I said, lighting up and turning to my left.

'Mikis,' he said, with a deferential nod. 'My apologies.'

'No need,' I replied, as the waiter arrived with my glass and filled it. 'And your friend?'

'Sorry?'

'The guy you were drinking coffee with at Nikos Taverna yesterday afternoon.'

'Ah, yes,' he replied. 'Albertos.'

I could feel Kate's eyes burning into the side of my head.

I took a sip of my drink. 'So, let me guess, Albertos was watching us at the beach today?'

'Boris was there too,' said Kate, before Mikis could answer. 'Don't worry, you weren't abandoned.' She smiled and reached for my cigarettes. 'May I?'

'Help yourself.'

'How's the wine?' asked Mikis. 'The glass doesn't offend you?'

'Sorry?'

'Tourists feel they must drink from a little short glass – a tumbler, I think you call it. But this warms the wine. A stem is more civilised, no?'

'Depends how quickly you drink,' I replied, annoyed to have been referred to as a tourist.

'Good man,' he said, with a snort of approval. 'In ancient Greece, everyone at a party would drink wine from a large urn called a krater. The poet Eubulus wrote that, after three kraters of wine, the wise guest goes home. By the fifth, everyone is yelling and shouting. The sixth one leads to prancing about, and the seventh to black eyes. The eighth brings the police, the ninth vomiting, the tenth, insanity and hurling the furniture.' He shook his head theatrically. 'Two thousand years later, not much has changed.'

'I promise not to throw any furniture,' I said.

Out of the corner of my eye I saw Kate smile.

Their coming together must have happened while I was waiting for Amara and Max at the villa. Probably just as Kate had

142

suggested it would play: Stelios instructs Gerald to hand over control of his men to the Greeks and renders him redundant.

'So, what happens now?' I asked, wondering how Gerald took the news.

Was that why he wasn't answering his phone?

'I'll let the boss answer that one,' said Mikis, sitting back and crossing his legs.

'Thank you,' replied Kate, exhaling a column a smoke into the sultry air. 'We're waiting for Xander to get the nod. As soon as we know the proposed time and location for the abduction, we will meet again to discuss the operation in detail. Along with the deputy chief of the Zakynthos police.' She slid my lighter over the table towards me. 'I wanted us to meet in advance to check we're all happy and up to speed. I've already briefed Mikis on everything you've told me so far.'

'Very clear,' confirmed Mikis, sweeping a hand through his thinning hair. 'She's good, this one.'

'If there's anything you need to ask, or clarify, Alistair,' Kate continued, ignoring Mikis's attempt at a compliment, 'now is the time. There will be little room for debate once we get the green light.'

Mikis gave a quick scratch of his ear and topped up his glass.

'I would like to clarify one thing,' he said, inspecting the bottle of Retsina. 'We will need another one of these.'

Kate acknowledged him with a polite nod.

As the hurricane lamps hanging from the rafters were switched on, I threw a quick glance around the terrace.

A handful of musicians dressed in the traditional Greek dress of white billowing shirts, black sashes and waistcoats were preparing for the night's festivities, smoking and laughing as they set up their kit in front of the bougainvillea on the north-east corner.

As for the clientele, a total of three tables were occupied, including us. No one eating yet – still too early.

143

'Where exactly will we meet?' I asked, turning back to Kate and tapping my ash.

I was wondering how they'd orchestrated their unification. Kate must have approached Mikis, because, as far as I understood from Kate, Gerald had had no idea there was a third party in the mix – that his own men were under surveillance.

'We have a safe house inland,' Kate answered, batting away an early mosquito.

'Far from here?'

Mikis's ears pricked up.

'We will bring you there when it's time,' she replied. 'But – no. Not far.'

I wasn't getting any more.

There was fleeting look of disappointment on Mikis's face, too.

'So – updates,' Kate said, drawing hard on her cigarette. 'How did it go at the beach?'

'We know that Xander stayed at the villa,' added Mikis, chipping in. 'Tired? Or is—'

Kate cut him off.

'How is Amara?' she said, with a brief wince of annoyance, as if she had found a fly in her drink. 'You had plenty of time to talk.'

Mikis took the hint and shut up.

'She didn't reveal anything particularly helpful about her husband,' I said finally. 'She appears to have no knowledge of his connection with the Seven Stars Mafia. As for his drug taking – she may have known of it in the past. Not sure she has any idea he's been at it recently.'

Kate nodded, waiting for me to continue.

'For what it's worth,' I added, 'I don't know how stable their relationship is.'

Kate's eyebrows lifted fractionally.

'And what of Takis?'

144

Mikis drew in closer and uncrossed his chinos.

'She refused to be drawn,' I replied. 'Oblivious, clearly.'

Kate frowned. 'To what?'

'The fact that her half-brother is trying to fleece her of her inheritance.'

I explained how I was now convinced that it was Takis who set up the whole idea of the kidnapping as a ruse to get his hands on Amara's money, using Xander as the fall guy.

Mikis smiled. 'This is only a theory.'

I pulled in my chair. 'There was no other way the Seven Stars could have known the family was headed to Zakynthos. Let alone how to find the telephone number of a private, unlisted villa. Only three people knew: Xander, Takis and Amara. Xander had just backed out of the whole thing – so he was hardly going to tell them. And as Gerald – or Kate – has no doubt informed you, Takis offered them the villa just three days after Xander walked out of the deal. A move completely out of character for her brother.'

'What makes you sure it wasn't Amara?' asked Mikis, gazing across the terrace behind me.

I paused, studying him closely.

'You're suggesting Max's own mother would have her son kidnapped?'

Mikis said nothing.

Kate let the moment hang before re-joining.

'We can't know for certain that Xander never mentioned the family villa,' she said finally, toying with the stem of her glass. 'And if he did, it wouldn't take them long to figure out that was where he'd disappeared to. Finding the number of the place would be—'

'He told me explicitly that he hadn't,' I interrupted.

'He was partying for weeks,' said Mikis. 'Drinking. Taking drugs. He could have said anything and not remembered it.'

Kate cleared her throat. 'We don't know for certain, that's

all I'm saying. Although your theory sounds good on paper, we have no concrete proof that Takis is behind this. What we do know categorically, however, is that Xander has confessed. Also, that he now knows you're working for a counter operation.'

Mikis pulled a face. 'Dangerous.'

'I told him because he was about to take his family off the island,' I said calmly. 'I didn't have a choice.'

'I'm with Alistair on this,' declared Kate. 'I can't see how Xander confiding in Haston would help their cause. Too much of a risk. It could easily backfire.'

'But if Xander has become suspicious of Alistair and reported back to the Mafia,' countered Mikis, 'they might have suggested Xander test him to flush out the truth. For all we know, Xander has already called the Mafia back, told them there is a counter operation, and the whole thing has been called off.'

'You're presupposing firstly that Xander has had reason to suspect me,' I said, slapping at a mosquito on my arm. 'And secondly, that the Mafia would necessarily walk away.'

'Of course they will walk away,' sneered Mikis. 'They don't want to get caught.'

'Not if they are operating at a remove,' I insisted. 'For all we know, the Seven Stars' commitment boils down to a couple of low-level hired hitmen. If it goes well, they sit back and watch, then collect their cheque at the end of it. If it goes tits up, the only people in the firing line are the hitmen and Xander. Under interrogation, the hitmen won't be a threat because chances are they'll have no idea who's paying them. And any testimony from Xander will only lead back to the client.'

'Takis,' said Kate, joining in.

'In this case.'

'Or Xander,' said Mikis, jaw thrusting. 'Well, we'll find out. If in a week's time no call has come through, then we know it's off.'

Once more, a silence descended upon the table.

Just the sound of Mikis's fingers tapping along to the music coming from the PA.

'I'm still in agreement with Alistair,' said Kate, by way of conclusion. 'We press forward on the assumption Xander's confession is legitimate.' She threw a look across the table. 'Mikis?'

'We have no proof.'

'We have no proof of anything,' said Kate.

Mikis shrugged.

'We can't rest on our laurels, however,' she continued. 'Whatever Xander's reasons for confiding in Alistair, he's trying to save his own skin. If pushed, he might feel inclined to swap sides again. Which means it's imperative you don't divulge anything of our plans. If he asks, you're to tell him you're being kept out of the loop – for yours and Max's sake. For his, too. You're simply following orders on a need-to-know basis. And he must do as instructed, if he's to stand a chance of avoiding prison.'

I nodded.

'And it's crucial you don't press Amara too hard,' continued Kate, turning to face me. 'Anything you say to her is likely to be shared with her husband.'

'Got it.'

'Which brings us back to today,' she concluded. 'Anything else of note?'

I explained how Amara had told me that Takis had a history with Ricky; that they knew each other briefly – the summer before I met Ricky, and how the latter had asked Takis to look after his finances.

'No doubt you'll think I'm shooting from the hip again,' I concluded, 'but I wondered if Takis still had Ricky's money and was planning to launder it along with the family inheritance, via his deal with the kidnappers.'

Mikis gave a sad shake of the head.

Kate waited until he'd stopped moving.

'It's possible,' she said finally. 'If your theory about Takis is correct. But I don't see how it has any practical implications. All the same, don't press Amara any more on it.' She looked over and eyeballed me. 'I trust you didn't share your thoughts with her?'

'Of course not.'

Mikis looked doubtful.

'Keep our plans to yourself. Keep Xander needy, and keep him in the dark.' She drew a fresh cigarette from my pack. 'Any questions?'

'Not from me,' said Mikis.

'Alistair?'

I lit Kate's cigarette. 'You said the decision had been made for us all to work together on this, but it seems you've taken charge.'

She smiled. 'Your point?'

'Do I still check in with Gerald, or is he redundant?'

'Gerald is taking a back seat,' she said, flicking a look to Mikis. 'His team, however stay in place. We need men on the ground.'

'And the plan is to intervene at the point of abduction?' I asked.

'How do you mean?' said Kate.

'I mean – whatever the scenario, you'll move in before anybody lays a hand on Max. Or me, for that matter.'

'Of course.'

The band struck up and the yearning chime of the bouzoukis filled the terrace.

'Well, if there's nothing else, I suggest we call it day,' Kate added cheerfully, knocking back the last of her wine. 'The Retsina's on me.'

Mikis stretched and sighed. 'We are wasting an opportunity.'

'Who are you expecting to catch?' I exclaimed, rounding on him. 'Between Xander and Takis you'll be able to make inroads into the minor players – as well as the Yiorgos character, who may well be higher up the chain of command, as you put it. Apply the right pressure, grant them witness protection, and they could easily be forced to sing.' I rubbed my temples and pushed back from the table. 'In any case, preventing the abduction of a five-year-old boy should be the fucking priority here.'

'I'm just saying—'

'Thanks to Gerald's tip-off we're already in a position to expose the culprits, once arrests are made – however low-key the players are,' interjected Kate, her voice calm but authoritative. 'Publicly exposing the cartel shames them in the eyes of the criminal fraternity. This can lead to in-fighting – which destabilises them. Secondly, being exposed means they will find it harder to do business because they'll be seen to be an unreliable entity. This emasculates them and eventually negates them as a viable organisation.' She extinguished her cigarette. 'It's the long game, but it's the one that works. If you want to play cowboys and Indians, go somewhere else.'

'Thank you for clarifying,' said Mikis, with an ingratiating smile.

Kate nodded. 'Now, if you don't mind, I'd like a moment with Haston alone.'

For a second, it looked like Mikis was going to protest, but then he hauled himself out of his chair, shook my hand and politely bid us both a good evening.

Once out of sight, Kate sat back in her chair and let out a groan.

'Where the hell did Gerald find him?' I asked, as the musicians ended their song to another round of applause from the surrounding tables.

'Mikis may talk shit, but don't be fooled. He knows all about our evening at the banana beach bar, for a start. And he's fully aware we were watching the meeting Gerald set up at Gerakas beach ...'

A squawk from the microphone on stage was followed by a summons from the lead singer that the ladies should leave their tables to join in a traditional dance.

'Gerald knew about you all along?'

'He admitted as much to Stelios when they did the handover.'

149

Again, Gerald had decided to keep the information from me – another power play.

'So where's the other guy?' I asked.

'Albertos? He's staking out Amara and Xander's villa with Boris,' she replied. 'Mikis will be taking over for the night watch. But don't worry, Albertos and Mikis won't be a problem. They want to get paid. They're not doing this for love.'

The band struck up once more, as a quartet of females – two mothers and their unwilling teenage daughters – were ushered to the dance floor.

'Do you think Gerald was seriously considering the option of having me and Max undergo the abduction?'

'Unfortunately, I think it's highly likely,' Kate said, rapping her knuckles on the table before reaching once more for my cigarettes. 'Another reason for effecting an early handover. To ensure something like that doesn't happen.' She withdrew a cigarette and tapped it against the palm of her hand. 'With the Piraeus drugs haul last year, he was the one to tip off the authorities with the time and location for the sting. He doesn't get that chance here. This time the information will come from Xander, via you, straight to us.'

In other words, harder for Gerald to claim the glory.

Kate looked up and smiled.

'Don't sweat it. Gerald knows the score. It's all part of—'

'The game. Right.'

I felt no sympathy for him, however. Having been prepared to put me and Max in jeopardy, I was happy to see the back of him.

Still, part of me wanted to pick up the phone and confront him . . .

We fell silent for a moment as a pair of foraging bats flew in under the vine trellises, performing a series of low-level aerobatics above the tables as they chased down their prey.

Eventually, Kate reached for the empty Retsina bottle and studied the label.

'Heading back to the villa?'

I told her that I'd been invited, but declined.

She looked up from the table. 'Go carefully with Amara.'

'Is that an instruction?'

'Friendly advice.'

I gave her a smile.

'And for all Mikis's attitude, he's right about Xander,' Kate added. 'The man's a liability. Watch your back.'

'Understood.'

For a moment, it looked as if she had more to say, but then she replaced the wine bottle on the table and rose from her chair.

'I'll leave you to it,' she said, lighting her cigarette. 'Thanks for the updates.'

By the time I'd got to my feet, she was gone.

After a shower back in my room, I sat at the window watching night fall across the bay, while trying to find fresh perspective on the last twenty-four hours.

But to no avail.

Thanks to the contrary Mikis, I had also started to question the legitimacy of Xander's confiding in me – as well as the validity of my theory that Takis was running the show. It was only the tiniest seed of doubt, but it threatened to undermine my entire resolve. Why? Because, ultimately, as both Mikis and Kate had ascertained, I had no concrete proof. It was all down to surmises, instinct and second-guessing. Well-informed and reasonable deductions, as far as I believed – but none irrefutable. Somewhere, there had to be a key piece of the puzzle that would connect the dots and bind everything together; but until I found it, had it confirmed, clarified and put into place, there was no use trying to string together a persuasive argument.

And so, at 9.30p.m., after a Greek salad and fries, I headed to the phone box inland to place another phone call to Athens. Seeing as it had all started with Gerald, my erstwhile handler, instinct told me that it was to him I had to return. He may have been made redundant in the proceedings, but now he was no longer directly responsible for me, there was a chance he'd be willing to offer some transparency and clarify the discrepancies. After all, it was he who had persuaded me to be part of the operation in the first place. I was owed a hefty dose of candour, at the very least.

Leaning up against the dusty glass, I dialled Gerald's number, watching the moths dancing in the headlights of the Nissan. But after ten rings the line cut out. No answerphone. Just a disconnection.

I tried twice more, with the same result.

Deciding to give it an hour, I paced the moonlit olive groves to the accompaniment of chirruping crickets and a solitary owl, wondering what the hell he was up to. He'd been adamant I update him every second of the way, and although he'd had to step down, he was hardly the type to shrink into the background. As Kate had said herself, that was his whole MO: he was a player, a contender, a wannabe spook. If he couldn't be in on the action, he'd be even more likely to want to hear it unfold, blow by blow, at the very least. He'd still want to make his presence known, offer advice – if nothing else, simply to ensure no one forgot about him, and that credit was given where it was due.

After a third attempt, I gave up and drove back to the Porto Roma, concluding it was possible Gerald's chagrin at being sidelined had got the better of him and he was out somewhere in Athens, letting off steam.

Arriving back at the hotel at 11.45 p.m., I pulled up a corner table overlooking the sea and spent the remainder of the evening watching the sweating bouzouki troupe perform their hypnotic sirtakis to an enraptured audience, doing my best to dull my brain with generous helpings of Amstel lager. An hour and a half later, sufficiently anaesthetised, I climbed the stairs to my room and crashed out on my bed.

*

I awoke to a knocking sound.

At first, I thought it was coming from within my head – the result of too much beer. But I soon realised someone was tapping on the door.

Fumbling for the bedside light, I switched it on and checked my watch.

Five forty-five a.m.

As the knocking resumed, more urgent this time, I peeled back my sweat-soaked sheet and crept over to the door to listen at the keyhole.

Two voices. Whispering.

One male. One female.

My immediate instinct was to look for a weapon – but there was nothing apart from a wooden chair to hand.

Pressing my ear closer against the lock, I realised they were speaking Greek.

The hotel owner's voice.

And the other . . .

Surely not?

Turning the key, I stepped back and swung open the door.

'Hey man,' slurred Xander, leaning against the door frame. 'Got a moment?'

Before I could say a word, he pushed past me into the bedroom.

'Amara's kicked me out,' he announced loudly, as the hotel manageress backed away down the corridor. 'Caught me doing powder on the patio.'

We stood opposite each other, immobile, as the sound of an outboard engine drifted up from the cove below.

'Shit,' I said finally. 'What did she say?'

'It's cool,' he replied, crossing to peer out of the window into the dark. 'It happens from time to time. She'll get over it.'

I stared at him, perplexed.

'How did you get here?'

He was still high as a kite.

'I walked,' he replied, through clenched teeth. 'She hid the fuckin' car keys.'

The outboard engine on the water choked briefly, then cut out.

Pulling the chair from under the table, Xander sat down, bolt upright.

'Yiorgos called,' he said, placing his hands carefully on each arm. 'It's on. Six o'clock tomorrow night at Agios Sostis marina. You and Max. There'll be a boat waiting for you. The *Anthea* . . .'

He paused, eyes wide from the stimulants coursing through his veins.

'You're going fishing.'

12

Perched on the windowsill of my hotel bedroom, I sucked on a Karelia Light, gazing out across the mirror-calm bay towards the silhouette of mainland Greece as it sharpened against the eastern skyline. Xander revisited his telephone conversation with Yiorgos. Helped along by the sobering effects of Greek coffee – courtesy of our accommodating hostess – his fractured ramblings grew increasingly lucid, and by the time the first rays of sun hit the trunks of the surrounding cedars, I had a workable understanding of what had been discussed.

A fishing charter, The *Anthea*, had been booked for four passengers, not including the captain of the vessel, and would set sail at 6 p.m. from the resort of Agios Sostis on the south peninsular just west of Laganas. The booking had been paid in cash by a third party, under Xander's name. Xander was to make out that the three of us would be going on the trip – him, me and Max – but once it was understood that there weren't enough places on board, Xander would offer to step aside. There'd been no mention as to the identity of other two passengers – or indeed, the captain – but they were almost certainly going to be Mafia plants, if not the abductors themselves.

'He didn't say where the boat would be heading?' I asked, breaking away from the sea view and turning back to the room.

Erect in his chair, Xander shook his tousled head. 'He just said I was to tell Amara it was a two-hour night-fishing trip, that's all. The boat would return just after dark.'

I lit a cigarette and passed it to him.

'No other instructions? No names?'

'Uh, uh.'

So, the Seven Stars were counting on a two-hour window; two and a half, possibly, by the time the alarm was raised and a search party dispatched.

Were they hoping to reach the Greek mainland? If so, why hadn't they chosen somewhere on the eastern coastline, where the landfall of Sparta was only twenty kilometres away? Unless they were looking to execute a hand-over at sea ... using the fishing boat as a decoy while a second vessel made the getaway.

Xander grunted and rose to join me at the window.

'I did what you suggested,' he announced, hitching up his jeans.

'You confronted him?' I asked, sliding him the ash tray.

'I told him I was confused, because we'd agreed to call it off...' He broke off and blew a lungful of smoke into the morning light. 'It was like he didn't hear me. He said it was natural to feel nervous, but that I had nothing to worry about. Everything had been well organised and Max would be well taken care of. But when I challenged him again, he turned nasty. Asked me why I was fucking with him – why I wanted to embarrass him by pulling out after all the time and money he had put in.'

He pushed away from the window and began to pace the room.

'I apologised and told him there'd been a misunderstanding,' Xander continued. 'Said I didn't mean any disrespect, and that I was still on board ... I'd just panicked, that's all. Then all of a sudden he's Mister Nice again. Tells me to relax. Says it's worked out better than they'd hoped for. Zakynthos is the perfect place – much easier than Athens. All I have to do is chill out and focus on the money.'

Xander stopped circling and studied the floorboards.

'He asked me about you. I said you wouldn't cause any problems. Told him you were waiting to find out the results of the DNA test, and, like, totally happy hanging out with Amara and Max.'

Outside the outboard motor fired up again, accompanied by distant shouts.

'What did he say to that?' I asked, looking back out to sea.

To the east, the horizon had turned a violent orange and purple.

'Nothing. Just told me to make sure I was on time. Then he hung up.'

'No plans to speak again?'

He shook his head, and crossed the room to lean up against the door.

'I'm fucked either way,' he murmured, staring down at his sandaled feet. 'If I back out, they come after me. If I go through with it, I'm in the slammer.'

I weighed my response carefully.

'You're on the right side now,' I said, extinguishing my cigarette. 'And in the hands of the police, you'll at least be safe.'

I checked my watch: 7.30 a.m.

High time I called Kate.

'Yeah, right,' scoffed Xander.

'They'll put you in a witness protection programme,' I added, trying to sound authoritative. It seemed feasible enough.

'With Amara and Max?'

'I imagine so.'

Not a fucking chance.

For a moment we faced each other, immobile, as the plaintive cry of a pair of swifts on dawn patrol drifted through the window.

'*Endaxi*,' Xander declared finally, stepping forwards, hands on hips. 'I've had enough of this shit. Just tell me what the fuck I gotta do.'

The supermarket was a single-story, low-slung white-washed chunk of concrete, built alongside a petrol station and a row of partially constructed villas in an area of wasteland just to the south of Zakynthos airport. Only a handful of cars occupied the expansive asphalt apron before it – all of them tucked into a thin band of shade offered by the north-facing wall, underneath an array of large posters offering the latest deals on Greek yoghurt, Papadopoulos biscuits and olive oil.

Leaving the sweltering car for the fifth time in an hour, I made another lap of the carpark perimeter, cursing Nissan for not having installed air-conditioning in the Micra, and eventually crossed the asphalt to wait in the shade of a row of cypresses on the embankment opposite the supermarket entrance.

It was now ten thirty.

Having dropped Xander back at Gerakas beach with the express command of doing whatever it took to patch things up with Amara, I'd put in two calls from the telephone kiosk outside the Beach Bar. The first, to Gerald, rang out unanswered. I then called Kate (she already knew about Xander being kicked out by Amara, thanks to Mikis on his overnight stakeout) and I relayed the night's developments, giving her a rundown everything Xander had told me at the hotel. Then, making me go back over all the pertinent details, she wrapped up the call and gave me instructions to meet Boris at the Galaxias Supermarket in Ampelokipoi, near to the airport, at ten o'clock sharp.

So, what was keeping him?

Over the next half hour, the sun continued its vertical ascent and the air around me began to cook. I tried to relax and focussed on the rhythmic strumming of a lone cicada high

158

up in the evergreen fronds above my head, but inevitably, my thoughts returned to Gerald and his radio silence.

As odd and unlikely though it was, that he should turn his back on the whole thing, it wasn't out of the question. Perhaps he'd left town to take a break and cool off – it was the weekend, after all. Then again, it was also possible the number he'd given me wasn't in fact his home residence; like Kate, he may have been working from an office, or a safe house of some kind (although, if that was the case, someone else, surely, would have picked up?). Or had he been physically removed from the equation: forced to go into temporary hiding, out of harm's way, until the deal was done?

Perhaps Kate could shed light on the situation.

Just then, a high-pitched whine heralded the arrival of Boris on his quadbike, as he swept in off the main road and pulled up in a screech of burnt rubber opposite the supermarket entrance.

I descended the embankment, keeping my eyes on Boris as he disappeared through the sliding doors, only to re-emerge moments later, unwrapping a fresh pack of Marlboros. Arriving back at the quad, he tucked his tank top into his Bermuda shorts and cast an eye about the car park, briefly catching my eye before hopping behind the wheel and lighting up. I checked no one was paying me any attention, then walked over and jumped on the back. Without acknowledgement, Boris kicked the machine into life and we skidded out of the car park in a pall of dust and dried leaves, joining the main road south in the direction of Laganas.

For fifteen bone-jarring minutes, we bounced and weaved our way into the blinding sunlight, barrelling across the parched valley plain with its half-built villas and rambling sunflower plantations, until, at the dusty Laganas T-junction, we swung west in the direction of Zakynthos mountain and began a laboured ascent through a myriad of olive and fruit plantations. A kilometre further, we passed through the village of Sarakina and the ruins of an old venetian villa, then climbed through a series of switchbacks, until the road levelled out on the edge of a dense pine forest.

Finally, after a further two kilometres of murderous pot holes and vertical drop hairpin bends, we eventually broke into a clearing and arrived at a newly built villa, surrounded by a thick wall of hibiscus and oleander shrubbery. Parked in front of picket fencing under the shade of a vast sprawling cedar, was a row of vehicles: Kate's Volkswagen, a Ford Cortina, a black Chevy truck, and a heavy-duty motorbike.

Boris pulled up next to the motorbike, killed the engine and, without uttering a word, strode off along the oleander-lined path towards the front door.

I hurried along behind him, catching a glimpse of a swimming pool and tennis court in the gardens behind the north wall of the villa, while, over to the south, beyond the cliff edge, an expansive panorama stretched away into the heat haze.

Not what I had been expecting. From my limited knowledge of the world of espionage, I understood safe houses to be uniformly nondescript abodes you wouldn't look twice at. But then again, on an island littered with picturesque villas, one presumably had to fit in.

Arriving at the door, Boris stopped to let me past. 'Please,' he muttered, flicking his cigarette into the flower beds. 'This way.'

I pushed open the glass door, crossed the threshold into a flag-stoned hallway and came face to face with Kate, dressed in jeans and a t-shirt.

'Sorry for the delay,' she said, turning on her heels and leading me along a corridor deeper into the villa. 'I thought it best to go over logistics with the rest of the team before bringing you in. Took longer than expected.'

'Not a problem,' I replied, following her past the kitchen and pausing momentarily when I spotted a pistol in its holster, set beside a row of walkie talkies charging on the counter. 'Glad Boris came to fetch me. I'd never have found it.'

She kept walking. 'After introductions, I'll ask you to repeat what you learned from Xander. By way of breaking the ice.'

'Sure.'

Then she stopped and turned to face me. 'Any word from Gerald?'

I hesitated before replying, transfixed by the stare of her unblinking blue eyes.

'None,' I replied finally. 'I was going to ask you the same thing.'

A muffled burst of laughter echoed along the walls from the far end of the corridor.

Kate stepped in closer, bringing with her a trace of jasmine. 'He went out on the tiles last night with his girlfriend. Stayed over at her place.'

'Girlfriend?'

'One of his students. He left her place briefly to pick up provisions and make a phone call from a telephone box before returning to the apartment. He didn't call us. I wondered if he'd tried you.'

'I haven't heard anything from him since yesterday afternoon,' I replied, trying to imagine what appeal a man like Gerald held for a woman less than half his age. 'After the hospital appointment – that was the last time we spoke.'

I was right though, about his wanting to let off steam. The chagrin at being sidelined.

'You think he called his contact – the Mafia informant?'

'We assume so.'

'Should we be worried?'

She shook her head. 'He'll have been checking in. Any moment now, we expect him to do the same with us. He knows the protocol – he needs to remain contactable at all times.'

'He's probably smarting from being made redundant,' I ventured.

'It certainly wouldn't be out of character,' she replied, offering a tight smile. 'Still, if you hear from him, give me the heads up.'

'Of course.'

'Excellent,' she said. 'Let's crack on.'

The briefing was held in an airy room at the end of the corridor, in the east wing of the villa, with a southerly view out over the hinterlands of Laganas bay.

On my left as I entered, beneath a large reproduction Monet, stood a lengthy glass table strewn with maps, files, coffee cups and half-eaten pastries. Across the room against the right-hand wall was a plush leather sofa set about a low-slung coffee table, a few feet back from a set of cracked-open French windows. Three occupants: the man nearest the windows appeared to be in his mid-forties; tall, balding, and dressed in a linen suit. A few feet away from him was a shrunken, lean-limbed man dressed in chinos and crumpled shirt; mid-fifties perhaps, with large sad eyes and a hawk-like nose. Lastly, sat at the table under the painting, was a military-looking type in his late thirties, thick set with a body-builder's neck, sporting a set of strikingly bushy eyebrows; dressed in jeans, boots, and a heavy black leather jacket – the owner of the motorbike, no doubt.

'Gentlemen,' said Kate, calling the room to order as she slipped past me. 'This is Alistair Haston. Max's father.'

There followed a muttering of Greek, as they came to attention.

'Mister Haston,' announced the linen suit, tugging at his collar as he stepped forward to greet me. 'I am Albertos. I work with Mikis and ... well – Gerald, of course.' Like Mikis, his English was flawless. Same easy charm.

I smiled and shook his hand. 'I believe I saw you having coffee at Nikos Taverna, my first day at the beach?'

'Ah, yes.'

'Nice to finally meet.'

162

Had it not been for his bald head, however, I would never have recognised him. He'd been sat opposite Mikis at the time, with his back to me.

'The pleasure is mine,' said Albertos, clicking his heels.

'And this is Markos, deputy chief of Zakynthos police,' Kate continued, as she steered me across the Turkish carpet towards the coffee table and the man with the hawk nose. 'He will be directing all land-based police units in tonight's operation.'

'*Yiasou,*' Markos grumbled, with a deferential nod, before proceeding in broken English: 'I am sorry I meet you . . . under this circumstance.'

'Thank you,' I replied. 'I appreciate your involvement.'

Markos smiled and frowned at the same time.

'And finally, Commander Argyris from the Coastguard,' announced Kate, turning to the glass table. 'He will be coordinating marine and air support.'

'A pleasure,' said Argyris with a grin, raising his Brezhnev-like eyebrows. 'I too am sorry for your – situation. We will do everything we can to help.'

I thanked him, shook his hand and turned back to Kate, who promptly summoned the gathering over to the table, before instructing me to brief the room on my conversation with Xander.

Accordingly, I repeated the entirety of what I had learned that morning (pausing every now and then to let Kate translate the odd phrase into Greek, for the benefit of the deputy police chief) and concluded by asserting my belief that, owing to their decision to depart from the resort of Agios Sostis in the south-west, the Seven Stars Mafia were most likely hoping to achieve a hand off at sea, rather than head directly to the mainland – otherwise they would have chosen a site on the east coast.

'It's possible,' said Kate, picking up a notepad and pen. 'But remember, there are two main areas for fishing charters. Laganas bay – which includes Agios Sostis next door; and

163

then Zakynthos town – which as you say, is indeed on the east coast. However, Zakynthos has more routing restrictions due to the commercial shipping and ferry lanes. There is far more leisure-boating traffic in the Laganas area. Busier waters offer a kidnapping team more cover in which to disappear.'

There were subdued grunts of agreement from Argyris and Albertos.

I nodded, feeling foolish for not having thought that one through.

'But your point still stands,' Kate added with a smile. 'It's certainly reasonable to assume they might try and effect a hand-over before reaching the mainland.'

Then she took possession of the map and moved to the head of the table while all three men lit up assorted brands of cigarette.

'However, as discussed earlier, and with Alistair last night, the kidnap scenario will not be allowed to develop. In light of our latest intelligence, this means it will be concluded at Agios Sostis. Not out at sea.'

She paused and flicked a glance over to Albertos – Gerald's man – but he remained implacable.

'Our aim is to use the sting to discredit the Seven Stars,' Kate continued, 'not score a headcount. As it is, we will have enough leads to work with. The two men on board the fishing vessel; the captain of the vessel; Xander – our key witness; and finally, Takis – who, crucially, we believe, may be one of the masterminds of the entire operation.' Kate threw me a glance and gave me the slightest of nods; vindication, finally, that my theory about Takis was being taken seriously. 'Above all, however,' she concluded, 'Max's safety is our priority.'

Interesting that she hadn't been ready to admit she was on board about Takis in front of Mikis last night at the Porto Roma. It also occurred to me that Gerald would surely be another useful candidate for interrogation; after all, he'd had direct contact with the Mafia. But then, I supposed, being the Intelligence Services' secret weapon, they might opt to protect their golden goose.

After a quick translation into Greek for the benefit of Markos, who thanked her for the gesture but said there was no need – although his spoken English was poor, he understood everything – Kate handed over to Argyris.

The youthful-looking commander pushed away his croissant and, beaming a smile as if he were planning a trip to Disneyland, proposed stationing a helicopter at Limni Keri, five kilometres west of Agios Sostis, along with a support motor launch moored at Laganas, less than a kilometre to the north. Both parties would set off for the kidnap location the moment the vessel was apprehended. The helicopter crew would be armed with standard-issue handguns; the marine patrol would be armed with assault rifles.

'We are not expecting to have to use the weapons,' Argyris concluded, his grin slipping into an earnest frown.

'Correct,' said Kate quickly turning to me. 'As I mentioned earlier: at six o'clock, Agios Sostis will still be crawling with tourists, both on land and at sea – something the kidnapping team will be hoping to use to use to their advantage. They're looking to disappear, not stand out. The show of force on our part is intended only as a deterrent.'

'*Endaxi* – exactly,' said Argyris, and reached once again for his pastry.

The floor was then handed to deputy chief Markos, who, aided by Kate's simultaneous translation, informed me he'd be supplying at least six police units: a combination of vans, cars and motorbikes; although, he proposed deploying only two cars – unmarked – in the immediate vicinity of Agios Sostis marina. Any more risked drawing unwanted attention.

'To which I agree,' Kate added, following on. 'The marina is made up of three jetties, primarily pedestrian and all very exposed. So yes – less is more.'

As all assembled murmured their assent, Markos beckoned me over to the map and continued with his brief, indicating the various locations with energetic sweeps of his leathery hands as he rattled off his directive in rapid-fire Greek. Once finished, he knocked back the remainder of his coffee and stepped back from the table, nodding to Kate, who translated his proposal.

One unmarked vehicle would arrive at Agios Sostis in the mid-afternoon, at approximately 3 p.m. The second unit would arrive an hour before the appointed fishing trip departure time of 6 p.m. The officers would be plain-clothed, posing as tourists. Two marked units would remain further afield: a patrol car, at the resort of Laganas; the other, a police van, at Lithakia, two clicks to the north. As soon as the arrests were made by the Agios Sostis contingent, the van would leave Lithakia and head for Agios Sostis to pick up the detainees. Meanwhile, the Laganas patrol car would assist Markos in coordinating the setting up of road blocks at Kalamaki, to the east; at Lithakia, on the main north-south highway; and finally, at Ampelokipoi – at the exit road leading to the airport. Markos himself would be driving an unmarked unit, his Chevrolet, joining us at Argassi and staying with us until we entered Agios Sostis; at which point, he would break off and head north to Lithakia, to be better placed to direct the operation.

When it was clear that Markos had nothing else to add, Kate left the room and returned moments later with a handful of walkie talkies, which she distributed to everyone apart from myself.

'Allowing for just over an hour to reach Agios Sostis from the Porto Roma, including stoppage time to pick Max and his family from Gerakas,' she continued, 'I suggest setting off no later than 4.30 p.m. Albertos and I will be waiting in a parked vehicle – the blue Volkswagen – on the coastal route from the hotel to Gerakas. When you arrive at the villa, we will overtake you and position ourselves at the north end of Gerakas beach car park. You will follow us from there all the way to Agios Sostis. As already mentioned, Markos will join at Argassi, and leave us again later, for Lithakia. At Agios Sostis, Albertos and I will break off and park facing the sea, on the southernmost of the three jetties. You will drive straight to the central jetty – the busiest of the three – and from there, seek out the fishing vessel, the *Anthea*.'

Markos nodded sagely.

They'd evidently worked this all out earlier that morning. Indeed, knowing there were only two ways off the island – by boat, or by air – they would already have had a skeleton strategy in place for some time. All they'd have been waiting for was the location.

'Do I need to know the exact route?'

Kate smiled. 'You don't – hence why we're travelling in convoy.' Then she beckoned me over to the map and traced over it with her finger. 'However, we will be taking the Laganas road turn off after Ampelokipoi, and once we've passed through Agrilia, we'll cut west across country to approach Agios Sostis from the south. There's a substantial hill to circumnavigate, so we'll keep to the north, to avoid getting caught up in the coastal traffic.'

'Will I too have a radio . . . a walkie talkie?' I asked. 'In case we get separated en route?'

Kate smiled. 'How would you explain it to Amara and Max?'

Good point.

'There's no reason we'd get separated,' Kate added. 'As long as you stay sharp and keep vigilant.'

I nodded.

There came a sudden crackle of a radio, and all eyes turned to Markos, who immediately began fiddling with his transmitter.

'This – noise . . . it is good?' he asked, fiddling with the transmitter and holding it up so we could hear the rhythmic pulse of static emanating from the speaker.

167

'They're all working fine,' said Kate, tight lipped, as Albertos too switched his machine on and began to fiddle with the nobs. 'Just interference – quite normal.'

Radios back on the table, she went on to explain what would happen at Agios Sostis.

In essence, it was simple enough: after locating the *Anthea*, Xander and I would approach the crew and initiate conversation while Max hung back with Amara by the car. When it was discovered that the vessel was overbooked, Xander would stand down and offer to remain on shore – as per the Seven Stars' instructions. Once this had been 'agreed' between Xander and me, and once the boat was departure-ready with the other passengers already embarked, I would then board the vessel myself. At the point Max was to leave his mother's side, the plain-clothed officers would move in from their positions on the adjacent jetties and arrest everyone on the *Anthea*, as well as Xander, on shore.

'Where's Mikis in all this?' I interjected.

Albertos obviously had a pivotal role alongside Kate, but there'd been no mention of Mikis, who, I presumed, was still in position at the villa in Gerakas.

'I was just coming onto him,' said Kate, coolly. 'But he'll remain back on the east coast – on standby to facilitate departure measures off the island.'

'Sorry – right.'

Reassuring, though, to know that non-believer Mikis was to be kept away from the front line.

'After the arrests have been made at Agios Sostis,' Kate continued, returning to the map, 'Albertos and I will take Amara and Max by car to the airport to be taken directly back to Athens on a security services aircraft. Albertos will stay on the ground, but I will travel with mother and son to Athens and take them to a safe house.'

She paused for a moment, checking that all present were still following her.

Indeed, they were; grunts of admiration were accompanied by the snap and fizz of cigarettes lighting up.

'They won't be able to go home?' I asked.

'Not initially,' said Kate, reaching into her jeans for her Camel Lights and lighting up. 'We will keep them under police watch until we have dealt with Xander. It is quite likely, irrespective of the quality of information we are able to extract from him, that Xander will be offered witness protection. The Mafia will be looking for someone to blame.'

'What about Amara and Max?' I ventured.

'What about them?'

'If they're merely innocent victims of the kidnap attempt, they wouldn't necessarily have to go into witness protection, right?'

Kate took a beat before answering.

'Technically that's correct, but you don't think the family would want to remain together?'

'Yes, of course.'

My heart leaped against my rib cage.

I hadn't for a second considered that scenario.

'So, what happens to me?' I added, quickly changing subject.

I had to keep the faith. Everything that she and Max had said or implied suggested Amara was looking for a way out.

Stay on your game.

Kate threw a glance at Markos before answering. 'You'll be debriefed, or should I say – interrogated. We need to keep up appearances. And we'll also, of course, require your official testimony on everything Xander, Gerald and Takis have said to you; not to mention an account of the events in London leading up to your arrival in Greece. Almost certainly you will be held at the police station in Zakynthos overnight. The following day, or possibly even the day after, once we have everything on record, you will be released to catch a civilian flight back to Athens, and then the UK. All expenses you incur will be paid by us.'

'Got it,' I replied, trying my best to sound blasé.

The real question I wanted to ask was how I'd be reunited with Amara and Max.

In good time . . .

Kate poured herself a glass of water and stepped away from the table, crossing to the middle of the room, where she paused briefly to peer out into the sunlight before turning back to the room. 'Mikis will be responsible for collecting all possessions and clothing from both the villa and your hotel, Alistair. These will be shipped onwards to their various destinations at a later date. Obviously, you won't be able to bring anything more than essentials with you on the drive to Agios Sostis.'

'Not even our passports?' I asked.

Kate took a sip of her water. 'Amara and Max – Xander too for that matter – have no idea about the intended evacuation. To ask them to bring their passports would only raise unhelpful questions.' She threw another glance at Markos. 'Mikis and a uniformed officer will collect passports and a change of clothes for Max and Amara from the villa, once you have left for Agios Sostis. Xander, of course, will have no immediate need of his. Mikis and the official escort will also stop by the Porto Roma hotel to collect all your belongings. However, if you'd rather keep your passport with you, that's fine. As long as you keep it out of sight.'

'Understood.'

Kate then emptied her glass in a couple of long pulls, before turning back to the others.

'You'll leave shortly to brief your respective teams, while Alistair makes sure the family are willing to go ahead with the fishing trip tonight. By "family", I mean, Amara. If she vetoes it, we are up against a brick wall.' She tapped her cigarette against the ashtray on the coffee table behind her. 'Not only must she agree to it, but she needs to be present on the expedition, in order to facilitate a quick and smooth evacuation off the island, following the arrests.

170

Out of the corner of my eye I saw heads nodding.

'Equally important,' she continued, 'we must consider Max's mental state. Even with our most favoured outcome, the events at Agios Sostis will cause him considerable stress, and potentially, trauma. We keep mother and son together at all times.'

'Absolutely,' I said, along with more murmuring assents from the Greek entourage. 'On the other hand, I can't very well force her.'

Kate turned again to me. 'It's highly unlikely she'd want to miss out on the expedition – for her son's sake if nothing else,' she added with a smile. 'But if she is feeling so inclined, you'll just have to use some of that ol' English charm.'

There was another deferential chuckle from Argyris and Albertos.

'Failing that, you'll have to tie her up and throw her in the back of the car.'

'Fair enough,' I said, joining in with the laughter.

Kate checked her watch, then extinguished her cigarette. 'Boris will take you back to the supermarket to collect your car. It's best you head straight to the villa. Mikis will leave the vicinity as soon as you arrive. He's been up all night and he'll need to get his head down before this evening.'

'Right.'

'Any questions?'

None came to mind.

'Make sure you call in every hour for any updates. And be ready waiting in your room at the hotel by 4 p.m.'

I nodded. 'It's safe to speak on the hotel phone?'

'At this stage, we don't have a choice. However, we're not anticipating any need to contact you, unless there's a problem.'

'Great.'

Kate turned once again to face her colleagues, dropping her arms to her side in almost military fashion.

'We have a plan, gentlemen. Let's put it into action.'

13

Boris delivered me back to the supermarket and the Nissan just before 1 p.m. By half past, having taken Mikis's parking space in the jam-packed field-cum-car park at Gerakas beach – Mikis's only attempt at communication being to honk the horn of his Peugeot as he pulled away – I was negotiating my way through the throng of tourists returning from the beach in search of shade and sustenance, en route to the villa.

As I passed through the front gate and followed up the flag-stone path to the front door, laughter from the back garden accompanied by the tuneless strum of a guitar suggested all was well with the family – well, with Xander and Max, at least. It sounded like the former was giving the latter a music lesson. Or, vice versa.

But what of Amara?

I knocked lightly on the door and waited, hoping that my announcement had been loud enough for Amara to hear, but not enough to alert the others round the back. I'd wait to broach the subject of the fishing trip in front of Max – for maximum impact – but I was keen to get a moment alone with his mother, to assess where she was at emotionally, and to find out what, if anything, had been discussed between her and her husband.

I was poised to knock a second time when Amara opened the door wrapped in a pair of white towels; one about her chest, the other, turban-like around her head.

'We were wondering when you might show up,' she said, standing back to encourage me in. 'Oversleep?'

'It's one thirty,' I replied with a laugh. 'I've been up and at it for hours.'

Her spirited response took me by surprise – Xander had obviously been quick to patch things up with her.

Bastard.

'We just got back from the beach,' she continued, tightening the lower towel until the bottom of the fabric rode up her thighs. 'Going to have some lunch soon. Wanna join us?'

For a moment, I couldn't tear my eyes away from her legs.

I'd known those legs. I'd felt them around me . . .

'I, erm . . . actually, I'm heading into Zakynthos town,' I said, bringing myself back on point, while at the same time realising that I hadn't given any thought as to how I was going to pass the time between then and the evening's operation. All I knew was that I had no desire to dissemble any more than I had to in Amara's company. 'Yeah, I need to get to the international phone exchange and check in on my flatmate.'

I had no intention of calling Vince, but it was the first thing that came into my head.

'What's up with him?' said Amara brightly.

'Been dumped by his girlfriend,' I answered, adding a dose of truth to support the lie.

'He'll be fine, though,' I continued. 'But hey – how's it going here?'

'All good, dude,' she said, pouring me a glass of water from the fridge. 'All good.'

Dude?

Whatever he had done, her errant husband had evidently worked some magic. She was even sounding like him.

173

'Guess who?' Amara yelled, stepping out onto the patio. 'Our favourite Englishman.'

There was no point in delaying things, so, after a hearty high-five with Xander – who, despite his haggard appearance, was doing a fine job of appearing to be his usual ebullient self – I squatted down in front of the guitar-clutching Max and, plucking at one of the strings, announced that I had a surprise in store for him: a special treat, as a reward for his great sailing the day before.

After a series of wrong guesses, Max became so worked up that he started foaming at the mouth.

'We're going fishing,' I announced finally, with a theatrical bow. 'Yours truly has organised a boat, tonight at six o'clock.' I threw a quick glance at Amara, whose eyes were wide with astonishment. 'Gonna catch ourselves some dinner.'

There followed a full minute of squealing from Max, as he leaped up and down the cobbled stones, swinging Xander's guitar above his head. Amara seemed equally delighted and gave me a prolonged thank-you hug. Even Xander played his part perfectly; accusing me of trying to steal the hearts of his family with my English cunning.

Turning down the offer of a beer, I gave them the low-down of the marching orders for the evening; how I would come and collect them in the Nissan just after four thirty to drive us all across to Agios Sostis, and how there was to be no hanging around.

Amara put paid to the question of whether or not she'd willing to come, by asking if I was also going to be taking them all out to dinner. I said it was exactly my intention, and suggested they come with a selection of suitable recommendations. Then I broke up the party, insisting I had to hit the road.

Xander clapped me on the back and said he'd make damn sure his family were all primed and ready to go no later than 4.15 p.m., and thanked me again with another hand-stinging high-five. When Amara's back was momentarily turned, he moved in closer, evidently hoping I'd shed some light on what was to happen that evening. But I shook my head and stepped away, at which point he grimaced and disappeared to the far end of the garden to rescue his guitar from Max, which was now being used as a tool to dead-head the geraniums.

Amara took me by the arm and walked me back to the front door.

'I called the hospital, by the way,' she said, leaning up against the door jam, as I slipped past her onto the steps. 'They're expecting the results as soon as tomorrow.'

'Great news,' I exclaimed, wondering if we'd be able to get the results over the phone.

Amara shook the towel loose from her hair and stared at me thoughtfully. 'You should go to Salamis Taverna on the waterfront. I'd come with you, but I've got washing to do before I pack.'

My heart skipped a beat.

'Pack?'

'Going back to Athens,' she said, holding my gaze. 'A friend of mine is very sick.'

I stared at her, uncomprehending.

'At least, that's what I'm going to tell Xander.'

'You've lost me,' I replied, straining to hear the laughter out the back . . .

Yes, they were still playing with the guitar.

'I don't understand,' I added, stepping in closer. 'What's happened?'

'Nothing yet,' she said, tilting her head and looking up at me. 'But as soon as we get the results of the DNA test, I'm taking Max home.'

Not today, though. Not until after the tests came in.

'Okay,' I answered, still none the wiser. 'Xander going with you?'

She smiled. 'He can do whatever he likes. But when I get to Athens, I'm filing for a divorce.'

I could only stare at her.

'See you later,' she said, taking a step back into the hallway. 'Enjoy the calamari.'

Then she shut the door.

Heart in my mouth, I drove straight to the telephone box at the convenience store and, pushing all thoughts of the soon-to-be single Amara out of my mind, called Kate; updating her on the fact that the fishing trip had been sanctioned by Amara and that she would indeed be joining the expedition; and also, that, although clearly nervous, Xander was holding up and putting on a brave face.

I kept Amara's bombshell to myself – that was no one's business but mine.

Thanking me for the heads up, Kate reminded me to call again within the hour and to be in position at the hotel from four o'clock.

I assured her I'd be ready.

'Hang in there,' she said finally. 'It'll soon be over.'

I decided against driving into Zakynthos town, and instead killed the remaining hour and a half at the cove beneath the Porto Roma, smoking my way through a packet of Karelia Lights as I poured over my map and went over the route we'd be taking that evening. Once confident I'd committed the journey to memory, I pocketed the map and lay back on the wooden pontoon, tuning out to the sound of the fisherman working on their nets.

Amara was leaving Xander ... and I'd be there to pick up the pieces.

I couldn't have wished for more.

Making a vow to quit smoking for good once back on British soil, I lit the last cigarette from the packet and, turning away from the sea towards the hotel perched on the cliff top, took in my surrounds: the shafts of sunlight in the cedars, the limpid movement of the fisherman at work ... the chorus of cicadas from the olive groves inland ...

I remained motionless in the golden light, my mind momentarily a blank, and was overcome by a profound sense of detachment. Only when the cigarette started burning my fingers did the spell break.

Remembering where I was, I set off through the lengthening shadows back around the cove and climbed the path up to the hotel, where, after a shower and a change of clothes, I packed up my rucksack and sat watching the phone on the bedside table, counting down the minutes.

Finally, at 4.20 p.m., a little ahead of schedule, I left my room for the last time, wished my hostess a pleasant evening, and, checking I was in possession of passport, map, and the birth certificates, set off in the Nissan along the coastal road towards the villa.

No turning back now.

14

I'd driven more than two-thirds of the two-kilometre journey before I eventually spotted the blue Volkswagen, tucked in off the road alongside an abandoned building site, some two hundred yards before the farmstead with the ducks and the plum tree.

After a glance in the rear-view mirror to check no one was following, I slowed down to a crawl, passing at a distance of a few feet. Kate was at the wheel, smoking, with Albertos riding shotgun, an arm out of the window, fingers tapping on the roof.

Neither acknowledged me.

Assuming all to be well, I continued on my way, up past the farm to the T-junction with the Gerakas beach road, pausing briefly opposite Nikos Taverna to check behind me before pulling out and turning left towards the track that led down to the villa. Sure enough, the Volkswagen was bouncing steadily up the road in a cloud of dust, at a distance of about a hundred yards.

In front of the turtle museum I was forced to stop and wait for a gap in the stream of tourists on their exodus from the beach, which was when I again caught sight of Kate in the rear-view mirror, turning right at Nikos Taverna before pulling up and parking under the cypress trees at the top end of the parade of restaurants.

Edging my way forwards in front of a group of sunburnt Brits peering at me over the tops of their ice creams, I turned off the along the track and began my descent down to sea level, arriving moments later at the villa to be met by an impatient Max, swinging on the front gate, sporting a Jurassic Park t-shirt and a baseball cap.

'Uncle Alistair!' he yelled, flashing his gap-toothed grin as I drew up to a stop. 'Let's go!'

'Ah, the fisherman!' I returned, hopping out of the car, seeing no sign of Amara or Xander; also wondering which one of the two had decided to name me 'Uncle'.

'I hope you're ready?'

'Yes, yes! Of course!' he squeaked, hugging me around the waist before grabbing my hand and dragging me through the garden towards the back of the house. '*Ella, pame!*'

I was just about to ask where his mother was, when we rounded the side of the building and all became clear:

Parked on the narrow track behind the rear garden, stood the jeep. Xander was leant over the bonnet, manically twirling a pair of Ray Bans, while Amara busied herself with something in the trunk. Dressed in a simple black dress and platform heels, she looked like she was about to go for a night out on the tiles, rather than a fishing trip.

I let go of Max's fingers, noting how the backlighting revealed the outline of her legs . . . as far up as the thighs.

'Right on time, Mister punctual Englishman!' hollered Xander, approaching me with his hand held ready for his customary greeting. 'Let's get out of here!'

The show of bravado was betrayed by a slight tremor in his voice. Which was understandable enough; in less than two hours he'd be in handcuffs.

But what was with the jeep?

'We're going in mine,' I replied, as Max pushed me across the grass to the back gate. 'My treat. You don't want to drive.'

'He's not driving,' said Amara, her head popping up from the boot as Xander slapped his hand against mine. 'I am.'

'What I meant was ...'

'We're not going in your little ... thing,' Amara continued, cutting me off. 'We're taking the jeep. It will be much more comfortable for everyone. And you don't know the roads.'

'She's right, buddy,' added Xander.

Shit.

Why hadn't I warned him we'd need to travel in my car?

Because Kate instructed me to keep him in the dark.

'I've got a map,' I protested.

'Then you can map-read.'

Amara kissed me on the cheek and walked around to the front of the jeep.

Xander looked at me questioningly. 'But we can ... go in your car if you want,' he ventured, finally sensing something was up. 'It's not so small.'

'*Ella*, Max, get in the back,' said Amara, ignoring him. 'Xander, you too. Alistair is riding up front with me.'

Max immediately shot round the side of the Jeep and jumped in, punching me in the leg on the way.

Xander stared at me, unmoving. 'Everything okay?'

'Yeah, sure,' I said brightly.

There was no arguing with Amara.

And the last thing I needed was a paranoid Xander.

'Yes, I erm ... just have to get my stuff,' I exclaimed. 'Won't be a second.'

'Stuff?' Amara hitched up her dress as she slid into the driver's seat and started the engine. 'You brought a fishing rod to Zakynthos?'

I acknowledged her with a laugh then took off back towards the Nissan.

To travel in the Jeep would be to give up all control.

But then, travelling in separate cars would be worse . . .

I checked my watch and stood hovering by the car, cursing Kate for not giving me a walkie talkie, and wondering what the fuck I should do next.

But there was no time for debate. Decision made, I ducked into the Nissan and grabbed the map off the front seat. It would have to be the Jeep. Kate would work out what had happened and radio ahead to Markos at Argassi and give him the heads up. Provided Amara didn't either drive too fast, or stop anywhere on the way, we'd be fine.

'*Ella*, Englishman, what's up?' yelled Xander, doing his best to sound authoritative. 'We're waiting.'

I shot back around the villa, waving the map in my hand. 'All good,' I said, jogging up to the Jeep. 'Found the map.'

Giving Xander a quick nod by way of reassurance, I jumped into the passenger seat and shut the door. Then we set off, swinging round to join the main track up to Gerakas beach.

'I mean – come on,' Amara exclaimed, peering past me in the direction of the Nissan parked against the wall. 'Your car's so diddy.'

As Max made Xander explain 'diddy' for him, I unfolded the map and checked ahead to see where Amara might be inclined to go off-piste. Markos joining us wouldn't be an issue – there was only one road north from Vassilikos, and one had no choice but to drive right through Argassi. Equally, there was only one route out of Zakynthos town in the direction of Laganas and the southern beaches. However, after the turn off point at Agrilia there was a myriad of minor roads on offer to reach Agios Sostis; keeping up with Kate's Volkswagen might prove considerably trickier, especially with Amara professing to know the roads.

'But if I'm map reading,' I said, affecting a supercilious tone, 'then you are to obey me at all times.'

181

'Yes, Sir,' replied Amara, turning on the air-conditioning.

'We're going fishing!' yelled the jubilant Max.

'Fishing!' echoed Amara, tooting the horn.

As Xander joined in half-heartedly with the celebrations, we exited the track, crossed the procession of retiring beach goers and approached the junction with the road that led to the Porto Roma.

Then I heard the indicator.

'Straight ahead,' I said quickly, with an eye on Kate's car up ahead.

Amara hit the brakes.

'The other way is prettier,' she replied, holding the jeep in the middle of the road. 'We get to drive by the sea.'

Xander stuck his nose back between the two front seats: '*Ti les?*'

'Just figuring out our route,' I replied.

No way could we turn straight off – Kate would be stuck behind us and then be forced to overtake, which could draw attention. And that was even if they noticed us leave; we were in Amara's Jeep, not the Nissan, as they were expecting.

'Both roads go where we want to go,' I said, improvising. 'But I haven't done the inland route before, and I want to see . . . something new.'

I had driven that way, of course – with Xander. On the way to the hospital.

Indeed, Amara had led the way.

'Humour him,' barked Xander, scratching at his stubble as he peered over my shoulder through the windscreen, trying to understand my reasoning. 'He's a tourist.'

'Xander, get back!' she hissed, elbowing him away.

For a moment, there came only the click-click of the indicator.

'But we drove that way yesterday,' said Amara finally, tapping her nails on the wheel. 'On the way to the hospital.'

'I was driving – following you,' I replied. 'Now I get a chance to sight-see.'

She turned to face me for a moment, a frown stitched across her brow, then sighed and switched off the indicator.

'Okay, just for you, Mister Tourist,' she sighed, kicking the Jeep into gear. 'Let's show you the olive trees.'

With that she drove on along the row of restaurants, passing the Volkswagen, which quickly pulled out and began to follow behind.

Wiping the sweat from the back of my neck, I exhaled deeply, checked my watch, and picked up the map.

Four forty-five p.m.

We were still on time.

With Kate's Volkswagen remaining sometimes two, sometimes three cars ahead of us, we left the arid Vassilikos peninsular behind us and made good progress up the coast, arriving at Argassi just after five o'clock, where we were joined by Markos in his black Chevy, who slipped into line two cars behind us after pulling out from the Shell petrol station in the centre of the bustling resort. From there, Kate led the convoy steadily north into the windswept Zakynthos harbour, with its cortege of yachts and motor cruisers twisting and bobbing against their moorings, before crossing over the narrow canal bridge at the marina and turning west onto the ring road. Pressing on through the suburbs with its plethora of bijoux hotels and tourist villas, we eventually merged with the main east-west route that ran through Ampelokipoi, just north of the airport.

Sensing I'd relaxed after our shaky false-start, Xander too had calmed down to a degree; nonetheless, every few minutes he would lean forward to peer through the windscreen, or twist back over his shoulder to check the road behind – to see who, in the way of police or Mafia, might or might not be tailing us. Luckily, Amara was oblivious to his fidgeting, thanks primarily to Max, who took it upon himself to regale us with his extensive repertoire of English nursery rhymes, before attempting to teach me the Greek lyrics to a song called 'Yianka 1-2-3' – which, according to Amara, was also a famous children's dance from the 1960s.

However, once we hit the straight stretch of road leading into Zakynthos's capital, Max tired of his endeavours and became sullen, asking over and over how much longer we had to left to drive, before eventually closing his eyes and dozing up against Xander's shoulder.

Without Max as a focal point, the tension in the jeep began to rise.

Negotiating the one-way systems of the Zakynthos ring road, I made several attempts to initiate a conversation – essentially, to keep Amara distracted so she'd be less likely to notice Kate's car up ahead – but each time I failed. Amara was unforthcoming about her kindergarten teaching, other than agreeing with me that its approach was probably akin to Montessori in style. Xander was equally reticent when I questioned him about his singing career. He wrapped up the inquisition before it had even started, by declaring that pop music was dead: *the Beatles invented it, they perfected it, and ended it.*

And so, as we continued along the valley plains due west towards Zakynthos Mountain, the three of us sat in a brooding silence. Amara, shifting restlessly in her seat, casting angry glances in the rear-view mirror at her soon-to-be ex-husband; Xander, resting his head against the window and staring morosely into the setting sun.

As for me: I was thinking of Amara – how exactly she'd respond once she realised I'd effectively used Max as bait to foil a Mafia kidnap plot. However much I'd claim safety precautions had been fully implemented, that Max had never been in any danger, and that I was saving them both from Xander's nefarious machinations, there was a chance she'd remain unforgiving.

Then what?

*

The sight of a signpost to Agrilia pulled me back to the present.

Sure enough, ahead of two tourist quadbikes in front of us, the indicator on the Volkswagen began to wink on and off.

I turned to Amara. 'Okay – we do a left here.'

Amara hesitated before answering. 'It'll be quicker if we stay on the main road.'

The jeep lurched as Xander leaned forwards to peer out of the windscreen.

I flicked my eyes to the map.

'Not necessarily,' I replied. 'It's a bigger road, but it takes us a long way north, and then we have to go back on ourselves.'

'Whassup?' piped up Xander, leaning forwards between the seats.

'*Xander, kathiste!*'

But Xander stayed put, scanning the vehicles ahead.

'Follow these guys,' I said, as the turn off rapidly approached.

The quadbikes had also begun to indicate left.

'They're going to Laganas,' Amara answered. 'If we go through Laganas, it'll take forever.'

I pointed to the map. 'Yeah, but we'll take a right-hand turn after Agrilia and cut across country. There'll be less traffic and it's more direct.'

The Volkswagen had already begun to turn.

As she reached for the indicator, Amara's face lit up. 'So, you do know where you're going . . .'

I returned the smile. 'I was going to drive, remember? Always plan ahead.'

She inclined her head coquettishly. 'But secretly, you wanna do some more sight-seeing?'

'You got it.'

'Okay, but don't get your hopes up,' Amara exclaimed, spinning the wheel to the left. 'Because there's nothing out there but trees and rocks.'

The two quadbikes in front pulled over outside a

mini-supermarket, and within seconds we had caught up with Kate.

I could sense Xander's head just inches from my left shoulder. He was keeping very still . . .

Had he noticed the Volkswagen?

'What's your favourite tree, uncle Alistair?' came a squeak from behind.

'Ah, you're awake.' I reached back and tweaked his cap, forcing Xander to retreat into his seat. 'Wanna teach me some more of that dance song?'

'No!' snapped Xander and Amara in unison.

I laughed and faced around to the front once more – but not before I'd spotted Markos's Chevy turn off and join us. We were now three in direct convoy.

'So, what shall we discuss?' I asked. 'Max – name a topic.'

'Topic?'

'Ask me a question – anything.'

The was a hiatus as Max tried to think of something.

'Go on then,' I encouraged, turning around to find Xander peering around the side of Amara's head in the direction of the Volkswagen. 'Test me.'

'Hey!' exclaimed Amara, nudging me in the ribs. 'Thought you wanted to see the sights.' She lifted her Guccis up on her head and peered ahead. 'Ooh, look – there's a petrol station . . . And a supermarket . . . Amazing, huh?'

'Okay – how about you ask me something else?' I said, turning around and catching Xander's eye. He was studying me intently, eyebrows furrowed.

'I have a question,' Xander said slowly, giving me a knowing look. 'What kind of fish will we catch tonight?'

He maintained eye contact with me and then nodded in the direction of the Volkswagen.

'An octopus?' asked Max, lifting off his cap and scratching at his blond locks.

'That's not a fish,' said Amara, giving a quick hoot on the horn. I turned back to the front.

'What's with these guys,' she exclaimed. 'They're so slow.'

'Well, you can give them a little more room,' I suggested.

I figured Kate didn't want to risk anyone getting between us at this point, in case we missed the turn off. Problem was, with the shadows of the apartment buildings blocking the glare from the low-lying sun, she and Albertos were vulnerable to being visible.

I checked my watch. 'We're not in a rush.'

Only five and a half kilometres to go.

'I thought you wanted to get to the olive trees?' Amara replied, finger and thumb on the silver necklace around her neck.

'I'm enjoying the build-up.'

Would it in fact matter if Xander recognised Kate? The more he joined the dots, the easier it might be for him to help me play Amara – such as siding with me on our routing.

Provided he keeps his cool and doesn't give it away.

'Okay, we've got a right-hand turn coming up in about four hundred yards,' I said, eyeing the map. 'So keep an eye out for signs to Ploumari.'

If Amara recognised Kate, however, it would be another matter entirely.

'Everyone keep an eye out for the sign,' I urged.

After a few more minutes we hit the industrial outskirts of Agrilia, where, taking advantage of the open road, Kate accelerated away.

'That's better,' murmured Amara, likewise opening up the throttle.

Moments later, a signpost appeared against the sky, backlit by the evening sun.

I turned around to the back. 'Hey Max, what can you see up ahead?'

Max leaned forwards and screwed his eyes up as he peered into the distance.

'The sign! The sign!' he yelled, bouncing up and down on his seat. 'I win!'

'*Bravo, Maxi mou,*' Amara exclaimed, flicking on the indicator.

'Looks like these guys are going the same way,' she added, with a frown.

'What's my prize?' asked Max.

'They're probably going to Agios Sostis too,' Xander offered, leaning in. 'It's the most direct route from here.'

'Says the man who lost his driving license,' said Amara brightly.

I made a point of studying the map. 'Well, they're getting on with it, at least.'

'If you keep up with them, maybe they'll show us the way?' Xander added.

'You, er ... doubting my map reading skills?' I said cheerfully, before twisting around and eyeballing him.

Don't overdo it.

As we swung briefly north-west, the countryside up ahead became clearer: in the distance lay the formidable silhouette of Zakynthos mountain, extending all the way up the western coast as far as the blue caves and Shipwreck Beach. In between them and us was a flat plain, dotted with the odd smallholding, but otherwise a relentless swathe of green olive groves extending as far as the eye could see. To the south, lay a large hill protruding out from the valley floor like a volcano plug or a drumlin; this was the high ground we had to circumnavigate to the north, in order to avoid the coastal traffic near Laganas. Beyond the hill, out of sight and a kilometre to the west, lay the resort of Agios Sostis and the waiting fishing charter.

'We've got a bit of wiggling to do,' I said, holding up the map. 'Once we hit Ploumari we head south again, but we've got to keep north of that funny-shaped hill, so we don't get sucked down onto the coastal route. Any number of possibilities – but bear with me, I think I have the way forward.'

Max had started to sing 'Yianka 1-2-3' again, but neither

Amara or Xander bothered to chastise him. If Max was happy, we were all happy.

'What did I tell you?' Amara said, pulling down the sun shade. 'Nothing but olive trees.'

'Looks good in the evening light though,' I said, noticing Kate had indicated left once more.

I checked the map.

'Yup, might as well follow these guys – they seem to know where they're going. Must be locals.'

'Not driving fast enough for locals,' countered Amara. 'You know the Greeks – we're crazy.'

I laughed but kept my eyes on the map, guiding Amara through a series of left and right turns, still following in Kate's wake, until we came to Ploumari. A deserted crossroads, the only sign of life was a lone venetian villa, just visible, a couple of hundred yards off to the right in the midst of the rambling olive groves.

'Looks like we're not the only ones heading this way,' said Xander from the back seat.

I twisted around to look.

Behind us, Markos's Chevy was following at a distance of around fifty yards.

'Now, he's a local,' announced Amara, peering into the rear-view mirror. 'It's a Chevy. They don't rent Chevys to tourists.'

Once again, I could feel Xander's eyes homing in on me.

'Well then, we're in good company,' I said, shouting over the top of Max as he reached a crescendo in the chorus. 'But you never know – they could be disappearing off to one of these farms.'

Kate pressed ahead and then turned left once more.

Her route was starting to become clear. Essentially, she was zig-zagging her way south towards the hill ahead, keeping to the more substantial roads, as indicated on the map.

Was it quicker than keeping on the main east-west route

and going via Lithakia – as Amara had suggested? Certainly, a shorter distance – by some five or six kilometres. One thing was clear: there were many more options on the smaller roads. If there was a hold-up in Lithakia or on the main road south to Agios Sostis, there was no way of turning off it. And we were still making good time, despite the uneven roads.

After maybe half a minute, I checked in the wing mirror, and saw no Markos.

Xander had also noticed, and was trying to catch my eye.

A quick glance at the map shed light on his disappearance: the right-hand turn at the crossroads led directly into Lithakia – approximately two kilometres to the north – where he would be coordinating the operation. He'd reached his appointed turn-off point.

As Kate turned left again, I told Amara to simply follow the Volkswagen, and then set-to joining in the singing with Max to prevent any further discussions about locals and their vehicles.

After another two hundred yards, we rounded a bend and nearly collided with the Volkswagen as Kate hit the brakes.

'*Apaniyamou!*' said Amara, slowing down and cranking up the air conditioning.

'What is it?' enquired Xander, silencing Max's singing as he leant forward between the seats.

Up ahead, a tractor had lost its load of watermelons off the back of the trailer. The vehicle was skewed, jack-knifed across the road, and a rustically-clad man was scurrying back and forth collecting the fallen fruit, while his accomplice was attending to the front offside wheel.

'He had a puncture,' declared Xander, craning his neck.

'Should I go around him?' asked Amara.

'Maybe,' I ventured, sticking my head out of the window to get a better angle.

The question was, firstly, what would Kate do about it?

And secondly: if she decided to turn around, how could I stop

190

Amara noticing her? She might even wind down the window in the hope of getting advice.

Kate had come to a stop, about thirty yards behind the truck.

Would she be tempted to get out?

Surely, she'd leave that to Albertos. After all, Amara had never laid eyes on the man.

'I'll turn around then,' declared Amara, throwing the jeep into reverse.

'Wait a second,' I said, eyes glued on the Volkswagen.

Kate's brake lights had gone out; but instead of doing a U-Turn, she backed up ten yards and then, indicating right, turned off onto a narrow sandy track cross-country.

Another glance at the map confirmed her intentions.

'Looks like there's a farm, or warehouse, off to the right,' I announced, tracing along the thin line of track that led to it. 'The track takes us through it and back on the road the other side – about a half kilometre further south.'

'Maybe it's where they keep the watermelons,' offered Xander, scratching at his neck.

'*Endaxi.*' Putting the car into gear, Amara crept forward and then turned right onto the farm track, following the cloud of dust kicked up by Kate and Albertos.

'Good move,' said Xander approvingly, peering over at the stricken truck. 'Those guys are gonna be there for ages.'

After a couple of minutes bouncing along the rutted ground, the track opened up into an expansive concrete apron, and we approached a row of derelict buildings on our left, which, judging by the illustrations on the dilapidated sign at the front, appeared to be a disused olive press.

'This area is famous for its olive oil,' said Amara, dropping into second and slowing down to avoid a series of potholes. 'There's a museum at Lithakia. They have a shop where you can buy it real cheap – if you wanna take some home to London.'

She turned and flashed me a smile.

I was about to reply, when all of a sudden, a container truck pulled out from behind the furthest block and ground to a halt in front of Kate, blocking the road where the concourse bottle-necked with the continuing farm track.

Kate slammed on the brakes and the Volkswagen came skidding to a stop.

For a moment, nothing happened.

'*Ti einai?*' said Xander, lunging forwards between the seats.

Kate started to honk the horn.

'Great,' exclaimed Amara, pulling up. 'Move, idiot.'

But the truck remained motionless.

Just the hiss of his air brakes.

'I think he's heading this way,' I said. 'He's waiting for us to back up.'

'What's going on?' asked Xander nervously.

'Are we there yet?' piped up Max, kicking my seat.

'I think you should back up and turn around,' I said, briefly checking behind us.

'He'll move in a minute,' replied Amara, also leaning on the horn. 'Come on!'

Then Kate stepped out of the Volkswagen and began shouting and gesticulating in the direction of the truck. Moments later, the doors on both sides of the vehicle opened, and two men came around from either side.

One of them, the driver, started yelling back.

'*Malakas!*' grunted Xander, reaching for the door handle.

'Xander!' exclaimed Amara, shooting him a filthy look in the mirror.

'Stay where you are,' I snapped.

Something about the other man's gait . . .

All of a sudden, Kate turned on her heels and retraced her steps back to the Volkswagen.

'Turn the jeep around, Amara,' I said calmly. 'Now.'

'We've seen that woman before,' said Amara, taking off her sunglasses.

'She was at the hospital . . . and the beach.'

'Turn around!' I snapped, as the driver's sidekick raised an arm towards Kate.

'Amara!' yelled Xander.

Arriving at the Volkswagen, Kate turned momentarily back to the truck.

'My God, is he holding a . . .?'

Amara never finished the sentence.

A gunshot ripped the air apart, and Kate fell, lifeless, to the ground.

15

With a shriek, Amara let slip the clutch and the jeep stalled, sending Max sprawling into the footwell behind me.

'Xander – take him!' I yelled, as Max tried to wriggle between the seats into his mother's lap. 'Amara, start the engine!'

But she didn't hear me. Rigid with shock, she stared transfixed at Kate's twisted body.

Unbuckling her safety belt, I reached over and attempted to wrestle her out of the seat, but two more shots sent me diving below the dashboard, pulling her with me over onto the handbrake.

'*Ella, Amara!*' bellowed Xander, pinning Max down on the back seat. '*Odigiste!*'

But while Max clasped his hands over his ears and howled, his mother remained inert.

Then came a cry from the truck cabin, followed by rapid gunfire from the rear of the vehicle as the driver leaped down and scuttled around the back to join his accomplice.

At the same instant, the Volkswagen passenger door swung open and Albertos's bald head popped up. Revolver in hand, he squeezed off three rounds at our assailant as he ran for cover.

The bullets fell wide of their mark, kicking up dust and

thudding harmlessly into the earth. But it bought Albertos time to reach Kate.

He fired twice more in the direction of the truck, grabbed Kate by the wrist and dragged her across the track until they were shielded by the Volkswagen. Reaching for her neck, he quickly checked her pulse ... then let her slide gently back to the ground.

'*Amara, pame!*' screamed Xander, apoplectic.

I seized her by the shoulders. 'Get in the back with Max. I'm going to drive!'

She turned her head and gave me a glassy stare. '*Ti?*'

A further brace of gunshots – from behind us this time.

Followed by what sounded like rain spattering the roof.

'*Mama!*' squealed Max, slipping free of Xander's grasp.

'*Poustis Malakas!*' roared Xander, diving back on top of Max. 'Motherfuckers!'

'Stay down,' I yelled, peering through the rear window:

The stricken tractor we'd encountered earlier was lumbering down the track towards us. Leaning out over the side of the trailer, amongst its cargo of watermelons, the man who'd been attending to the 'puncture' was now brandishing a shotgun.

We were trapped.

Ambushed ...

As my brain struggled to understand how the Mafia could possibly have had the jump on us, another shot ripped through the air and the ground exploded in a fountain of grit less than ten feet from the jeep.

Amara sprang to life and launched herself head-first through the front seats into the back. Dragging Max free of Xander's grasp, she pulled him down into the footwell and began to hyperventilate.

In an instant, I was at the wheel.

Firing up the engine, I slammed the jeep through a three-point turn until we were facing the advancing tractor.

But then Xander did the unthinkable.

Seizing the handle, he flung his door wide, jumped out and ran across the wasteland towards the abandoned distillery.

I wound down the window, desperately calling after him as he crossed over the concrete forecourt between the warehouses. But my shouts fell on deaf ears . . .

Then came a cry from over by the Volkswagen, and in the wing-mirror I spotted Albertos leaning up against the side of the car, shouting at Xander to get down as he reloaded his revolver.

Up ahead, meanwhile, the tractor was a hundred yards away, and closing.

At first, I thought my only option was to break through the rusty wire fencing, either to the left or right and escape through the olive groves. But then I noticed a steep drainage ditch running the length of the entire track on both sides. The jeep would never cross it without rolling. I'd have to try and squeeze past them instead.

But what about Xander?

I had to leave him.

He'd made his choice, abandoned his family . . .

However, as I slammed in the clutch, throwing a last look in his direction, Xander drew up to a halt on the edge of the overgrown concourse and turned back to the jeep.

'Drive! *Grigora!*' he yelled furiously, waving at me. 'Go, go! *What the hell?*

He wasn't making a break for it, he was creating a diversion.

Amara's head suddenly appeared beside me. 'What is he doing?' she croaked, one hand trying to thwart the hysterical Max's advances up out of the footwell.

As words failed me, there came another shot, followed by the high-pitched whine of a ricochet. Scuttling low to the ground, the driver of the truck emerged from behind the vehicle and shot off around the side of the warehouse.

Xander spotted him and bolted to the nearest entrance.

But the rusted door was locked.

Xander spun on his heels and froze . . .

As my hand hovered over the gear stick, prevaricating as to whether I should put Amara and Max's lives at risk by attempting to drive to his assistance, there came a flash over to my right, followed by a hollow 'crack'.

Xander jerked violently, then folded like a rag doll to the ground.

For a split-second all was still. Then Amara began to wail.

Clinging onto the steering wheel, I sat frozen as the world around me dissolved into static.

I struggled to breathe . . .

Why was the jeep rocking?

Amara, fighting to keep Max down on the floor.

Another shot from the truck . . . a yell from somewhere in the factory . . .

Xander?

Drive Haston!

One more minute and it would all be over.

I couldn't just leave Xander there.

What if he's alive?

An arm tore at my shoulder, and I twisted around to find Amara, eyes locked onto the square of broken concrete where her husband lay.

'Is he . . .?' she whispered, unable to finish the sentence.

'I . . . I think—'

'Get us out of here!' she moaned, sliding to the floor of the jeep.

Drawing Max into her, she wrapped her arms around him and buried her face in his hair. '*Mihn anisycheis, glykia mou,*' she intoned, over and over into his neck. *Don't worry, my darling . . .*

Heart hammering against my ribs, I turned to the advancing tractor.

'Stay down!'

Gripping the wheel, I tried to assess whether to pass to the left or right of the vehicle. Either way risked collision. It was just too tight . . .

'*Pame!*' howled Amara, thumping a fist into the back of my seat.

At once, my door flew open and Albertos's puce face loomed before me.

'Move over!' he yelled, showering me in sweat as he thrust his way in. 'I'll drive!'

Unhesitating, I scrambled backwards. Albertos slid into the driver's seat, threw the jeep into gear and accelerated down the track.

As we hurtled head on towards the lumbering tractor, Amara sprang up from the footwell and screamed a string of abuse at our intruder.

'*Katse kato!*' Albertos roared, producing his revolver and thrusting it out of the window. '*Eimai filos . . .*'

Before Amara could take further umbrage with our 'friend', the gunman in the trailer levelled his shotgun and let loose both barrels.

The percussion slammed through the interior of the Jeep as the ground in front detonated in a shower of sand and rocks.

This was insane – we didn't stand a chance.

'Amara!' I yelled, fumbling for the door handle. 'Hold Max . . . Get ready to jump!'

Then Albertos levelled his revolver and pulled the trigger.

Max and Amara squealed in unison as the tractor swerved violently, slinging the trailer out across the track, which then tipped, launching its contents, along with our assailant, over the side.

Albertos fired again, and a pair of watermelons exploded in a mulch of green and red.

The gunman bolted for cover.

'Hold on!' Albertos yelled, holding his line as he stamped on the accelerator.

Seconds later we shot between the upturned trailer and the fencing, ploughing through a sea of rolling watermelons. Then Albertos lost control and the jeep skidded, lifting onto two wheels before slamming into a pothole, causing him to lose his revolver out of the window.

The opposite fence and drainage ditch were upon us . . .

It was all over – we were going to roll . . .

At the last moment, inches away from the barbed wire, Albertos wrestled back control of the wheel and, straightening out, gunned the jeep back down the track to the junction with the main road.

Blood pounding in my temples, I waited for the sound of gunfire and breaking glass, but it never came. In a cloud of dust, we slid to a grinding halt at the junction, bounced down onto the tarmac and swung left before accelerating north towards the crossroads whence we came.

I wound down the window, stuck my head out into the rush of air and threw up.

Hunched over the steering wheel, his linen suit flapping in the headwind from the open window, Albertos produced a handkerchief from his jacket pocket and wiped the sheen off his balding pate before finally breaking the silence.

'Tha miliso sta Anglika, endaxi?' he said, twisting around to Amara.

He was asking if he could speak to us in English.

Amara murmured something indecipherable and continued to cradle her son.

Albertos nodded thoughtfully and turned back to the front.

'I am sorry for my driving,' he announced, raising his voice so he could be heard in the back. 'Nobody is hurt, I hope?'

Flip though it sounded, there was nothing ironic in his

apology. If the jeep had rolled, we would have been at the mercy of the gunmen.

His question hanging unanswered, Albertos pressed on, introducing himself by name and explaining that he was working on behalf of the Greek government on a case that we had tragically found ourselves caught up in. Expressing his deepest sympathies for 'the terrible accident', he informed us that his chief concern now was for our continued safety.

'I will explain when we get to the airport,' he concluded, pinching the bridge of his nose between finger and thumb, 'but it is of some urgency that you leave Zakynthos as soon as possible.'

One hand braced against the dashboard in a bid to dispel another wave of nausea, I turned and studied his hawkish profile.

Leave the island?

'We can't just leave,' I retorted. 'We need to go to the police.'

'Of course,' Albertos replied, throwing me a look. 'In Athens.'

He maintained eye contact for a moment before turning back to the road ahead.

Athens?

Because with Kate down, there was no official representative of the Greek Intelligence service on Zakynthos?

There was a rustle of fabric behind me as Amara hauled herself and Max up out of the footwell. Whatever plans she'd entertained for divorcing Xander, there was no way she'd agree to leaving his body behind.

But she was too in shock to speak.

'Explain yourself!' I demanded, rounding on Albertos. 'Her husband is . . .'

I broke off, remembering Max was still oblivious to his stepfather's fate.

It was crippling, not being able to talk openly. Now was the time for us to lay our cards on the table; for me to come clean to Amara and tell her all about the Mafia plot and Xander's involvement in it; for Albertos to explain why the hell we

200

weren't putting ourselves in the hands of the authorities. And yet, it was inconceivable I should break the news to Amara in her current state. Let alone in front of her child.

'As I said, your safety is our priority,' Albertos insisted, once more producing his handkerchief and dabbing at the sweat beading on his lip. 'We will be at the airport soon.'

Surely, we weren't still in danger?

I was about to ask him, then realised that, if we were, it would be prudent to keep the fact from Amara and Max.

Again, I'd have to wait for a private moment.

Behind me, Max coughed and reached a hand out to his mother.

'*Dipsao*,' he sniffed. '*Pou einai to poto mou?*'

He was asking after his drink.

Amara fumbled about in her handbag and pulled out a carton of apple juice.

'What about our possessions?' I objected, turning again to Albertos. 'We can't just leave everything here.'

I was well aware of the proposed plan of action, as set out by Kate at the safe house, but, for the purposes of keeping up appearances, it was an obvious question to ask. And Amara, mute though she was, would no doubt be wondering the same. I also hoped it would prompt Albertos into a coded revelation of what he was withholding from me.

Turning over his shoulder, Albertos tried to catch Amara's eye.

'My colleagues will return the car for you – it is a hire car, yes?' He pressed on without waiting for an answer. 'And your belongings will be packed up and brought to your home.'

Still, Amara said nothing. Struggling to remove the straw from its plastic wrapping, she eventually succeeded and stabbed it into the juice box before handing it to Max.

'The same for you,' Albertos continued, eyeballing me as he brushed the back of his hand against his chin. 'Everything will be taken care of.'

201

Confirmation then, that I too was to be evacuated along with Amara and Max.

Who'd made that call?

When?

'And how are we supposed to get back to Athens?' I countered. 'We just turn up and beg for a ticket? Are there even any flights at this time of day?'

The question wasn't wholly disingenuous; Kate had already explained back at the safe house that a secret service aircraft had been assigned for the evacuation. And yet, everything had changed. We were in completely uncharted territory. For a start, Kate herself was supposed to have been escorting Amara and Max back to the mainland. Who would take her place?

'Don't worry about the arrangements,' Albertos answered, as if reading my mind. 'I am flying back with you.' He lifted his eyes briefly from the road to peer up at a bank of clouds building on the eastern horizon.

Was he improvising?

No contingency plans had been raised at the safe house – at least, not in my presence. Everyone, especially Kate, had been certain of a slam dunk. A misplaced confidence, for which she'd paid the ultimate price.

We drove on in silence for the next kilometre, passing through the desolate Ploumari crossroads before setting off through the next acreage of olive trees. Then, just as I was about to take Albertos to task once again as to why we weren't putting ourselves in the hands of the authorities, he reached into his pocket and pulled out a walkie talkie.

There was a hiss of static as he hit transmit.

'*Ella, Markos!*' he barked. '*Albertos . . . Me akous . . .?*'

No response.

Just the hiss of interference.

'*Markos!*' he urged again, holding the radio closer to his mouth as if it might help.

Intrigued by the sight of the gadget, Max craned his neck forwards for a better view. Amara pulled him gently back.

Albertos jabbed his thumb repeatedly into the transmitter key . . .

'*Markos, pou eisai . . .? Ella, Markos . . .? Markos!*'

Still nothing.

Just static.

Swearing under his breath, Albertos tucked the radio in between his thighs and with one hand, fiddled furiously with the set of nobs on the top.

A further crackle of static was interrupted by a flurry of Greek on the other end.

Markos?

No – the voice wasn't gravelly enough.

Boris, maybe?

As the exchange became more urgent, Amara shuffled forwards between the seats and leaned in to listen.

Eventually she turned to me: 'He is telling the other man what happened . . .'

What happened?

Albertos had surely already radioed for back up from the Volkswagen?

'Something about needing to change cars . . .' Amara croaked, screwing up her puffy features in a bid to catch the broken words skittering through the interference. 'In Ampelokipoi . . .'

Ampelokipoi? That was next to the airport.

'No, they are coming *from* Ampelokipoi . . .' she mumbled, correcting herself. 'They are going to meet us in Agrilia. With our passports . . .'

She turned to me, eyes wide with fear.

'How do they have our passports?'

'I . . . have no idea,' I lied.

The person on the other end had to be Mikis. Kate had put him in charge of departure procedures, collecting passports.

But, why the need to change cars? Why not simply meet at the airport?

Albertos barked a final instruction into the microphone and signed off. Holding the walkie talkie out in front of him, he studied it for a moment and, after throwing me a look, switched it off and slipped it back in his pocket.

Why had he turned it off? The last thing we needed was radio silence.

More importantly, where the hell was Markos? Why hadn't he picked up?

Or Argyris, for that matter?

Only then did it occur to me that not a single police car had passed us. No sirens, even, in the distance. No helicopter overhead . . .

I felt a hand reach over the back of my seat and touch my shoulder.

'What is happening, Alistair?' Amara murmured, her voice wavering.

I shook my head slowly and, taking her hand in mine, interlocked fingers.

For all my involvement hitherto, I was as in the dark as she was.

For the next two kilometres, we drove on in an eerie quiet, punctured intermittently by the sound of Max slurping on his drink as we passed through the industrial outskirts of Agrilia with its sterile parade of car showrooms, bike rentals and supermarkets.

When Amara began to sob softly into my shoulder, I squeezed her hand tighter, pressed back against the seat and tried to still my mind. But each time I closed my eyes, Kate and Xander appeared before me, their twisted bodies lying prone in the dust.

What the hell had gone wrong?

How had the Mafia found out? How long had they known?

Was Mikis right, after all? Had Xander weakened at the last minute and told his contact, Yiorgos, that he'd been compromised? Or had Xander in fact played me the entire time, stage managing his confession in the car to turn me into an unwitting facilitator, helping the Seven Stars stay one step ahead?

Although, if Xander was behind it, why had he put himself in the firing line?

Had guilt propelled him to a final act of altruism, sacrificing himself in exchange for his family?

The jeep swung hard to the right and I opened my eyes to see we were pulling off the main road into the Agrilia Total petrol station – the one Amara had sarcastically pointed out earlier as a sight worth seeing.

Time for the car swap.

Scanning the forecourt, I counted four vehicles: a quadbike at the diesel pump; two hatchbacks parked side by side outside the shop; and the third, positioned in the shadows alongside the out-of-order air and water station ... Mikis's brown Peugeot. Leaning up against the bonnet, illuminated by a shaft of evening sunlight breaking through the row of poplars along the perimeter, stood its slick owner, tapping an unlit cigarette against the palm of his hand.

Albertos killed the engine and, after a quick exchange with Amara in Greek, jumped out.

As Amara tended to Max, I joined Albertos at the front of the jeep.

'What the fuck are we doing going to the airport?' I hissed, keeping my back to the others. 'Kate and Xander are dead!'

'*Meta*,' Albertos replied, tightening the belt on his linen suit and walking around to help out the others. *Later.*

'I suggest you use the facilities while we have the chance,' Albertos advised Amara coolly, pointing in the direction of the toilet sign as they stumbled, hand in hand, out of the jeep. 'Is there anything you need from the car?'

205

Still dazed, Amara shrugged: 'In the trunk, there is a cool-box with drinks and snacks . . . A blanket . . .' She tailed off, her eyes misting over.

'We will bring everything and you can decide later,' said Albertos gently. '*Endaxi?* Please . . .'

He gestured again towards the red-brick out-house with the rusty toilet sign.

Amara looked dubious. 'We can wait.'

'Best to go now,' urged Albertos, indicating Max. 'At the airport, it may get complicated.'

Amara turned and frowned.

'He's right,' I said. 'Take the chance while you can.'

It would give me the time to grill Albertos.

Which I now realised was why he'd arranged the car swap – to regroup.

Albertos gave Amara a reassuring nod. '*Tha eisai asfalis,*' he said, casting an eye over the other occupants milling on the concourse. *You'll be safe.*

As Max shuffled across the concrete with his bowed mother, Albertos whistled to Mikis, who, sticking the unlit cigarette behind his ear, sauntered over.

'You have everything?' Albertos growled.

Mikis nodded. 'Passports are in the car. There is also a change of clothes for the boy.'

I checked my back pocket to be sure my own passport was still in place.

Mikis raised his eyebrows at me. 'You okay?'

I nodded.

The smile faded on his lips. 'It's a bad day, my friend. I'm sorry.'

Why was it I still didn't trust Mikis?

Something snake-like about his smile . . . the dead eyes.

Then followed an exchange in Greek which I didn't catch, culminating in Albertos handing Mikis the keys to the jeep. I presumed he'd be heading for the villa to start the packing.

Mine was already done, my rucksack sitting on the bed back at the Porto Roma.

'*Ella*,' Albertos murmured, setting off in the direction of the toilets. 'We should stay close.'

But as soon as Amara and Max had disappeared into the building, I spun around and seized his elbow.

'It was Xander, wasn't it?' I exclaimed. 'He was playing us all along.'

Albertos slowly prised my hand off his arm.

'We were set up,' he said, eyeballing me. 'But it wasn't Xander.'

Thrown, I paused to let a pair of tank-topped Brits laden down with cigarettes and alcohol pass between us, on their way back to their quadbike.

As soon as they were out of earshot Albertos stepped in closer, eyes blazing.

'The attackers' timing was perfect. The truck – the tractor with the watermelons. They knew exactly where we would be, and they co-ordinated it perfectly.' He paused, casting an eye over to Mikis who was carrying the cool box from the jeep to the Peugeot. 'Xander didn't know the route we were going to take. It was only decided this morning, at the safe house.'

I stared at him as the implication sunk in.

There'd been five of us at the safe house: Kate was dead, Albertos had saved us from the ambush ... That left Boris, Markos and Argyris.

'But ... if the Seven Stars had known all along,' I stammered, 'they could have put tracking devices on the cars. Or had scouts watching ...'

Not one of our own team, surely?

Albertos nodded thoughtfully. 'It is possible. But there is more ...'

Distracted momentarily by the sound of a cistern flush, he broke off and flicked a glance over to the toilet outhouse before turning back to me.

'When I called for back-up in Kate's car, the channel was jammed.'

Jammed?

'Someone blocked the signal,' he explained, as, behind him, Mikis walked back from the Peugeot and jumped into the driver's seat of the jeep.

I stared at him, heart racing.

Was that why Albertos hadn't been able to reach Markos earlier?

'But, the Mafia could have done it,' I insisted. 'If they'd known the frequency—'

Albertos cut me off. 'The signal was jammed by something we call a "dead key" method. You hold down the transmitter key so no one can use the channel.' He pulled me away from the pumps as a burly local on a moped swept in off the road to refuel. 'It's simple, but it's risky. First of all, you have to be in close range. Secondly, walkie talkies have their own signature – recognisable clunks or clicks. This can give away your identity.'

One of the five was most certainly in our vicinity – or at least, could have been there in time for the appointed moment.

After he'd left us at Ploumari . . .

Albertos held my gaze, unblinking. 'When I spoke to Markos on the way from Gerakas, I noticed his transmitter had a pulse . . .' He stepped in closer still, until I could feel his breath against my cheek. 'I heard the same pulse through the static when the signal was jammed.'

I too had heard that pulse – back at the safe house when Kate handed them out. Markos had believed his transmitter to be faulty.

But . . .

Markos – the deputy chief of police?

Rendered speechless, the sweat broke out along my neck and I was once again back on Paros, in the police station, being walked to that shit-stinking cell . . .

This couldn't be happening.

Not again . . .

There came a sudden revving of an engine as Mikis pulled the jeep out of the petrol station, and with a brief nod in our direction, shot off in the direction of Zakynthos town and the coastal road south.

'But why?' I whispered.

'Good question,' Albertos replied, motioning me towards the Peugeot. 'All I know is that, whatever their intentions, they fucked up. And now they have a serious problem on their hands.'

Just then, the toilet door opened and Amara and Max stepped out onto the concourse.

'Which is why I can't let you go to the police station.' Albertos turned back to face me, jaw clenched. 'Once inside, you will never come out.'

16

At 6.35 p.m., forty minutes having passed since the attack, we pulled sharply off the Zakynthos-Laganas highway and swung into the sweltering airport car park, slamming to a halt alongside a dusty oleander hedgerow.

No police cordon. No sign of any police presence at all.

Just a handful of sunburnt tourists struggling with their suitcases.

And Boris. Cigarette in hand, standing beside his dust-covered quadbike.

Corralling Amara and Max out from the back seat, I kept half an eye on Albertos and Boris as they distanced themselves and set to an urgent discussion at the kerbside. It was impossible to make out what they were saying – but after handing Albertos a set of papers, Boris appeared to be attempting to placate his colleague, who had become uncharacteristically animated.

Max, in the meantime, began to complain he was tired – he wanted to go back to the villa and see *Papi*. Amara took his little hand, lowered her sunglasses down over her eyes and assured him they'd be home soon.

What else could she say? Max knew something had happened to Xander, but appeared oblivious to the finality of his absence. He'd heard the gunshots, witnessed his mother's distress . . . the terrifying ordeal with the tractor. But it seemed he had yet to connect the events. As if he was expecting Xander to re-appear at any moment.

'Where is *Papi?*' urged Max for the second time, tugging impatiently on his mother's arm. 'Why are we at the airport?'

Amara looked to me in desperation, but before I could speak, Albertos appeared and took Max by the shoulders. 'It's a surprise.'

'*Ti?*'

Max peered up expectantly at his mother as Albertos stepped in closer.

'Hey – you want an ice-cream?' he continued hastily, casting an eye over the car park. 'We go inside – to the café.'

'Anything but chocolate, right?' I said, pulling his cap down tighter on his head.

'*Pame,*' barked Albertos. 'Let's go!'

Producing Amara and Max's passports from a leather satchel, he waved them in the direction of the airport terminal and set off at pace across the tarmac.

What had Boris said to him?

Hurrying Amara and Max along, I checked behind us and caught sight of Boris in the Peugeot, setting off in the direction we'd just come.

Hiding the getaway car, I presumed.

Although, we'd already changed vehicles – wasn't that the point?

'Go and choose,' said Albertos, steering Max in the direction of the airport café as we entered the terminal. 'Your mother will come with you.'

Amara was about to protest, but Albertos thrust a handful of drachma into her hand. 'It's a surprise, remember?' he repeated, holding her gaze. 'Don't spoil it.'

Nodding obediently, Amara grabbed Max by the hand and whisked him over to the café.

Albertos spun back around to face me:

'The aircraft has been delayed by a thunderstorm,' he panted. 'It will now land on the mainland – a place called Varaxos. We must take a helicopter and meet them there.'

I stared at him, incredulous.

'Why can't it come here?'

'If it lands in Zakynthos, it will be an hour at least before it can turn around for Athens. Varaxos is a very small airport – we will be able to leave immediately.'

In an hour, it would all be over.

'How the hell do we find a helicopter?'

'Boris has arranged a private charter,' he said, turning back to the entrance to the terminal. 'It is only a thirty-minute flight to Varaxos.'

'Why don't we go straight to Athens?'

'Because you will need the protection of the secret service. Without them, you are no better off than being here.'

'What about you?'

He shook his head. 'I don't have clearance. Kate was their representative. I will be with you, of course, but we need an official agent.'

'Stelios, Kate's boss?'

'I don't know who,' he murmured. 'Boris's brief was only that we must go to Varaxos.'

'Well then, let's get out of here,' I hissed, turning back to the café. 'What the hell's taking them so long?'

'Don't draw attention to yourself,' he said, scanning the concourse. 'We are still ahead.'

For now.

All it would take was a phone call.

'We've got to bring Amara up to speed,' I urged. 'It's not fair to keep her in the dark. Besides, she'll be less resistant when she knows the truth about Xander.'

'You want to tell her of your involvement in this?' he shot back, eyebrows furrowed. 'I don't advise it.'

'No – for now we have to keep up the pretence. I'll play along.'

He nodded. 'Once we get to the departure gate. But we will need to distract Max.'

'Got it.'

Assuming we weren't stopped at security.

With that, Amara and Max returned – the latter brandishing his ice cream.

'I want my *papi*,' he demanded, peeling back the foil. 'Can we go now?'

Albertos was primed and ready.

'Hey, Max, *fili mou* – you ever been in a helicopter?'

The woman at security control couldn't have been less interested.

Casting a fleeting eye over the papers Albertos had received from Boris in the car park – which I now understood to be our tickets – she flipped open our passports without actually looking at them, gave a quick feel of Albertos's satchel and Max's holdall, then promptly waved us through, wishing us a pleasant flight and instructing us not to miss the beautiful Zakynthos sunset. All of this, as if on automatic pilot.

Albertos was right, we still had the initiative.

Once through to departures, the newly restored Max made a beeline for the souvenir shop to inspect the toys on offer. The knowledge he'd be travelling in a 'chopper' had triggered an extraordinary transformation – as if the past few hours had simply been erased.

'Max, get back here!' snapped Amara, setting off after him.

'Please,' exclaimed Albertos, taking hold of her shoulder. 'Buy him a gift.'

'Get your hands off me,' she hissed, shrugging him off. 'And tell me what the fuck is happening.'

'As I promised,' Albertos replied. 'But not in front of the boy.'

Understanding Max needed a distraction, Amara paid for a

toy jet plane, along with provisions of water and sandwiches, which she packed into the holdall, then we followed Albertos down a narrow side corridor displaying signs for Zakynthos Helicopter Tours, until we arrived at the entrance to a bleak departure lounge, the walls of which had been plastered with fading posters of Shipwreck Beach and the Blue Caves.

Which was when I saw the officers:

Two of them, walking slowly along the glass corridor towards us, one of them resting a hand on her firearm.

For some reason, I hesitated.

'Come on,' muttered Albertos, gesturing for Amara and Max to approach the gate. 'Go inside.' He'd spotted them too, but was doing his best to ignore them.

Having caught my eye, however, the policewoman changed course and ambled over.

'You go to Shipwreck beach?' she asked, casting a glance in the direction of Amara and Max as they entered the departure lounge.

'I'm sorry?'

Albertos turned and nodded at the officer's companion.

'It is forbidden to land on the beach,' she continued, facing me squarely on. 'You can only look at it from the air.'

'Oh, right.'

My cheeks were flushing like a schoolboy's.

'And at this time of day there is often a strong wind. It can be very uncomfortable.'

'Got it. Thank you.'

The male officer unleashed a stream of Greek at Albertos.

Albertos listened attentively, then nodded.

'We are not to encourage our pilot to land on the beach,' Albertos said, turning to me. 'People sometimes try to bribe them – but if they are caught, everyone on board is fined.'

'Of course,' I said, forcing a grin. 'No – we're erm ... not going to be landing on any beaches.'

She smiled and backed away. '*Kala.*'

As they set off again towards the main terminal, Albertos quickly confirmed with our gate attendant that the flight was still on schedule, then led me over to where Amara was slumped on a wooden bench, watching Max as he stood at the floor-to-ceiling windows, nose pressed to the glass, gazing out at the runway.

Removing her sunglasses, Amara rubbed the smudged mascara from under her eyes and turned to Albertos.

'I'm listening.'

After a quick glance in Max's direction, Albertos apologised for what he was about to say, then announced in a detached, almost business-like manner, that it was Xander himself who had been responsible for the attack; that he had been working with a Mafia cartel called the Seven Stars, planning to kidnap Max and ransom him as a way of paying off his gambling debts. Going into still further detail, he explained how he and his colleagues had expected the attempt to take place at Agios Sostis where the fishing boat was waiting; officers and intelligence agents had been standing by, ready to move in, but they'd been betrayed by a senior member of the police force, who, unbeknownst to them, had been working with the Mafia all along – resulting in the ambush.

At which point Albertos paused, wiped his neck with his handkerchief and flicked a look to Amara, awaiting her reaction.

Unblinking, she kept her eyes on Max.

I too remained silent, feigning incredulity.

'This is hard for you, I know,' Albertos concluded, turning to Max, who was now up on a chair, flying his plane along the windowpane. 'But your boy, at least, is safe.'

'This doesn't make any sense at all,' I said finally, dissembling. 'Xander was shot. He couldn't possibly have been part of this . . . this – kidnapping attempt.'

'It is confusing,' agreed Albertos. 'We believe Xander had a last-minute change of heart. His sacrifice allowed us to escape.'

Not the whole truth.

And yet, to reveal that Xander had wanted out of the whole scheme wouldn't have helped. Amara needed closure; she needed to know that Xander was the bad guy. For now, at least.

Finally, she lifted her head. 'How long have you known this?' she asked, her gaze still fixed upon on her son. 'Why didn't you do something sooner?'

No disbelief, then, at the accusations thrown at her husband. Indeed, why would she refute it? She'd been ready to divorce him.

There came a loud 'vroom' as Max jumped off the chair, his toy held aloft.

'We needed more evidence,' Albertos replied. 'It wasn't certain the kidnap attempt would go ahead. These things are complicated. They take time and patience and, well – they don't always go to plan.' He looked up and tried to catch Amara's eye. 'I am sorry for your loss.'

'You used us,' she spat, still unable to look him. 'Deliberately put my son's life at risk – our lives at risk.'

Succumbing to a rush of guilt, all I could do was nod along in agreement.

Albertos pursed his lips, taking a moment to compose his answer, knowing full well there was no satisfactory riposte. Amara and Max had indeed been used as bait, and the moral implications stank. 'I can only apologise for subjecting you and your family to this,' he eventually answered. 'But what you must understand, is that whoever betrayed us will try and cover their own tracks. They need someone to blame. That is why you must leave Zakynthos immediately.'

'We've done nothing wrong,' exclaimed Amara, turning to him finally, her face aghast. 'How could they blame us? Max is my son, for God's sake!'

Hesitating, Albertos puffed out his cheeks and drew closer still.

'The Mafia and Xander were intending to frame Alistair for the kidnap,' he murmured, glancing over in the direction of our gate attendant, who had begun to take an interest in our conversation. 'With the help of at least one police informant. Maybe more.' He cleared his throat. 'But because the attack failed, whoever is responsible in the police will be even more desperate to blame Alistair – or worse.'

'Jesus Christ,' I whispered, affecting as much astonishment as I could muster. 'Frame me? Why? *How?*'

Albertos pulled a face. 'My understanding is that they would have taken you, along with Max, and made out that you were the kidnapper. Then they would have disposed of you. Once the ransom was paid.'

'*Disposed?*'

Amara let out a gasp.

'I don't believe it,' I objected, knowing I couldn't be too quick to concede. 'It just doesn't . . . make any sense.'

It was crystal clear to Amara: 'It was Xander who called you in London,' she announced, pulling herself slowly upright. 'He knew you'd come to investigate the truth about Max. About you being his father. He is the one responsible for bringing you here.'

'But . . .' I broke off and let my incredulity hang.

Amara was now fully in the loop; aside from my own part in the proceedings, of course.

Albertos smoothed down his linen trousers and said nothing.

For a moment, nobody moved. All eyes were on Max, who was edging his way across the flagstones towards us, making his jet do loop-the-loops.

Albertos had played his hand well. But where the fuck was our helicopter?

As I checked my watch, fearing the officers would reappear at any moment and detain us, Amara reached over and interlocked her fingers in mine.

'I'm so sorry,' she whispered, her chin quivering. 'I knew nothing about . . .'

'No, I'm sorry,' I replied, unable to look her in the eye. 'For you – for Max.'

Then, as quickly as she had taken it, she dropped my hand and slumped forwards, burying her face in her fists.

'Oh, God . . . Xander.'

At that moment, the departure doors swung open and a uniformed flight attendant stepped in, calling us forward for our flight.

A rickety minibus took us away from the terminal building in the opposite direction of the main runway, passing behind a pair of rusting aircraft hangers before pulling up sharply in front of a brace of helicopters parked at the barbed-wire perimeter fence. Hastily disembarking, Albertos dismissed our flight attendant and led us over the still-baking asphalt to our ride: a four-blade, single engine affair, with seats for two crew and up to four passengers – so he informed Max, who was hanging on his every word.

'The flight will take half an hour or so,' Albertos continued, checking his watch as we reached the open passenger cabin door. 'We might even get a view of Shipwreck Beach and the Blue Caves.'

Amara took hold of Max's hand, studying the aircraft in apprehension.

Albertos's tour-guide act, understandable though it was in terms of keeping Max distracted, seemed to be having the opposite effect on his mother.

'Helicopters are extremely safe,' he assured us. 'Safer than a plane. If the engine fails, they float to the ground like a leaf.'

Too much information, perhaps.

'I say we get in,' I said, shouldering Max's holdall as I peered back to the gap between the aircraft hangers, expecting at any moment to see the tell-tale approach of flashing red and blue lights. 'Max – you wanna go first?'

Entering the cabin, we took our places in the upholstered seats, Amara fastening Max's safety belt while Albertos closed the door then cross-checked with me via hand-signals through the window to check it was secured. He then jumped into the passenger seat in the cockpit and, attaching a headset, proceeded to brief the helmeted pilot, who was busy checking our routing. Peering through his aviators at the map on his lap, the latter nodded along attentively, until finally he turned and gave Albertos a confirmatory nod, then hit the ignition.

At once, a high-pitched whine reverberated through the cabin and the rotors began to turn, accelerating ever faster until they became nothing more than a thrumming blur.

I tried to catch Amara's eye, but she was gripping her seat arms, steadfastly focussing on her excited son.

Moments later, the helicopter rocked, lifted a few feet off the ground, and after rotating forty-five degrees to the west, accelerated swiftly up and out of the airport compound, climbing steadily higher over the arid Laganas basin, before banking slowly around to our right in the direction of Zakynthos mountain.

Overcoming a rush of vertigo, I peered down to the rapidly shrinking airport grounds below . . .

Still no sign of police activity.

It looked like we were going to make it.

The helicopter levelled as we passed over the mountain peak, still bathed in the last rays of the setting sun, before descending once more and heading north along the windswept coast.

After a glance across the cabin at mother and son, who had now withdrawn into their private universes – the former, gazing forlornly at the blood-orange sunset on the distant horizon; the latter, enrapt by the jigsaw of turquoise coves and inlets directly beneath us – I pressed back in my seat, closed my eyes and tried to still my mind.

The adrenaline having run its course, my body now felt limp, raw and useless; a slow pounding in my temples exacerbated the nausea sitting low in my gut. We had been so intent on escape, there'd been little time to breathe, let alone process anything. The attack; Kate's death; Xander's self-sacrifice; the police betrayal . . . it was all too surreal. Fragments of a waking dream that had yet to fully piece itself together.

And it wasn't over yet.

Amara and Max would no doubt be taken to a safe house as Kate had determined, while I would be de-briefed – or, cross-examined, rather, in light of Xander and Kate's deaths – by the intelligence services. But who would have my back? Stelios? A lawyer? Inconceivable though it was that the secret service should in any way be compromised by the police conspiracy, the thought of having to face interrogation on my own was a terrifying prospect. At the very least surely I'd be given access to a British Embassy official, if not a member of MI6?

Dismissing the idea that Gerald might deign to make a re-appearance, my mind continued to drift and I wondered at one what point I'd be allowed to reconnect with Amara and Max.

And do what, exactly?

Apologise?

Succumbing to the comforting rattle and hum of the rotors, I slipped into a restless half-sleep, only to be jolted back to my senses by a sudden change in the cabin air pressure. Prizing open my eyelids, I found the helicopter to be banking steeply to starboard, while, across from me, Max jabbed his finger excitedly at the windowpane:

A few hundred feet below, an extensive ridge of chalky cliffs broke away on three sides to reveal a perfect sliver of white sandy beach, disappearing out into slow-shelving shallows. In the middle of the strip, a rusting, broken skiff lay perfectly positioned, as if it had been dragged up the sand and set as an ornament; while, out in the cove, a handful of moored pleasure boats awaited the return of their passengers, who were scuttling, ant-like on the sand, cameras in hand, capturing the iconic landmark in the thickening light.

Shipwreck Beach.

Albertos twisted around in his seat and thumped on the cabinet before giving a thumbs-up. Max grinned and returned the gesture, then pulled his cap down tighter on his head and glued his elfin face back to the window as the pilot pulled back on the stick and we rose up higher, turning once more to starboard before levelling off and heading east over the channel towards the mainland.

As we bounced and jigged our way ever east towards the Peloponnese promontory, alternately climbing and dropping to evade the stronger gusts of wind, I struggled desperately to come up with a persuasive argument that stood a remote chance of appeasing Amara, knowing that nothing short of total transparency would be acceptable. And yet the truth itself was utterly unpalatable. I had lied consistently to her and Max and put them both in serious danger.

How would she ever be able to trust me again?

Just before 7.30 p.m. we made landfall, and our first destination: a desolate airfield consisting of a surprisingly lengthy runway, running east to west on a low-lying plateau at the edge of the headland.

Our pilot made a pass over the runway, during which I made out a pair of Cessna aircraft parked at the edges of the cleared scrub, along with a solitary low-slung building that I imagined served as the terminal. Then, as we circled back around, momentarily drifting out to sea above a cluster of uninhabited islets, I looked inland and saw our plane: a Lear-Jet, or something similar, standing before a strip of windblown myrtle at the easternmost end of the airfield.

There didn't appear to be any other sign of life down below; indeed, it looked as though the place hadn't been used in months. No evidence of any airport lighting either. It must have been a daytime-only set up.

Passing over the terminal building, we rapidly decelerated, then, remaining some thirty feet off the ground, crept forward along the edge of the runway to where the jet stood waiting, step-ladder already in position.

Max turned to Amara and asked something – but I wasn't able to tell if it was even in Greek or English; I only knew from his mother's response that she didn't have an answer.

All at once we slowed to a mid-air halt, around a hundred yards or so from the jet, before finally touching down on the concrete; whereupon the pilot killed the throttle and the rotors began to slow.

Albertos took off his headset and craned his neck around.

'This airfield was built by a businessman in the seventies,' he announced, unfastening his seat belt. 'He was hoping to attract interest from the airline companies, but it is too poorly positioned for commercial use. Now it is used by a local flying club, as well as the coastguard and sometimes the postal service.'

When the rotors had all but stopped, the pilot opened his door and jumped out.

Shouldering his satchel, Albertos followed suit and came to stand before the cabin window – giving me another thumbs-up as an indication I could unlock the door.

'Where are we?' asked Max nervously, watching me unclip my belt and remove the safety catch.

'We're going to be getting onto an aeroplane now,' murmured Amara, shakily unfastening Max from his seat. 'It is part of the surprise.'

Max frowned. 'But where are we going?'

'You'll see,' said Amara, catching my eye.

Until we reached Athens, there was no other way through

222

this but to bluff; to turn the trip into an adventure, a game of sorts – macabre though it seemed.

How to eventually break the news that his *papi* was dead, however, was beyond me.

'*Ella, pame!*' called out Albertos, as he held back the door.

As we left the confines of the cabin and stepped out into the salty air, we came face to face with a woman dressed in a suit, who had seemingly materialised out of nowhere; around five feet tall, thick curls of hair down to her shoulders.

'Good evening,' she said, giving Max a warm smile while maintaining a respectful distance. 'I hope the flight from Zakynthos was not too uncomfortable?'

Albertos spoke on behalf of all of us, assuring her we hadn't encountered any difficulties.

'I will be looking after you for the rest of the journey,' she continued, fastening her suit jacket and shuffling the folder from one hand to another. 'My name is Alexandra.'

'Thank you,' said Amara, stepping in closer to her, evidently relieved to be in the presence of another woman.

I, on the other hand, could only stare in wonder.

'Look what I got,' piped up Max, showing her his toy jet.

There was no mistaking those cheekbones, the cascades of black hair . . .

'My – what a beautiful aeroplane,' Alexandra purred.

The blood red lipstick.

'Mommy bought it for me.'

It was the woman from Athens airport.

The one with the suitcase . . . who'd let me share her taxi.

'It's very nice.'

'Thank you, for everything you're doing,' I said finally, catching Alexandra's eye as she turned to face me. 'We, erm . . . appreciate it.'

She gave me a sad smile. 'Whatever I can do to help.'

Did Albertos know her?

Did he know that I knew her? Alexandra was, after all, of Gerald's stable.

She straightened up and eyeballed Max. 'Would you like to see my jet, young man? It is big and fancy – although not as cool as yours.'

'We can't go without my *papi*,' replied Max earnestly. 'We have to wait.'

Alexandra nodded, smile fixed in place, waiting for Amara to take the lead.

'*Papi* will join us in Athens,' said Amara, clearing her throat to mask the tell-tale catch. 'It is a surprise, remember?'

'Very good,' said Alexandra.

'Perfect,' added Albertos, rubbing his palms together. 'Let's go see our new plane.'

Following on behind Alexandra, we passed our helicopter pilot, who was stood at the edge of the runway nursing a cigarette, the smoke adding a sulphurous tang to the rosemary and thyme hanging in the evening air. He'd not bothered to remove his helmet or aviators – he was no doubt taking a quick break before returning to Zakynthos – but now I had a fuller view of him, there was something about his physicality that was also familiar. Was it the set of his shoulders? His thick neck? Or maybe it was his stance: wide and grounded, reflecting that unshakeable confidence that was the prime requirement for any pilot . . .

Who, though?

I gave him a nod and hurried on to catch up with the others.

Reaching the aircraft, Alexandra stopped and drew herself up to her full height. 'You can board straight away. We have drinks and snacks, and you only have to wear your seatbelt for take-off and landing – unless the captain asks you to do otherwise.'

Max reached out and took his mother's hand.

Albertos looked expectantly at the three of us. '*Endaxi*. Are we ready?'

Amara nodded, drawing her son in towards her.

'I trust you have your passports?' Alexandra asked, almost as an afterthought.

I reached into my back pocket and held up my passport, stuffing the birth certificates back into place as they slipped out between the pages, then turned to Amara. She shrugged and passed the look onto Albertos.

Albertos jumped to attention. 'Yes, of course – forgive me.'

Reaching into his jacket pocket, he pulled out a passport, checked the identity, and offered it to Max, who grabbed it and thrust it into his pocket before Amara could take it off him.

'Wait a minute,' mumbled Albertos, checking his other pocket, and then his trousers, before taking off his satchel and rifling through the contents. 'I gave it back to you already, no?'

Amara shook her head. 'You have had it whole time.'

Alexandra looked politely away and gazed out over the channel to the brooding silhouette of Zakynthos.

'No, but where is it?' said Albertos, slapping at a mosquito on his neck. 'Maybe it is in the helicopter?'

Swearing under his breath, he handed me his bag, then took off at a jog, calling out to the helicopter pilot who had finished his smoke and was inspecting the rotors in preparation for his return flight.

'Please – you can board now,' urged Alexandra, checking her watch. 'Albertos will find it.'

The three of us looked at each other and then, shouldering Max's holdall and Albertos's satchel, I led the way up the steps up to the cabin door, pausing at the top to glance back to the helicopter where the pilot and Albertos were now in animated discussion.

Max followed after, with Amara bringing up the rear.

'Madam, may I speak with you for a moment?' asked Alexandra, reaching into her pocket for a pen. 'In private?'

'Yes, of course,' Amara replied, handing her son the holdall. 'Max, go with Alistair.'

I let Max pass by me into the cabin and checked on Albertos, who had now disappeared into the helicopter interior with the pilot to conduct their search.

'*Menete stihn Athina?*' I heard Alexandra ask as she clicked her pen and opened up her folder.

Amara replied in Greek that they did indeed live in Athens, whereupon the two of them fell into a polite discussion – about what, I couldn't tell. Preliminary niceties, I presumed, before tackling the difficult stuff.

'Mister Alistair, come and see!' came a muffled shout from behind me.

I turned around to see Max half way down a far larger cabin than I'd expected, judging from the exterior. A quad of forward-facing and rear-facing leather seats were set around a mahogany side-table, along with a further two forward-facing chairs at the rear of the aircraft, and a single seat up front by the cabin door. Max had thrown himself down on the port side seat of the quad and was kicked-back, legs splayed, hands behind his head, gazing admiringly up at the ceiling lights.

'I'm hungry,' he exclaimed with a yawn, pulling his cap off his head and tossing it onto the seat opposite. 'Where are the snacks?'

'Your mother bought you some sandwiches,' I said, dropping the holdall at his feet.

'I want potato chips.'

'You have to wait for Alexandra,' I said, peering out of a window, noticing that the conversation between the two women had taken a serious turn. Amara now stood, head-bowed, clutching the folder and pen, nodding along to Alexandra who was talking quietly into her ear, one arm protectively around her shoulders.

And Albertos?

226

He was jogging back from the helicopter . . .

Empty handed.

After a moment's hesitation, I opened Albertos's satchel and peered inside: a pair of fresh handkerchiefs, a pen and notebook – blank – and his worry beads. No sign of a passport. I also checked the two inside zip pockets – empty.

Hastily closing it up again, I made my way back up the cabin towards the door in time to hear Albertos apologising profusely to the two women, who were still in huddled discussion.

'I will check once more,' I heard him say as he leaped up the steps two at a time.

'I've had a look myself,' I said quickly. 'Sorry – I thought it best.'

He stopped and frowned. 'You looked in the pocket at the back?'

I hadn't noticed one at the back.

'Here – let me see.'

As he whipped the bag out of my hand and pushed past me into the cabin, I spotted the helicopter pilot advancing at pace along the runway.

Had he found the passport?

'There was an envelope of cash in here,' Albertos growled accusingly, now on his knees as he searched under the seats. 'Where is it?'

Was he serious?

'Christ, Albertos – I'm hardly going to steal from you!' I protested, bending down to look under the chairs. 'I didn't see an envelope.'

Suddenly there came a loud 'clang' from the front of the cabin and the aircraft shook.

I stopped and sat up on my haunches, in time to see the partition doors to the cabin slide shut.

'What's going on?'

Albertos hauled himself off the floor and peered down the cabin.

'I have no idea.'

Then came a growl from the rear of the aircraft, as the engines fired up.

What the hell?

'Has he closed the doors?'

'Mommy?' squeaked Max, jumping up off the sofa. '*Pou einai i mitera mou?*'

'She's – hang on . . .' I answered, trying not to sound alarmed.

But when I reached the panelled partition, I found it to be locked.

'Open up,' I yelled, hammering on the panelling. 'Albertos, help me!'

Albertos grunted and loped down the aisle to join me. But after attempting to slide the doors open, claimed they had been secured from the other side. Only the pilot could open it.

Then to my utter astonishment, the aircraft began to push back onto the runway.

'For Christ's sake stop the plane!' I screamed into the gap in the door panelling, before charging down the aisle to where Max was standing stock still – his gaze fixed on the window.

As I joined him, telling him not to panic, I turned to the window and likewise froze.

Amara had collapsed against Alexandra's chest; the helicopter pilot, meanwhile, appeared to be desperately trying to revive her.

Or, so I thought.

At a nod of the head from Alexandra, the pilot whipped Amara off the ground and, holding her limp in his arms, set off as fast as he could to carry her back towards the helicopter, with Alexandra close on his heels.

'What are they doing with my mommy,' cried Max, pawing at me with his little fists. 'I want my mommy!'

Then the aircraft began to rock, as it spun 180 degrees to face the runway.

228

I wrapped an arm around the hysterical Max and twisted around to Albertos to challenge him again as to what the hell was happening.

But the expression on his face left no doubt.

'I suggest you sit down,' he intoned, sliding into one of the quad seats behind the side table and fastening his seat belt. 'And keep the boy calm.'

'I don't understand,' I shot back, understanding everything with sickening clarity.

Turning to the window again, I caught sight of the pilot and Alexandra manhandling Amara into the helicopter . . .

But there was nothing to be done. The engines increased to a deafening roar as the plane jolted forwards over the concrete and commenced its take-off roll.

I picked up the hysterical Max, dragged him to the rear two seats and strapped him in, as the jet accelerated inexorably down the runway.

As the boy pressed his face against the window, desperately trying to catch sight of his mother, Albertos caught my eye and leaned in over the table towards me. 'Nothing will happen to his mother,' he growled, extracting his string of worry beads from his jacket pocket and wrapping them around his wrist. 'Provided you do exactly as I say.'

Then with a sudden lurch, we were airborne.

17

As Max's shrill sobs reverberated through the cabin, I sat rigid with disbelief, staring dumbly across the table at our abductor.

This couldn't be happening.

Albertos ...?

How?

Why?

He'd saved us from the ambush. He'd been one of ours.

It didn't ...

I couldn't ...

Breathe ... I couldn't breathe.

My throat began to close up; tongue sticking to the roof of my mouth ... peripheral vision shrinking, as a veil of darkness closed in around me ... Heart, unable to cope, smashing itself against cartilage and bone, desperate to break loose ...

Then a sudden flailing of an arm against my shoulder ...

Max – screaming. Twisting, writhing in his chair.

Spurred into action, I lunged across the gap between the seats, clasped Max's hands tightly in my own and frantically reassured him he'd soon be seeing his mummy again ...

She'd been taken ill ... Not seriously so, but she'd had to go to hospital in the helicopter just to make sure everything was fine. We'd only continued on without her, because she hadn't wanted to spoil the surprise ...

Max wasn't having any of it.

Thrashing his head from side to side, his protestations grew increasingly desperate; shrill, piercing shrieks giving way to silent gasps as he struggled to draw breath.

I leaped out of my seat, released his safety belt, and carried him down to the rear of the cabin, where I rocked him back and forth in my arms, whispering hollow assurances over and over in his ear, until exhaustion got the better of him and he fell limp in my arms.

Finally, as the aircraft reached cruising altitude and levelled off, I led him back to his seat and, in a bid to keep him further distracted, reached into the holdall and offered up the provisions Amara had bought at the airport.

He took one look at the cellophane-wrapped sandwich and knocked it to the floor.

'Don't like it, Mister Alistair,' he croaked, gazing up at me, snotty and wide-eyed. 'I want potato chips.'

Crouching in front of him, I explained we didn't have any crisps, but that he should eat the sandwich because his mummy had bought it for him and she wouldn't have bought something for him that he didn't like.

At which, he burst into tears once again.

'You want something to eat?' came a growl from across the aisle. '*Ella.*'

'Keep your mouth shut!' I roared, twisting around to Albertos. 'Stay in your fucking seat.'

'Easy, man,' he purred, 'I'm just offering the boy some refreshments.'

'You're not fooling anyone.'

'Mister Alistair!' yelled Max.

'Not in front of the boy.'

'Fuck that!'

231

'Mister Alistair, stop!'

I was a split-second away from launching myself across the seats and seizing Albertos by the throat, but was thwarted by a pair of tiny fists pummelling my shoulder blade.

'You mustn't say that word,' howled Max, incandescent. 'Mommy says it is rude.'

Quivering with rage, I hovered by the edge of the table, glaring at Albertos, who, in turn met my gaze with placid indifference.

'All in a day's work, is it?' I spat, balled fists at the ready. 'Taking children from their mothers? Ripping families apart?'

'As you yourself explained to Max,' replied Albertos calmly, 'there was no time for goodbyes. We had to get his mother to hospital as soon as possible.' He threw Max a crocodile smile. 'The boy is hungry ... and I am only trying to help.'

'Let him help, Mister Alistair,' wailed Max. 'I want potato chips.'

Astonished, I turned back to face him as he gawped up at me from his seat, baseball cap in hand, tugging at the thick locks of hair over his ears.

Levering himself up from his seat, Albertos made his way up the aisle to a cabinet adjacent to the partition doors. 'Potato chips, *nai, fili mou?*' he mumbled, rummaging in a drawer. '*Theleis mia Cola?*'

Chest still heaving, Max kept his unblinking eyes on me and nodded.

Albertos turned around, a can of Coke in one hand and a bag of nuts in the other.

'*Then echoume patakia,*' he grunted. 'But we have peanuts. You want peanuts?'

Again, Max nodded, eyes still fixed on me.

'And for you?' Tucking the packet under his chin, Albertos stuffed the loose end of his shirt back into his trousers with his free hand. 'You need something?'

With a shake of the head, I turned back to Max.

Albertos was again fostering an alliance of convenience; just as we had done with Amara on the way to the airport.

To what end, though?

We were his prisoners – he could do with us whatever the hell he liked.

Returning to his seat, Albertos slid the Coke and peanuts across the table towards me, then returned to his worry beads.

I took hold of the can, cool and solid in my hand, thinking that such an object could make for a useful weapon.

Smashed into a face … across the bridge of the nose …

'Please, Mister Alistair, I'm thirsty,' whined Max, jabbing at my shoulder.

'Yes, of course.' I cracked the ring-pull, then passed the Coke, along with the peanuts to the impatiently awaiting Max.

As he ripped open the packet and tipped the contents into his mouth, I twisted around to peer through the portside rear window, through which I could just make out a purple and orange halo spanning the low-lying horizon behind us.

We were travelling east, away from the Greek mainland.

To one of the outer islands?

Or leaving the country?

At which point, Max turned to me and, with a mouth full of nuts, demanded once again to know where we were going and how long it would take.

I confessed I wasn't sure. His mummy hadn't told me; it was all part of the surprise.

'Can you ask the man?' he whispered, leaning in towards me. 'Maybe he knows?'

The ever-watching Albertos was already primed.

'Don't worry about your mommy,' he murmured, pocketing his worry beads. 'You will see her soon. But if you ask too many questions you will give away the surprise.'

'Okay,' sniffed Max. 'I don't want to spoil my surprise.'

'*Kala, fili mou,*' said Albertos with a lopsided grin. 'Good boy.'

Albertos mimed zipping his mouth shut, then fished out a pack of Lucky Strikes from his suit pocket and lit up.

With that, conversation ceased.

While Max washed down the remainder of the packet of peanuts with noisy slurps of Coke, I sat motionless in my leather seat, studying Albertos as he gazed out into the night, mechanically raising and lowering his cigarette from arm-rest to a pair of thin, cracked lips.

Now what?

Further confrontation would achieve nothing, except to heighten the risk of Max learning the truth about what was happening to him. Physical confrontation was equally out of the question. Even if I managed to get the better of him, there'd still be the pilots to contend with, not to mention whoever was waiting at the other end. Nor did I have the option of grabbing Max and trying to make a break for it, because, as had been made clear only minutes earlier, Amara was being held as leverage.

My only recourse was to try and negotiate. To strike some sort of a deal. As a member of an organised crime gang, Albertos was in this for one thing only: money. Which made him vulnerable to turning.

Averting my eyes, I followed a lone wisp of smoke coiling its way across the aisle up towards the ceiling.

To negotiate effectively, however, I needed a firmer grasp of the facts. And yet everything that had happened in the last twenty-four hours left me utterly baffled. There were contradictions at every turn.

Of one thing, though, I was certain. There'd been no police conspiracy.

Albertos had spun the lie in order to frighten us into agreeing to be escorted off the island. I'd bought into it at the time, because it was the only way to explain how the attackers had got the jump on us. It was now all too obvious that, while

Albertos had been apparently working for Greek Intelligence, he, along with his accomplice, Mikis, had been feeding the Seven Stars updates to keep them in the loop, allowing them to play us at our own game; feeding Xander false intelligence of the proposed kidnap time and venue so they could create a diversion event and carry out their assault, unhindered, at an entirely different location.

Casting an eye over the packet of cigarettes on the table in front of me, I pulled myself forward on my elbows and gazed through the stratum of smoke to the partition doors at the head of the aircraft.

Exactly how Albertos had managed to pull off the coup would remain beyond my grasp. But there was no mystery as to how he'd infiltrated Kate's operation in the first place: through the man who had hired not only him, but also his colleagues Mikis and Alexandra; the other key players integral to our extraction off the island ...

The man who'd gone AWOL to apparently lick his wounds after having been sidelined from the action; who'd collared me on my first night in Greece at a sleazy hotel bar in downtown Athens and broken the news to me of a Mafia plot to abduct the son I never knew I had.

Gerald.

There came a sudden clunk as the empty Coke can hit the floor and rolled across the aisle towards me. Trapping it with my foot, I looked up to see Max slumped in his seat, head down on his chest; a hand dangling over the side of the chair arm.

Asleep, finally.

After checking his breathing wasn't restricted in any way, I fastened the seat belt loosely over his legs, then turned back to Albertos, who was studying me with an expression of amused curiosity.

Gerald had been Albertos's way in.

The British expat might also be his way out.

'Do you mind if I have a cigarette?' I asked amiably, reaching across the table for the packet of Lucky Strikes. 'It's been a long day.'

Albertos gave a grunt and turned back to the window.

I took hold of his Zippo lighter and lit up, sucking the smoke deep into my lungs.

'It's funny, I never really trusted Gerald,' I said with a smile. 'I guess it only goes to show ... always follow your instincts.'

Albertos licked his lips, but remained silent.

'He wasn't in from the beginning, though, was he?' I mused. 'Because this all started with Takis, right? He exploited Xander's debt as a way of stealing Amara's inheritance. Used his dodgy connections in the banking world to engage Yiorgos of the Seven Stars Mafia to court Xander. To propose the idea of a ransom kidnap. Yiorgos, in turn, hires the likes of you, Mikis and Alexandra to assist in the operation. And then finally, Gerald, a bumbling British expat with the gift of the gab, is assigned to help lure me into the conceit, the minute I arrive in Greece.'

I took another drag and blew the smoke up to the ceiling.

Albertos said nothing; kept his eyes front, staring down the aisle towards the rear of the aircraft.

'Who brought him into it, though?' I continued, leaning in across the table towards him, 'Yiorgos, or Takis? How does a gone-to-seed university lecturer like Gerald even show up on their radar?'

I hesitated for a moment, as if waiting for an answer, allowing the palliative effects of the nicotine to flush through my limbs.

'Actually, I do have an idea,' I admitted, tapping my ash into the empty Coke can. 'Did you know Gerald was responsible for sabotaging your drugs deal, a year ago? That forty million dollars' worth of cocaine hidden in a boat at Piraeus? Kate told me that was down to Gerald. He got tipped off by an inform-ant from a rival cartel of yours based in Thessaloniki. Gerald watched and waited, and then at the last moment, handed the gig over to Greek Intelligence to carry out the bust. Came away looking like a hero.'

Albertos didn't move a muscle.

'But get this,' I continued. 'A few months ago, Gerald is contacted again by the same informant about a Seven Stars plot to kidnap a five-year old boy. Except, this time, Gerald ends up working for the very cartel he was supposed to stitch up. How does that happen?'

Eyes still averted, Albertos reached languidly into his jacket pocket, pulled out his worry beads and commenced his mesmeric ritual once again, whipping them back and forth across his palm.

I pressed on. 'I think our maverick Gerald got a little ambitious. He let his previous success go to his head, and, upping the ante, decided to switch teams. Approached the Seven Stars in Athens, told them about the tip off, and how he'd been signed up by Kate and Stelios of Greek Intelligence to help foil their kidnap plot, then offered his services as double agent.'

Catching the beads in his fist, Albertos finally met my gaze.

'If you have all the answers,' he murmured, 'why are you asking me?'

I smiled again. Tapped my ash.

'It just seems unfair that a chancer like Gerald should share in the loot,' I replied, throwing a glance out of the window. 'Especially when he was responsible for busting your drugs haul last year. To be honest, I'm surprised he lived to tell the tale.'

Turning back to the cabin, I took a final pull on my cigarette and dropped it into the empty Coke can.

'Anyway, enough of Gerald,' I said, sitting back and folding my hands in my lap. 'What's in it for you — a gig like this? A share of the spoils, I suppose, along with everyone else?'

Breaking eye contact, Albertos set down his beads and picked up the pack of Lucky Strikes. His Zippo, however, was just out of reach.

'I hope it's worth it,' I added, sliding the lighter across the table. 'Because the expenses must be racking up. The helicopter, private jet ... all the manpower. Once Takis, Yiorgos and Gerald have taken their split, I'm not sure there'll be much left in the pot for the likes of you. A whole lot less than you deserve, that's for sure.'

Albertos said nothing. Cigarette hanging out of the corner of his mouth, he toyed with the Zippo, turning it over and over in his fingers.

'Sure, Yiorgos had to deal with the admin, the rounding up of the troops,' I continued. 'Hardly counts as work, though. As for Takis, he's sitting pretty in Athens, waiting for his sister's cry for help. Gerald's probably shacked up with his student girlfriend, wondering how to dump her when his money comes in ...'

I paused, watching the Zippo slowly revolve in Albertos's hand.

'All these guys, safely out of harm's way, waiting for their foot-soldiers to bring in the cash cow, while you're on the front line taking the heat. Sounds like a bum deal to me.'

Albertos finally lit up, took three consecutives drags on his cigarette, then sat back and fixed me with his hawk-like gaze.

Flicking a glance at Max, I lowered my voice. 'But what if all that money Takis was going to keep for himself, along with the cash he was going to divide between Xander, Gerald, Yiorgos, and all his hired hands ... what if it could all be yours?'

Albertos didn't move a muscle.

I leaned in over the table towards him.

'Five years ago, I walked free from a Greek prison,' I began. 'The chief of police on Paros who helped clear my name will be more than ready to hear what I have to say about Takis.' I leaned in further still, until I could smell Albertos's pungent aftershave. 'All it'll take is a phone call. I instruct Takis to assign the entire inheritance funds over to you, or face the consequences of a police enquiry. However badly he wants that money, I guarantee you he sure as shit doesn't want to go to jail.'

A sudden bump of turbulence shook the aircraft, causing Max to stir.

Opening his eyes briefly, he rubbed his nose and coughed back some phlegm that had stuck in his throat, before falling back to sleep.

I pulled his t-shirt back down over his stomach, then turned once more to Albertos who was studying me intently, a frown of consternation etched into his forehead.

'You want to know how much?' I continued. 'Ten million dollars. Maybe more.'

He stared at me, unblinking.

'As it stands, The Seven Stars will get a cut of that, as a commission. And you'll get a cut of that cut.' I paused, holding his gaze. 'But I'm offering you the lot.'

He grunted and turned away.

'Even after you've paid off Yiorgos, Mikis and Alexandra, and whoever else you have to,' I continued, lowering my voice still further, 'you'll still be left with a fortune. We're talking the best part of ten million dollars, Albertos.'

Turning back to me, he slowly tapped his ash into the armrest ashtray.

'You think Amara will be happy with you spending her inheritance?' he murmured, a smile forming at the corners of his lips. 'It is because of you that she has been separated from her boy. It is because of you that her husband is dead . . . It is because of you that her life has been turned upside down. If I was her, I would use my inheritance to make sure you disappeared from my life. Permanently.'

I stared at him, lost for any comeback.

He couldn't have been more right; but that was now out of my hands. Right now, I had to look after Amara and Max's interests. Not mine.

'If it means an end to what Max is having to suffer,' I exclaimed, going on the offensive. 'If it means Amara is reunited with her son at the earliest possible fucking moment – of course she'll be happy to pay the money.' Scratching at the back of my head, I allowed the indignant tone free reign. 'Takis will pay it all back. Sell his fucking house, at the very least. Gerald – he'll have to stump up for it, too. Neither of them gets off the hook until they've replenished every penny of Amara's funds.'

'It will take them a long time to pay back ten million dollars, no?'

'What's that to you?'

Albertos nodded along, scratching at an itch under his collar.

'All you've got to do,' I urged, 'is turn the plane around and take us back to Varaxos. Have Alexandra meet us with Amara. I'll make the phone call to Takis. He'll arrange the bank transfer. You pay off the pilots, send Amara, me and Max back to Athens in either the helicopter or the jet, and then disappear off the grid a seriously wealthy man.'

Maintaining eye contact, I sank back into my seat and casually folded my arms across my chest. 'Xander alone will be accountable,' I concluded. 'And he's dead. No one will ever know any better.'

At first, Albertos remained inscrutable, watching a thin line of smoke snake up from the tip of his shrinking cigarette. Eventually, he sighed, slid out from behind the table and, making his way up the aisle to the cabinet by the partition doors, reached into a drawer and pulled out a manila envelope. After a brief examination of the contents, he returned to his seat, tapped his ash into the Coke can and dropped the envelope onto the table.

Was that a 'yes' or a 'no'?

'We will be landing in Cyprus,' he announced, spreading the documents out on the table. 'You and Max have reservations at the Limassol Hilton. You are waiting for the arrival of Amara from Zakynthos. As you explained to Max, she has been delayed

240

for medical reasons, but she will be joining you in twenty-four hours. A family gathering to celebrate the boy's birthday . . .'

Sucking hard on his cigarette, he glanced up at me, as if to check I was paying attention.

I could only stare at him, utterly bewildered.

'The passport in Max's possession is a fake,' he continued, puffing smoke out of the side of his mouth. 'In it, his date of birth is given as the 12th of July. Two days' time. You are named as one of his emergency contacts. Your relationship is given as his father.' He paused, eyeballing me. 'So, no need for you to produce the birth certificates in the back of your own passport. It will only confuse things.'

Again, he looked up at me, as if expecting me to reply, but I remained too dumfounded to speak.

Albertos ploughed on: 'There are two UK immigration stamps at the front of Max's new passport,' he declared, thumbing his jacket lapel. 'One dated for December last year, and the other for the previous summer. When Max travelled with his mother to visit you in London.' His pursed lips gave way to a weary smile. 'There shouldn't be any reason for the officials to question you. But if they do, you can simply explain that the trip is a birthday surprise.'

As I had done earlier, he reached over and extinguished his cigarette in the empty Coke can.

For a moment, a stillness befell the cabin.

Just the sound of Max's snuffles punctuating the hum of the air conditioning.

'If Max plays up, it's all over,' I countered, unable to accept that Albertos had dismissed my proposition out of hand. 'You lose your money.'

'If Max plays up, he loses his mother.'

'Takis isn't going to murder his own sister, for Christ's sake. He'll just pull the plug.'

'Amara will be silenced,' said Albertos, grim-faced. 'The

Seven Stars cannot afford to leave loose ends. Takis knows the deal. He, along with Gerald, will testify that the kidnap plot was initiated by you, and that they were blackmailed into taking part.'

Rearranging his suit jacket, he eased himself back into his seat.

I thrust myself forwards over the table until I was inches from his face.

'You don't have to do this,' I urged. 'This isn't what the Mafia is about . . . abducting children? Killing their mothers? For Christ's sake Albertos, you're a good man. In your heart. I know it. I'm offering you a solution. A way out, that stops this thing in its tracks and makes you—'

'When we land, you and Max will continue alone,' he snapped, interrupting me. 'A driver will meet you in arrivals. He will take you where you need to be.'

'You're not disembarking?'

'I have no need. With Amara's life at stake, you won't do anything stupid.'

It made sense. Why would he risk being caught, when I could be handled at a distance?

But not for a minute did I believe we were actually going to the Hilton in Limassol.

'Where are we going then?' I demanded. 'Somewhere they won't be offering room service, I take it.'

But Albertos had lost interest. Signalling the end of the discussion, he produced his silk handkerchief and dabbed it at his neck before folding it away into his suit jacket and peering once more out of the window into the dark.

'And if you try to bribe me again,' he murmured, stroking his chin, 'I will cut your throat myself.'

18

We continued our easterly trajectory for close to an hour, until, shortly before 10 p.m., the captain announced in Greek that we'd be landing in twenty minutes.

There had been no further conversation.

Unable to shake off a growing sense of dread, I'd simply sat, catatonic, in my seat while opposite me, shrouded in strata of slow-swirling cigarette smoke, our captor gazed inscrutably out into the night.

At some point in the journey the aircraft encountered a spate of turbulence, causing Max to whimper in his sleep. Reaching out to lay a hand on his shoulder, I'd experienced a flashback: picturing Amara at her father's restaurant on Naxos, dressed in a white crop-top and jeans shorts, straddling a wicker chair under the eucalyptus trees in the rear garden. And then later, on the roof terrace of her father's house . . . alone together under starlight, shutters thrown wide. That night of Retsina, olives and fireflies . . . of cotton sheets, honeysuckle and sweat . . . The night we'd made Max.

A night that would remain forever firmly in the past.

The Mafia had won. I was to be framed for the kidnap – and then silenced.

Turning back to my window to stare vacantly out at the sweep of frozen stars stretching away across the firmament, I recalled my grandfather's funeral, and the reading my mother had delivered from the pulpit:

'*Death is nothing at all. I have only slipped away to the next room . . .*'

At the time, the words had brought comfort to all assembled. Not so, now.

I didn't want to be in the next room.

I was too young to be in the next room.

A string of lights eventually appeared through the starboard windows, heralding the approach of the Cypriot coastline, upon which our aircraft threw a stomach-churning 180-degree-turn before reducing throttle in order to commence its final approach, dropping rapidly over a period of several turbulent minutes towards sea level.

At the very last moment, just as I thought we were sure to crash-land in the water, a runway flashed by under our wings. A screech of rubber from the undercarriage was followed by a second bump, as the nose-wheel hit the asphalt, at which point the engines reversed, slowing the aircraft to a walking pace before coming to a juddering halt, a stone's throw from the terminal building.

'*Ella*, wake the boy,' growled Albertos, from across the table.

I rose from my seat and, unclipping Max's safety belt, began to gently call his name.

'*Moumia?*' he mumbled, rubbing his eyes as he hauled himself upright. 'Is my mummy here now?'

'Not yet,' I whispered. 'We're getting off the plane.'

'Where are we?'

'We're in Cyprus.'

'*Kypros?*'

'That's right. Have you been here before?'

'*Oxi.*'

244

It was possible Max might return.

Not I.

I would never leave.

'Come on then,' I said, unable to think of how to delay the inevitable. 'Let's check it out, shall we?'

And then, a shadow, clawing into my brain . . .

Heat rising up my spine; my breathing becoming more rapid . . . sweat breaking out along the nape of my neck . . .

Tend to Max, I told myself.

Take care of the boy.

There was a rush of warm air behind me as Albertos threw open the cabin door and began shouting to a member of the ground crew outside.

Shouldering the holdall, I placed Max's cap back on his head, slipped his passport out of his back pocket and propelled him up the aisle to the cabin door.

'You look after Mister Alistair now, *endaxi?*' said Albertos, bending down to Max and chucking him under the chin. '*Kali tihi.*'

Having wished Max good luck, he pulled himself upright and looked me in the eye.

Before he deigned to wish me the same, I dragged Max straight past him to the stepladder, and then on down to the tarmac where a member of the ground crew in oil-stained over-alls and ear defenders collected us, then led the way across the apron to the entrance of the terminal building.

Barking instructions to follow signs to Baggage Reclaim, he gave us a quick thumbs-up and slipped furtively back out into the night.

I grasped Max's hand and glanced back over my shoulder through the plate glass to see Albertos's shadowy figure looming in the doorway of the jet. In the cockpit, meanwhile, the two pilots leaned over their controls doing their post checks. Neither of them turned in our direction.

As a familiar light-headedness began once again to take hold, I ushered the weary Max along a series of deserted echoing corridors, stopping off for a brief toilet visit, until finally, we reached Immigration.

There was no queue; just a uniformed official leaning up against the counter with his female assistant standing by, listening to a portable radio.

I came to a halt and studied the couple up ahead.

There was still time.

All I had to do as walk up to the officials and put ourselves in their custody.

Everything would stop.

Max would be safe.

I would live . . .

'Come on Mister Alistair,' squeaked Max, staring up at me with his bright blue eyes. 'I want to see my surprise.'

Amara, however, would die.

Down the hall, the uniformed guard was gesturing impatiently for me to bring Max up to the gate; but my attention had been taken by the scuttling of a gecko halfway up a concrete pillar, a few feet to my right.

Max spotted it too, and moved over to the base of the column, baseball cap in hand, to admire the translucent reptile as it paused to eye a moth fluttering around the ceiling light.

'Can we catch him, Mister Alistair?' he asked, twirling his cap in his fingers.

'I don't think so,' I murmured. 'Another time.'

'Oh,' he replied, amenably. 'Okay.'

Shuffling back over to me, he took my hand.

'Are you sad, Mister Alistair?'

'No, I'm just . . .'

'Yes?'

'Nothing.'

246

'Do you miss my mommy?' he asked, frowning. 'Because you mustn't worry. She is coming soon. The man told us.'

'Of course.

'Why are we waiting?' he continued, picking his nose. 'There's no one else here.'

'I know.'

'Maybe they are all sleeping?'

'Maybe.'

'I'm looking forward to tomorrow,' he declared with a sigh. 'I'm bored of today.'

'Me too.' I tightened my grip on his hand and pulled him in closer.

'I'm glad I'm with you, Mister Alistair. I think I would be frightened on my own.'

I nodded, unable to speak.

Because, in that moment, everything became clear.

I had failed Max; I'd failed Amara; I'd even failed the errant Xander . . .

But if nothing else, I intended to reunite mother and son.

Whatever it took.

'Don't ask any questions,' I said gently, bending down and placing his baseball cap back on his tousled head. 'We don't want to give away the secret.'

As Max nodded and pulled his cap down tighter, I led him calmly up to the security counter and wished both officials a good evening.

The dapper young man peered over his aviators, stamped each of our passports with an impatient flourish, then sent us on our way without uttering a word.

I'd sealed my own fate. But I was meeting it willingly.

Robbing death of its sting.

The arrivals concourse was all but empty; a handful of staff manning the rent-a-car and tourist information desks, along

247

with a group of subdued elderly holiday-makers drinking coffee at the tourist-shop-cum café.

Just as I was beginning to wonder what action we should take if our contact never materialised, I spied a figure hovering beyond the entrance to the terminal. Dressed in jeans and a light denim jacket, he was leaning up against a concrete bollard, idly flicking a set of keys in his hand.

Exhaling in and out over a slow count of ten, I pulled Max forward to the entrance.

As we drew nearer, the man clocked us and lifted up a cardboard sign:

Mr Alistair Haston.

'Come on Max,' I said, tweaking his baseball cap. 'This is us.'

Approaching our driver, I nodded a greeting, upon which he grunted something indecipherable in Greek, then led us out into the moonlit carpark to a lone Ford Escort parked up against a row of cypresses. Moments later, we were pulling out of the airport perimeter onto a road lined with poplars that led away from the coast across a broad, open plain.

With an arm across Max's shoulders, I surrendered to the rhythms of the plaintive mandolins emanating from the car radio and let my mind float unfettered through the unfolding moonscape.

I no longer had a sense of self.

Because there was no 'I'.

I was simply part of everything else.

Before long, the arid wasteland gave way to a series of scattered olive groves and fruit plantations, which, in turn, began to peter out as we left fertile pastures behind us and headed into mountainous terrain, with perilous switch-backs and vertical drops plunging hundreds of feet down into the valley below.

At length, even the moon abandoned us and went into hiding, obscured by a swelling bank of cloud, pulsing with periodic flashes of lightning.

Climbing steadily higher into cooler air, we eventually reached the limit of the tree line, at which point we turned off the tarmac road and dropped down onto a winding pitted track that led away around the south face of the mountain along the border of a conifer plantation, with only a three-foot-high stone wall between us and certain death.

Just shy of a kilometre later, we skidded around a corner and hit a dead end.

Well, not quite.

Beyond the end of the track, emerging from the trees, stood an ancient, sprawling Villa.

Slamming on the brakes, our driver brought the car to an abrupt stop amid a cloud of pine needles and dust. We sat in silence for a moment, as another flash of sheet-lightning lit up the valley, fleetingly revealing the villa in more detail: a rambling stone structure, with arch windows and a bell-tower, lending it the air of a medieval castle.

In the driveway, bordering the entrance to a concealed court-yard, stood a Mercedes van, a moped, and, closest to the villa, going by the low-slung profile, what appeared to be a sports car, hidden underneath a canvas tarpaulin.

'Is my mommy here?' whispered Max nervously, craning his neck to the window to look up at the imposing residence.

I pretended I hadn't heard.

Realising our driver had no intention of getting out of the car, I helped Max out of the back seat into the cool, resinous air, and for a moment entertained the notion of grabbing him and making a run for it . . .

But then the villa door opened and a bowed, elderly man emerged, dressed in a black suit and white shirt, looking to all intents and purposes like a butler. In the crook of his right arm, the unmistakeable shape of a double-barrelled shotgun.

Shielding his eyes against the Ford's headlights, he peered over at us, then disappeared back inside. Moments later he re-emerged, without the weapon this time, and, hands on hips, beckoned us over.

I took Max by the wrist and led him up the shingled path to the portico.

'Welcome, Mister Haston,' mumbled the ancient in a thick Mediterranean accent, as, behind us, the car pulled a three-point turn and shot off back the way we'd come. 'And Mister Max,' he added, ruffling Max's hair. *'Kala eisai?'*

Max pulled himself in closer to my legs.

'Come – please.'

Stepping over the threshold, we followed him across an expansive flag-stoned hallway towards a formidable spiral staircase in the far-left corner.

By the light of a sizeable industrial lamp overhead, I could make out a series of entrances leading off the quadrant: a pair of swing doors dead ahead, pinned back by door stoppers, revealing a kitchen sink and cooker; to my right, a heavy iron door, ajar, leading to what appeared to be a basement, or cellar. Finally, behind me, in the corner by the main entrance, an archway led to what was evidently the store-room – judging by the shelves stacked with tinned produce – along with a bucket and a mop.

Was that where he'd stashed his shotgun?

'Sorry about gun,' the butler grunted, as if reading my thoughts. 'Many peoples here bad ... they come to steal.'

Thrown by his air of geniality, I kept quiet and followed close on his heels, one hand tight around Max, as the old man led us up three flights to a spacious, high-ceilinged drawing room, complete with an expansive pine table and high-backed, ornate chairs sprawling under a low-hanging crystal chandelier; candelabras on every available shelf; a disparate collection of reproduction Picassos and Van Goghs on the walls.

As the first rumbles of thunder drifted in through the open terrace windows, our host led us on through an archway off to one side of the drawing room and on up yet another staircase, leading to a stiflingly hot attic.

Pushing open the wooden door, he stepped back and gestured us to enter.

In the middle of a terracotta-walled room lit entirely by candles, stood a large four-poster bed enclosed in mosquito netting. Off by the window, underneath an open set of Venetian blinds, a second, smaller bed had been made up. On it was a box, gift-wrapped in silver paper.

Other than the two beds and a washbasin in the corner of the room, there was not a single other piece of furniture. Just an array of Turkish carpets spread out across the stone floor.

Crossing over to the window, Max warily approached the single bed and picked up the box.

'Is this mine?' he enquired, turning to face me.

Without thinking, I nodded.

Where the fuck were we?

Tearing off the wrapping paper, Max squeaked with delight:

'A remote-control car!' he yelled, brandishing it above his head. 'Has it got batteries?'

But my attention was taken by a tapping noise from behind.

At first, I thought it was the knocking of a loose water pipe, except it seemed to be getting louder. Only after a good half minute did I realise the sound was, in fact, drawing closer.

When the door jamb creaked, I turned, expecting to see our host. But as my eyes adjusted to the light spilling in from the stairwell, I realised someone else had taken his place.

Someone younger.

Taller.

A walking stick in one hand. Candle in the other.

Casting a shadow across the carpet at my feet, the figure stood stock still in the doorway; the ochre light from the flame catching his white t-shirt and cowboy boots.

It was as if the room had tilted.

I reached out at thin air in a bid to stabilise myself.

But nothing had moved.

Before me, however, the figure loomed larger in the flickering light.

Impossible . . .

I froze, rooted to the floor.

I didn't believe in ghosts, and yet . . .

In front of me stood a man who shouldn't exist.

A man who'd bled to death before my very eyes.

The man I'd killed in self-defence, for fear of being butchered in cold blood.

Stepping forward out of the doorway, the figure chuckled and raised his candle, revealing a mahogany tan and trademark Hollywood grin.

'Haston, you pommie bastard,' he drawled in a thick Australian brogue. 'Gimme some fuckin' skin . . .'

Ricky.

19

Spreading his arms wide, Ricky took a step in towards me.

'Don't be a stranger mate,' he exclaimed, grin still plastered across his face. 'Hug it out.'

Without waiting for a reply, he shuffled another half-step closer and, still bearing his cane and candle, wrapped his sinewy arms around me.

'You lost weight?' he murmured into my neck. 'Muscle tone, too.'

Max sidled over, head cocked, remote control car in his hand.

'Get your arms around me, brother,' Ricky demanded, turning out to face Max. 'Don't want to give the kid the wrong impression.'

Still unable to speak, I lifted my arms and put them around his taut frame.

'Who are you?' asked Max tentatively, circling around to examine Ricky's face resting on my shoulder. 'Are you Mister Alistair's brother?'

'Too right,' said Ricky, squeezing me harder, his stubbled jaw scratching at my exposed collarbone. 'He never told you about uncle Ricky?'

Max shook his head and dropped his gaze to his car.

'Is this for me?' he asked shyly.

I tried to pull away, but Ricky gripped me tighter.

''Course it's for you,' he replied with a chuckle. 'In a minute, I'll get Besnik to get you some batteries.'

Max frowned. 'Who's Besnik?'

'Besnik's the old codger who brought you all the way up the fuckin' stairs instead of using the elevator,' Ricky said, in mock indignation. 'Don't be fooled. He pretends he doesn't understand anything, but his English is better than mine. Speaks a ton of languages. Greek. French. Even Russian.'

'You mustn't say "fucking",' objected Max.

Ricky roared with laughter then pulled back to face me.

Still, he wouldn't let go.

'Sweet kid,' he murmured, levelling me with his translucent green eyes. 'And you, Haston ... you don't look a day older. Nice to see you with hair for a change.' He craned his neck around to Max, revealing a matted ponytail hanging down between his shoulder blades. 'Hey, Max, grab the walking stick and candle will ya?'

A familiar sickly scent of Kouros aftershave wafted up from his neck ...

Followed by fleeting images of a forgotten summer:

Sun-cream and dried salt ... The red light on Ricky's video camera ...

Heinrich's yacht ...

Snorting cocaine off flat stomachs ... Paintbrushes and oil paints.

Roland's severed head in a cool box.

Max relieved Ricky of the cane and candle and retreated over to the bed.

'Can we get the batteries now?'

'Just a minute, son,' said Ricky, seizing my hands and wrapping them around his back.

Gripping my wrists tight, he slid them under his t-shirt and

254

inched them up along his spine until I could feel a strip of rough skin; a scaly protrusion, brushing against my knuckles.

'Feel that, mate?' he whispered into my ear. 'That's three years of surgery.'

Locked in our grisly embrace, the villa shook as an extended peal of thunder rolled down the mountainside.

'Just thought you'd like to know,' he said, kissing me on the cheek.

Finally, he let me go and stepped back.

'No standing on ceremony,' he declared, raking a hand through his sun-bleached hair. 'We're gonna get some batteries for Max's car, and then I'm going to fetch us a cold one. Don't know about you, Haston, but I can't get through these summer nights without a fuckin' brew in the hand.' He twisted around to Max and winked. 'Sorry, son. You'll get used to my French.'

'That's not French,' objected Max.

'No flies on you.'

Ricky flashed a grin as he walked stiffly over to the bed and picked up his cane. 'You can keep hold of the candle,' he added, turning to Max and arching his back in a stretch. Then he whipped the baseball cap off the latter's head and balanced it on his own. 'Lead the way, little one,' he exclaimed. 'Let's find that rascal, Besnik.'

Approximately twenty yards wide and ten deep, the flag-stone terrace overlooked a sheer drop down into the valley; perimeter stone walls covered with honeysuckle and sprawling bougainvillea.

Protected from the elements by an overhanging awning, a cluster of metalwork chairs had been grouped around a sturdy slate-topped table, set with hurricane lamps at either end, along with a brace of porcelain ashtrays.

'If you keep going south as the crow flies,' came Ricky's voice from behind, 'you hit the port of Limassol. A shit hole – no need to go there. But if you follow the coast west, you get to Paphos. The *Akamas*. A whole different kettle of fish. Paradise.'

Delivering two beers to the table, he shuffled past me and pulled up a chair.

'Keo – Cyprus's own brew,' he said tapping his bottle. 'Better than the imported crap the tourists drink.'

Reaching into his pocket he pulled out a packet of cigarettes and lit up.

'I've been trying to quit,' he said, waving his cigarette in the air. 'Too weak willed.'

Still too shocked to speak, I collected my drink and, stepping out into the sulphurous air, made my way, as if on autopilot, over to the wall.

'Mind your step,' warned Ricky, breezily. 'It'd take you a while to climb back up.'

A dazzling flash of lightning was followed by an ear-splitting crack over the mountain ridge behind.

Instinctively, I ducked and quickly returned back under the awning.

'Been due a storm for weeks,' Ricky said, swigging from the bottle. 'Usually we get one every four or five days in the summer. The cold air off Mount Olympus meets the heat in the valley and delivers a nifty *son et lumière* show. But it's been super dry this month. Conditions haven't been right.'

He blew a coiling smoke ring out across the table into the night.

Childish laughter from within was followed by a weighty guffaw, then the high-pitched whine of an electric motor as Max's remote-control car shot out briefly onto the flag-stones at my feet, before pulling a U-Turn and disappearing back inside.

'Besnik and Max are bonding,' chuckled Ricky, taking another pull on his beer.

Experiencing a surreal sense of disembodiment, I gazed

dumbly at the bobbing motion of his Adam's apple; rippling the leathery skin of his throat as he drank.

A ghost . . . a reptilian ghost.

'Sit down,' he chided, peering sideways at me, lips around the bottle neck. 'Put yer feet up.'

I hesitated a moment, then, after several long, slow breaths, pulled up a chair a few feet distant from him. 'So much for a ransom kidnapping,' I said slowly. 'Want to tell me the real reason we're here?'

Ricky shook his head and took another hit on his cigarette.

'Slow down, detective,' he sighed. 'You've just arrived.'

Then he lifted his right leg up with both hands and rested it on the table.

'I forgot what an infuriating bastard you can be,' he added. 'Relax. Enjoy the moment. *Twenty-first century's yesterday . . .*'

And then he broke into song: 'Need You Tonight', by INXS; a hit that was playing in all the clubs on Paros five years ago.

'Hutchence is a genius,' he concluded.

I had been of the same opinion at the time. To hear the song now only brought on an attack of the sweats.

'You brought me all the way out here to shoot the breeze?' I said, revolving my beer bottle on the table. 'You could've dropped me a line. Sent a postcard. I'd have written back.'

'Clever fuck,' he replied, breaking into a grin. 'Anyway – I did send you a postcard. Never heard back.'

The postcard I found on my bed in the halls of residence at St Andrews . . .

Missing you. Rx

'Fair enough,' I murmured, before taking a sip of my beer. 'But no return address.'

'Fuck off, Haston,' he grunted, eyeballing me. 'Bet it freaked the shit out of you. Tied that ol' detective brain of yours into right little knots . . .'

'Didn't give it a second thought,' I lied.

'Mister Alistair!' yelled Max from within. 'Come see my car!'

'In a minute, son,' answered Ricky on my behalf, massaging his thigh. 'Just catching up with the English dude.' The he turned and frowned. 'Does he call you "dad"?'

'He doesn't know.'

'Better tell him soon, though, eh?'

'All in good time.'

He gave a derisive snort. 'Not sure you got much of that. Want me to do it?'

Ignoring his remark, I peered out across the terrace into the abyss.

What were the chances I could pick Ricky up and throw him over the edge?

With his gammy leg . . .

The odds were surely in my favour.

'Oh, by the way . . .' Ricky continued with a grin. 'Don't get any ideas.'

He jabbed his cigarette up towards where the awning met the side of the stone wall.

A shiny CCTV camera pointed straight at us.

'I'll introduce you to the boys later,' he continued. 'They're probably stuffing their faces with kebabs, but if you so much as come within two feet of me, they'll put a bullet in your brain faster than you can shout "I'm a cunt".'

I took another sip of my beer. 'A cunt, you are. No need to shout about it.'

'Touché,' he chuckled. 'Same ol' Haston.'

Two security guards, then. At the very least.

Plus Besnik.

'Got cameras all over the place,' Ricky added, belching. 'Big brother is definitely watching.'

At which point, Besnik poked his head around the door, holding the controller for the car in his hand. 'You will be needing anything to eat, Mister Ricky?'

'I'm good. What about the pommie bastard?'

I hadn't eaten for over eight hours, but my appetite had been killed by the presence of the man before me.

'Gone off Greek food,' I replied. 'I'll stick with the beer.'

'I will bring bread with olives,' said Besnik decisively, catching my hesitation.

'And potato chips for me!' squealed Max from within.

Besnik gave a brisk nod then disappeared inside; his footsteps echoing along with Max's as they descended the staircase to the floor below.

'This place belonged to Besnik's dad,' said Ricky, continuing to massage his leg. 'Albanian dude. He was head boy here when it belonged to a Czechoslovakian countess. The woman was a fruitcake recluse. When she got terminally ill, she sold the place to a French developer who wanted to turn it into a hotel. Never got around to it. Anyway, she insisted Besnik's father was kept on as permanent staff – part of the deed of sale.' He took a final draw on his cigarette then stubbed it out in the porcelain bowl. 'This was sometime between the wars. After that, it was taken over by a Greek family who split their time between here and Athens. Again, Besnik's old man stayed on with the property. Besnik was born here and took over his father's job when he died. The Greeks eventually sold up – the bloke went to jail for money laundering – and the place stood empty for about ten years. Then I bought it.'

He tipped back his bottle and reached again for the cigarettes.

'Ready for another beer?' he mumbled, lighting up. 'No drugs, I'm afraid. Don't do that shit any more. Body can't cope. Although, if you want, I can send Besnik out on the moped. There's a Dutch playboy a few clicks down the road who, I hear, does a good line in marching powder.' He grinned. ''Scuse the pun.'

I shook my head, straining to listen out for signs of Max.

'Don't worry about the ankle-biter,' Ricky murmured, as the

first fat drops of rain began to fall beyond the awning. 'Besnik is a sweetheart. He'll be giving him a guided tour, most like. Big ol' fucking house. Don't use half the rooms.'

'Maybe you should turn it into a B&B,' I said, gazing out over the valley as the rain began to fall in earnest. 'Bring in some extra income.'

He threw his head back and guffawed into the night.

'You can come and run the place for me,' he said finally with a shake of the head. 'Just like the old days.'

'Not quite,' I replied. 'You don't do drugs any more, after all.'

'Yeah – right,' he said with a chuckle.

Whatever Ricky was planning, he was biding his time.

For what?

Or whom?

Tossing back his head, Ricky re-tied the band around his ponytail.

'Now, come on – spill the beans. What's going down? How's London treatin' ya?'

A blinding flash overhead was followed by an instantaneous crash of thunder. Then all at once, the clouds burst; sheeting rain reducing visibility across the terrace to zero.

A second later, all the lights in the villa turned off.

'Power cut,' announced Ricky – his face lit by the flickering flame of the hurricane lamp. 'It'll be back on in a second. The storms wreak havoc with the power lines.'

Sure enough, a moment later the lights flickered back on again.

'Happens all the time,' he added. 'We got a generator out the back, in case it stays off. Self-sufficient, up here.'

Steeling myself, I turned and faced him.

'Let's cut the shit, shall we?' I exclaimed, raising my voice to be heard above the deluge. 'Just tell me what the fuck I'm doing here.'

Ricky blew out a long, slow plume of smoke into the curtain of water cascading from the awning's edge.

'All in good time,' he said, with a wink.

Ricky had no intention of cutting to the chase. It wasn't his style. He was going to draw it out. It was all part of the game; foreplay, before delivering the coup de grâce.

I took another pull on my beer and cast an eye to where the stone wall met the shadows of the cypresses at the western end of the terrace.

Would it be possible to jump into the trees ... slide down through the branches to the forest floor?

Not with Max in my arms.

'Takis bought this place for me,' Ricky continued, sucking on his cigarette. 'Two years ago. He's been looking after my finances since – well ... since I met the guy, really. That's when he told me about Max ...'

He tapped his ash.

'I was astounded ... Haston has a kid? With Amara? Fuck me sideways! Then he told me that their dad had known all along. That he'd forced Amara to put your name on the birth certificate before he died, 'cos he didn't want his grandson kicking about without a father to his name ...'

Just then, Max appeared at the French windows, followed by Besnik; Pepsi bottle and straw in one hand – in the other, a plate of bread and olives.

'Here you are Mister Alistair,' he announced proudly, placing the plate before me. 'Wow, look at the rain!'

I reached out and tried to take his hand.

He withdrew a step. 'Uncle Ricky, are you sure you aren't hungry?'

My stomach churned at the epithet. But I said nothing.

'Don't fret,' said Ricky, shifting his chair to one side of a rivulet of rain pooling on the flagstones between us. 'Go enjoy yourself. It'll be bedtime soon, right?'

Max shook his head vehemently. 'Besnik said I can take the car down to the basement.'

'Besnik looking after you?' I replied.

'Yeah – he's cool,' Max shot back. 'He reminds me of *Pappous*.'

His grandfather – Amara and Takis's old man.

'Well, don't tire him out,' I said, turning back to Ricky with a smile. 'I'm sure he's got work to do.'

Besnik wasn't of Ricky's ilk – chances were, he knew little of Ricky's past . . . or present.

Might he be a potential ally?

'Whatever the old man says,' Ricky called out, studying me closely. 'Massive wine cellar down there. Great place for a kid to have a den.'

Max let out a whoop and, calling out for Besnik, shot back indoors.

Ricky sat back and laughed as a streak of forked lightning earthed itself down in the valley.

'The boy's a hoot,' he said finally. 'Takes after his old man.'

For a moment, neither of us moved.

Beyond the awning, the rain hammered on the terrace, underscored by fading echoes of thunder across the mountain.

'At some point, he's going to ask after his mother,' I said finally, as the rumbling died away. 'He may be five, but he's not stupid.'

Reaching for his cane, Ricky sighed and rose from his seat.

'Another beer coming up,' he called out, as he shuffled over to the French windows and disappeared inside. 'I fuckin' spoil you.'

I waited for the tapping to recede, then rose from my chair and ventured out into the downpour to recce the side of the terrace.

It was all sealed off – self-contained. No other way in or out, except through the French windows. Or over the edge . . . onto the rocks, hundreds of feet below.

Soaked to the skin, I stared dumbly out into the void.

It was conceivable, after all, that Ricky intended to ransom Max . . . get his hands on Amara's inheritance. It was a shortcut to easy winnings that would save him having to get back out into the field and graft for his money. But it didn't explain what he intended for me. His revenge would hardly be limited to framing me for the abduction; too pedestrian for a self-styled Machiavelli such as Ricky. He'd have something far more theatrical in mind.

'Tuck into the bread and olives, mate,' muttered Ricky, re-emerging from the villa. 'Must have been a while since you last ate.'

I waited until he had sat down, then returned, sodden, to my chair, noticing that he had brought me out a beer, whereas he himself was now nursing a bottle of mineral water.

'You'll forgive me for not joining you in another brew,' he apologised. 'I try to limit myself to a couple of beers a day. Gotta look after your health, right?' At which point, he reached into his pocket and, producing a bottle of pills, popped a tablet into his mouth. 'Besides, it doesn't mix well with the morphine,' he added, washing the pill down with water. 'Makes you sleepy.'

Helping myself to a wedge of bread, I ate in silence, keeping an ear out for signs of Max.

I was convinced now that nothing would happen until the morning – at least, not on Ricky's part.

Night would be the best time to make a break for it . . .

Not with his security guards on constant surveillance.

And I could hardly approach Besnik and persuade him to kindly hand over the keys to Ricky's car . . .

Besides, any attempt to run for it would cost Amara her life.

Still . . . there'd be an opening. There had to be a way . . .

'Once I heard about you and Amara having a kid,' Ricky continued, picking up from where he'd left off, 'I thought I'd better move things along . . . Told Takis to find someone in Athens who might be of help in getting you on board. A fellow Brit, you'd feel inclined to trust.'

He threw me an expectant look; master, to student.

'Gerald,' I replied, flatly.

'Bingo,' said Ricky with a grin. 'He was Takis's tutor at the uni in Athens. Takis said he was a wannabe spook, but never made it 'cos he couldn't handle his booze, or keep a secret. Then last year, I decided to help the bloke out. Anonymously tipped him off about a drugs delivery in Piraeus. He took the credit for the bust; teamed up with an old school mate in Greek Intelligence to help him bring off the sting. I paid a shedload of cash into his account – well, Takis did – pretending it had come from a rival cartel based in Thessaloniki, then sat back and waited. Six months later I call him up again, disguise my voice, and tell him I'm from the cartel he'd stitched up first time around, and that if he didn't help out on a certain project, he'd get his throat cut.' He broke off and grinned. 'Gerald put on his best 'I'm a diplomat' act – as instructed by yours truly – and made you an offer you'd never refuse. Honourable fucker and all, that you are.'

I stared at him, trying to join the dots.

Kate had told me the same story in almost the same words.

Except she'd been a step behind.

'You were the informant, then – supposedly from a Thessaloniki cartel?'

Ricky frowned. 'As I just said.' Then he broke into a smile. 'I gather Gerald's quite the bullshit artist.'

The overbearing threat to his own life no doubt greased the wheels of invention.

'And the cartel you stitched up was the Seven Stars?' I asked, another puzzle forming at the back of my mind.

'Correct.' He threw me a grin. 'You see – look at us here . . . havin' a right ol' chinwag.'

'But Albertos, Mikis and Alexandra,' I pressed on, ignoring his remark. 'They're all from the Seven Stars. I take it they don't know you're the reason they lost their forty million dollars-worth of cocaine?'

Ricky slapped at a mosquito on his neck.

'Bastards. The rain's gonna bring 'em out in droves.'

'How did they end up working for Gerald . . . Or vice versa?'

A deeper knowledge of Ricky's machinations might hold clues to a way out – to a weak link in the chain of command.

Although, Ricky was the end of that chain.

And I'd already failed to turn Albertos.

Ricky scratched at his chin. 'When you asked Gerald to prove he had men watching you . . . he called Yiorgos, then Yiorgos called me. I told him to assign whoever he trusted.'

'Yiorgos was the guy who initially roped in Xander on the nightclub circuit in Athens?'

Puffing out another smoke ring, Ricky nodded.

'And he's also Seven Stars?'

Ricky smiled. 'You're doing so well, mate . . . but I gotta set you straight. None of my guys are from the Seven Stars Mafia. Yiorgos belongs to an outfit based in Crete. They're all his crew.'

I stared at him, stumped.

'Albertos told me he was Seven Stars,' I objected, still trying to keep a grip on what I'd understood to be the truth.

'''Course he fucking did.'

Although, it was Kate who'd informed me first.

'Greek Intelligence were of the opinion it was the Seven Stars too,' I added, wincing as a bolt of sheet lightning ripped through the clouds directly overhead.

'That right?' Ricky replied, head angled to one side, as thunder rolled across the mountain.

'The woman who was shot – Kate. She told me.'

I didn't need his answer. I now understood that Albertos had simply played along with what Kate had mistakenly believed to be the truth.

Which begged the question as to how Kate and her colleagues had been so wrong.

Not that I could point fingers. It was I who'd insisted Kate bring Gerald's team in to work with her – which had ultimately brought about her death. One of many errors in a long line of mistakes; on both my part, and Greek Intelligence's.

What did it matter? It was all too late now.

'You won't get away with this,' I said quietly, staring into the hurricane lamp. 'Whatever you do to me, the police and coast-guard on Zakynthos will already be making investigations. As will the Greek Secret Service. They'll want payback for what happened to Kate. They'll get you in the end.'

'Whatever you say, chief.'

We sat for a moment in silence, as consecutives flashes of lightning threw ghostly shadows across the terrace.

'Bet you thought Takis was after Amara's inheritance, right?' Ricky eventually continued with a smirk. 'Along with Xander? That the two of them were in cahoots?'

I pushed back my chair and rose to my feet.

'If you're not going to tell me what the fuck we're doing here,' I said, taking a last pull on my beer, 'I think Max and I will turn in. Been a long day.'

'Sit down, you impolite prick,' he snapped, flicking his eyes to the CCTV camera above us. 'I'm telling a story.'

After a brief nod to the camera, he turned back and grinned.

I reconsidered, and lowered myself back down into the chair.

'Well, if you're gonna be quick about it,' I replied, reaching once more for my beer. 'Got to be on good form for—'

'As I was saying,' he continued, cutting me off, 'Takis had nothing to do with it. For the last six or seven years, he's been looking after my money. Laundering it. Investing it in this and that. Taking his cut. I told him if he didn't do what I asked of him, I'd anonymously dob him in to the cops. All that commission he's creamed off the top of many a dodgy investment ... that's a tidy prison sentence.' Ricky paused and picked at a nostril. 'Actually, to be fair to the guy – he took a little more persuading. When I told him that the coastguard would be picking bits of his body out of Athens harbour for the foreseeable future, he came on board. He's good like that. A team player.'

He turned and held my gaze.

'You made Takis persuade Xander to take the villa on Zakynthos when he got cold feet and backed out of the plan to kidnap Max?' I eventually replied.

'Spot on, detective,' he answered, clicking his finger in approval. 'Yiorgos is pretty persuasive usually. Charming, smooth motherfucker – you've met him right?' But Xander wasn't buying it.

I met Yiorgos?

'In Athens,' Ricky continued, holding my gaze. 'With Gerald.

'I met a guy called Stelios,' I said slowly. 'Works for Interpol. Well – that was his cover. He's Kate's boss in Greek Intelligence.'

'Ah, yes – one of his aliases,' said Ricky, batting away a mosquito from his face.

I stared at him, lost.

'I made Gerald give away the name of his old school friend in Greek Intelligence,' he continued, drawing his seat closer to mine. 'Who – yeah, you got it – goes by the name of Stelios. Yiorgos adopted the alias of Stelios to maintain credibility when Gerald introduced him to you at the hotel. In case you felt inclined to check the validity of a certain Stelios working for Greek Intelligence.'

Which explained why, at the Banana Beach Bar, Kate was puzzled when I told her I'd met Stelios with Gerald, claiming that Stelios had never mentioned the meeting to her.

Because Gerald's Stelios was in fact Yiorgos.

But then again, Kate mentioned she was going to challenge Stelios as to why she hadn't been kept in the loop. Had she decided against asking?

'How do you know Gerald wasn't feeding back everything to the real Stelios?'

'Because Gerald wanted to live,' Ricky shot back, stretching out his back.

I noted his use of the past tense.

'Is he still alive?'

'Enough of Gerald,' Ricky said, shifting in his seat to get comfortable. 'Now, you're wondering how I ever made it off that beach, eh? Or am I boring you?'

Knowing the question to be rhetorical, I waited for him to get on with it and turned my mind back to Besnik and his shotgun.

He'd disappeared with it and returned only moments later . . .

Which meant it had to be stored somewhere close to the front door.

In a locker – or cupboard?

Ricky remained silent for a moment.

'A bunch of tourists on a passing yacht heard the gunshots,' he said eventually, following the progress of a pair of tumbling bats on the hunt for insects that had taken wing, now the rain was over. 'They stopped by. Took me to a hospital on the mainland . . .'

He stubbed out his third cigarette into the porcelain bowl.

'They left Heinrich there?' I exclaimed. 'His sister, too?'

Ricky shook his head. 'The tourists never made it up to the villa. The Krauts' bodies must have been found a whole lot later by the dude that owned the other house.'

Heinrich's Italian film-star friend.

'But, hey – no more interruptions please,' Ricky objected, with a wink. 'It turned out the propeller blades missed an artery by a whisker, but it left some major tissue and nerve damage. Hence my dodgy leg. To be honest, like you probably did, I thought I was a gonner. Slipping in and out of consciousness while you and your bird were getting lovey-dovey on the beach.' He broke off and slapped at another mosquito, on his forearm. 'See? Here they come. Wankers.' Then paused. 'How is she by the way? Ellie?'

I shook my head, catching sight of the lizard tattoo on Ricky's neck.

'No idea,' I replied.

It seemed less striking, less potent than I'd remembered – poking out from under his t-shirt.

'She was a keeper,' Ricky said thoughtfully, eyeing the foraging bats as they returned to the terrace, swooping low above the hurricane lamps. 'I'd love to have shagged her.' He pulled a face. 'No wait – I did.'

I sipped in silence as he laughed at his own joke.

'Had to go through fuck-loads of surgery,' he eventually continued, clawing through the end of his ponytail with his fingers. 'In Barcelona at first. Stayed there for a year. Then moved to Munich in Germany for a while, before ending up on Crete doing some favours for a gang I'd made connections with in the '80s. Smuggling booze and drugs. You know – same old, same old.' He rose from the table and walked stiffly towards the wall. 'Sorry – my back. The morphine works wonders, but, sometimes you gotta keep moving, yeah?'

Approaching the wall, Ricky levered himself up and turned to face me.

Sitting on the wall?

Why had he done that?

I could rush him . . . right then and there.

'I know what you're thinking, Haston,' he said with a smile. 'But I wouldn't bank on it. Not with Elias standing by.'

He gestured with a lift of his chin, over my shoulder.

I spun around.

In the doorway stood a stocky, shaven-headed man in smart jeans, leather jacket and trainers, leaning causally up against the door frame.

I'd never heard him arrive.

Ricky must have signalled to him with that nod to the CCTV camera earlier.

Big brother is watching . . .

'Elias, this is Alistair Haston,' said Ricky politely. 'He's a

269

mate, but if he takes one step out of his chair you will please shoot him, won't you?'

Elias gave a single shake of his head.

Greek for 'yes'.

'Elias and Grigoris are in charge of security,' added Ricky, grinning. 'They run a tight ship.'

Grigoris was evidently manning the CCTV cameras in the control room.

'Do you always live like this?' I asked lightly, wondering how far we were from the nearest village. 'Live-in armed guards? Security cameras? An armed butler?'

'Besnik brought out that ol' shotgun relic, eh?' Ricky said with a chuckle. 'He takes it out hunting for pigeons. Never gets anything. But it helps keep away the nosey tourist or two, when they come knocking on the door.' He tugged at his ponytail and grinned. 'Elias is the one you want to watch out for. The trigger-happy fucker keeps an AK-47 under his bed – don't you, Elias? You're desperate to put it to good use.'

Elias gave a polite nod.

Stamping out his cigarette, Ricky pulled out the packet from his pocket and immediately lit a fresh one.

'Nah, I'm all for a quiet life, mate,' he continued. 'Time to spend what I've earned.' He glanced over at me with an air of wistfulness. 'I got these guys in when I knew you'd be coming to visit. You're a shifty fucker, you are.'

Refusing to be drawn, I kept my thoughts to myself and turned away.

Over the valley, the clouds had begun to peel away, revealing the moon in her lonely ascent. Off to the side of the villa, in the undergrowth, a chorus of crickets resumed their nightly serenade.

I was trying to remember how old Ricky was. Seven, eight years older than me?

Still, despite his physical affliction, he'd somehow retained the supremely youthful, panther-like quality I remembered from that ill-fated summer; a coiled spring ready to unleash itself in the blink of an eye.

'Now, where was I?' said Ricky finally, scratching at his chest through his t-shirt. 'Oh yeah. I kept having to nip to the mainland for surgery in Germany. Great country, by the way. All that work on my back done for free. Including the new tattoo ... Which you haven't seen yet, right?'

Leaning forward, he pulled his t-shirt up over his head, then twisted around to show me his back.

'Check this beauty out.'

It was a cobra.

The tail began out of sight somewhere below the waistline, with the body of the snake twisting up his back, over the scar tissue – not quite concealing it – and on up to the base of Ricky's neck, where the cobra's head loomed, mouth agape, fangs exposed in a display of aggression.

'They had to do a skin graft first,' he said, rolling the shirt back down. 'Took a strip of the stuff off my other leg – the good one. Then slapped it over the scar tissue. Sweet artwork, though eh?'

'Reminds me of an ex-girlfriend,' I replied, eyeing the cobra. 'After too much Pinot Grigio.'

'Anyone I might have shagged?' he shot back without missing a beat. 'Because, hey – you never know ...'

'Well, when it comes to swapping girlfriends ...'

'Careful matey,' he snapped, holding up a finger. 'Remember where you are.'

I took a sip of my drink and cast another glance at the CCTV camera.

The other guy – Grigoris – was no doubt manning the controls in Elias's absence.

'Got any tats?' continued Ricky, sucking at the dregs of his beer. 'Course you haven't. Philosophers don't have tattoos.'

I turned and caught Elias's eye.

'I'm just going to check on Max,' I said, rising slowly to my feet. 'He's been down there for ages.'

Elias frowned, glanced at Ricky.

Ricky held up his hand.

'Leave Max,' he murmured. 'He'll be fine.'

'That's alright,' I began, taking a step towards the doorway. 'I'm . . .'

'Sit down, you fuck,' snarled Ricky, eyes flashing.

I resumed my seat and picked up my beer.

Ricky eventually plucked a flower off the bougainvillea and sniffed at it. 'I was in Crete when Takis told me the news about you being Max's father. That's when I decided to put a team together and figure out a way of getting you and Max in the same place. And deliver you to me, of course.'

Polishing off his bottle, Ricky lobbed it over the wall behind him.

'Wait for it . . .' he said, cupping his hand to his ear.

A good few seconds later, the distant tinkling of shattering glass cut through the chorus of crickets.

'In a nutshell . . .' he continued, 'because, yeah, I know you're tired and all I've done is sit on my arse by the pool all day – which, by the way is a nice little number. Not too big, but it does the trick . . . got it overhauled and fitted with those blue and white mosaic tiles. Know the kind?'

He broke off, straining to identify the approaching footsteps emanating from within the villa, before pressing on.

'Anyway, when Takis told me of your kid, he also told me how Xander was treating Amara like shit. Gone bankrupt. Doing too many drugs. Figured I'd come up with a way of pretending to help the loser, that would, in turn, help me. And hey presto, here we are.'

Besnik appeared in the doorway carrying Max in his arms.

'He is sleeping, Mister Haston,' the old man murmured. 'I put him in his bed, yes?'

'We're all going to hit the sack, Bezzy,' said Ricky, rising unsteadily to his feet.

Besnik nodded and disappeared back inside carrying the boy.

'And in the morning?' I said, as the shuffling footsteps receded. 'Trip to the beach, is it?'

'Cheeky fucker,' replied Ricky, jabbing an admonishing finger at me.

'Or are you gonna drag me from my bed in the middle of the night and throw me over the wall – make it look like an accident?'

Ricky took a long pull on his cigarette.

'Not a bad idea,' he said thoughtfully, running a hand across his neck. 'Not a bad idea at all . . .'

Transfixed, I watched him lift himself off the wall and cross the sodden patio to the table, finally turning back to face me.

'But I've got something much more fun in mind.'

With that, he picked up his cane, tapped it decisively against the flagstones and made his way past me to the French windows.

'If you need anything during the night,' he added, turning over his shoulder, 'just wave at one of the cameras. The boys will be watching.'

20

At some point, I slipped into unconsciousness. For how long I was under, I had no clue, but I awoke with a start, dripping in sweat, with the cold certainty that a third person was in the room with me and Max.

Lying motionless under the sheets, staring straight up at the ceiling, I began to detect two sets of breathing coming from my right.

After a further minute, I inched my head over on the pillow until I was facing the venetian shutters, and, sure enough, through the blur of the mosquito netting, locked onto a silhouette materialising in the half-light: a figure huddled on the floor by the head of Max's bed.

Ricky.

Arms stretched out protectively over Max's shoulders . . .

Slow, regular breaths . . .

Fast asleep.

What the fuck was he doing?

How long had he been there?

But then, as my eyes gradually adjusted to the gloom, I realised I'd been mistaken.

It couldn't be Ricky. Too slight.

Besnik?

Slowly, I raised my arm and glanced at my watch, able to make out that it was just gone 7.15 a.m.; then, millimetre by millimetre, I made my way to the edge of the four-poster bed and slid onto to the Turkish carpet, pausing momentarily.

The figure stopped breathing and shifted to the right.

I hung there, suspended, one foot off the ground, until, confident he was still asleep, I continued my advance, creeping ever closer to the bed . . .

And then froze in my tracks.

There was now no mistaking . . . a cascade of hair falling onto the floor.

The emerging contours of a dress catching the diffused light.

It was a woman.

Surely, it couldn't . . .

Before I could complete the thought, the figure lurched up and away from Max and, stumbling swiftly to its feet, dealt a stinging slap across the side of my head.

'Jesus Christ!' I exclaimed, recoiling, slamming into a bed post. 'Amara! How the hell did you . . .?'

She slapped me again. Harder.

The blow caught me off my guard and I fell backwards onto the bed, before immediately sliding back off, ripping the mosquito netting as I crashed onto an exposed section of wooden flooring between the carpets.

Fists clenched, Amara ran around the bed and hurled herself on top of me, pinning me with her thighs before unleashing a flurry of punches.

'Bastard!' she spat, arms whirling their payload down on my head and chest. 'Fucking bastard!'

'You'll wake Max!' I exclaimed, arching my back off the floor in an attempt to move out of range.

Locked in adversarial embrace, we rolled back and forth across the floor until we slammed into the wall by the sink.

'Amara – stop, for Christ's sake!' I hissed, on top of her now. 'Let me talk!'

Dislodged from its footing, a candelabra tumbled from the shelf above, narrowly missing our heads. With a flailing arm, Amara tried to reach it, but it had been caught up in the bed-sheets and netting.

Thrusting down harder upon her with my hips, I quickly immobilised her, trapping her hands beneath mine.

'Amara – please!' I panted.

'Fuck you!' she shot back, her voice breaking.

And then a snuffle from across the room.

'Mommy?' groaned Max, stretching his arms above his head. *'Pou einai?'*

When he called out a second time, I hauled myself up with the help of a bed post and let Amara slide out from under me.

Tugging her dress into place, she stumbled over to the venetian windows, where Max was now upright on his bed, rubbing his tousled head.

'I'm still here, baby,' she gushed, throwing her arms around him. 'I'm not going anywhere.' Then she proceeded to mumble a stream of incomprehensible Greek into his ear.

Max eventually yawned, giggled, and promptly fell back to sleep.

I stood silently watching as the light in the room grew stronger, until finally Amara released her son back onto his pillow.

Backing up towards the four-poster bed, she dropped down onto the sheets.

'How could you?' she whispered, nursing her neck. 'Why?'

My ears still ringing from her blows, I cautiously approached.

'How did you get here?' I murmured. 'Albertos brought you?'

She lifted her head, the side of her face just visible in the gloom.

'They told me you have known all along,' she said, choking back tears. 'How could you do this to me? To Max?'

'Amara – slow down!'

I paused, to check that Max was still out cold, then sat down on the crumpled sheets beside her.

'Yes, it's true I knew about a plan to kidnap Max,' I continued, massaging my cheek. 'Xander's plan. Or so I believed at the time. I didn't tell you because I was trying to protect you . . .'

She reached out again to hit me, but I ducked out of the way and quickly crossed to the far side of the bed by the sink.

'Liar!' she spat. 'This was all your idea. Kidnapping Max. Trying to steal my inheritance money . . .'

'Amara,' I pleaded, steadying myself, 'I promise you, it's not true. I was brought in by the authorities to help try and stop the kidnap attempt. By the time I'd agreed to help, it was too late for me to tell you. I wanted to . . . of course I did. Every moment I had to lie to you was unbearable. But I did it to protect you both.'

'Protect us?'

'It's complicated,' I replied. 'But I'm telling you, I was set up. Whoever said it was my idea is trying to mess with your mind. To divide us . . .'

'To divide us?' she exclaimed, recoiling. 'You have already divided us. You divided me and Max. Xander is dead because of you . . .'

She broke off and sobbed silently into the crook of her elbow.

Her words echoed what Albertos had said on the plane, how I had been responsible for the break-up of her family . . . for Xander's death.

I cast my eyes to the mirror:

Perhaps Albertos was watching us right now, along with Elias and Ricky . . . Enjoying the denouement of Ricky's masterpiece.

Rounding the bed, I slowly sat down beside her once more and caressed her face.

'You know where we are, don't you?' I asked, shifting closer, until I could feel the touch of her thigh against mine. 'They told you who owns the villa?'

277

The last time Amara and I had sat together on a bed was in her father's house in Naxos.

Naked ... exhilarated ...

Flushed with post-coital afterglow.

She shook her head. 'An old man took me up to this room and said you and Max were sleeping here.'

Ricky was holding back his entrance onto the stage, for maximum impact.

'Why?' she continued, drawing herself closer; her warm breath meeting my mouth. 'Who lives here?'

Climbing up onto the bed, I turned back to face her, shuffling backwards until my back met the cool of the terracotta wall behind.

'Ricky,' I answered, holding her gaze.

For a moment, the room fell silent.

Just Max's rhythmic breathing from over by the window.

Amara twisted around and, hitching up her dress, climbed on to the bed to join me.

'Ricky?' she whispered, crawling towards me over the sheets.

'Everything that has happened is because of him,' I said, glancing over to the door. 'Luring me to Greece. Kidnapping me and Max ... and you. Killing Xander. Bringing us out here ...'

Through the window the whistling call of a swift heralded the break of day.

The nocturnal hunters had drawn back into the shadows to make room for the more brazen daylight predators.

'But ... Ricky is dead,' said Amara, a fingernail pulling at the corner of her lip.

I cast another look to Max as he rolled over onto his opposite side. 'Christ knows he should be.'

As the rising sun began to gild the tops of the conifers higher up the mountain slopes, I relayed the conversation I'd had with Ricky; explaining how he had been rescued by the tourists on

278

the yacht, and how he'd then convalesced in Spain and Germany over the next two years before heading to Crete to work with an organised crime group, smuggling alcohol and cigarettes.

'Although, it wasn't until he'd spoken to Takis,' I added, leaning forward and taking her hand, 'that he began planning his revenge.'

'Takis?' Huddled on the bed sheets before me, Amara's ashen face was now clearly visible in the early morning light. 'I don't understand.'

Drawn and pallid though her features were, she looked as exquisite as ever.

Keeping hold of her hand, I pushed off the wall and inched closer.

'Two years ago, just before your father died,' I continued, 'Ricky found out through Takis about Max being born ... about him being my son.' I paused, thinking I'd heard a noise on the landing below. 'Since then – yes. He's devoted every waking moment to engineering our capture.'

Hiking a fallen dress strap up onto her shoulder, she reached out her left arm and clasped the bed post.

'Takis knew all this time that Ricky was alive?'

I nodded. 'He has been looking after Ricky's finances all this time.'

'But he has been lying to me ... his own sister.'

'He didn't have a choice.'

She frowned. 'Because he was in love with Ricky?'

'No, because Ricky literally gave him no choice.'

'Ricky did all this?' Amara murmured. 'Because of you?'

I nodded.

I realised now that it almost certainly had been Takis who phoned me in London – except for none of the reasons I'd hitherto suspected.

Amara shivered and turned over her shoulder to look about the room.

'He's watching us now,' I whispered, gesturing over to the mirror by the door. 'If not him – his security guards.'

'How?'

'There'll be a camera behind the mirror,' I explained. 'There's CCTV all over the villa.'

Amara drew her knees up under her chin and turned back to gaze at her still-sleeping son. 'But I still don't understand,' she murmured. 'If Ricky wants revenge on you, why are Max and I here?'

I shook my head and gazed over to the window.

'I'm not sure,' I said, avoiding an outright lie. 'So far, all he has done is explain how he put his operation together.'

There was no telling what Ricky had in store for us, but I now understood all bets were off. This wasn't just about me. Ricky was looking to level the score on all accounts. Amara had betrayed him when she assisted in my bid to bring him down in '88. And then there was Max, guilty by association: the progeny of our alliance.

We were all going to be made to pay.

All of a sudden there came a thud from somewhere downstairs, followed swiftly by a second, more distant.

Someone was up.

Amara cleared her throat. 'And Xander?'

I held up a hand.

Whoever it was, it sounded like they'd gone outside.

Besnik, perhaps – to fetch breakfast supplies?

'Go, on,' I said finally, satisfied the coast was clear.

'Xander wasn't part of this?' Amara continued, brushing her hair from her face.

'He agreed to the kidnap operation,' I said, tearing my gaze from her lips. 'But he'd genuinely believed no harm would come to Max. When he got cold feet, and tried to get out of it, they wouldn't let him.'

'They?' she said, inclining her head.

At which point there came another clunk from the landings below.

For a moment, we held each other's gaze as the sound of footsteps receded away down the stairs . . .

Followed by yet another distant thud.

Was that Ricky?

The footfall sounded too brisk.

'Ricky's men,' I finally answered. 'Nothing to do with the Seven Stars Mafia. A handful of gangsters – hired hands he found in Crete.'

Amara said nothing.

'Did Albertos say anything to you on the plane?' I continued, 'about where you were going?'

'He didn't speak at all,' she mumbled, wiping her mouth with the back of her hand. 'It was the woman who did all the talking. The one who brought me here – to the villa.'

The woman?

'Alexandra?' I ventured. 'The one who met us at Varaxos?'

Amara gave a soft click of the tongue. 'The other one.'

I stared at her baffled.

'The woman whose sunglasses you picked up when we were in Gerakas,' she continued, furrowing her brow. 'The one who was shot.'

Shielding my eyes against the low-lying sun, I rounded a sprawling hibiscus shrub at the corner of the villa and drew up short on a gravel path leading to a terrace of similar proportions to the one where Ricky and I had sat last night. Sunk into the flagstones in the centre of the patio, a narrow ten-metre swimming pool reflected the dappled early morning light; complete with a diving board at one end, and a brace of stone gargoyles spouting arcs of bubbling water into the shallows.

A few feet away from a set of step ladders, Ricky was leaning forwards on his elbows at a small table under a sun umbrella, shirt off, in a pair of neon-red Bermuda trunks. Next to him, slowly stirring a cup of coffee, sat Kate.

Sporting a pair of sunglasses and dressed in a white bikini that accentuated a tanned, athletic physique, she remained motionless, save for the movement of her fingers turning the spoon; her mouth fixed in a faint smile.

'Always enjoyed a swim before breakkie,' said Ricky jovially, calling out across the patio. 'Later in the day, it gets too damn hot. Right, Bezza?'

Besnik, who had escorted me down from inside the villa, was stood to my left, hands clasped behind his back.

He remained mute.

'The others are still kipping?' added Ricky, pulling himself to his feet and stretching. 'Lazy sods.'

All I could do was stare, gobsmacked.

As Besnik ducked away and retreated back along the path towards the villa, Ricky approached and came in for the hug.

'Kate's a real find,' he murmured, embracing me tightly. 'Without her, none of this would have been possible. All thanks to our man, Yiorgos.'

Without letting me go, he pulled back and gave me a wink.

'And a tidy little arse, too.'

Arms limp by my side, I continued to gawp at Kate, as she rose from the table with her coffee cup in hand and made her way barefoot across the paving stones to the deep end of the pool, where, taking up position on the diving board, she sat side-saddle and lowered her legs into the water.

'Close your mouth, mate,' Ricky quipped. 'You're dribbling.'

Releasing his grip on me, he placed a hand on my shoulder.

'Kate tried to join the French Foreign Legion at eighteen, but they wouldn't allow it,' he continued. 'They've only ever once allowed a woman in their ranks – isn't that right, Kate?'

Running a hand through her peroxide hair, Kate removed her sunglasses and lifted her face up towards the sun.

'Susan Travers,' she answered, eyes closed. 'Assigned as a driver for the Free French Brigade in the Second World War – proved herself to be a bit of a hero. At the end of the war she applied to join the Foreign Legion. Didn't mention her sex on the application form, and they accepted her into their ranks. She was eventually sent to Vietnam during the First Indo-China War. By the end of her career, she'd earned the *Médaille Militaire*, the *Croix de Guerre*, and the *Légion d'honneur*.'

Then she slipped off the diving board and disappeared under water, before surfacing and swimming a length of breaststroke to the shallow end.

'Now, that's some badass fuckin' Sheila,' snorted Ricky, applauding.

Except it still didn't explain how Kate had survived the gunshot.

Or how a member of Greek Intelligence had ended up working for Ricky.

'But they wouldn't take on any more,' said Ricky, patting me on the back before moving off towards the edge of the pool; his tattoo glaring defiantly at me as he turned his back. 'Their loss, eh? Chauvinist pigs.'

I tore my eyes away from his leathery skin and scanned the immediate vicinity.

Off to my right, thick forest met with the villa perimeter; no sign of any path, or thoroughfare down the mountain. Directly in front, the patio extended some thirty feet until it met the stone wall and the drop down to the valley. To my left, the patio stretched approximately the same distance to the eastern limits of the villa, which, again, bordered with the dense coni-fers, spreading out across the mountain. A table . . . a few more scattered deckchairs and another pair of sunbeds . . .

No sign of Elias – or the elusive Grigoris.

As ever, Ricky knew exactly what I was thinking.

'Up on the side of the house,' he said, keeping his back to me. 'You'll spot it.'

Turning away from the pool, I spied two CCTV cameras mounted on the walls of the villa – one facing out over the patio, the other covering the approach around the side of the house.

Then a loud splash brought me back round to Ricky, who was now frog-kicking backwards across to the far side.

'And Greek Intelligence . . .?' I began, drifting towards Kate, who had swum back to the deep end and pulled herself out of the water, and was now sat sipping her coffee, eyeing me with an air of amused curiosity. 'I take it they don't know you're here.'

Ricky got in there first.

'You're hilarious, Haston,' he jeered, blowing water from his nose. 'Kate doesn't work for the fuckin' secret service. No more than the guys you met on Zakynthos worked for the police – or the coast guard.'

Turning away with a chuckle, Kate lowered her head and studied the reflections in the water.

'Whole thing was rigged, mate,' Ricky continued. 'Yiorgos hired Kate to put a team of misfits together that would be sure to dupe you.'

As a lone swift dive-bombed a column of insects hovering above the pool, I remained silent, digesting the information. For the last seventy-two hours, I'd been trying to identify the missing piece of the puzzle that would make sense of all the contradictions; and here it was, finally . . . standing opposite me in three feet of water, a spitting cobra etched into his spine.

Except . . .

'What about Xander?' I began. 'He's dropping by for a swim too, is he?'

Mounting the steps in the shallow end, Ricky dripped his way over to the table under the sun umbrella, picked up a pack of cigarettes and lit up. 'Ah – now, yes . . .' he began earnestly, turning back to face me. 'Sorry to say, that fucker is indeed dead. The boys aimed off, to give you guys a good scare – used blanks on Kate. But I'm afraid they popped a couple of live

284

rounds into the popstar. He deserved it, right? For trying to ransom kidnap his own fucking son. Jesus!'

Puffing out a smoke ring, he held up the packet. 'Smoke?'

'So, this is your revenge?' I said, turning my back on him and calling over to Kate. 'A reject mercenary, sticking two fingers up at the system?'

'Something like that,' she replied, languidly drawing one foot out of the water and resting her glistening leg on the diving board.

'Don't get any fancy ideas, Haston,' said Ricky, eyeballing me. 'Got to watch this one, Kate. He'll be on you like a rash, give him half a fuckin' second. Workin' that British charm.'

'I think I can cope,' Kate replied, flashing Ricky a brilliant smile.

'Mate, get your ass over here,' hollered Ricky, prizing his eyes away from Kate. 'Check out the view.'

It wasn't as if I had a choice.

Circling the pool around to the east side of the terrace, I joined Ricky at the wall, keeping several feet distant.

'Some chick, eh?' he murmured, glancing admiringly back at Kate. 'She's got a business head on her too. Gonna bring me in on a couple of projects she's cooking up on mainland Greece. Pity she can't stick around.'

Still salivating, he took a pull on his cigarette then swung around to face the valley.

'So ... what can I tell ya?' he continued, squinting against the sun. 'The nearest village is over ten kilometres away. A place called Fikardou, which – wait for it – translates as "den of thieves."' He grinned and licked his lips. 'An old medieval settlement. Pretty much deserted nowadays, apart from a few nosey tourists. You probably took the other road though, if you were coming up from the airport.'

Remaining silent, I stared out over the drop.

Dead ahead, the distant valley floor shimmered in the morning heat haze; a patchwork of sun-bleached scrubby terrain broken by the dark green splash of fruit plantations. Beyond that, a pale, grey-blue streak marked where the sea met the southern horizon.

'Worth every penny,' Ricky sighed, towelling his hair. 'Get the best views in the morning. In the arvo, it's too hazy. Now, don't look down, whatever you do ...'

Succumbing to a reflex response, I nonetheless peered over the edge.

It had been unnerving enough in the dark, but daylight left no room for doubt: after an initial fifteen to twenty feet of steep, scrubby incline, the chalky cliff dropped vertically away down to a dry riverbed, dizzyingly far below.

'Every man needs his own castle,' murmured Ricky, scanning the valley floor. 'They don't come much better than this. Or more secure, for that matter.'

I turned away and glanced over to the pool.

'And Kate?' I said, eyeing her as she gazed into the water. 'Let me guess – she's still under the impression this is a ransom kidnapping?'

'A good soldier doesn't ask questions,' he replied, with a wink. 'They just do what they're told.'

'That includes dressing up for you?' I shot back. 'Don't tell me she packed a bikini too, on this business trip?'

'I look after my guests – what can I say,' he replied, casting a lascivious glance in Kate's direction.

'So where are my swimming trunks then?' I said, also turning to Kate, who was now sat on the wall under the shade of the cypresses with her coffee. 'Or are you going to lend me a pair of yours?'

'Sorry mate – you'll have to make do,' he said, nudging me in the ribs. 'But don't worry, I got a surprise for you guys, for later.' He stepped in close and rested a hand on my shoulder. 'She wanted to go for a fuckin' onesie, but I persuaded her to take the bikini.'

286

'I guess you've still got it,' I said, resisting the urge to move away.

'Guess I do, matey. Guess I do.'

How much did Kate know about Ricky?

It was probable none of his mercenaries had any clue as to his real intentions, but someone like Kate would surely know what Ricky was capable of. The horrific events of the summer of '88 had been well documented in the press – and from the way she had played me on Zakynthos, she'd clearly done her research.

'Shame she's gotta shoot off,' continued Ricky, taking a final drag on his cigarette. 'She's a keeper, that one.'

Just then, a phone began to ring somewhere in the depths of the villa.

Extinguishing his cigarette between finger and thumb, Ricky flicked it over the wall.

'Got to be careful you don't start a bush fire,' he added wistfully. 'Dry as tinder, the Troodos mountains.'

As the phone continued to ring, a shout from behind heralded the arrival of Max stumbling along the path in his underwear, followed by Amara, clutching his Jurassic Park t-shirt and shorts.

'Max! Get your ass in the pool,' yelled Ricky. 'Amara – let me guess – you didn't bring a swimsuit either . . . shame on you.'

Amara stopped dead in her tracks and stared, transfixed, at her ex-boyfriend.

'But don't sweat, it guys,' he continued, approaching the edge of the pool. 'We're all family, here. Nude bathing absofuckinglutely permitted.'

'Don't say "fucking",' yelled Max gleefully, as he cannonballed into the water.

Inside the villa, the ringing ceased.

As Max swam towards Ricky and began to splash him, Kate drifted steadily across the terrace in my direction, all the while gazing admiringly out to the southern horizon and the sea.

'You've got balls,' she murmured, once she was in range. 'I'll give you that.'

For a moment, I thought I had misheard.

'Sorry?'

'Albertos told me about your offer,' she added, still without looking at me. 'Nice try.'

With that, she set off again, padding over to the south facing wall.

'Don't bother,' yelled Ricky, as he wrestled Max in the shallows, 'English charm ain't gonna work on a bird like Kate.'

Besnik arrived at speed from around the corner of the villa.

'Telephone call for you, mister Ricky,' he panted, bending forwards and leaning his hands on his knees. 'You take it, yes?'

'I'll be right up,' replied Ricky, dunking Max underwater before hauling himself out of the pool. 'Bring out a couple of towels and the collection of swimsuits we bought the other day, will ya? Amara's got nothing to wear. Oh, and two more coffees for me and Kate – we'll take 'em inside.'

Besnik nodded and spun briskly on his heels.

'Shall we?' continued Ricky, calling over to Kate as he took a towel off the table and dried himself off. 'Cooler in the villa – easier to think.'

Then he turned to me and lifted the cigarette pack off the table.

'Help yourself to these, matey,' he declared, lighting one for himself. 'Kate and I got shit to discuss. Grigoris will look after you.'

Behind Ricky, Besnik disappeared around the side of the building, replaced, in the same instant, by a new arrival – Grigoris, I presumed.

Ambling a few paces up the pathway, he came to a halt, pulled out a packet of Marlboros and lit up. In his late forties, with a thick crop of greying curly hair, leaner and craggier than the youthful-looking Elias, he, like the latter, was also sporting a weighty leather jacket . . . bulky enough to conceal a pistol.

'Any chance of breakfast?' purred Kate, approaching Ricky and laying a hand on his shoulder as she slipped on her trainers. 'I'm not getting back on the plane without a decent bloody meal.'

'You've got time?' said Ricky, turning to her with a lascivious grin. 'I'll get Besnik to whip up a little something.'

'And I expect a guided tour,' she added. 'Of your bachelor pad.'

'Well, naturally.' Pulling on his t-shirt, he slid an arm around her waist and ushered her in the direction of the footpath.

'Go on ahead,' he instructed. 'I won't be a minute.'

Then he reached under the table and produced a leather holdall.

'How about that?' he murmured, rummaging in the holdall. 'Kate's staying for breakkie.'

'Maybe we should leave you to it and get on our way,' I said, turning away in time to catch Kate glancing over her shoulder back at Ricky. 'Don't want to cramp your style.'

'No such luck, matey,' he said, fiddling with something at the bottom of his bag. 'Who says you can't mix business with pleasure?'

Watching Kate as she rounded the corner of the villa, clothes in one hand, towel in the other, I wondered if her flirtatiousness was born of genuine attraction, or innate business acumen – instinct telling her exactly how to play a man like Ricky.

More puzzling, though, was her jibe at my attempt to buy Albertos. Schadenfreude didn't seem her style.

A shout from the pool drew my attention back to the terrace.

On the opposite side of the pool, Amara hovered indecisively, staring over at me with a rabbit-in-the-headlights gaze. Off to my right, meanwhile, Grigoris had finished his cigarette and drawn back under the shade of the hibiscus trellis on the villa's western wall, gazing up at an aeroplane cruising high above the valley.

'Too cute, that kid,' mumbled Ricky through his cigarette, as he unzipped the holdall. 'Resilient little fucker, too.'

Then he pulled out a video camera and swung it in my direction.

'Smile, mate,' he said cheerfully, as a red light switched on by the lens. 'I'm recording.'

I stood rooted to the ground as Ricky crept closer.

My heart stuck in my chest . . .

A contraction in my gut, urging bile into my throat.

'I've got something much more fun in mind . . .'

There was only one reason Ricky would bring out such a contraption; the same reason he'd deployed a video camera in the summer of '88.

To make his snuff films . . .

Inches from my face, Ricky switched off the videorecorder and lowered the lens.

'They make 'em even better now,' he murmured, holding my gaze. 'Sharper picture. More depth of field. Translates like a beauty onto the bigger screen.'

'Do whatever you want with me,' I stammered, recoiling. 'But let Max and Amara go. They've done nothing to you . . . Max is a child, for Christ's sake.'

'Au contraire, my friend,' he grunted, blowing a smoke ring into my eyes. 'Children are the worst – they grow up to be cunts like you.' He broke off and frowned. 'But don't fret – the boy won't take part. You think I'm sick? You and Amara are my protagonists.' He lifted his chin and blew another column of smoke into my face. 'Don't worry, Max won't see a thing. He'll be dead by then, anyway.'

With that, Ricky turned and, switching on the camera, pointed it over at Max.

'Hey, Max!' he hollered, waving his free hand. 'Say something to camera.'

As Amara shot forwards to come between the camera and her son, Max joyfully blew a raspberry and dived back into the pool.

Oblivious to the horror soon to be unleashed.

Amara, meanwhile, had turned ghostly white. She knew all about the films Ricky made.

'Now, I know you're one for an itinerary – so here's the plan,' said Ricky, turning back and filming me once again. 'Kate and I are gonna talk business. Then we'll have some breakkie. Soon as we've waved her goodbye, the rest of us will gather together, for old time's sake . . .'

Switching off the recorder, he tapped his ash at my feet.

'And have ourselves a party.'

With a final grin, he sauntered off down the path, flicking his still-smouldering cigarette into the dry earth under the hibiscus, before disappearing out of sight.

Head reeling, I turned to face Amara; her pallid complexion signalling she too was under no illusion as to what fate awaited us. She may not have heard Ricky's declaration, but the presence of the video camera, along with my reaction, left no room for doubt.

And yet, as I stared dumbly across at both mother and son, digesting the full horror of Ricky's words, I was struck by a revelation of an entirely different nature: for the last twelve hours, the enforced separation of Amara from Max and me had allowed Ricky's entourage to maintain the advantage of leverage; we'd had no choice but to blindly toe the line for fear of repercussions to the other party. Now that we'd been brought together, however, an option was available that had hitherto been denied.

We could make a run for it.

21

Not quite, however.

Unable to talk openly in front of Max – with the surly Grigoris standing sentinel and Elias monitoring us on the CCTV cameras – there was no chance of conferring with Amara, let alone planning such an attempt.

Confined to the sweltering patio while Ricky conducted his affairs with Kate inside the villa, we were instead forced to maintain the same macabre façade of cheeriness that both we and our enemy had deployed over the last twelve hours in order to keep Max oblivious and compliant – albeit for different reasons. We played with the boy in the shallows of the pool, before heading every so often into the shade of the sun umbrella to sip from the water bottles Besnik delivered to the terrace shortly after Ricky made his exit.

As the temperature rocketed, I desperately tried to envisage a way forward.

It wasn't just a question of slipping through Ricky's security net and fleeing the confines of the villa. We then had to navigate swathes of steep, forested terrain and find a safe haven, all the while being pursued by hardened criminals, who, for the most part, were familiar with the region. Indeed, any attempt at a breakout, in daylight, as a threesome, would be tantamount to suicide. At night, we might face fairer odds, but that luxury wouldn't be afforded us. If Ricky's plan evolved unchecked, we would be dead long before darkness fell.

There was nothing else for it in the end, I realised, but to create a diversion which would allow Amara and Max to make a break for freedom as a pair. With enough of a head start, they stood a fighting chance of reaching a homestead, or farm, from which they could call the police. I would make my solo attempt after they had fled.

As to how and when I'd initiate said diversion, of course – not to mention how I hoped to extricate myself after the event – was another matter entirely.

At 10.05 a.m., almost an hour after Ricky had left us, Max declared he'd had enough of the pool and wished to go inside. For a start, he was hungry, and he also needed his baseball cap – mummy's fault for letting him out in the sun without protection. Furthermore, he was missing *Papi*, and, quite frankly, he felt we'd been in Cyprus long enough. He wanted to be back in Athens, playing with his dinosaurs in his bedroom.

Breaking away from Amara, he marched in his sodden underpants up to Grigoris, demanding to know where Uncle Ricky had disappeared to. Resorting to Greek, the bemused Grigoris grunted something at him and waved his cigarette in our direction – instructing him, no doubt, to return to his mother.

I spun on my heels and bore down on Amara.

'You've got to make a run for it,' I hissed, once I was in earshot. 'You and Max.'

She froze – her eyes wide with panic.

'Now?'

I shook my head. 'When I say.'

'But . . . how?' she whispered, her eyes darting over to Max. 'What about you?'

'Don't worry about me,' I replied, keeping an eye on our sentry. 'I'll find you.'

'Hey – come get the boy!' barked Grigoris, taking Max by the arm and steering him back across the patio. *'Ella! Grigora!'*

I put an arm around Amara's waist and turned to face the advancing Grigoris.

'When it's time,' I continued, murmuring out of the side of my mouth, 'you'll simply walk out the front door. Don't follow the road – stick to the forest. And don't go into the valley, they'll be expecting that. Make your way towards the summit, up as far as the tree line, then head around to the east before coming back down. Go to the first farm or house you find and call the police.'

'But . . .'

Amara was cut short by the arrival of an indignant Max.

'I don't like this man, he's mean,' he declared, rubbing his arm as he broke away from Grigoris's grip. 'Why can't we go inside?'

'Uncle Ricky has work to do,' I said, raising my voice so Grigoris would catch it. 'I'm sure he'll be out soon. Come on – let's see if we can find any lizards along the wall.'

'But I'm really hungry,' insisted Max, glowering at Grigoris who was stood only a few feet away now, his right hand tucked under his leather jacket.

Surely, he wasn't about to produce his gun?

'Stay in the shade,' I said to Amara, taking Max by the hand.

She remained immobile, fingers clawing at the hem of her dress.

'Haven't seen you catch a lizard yet,' I continued breezily, mussing Max's hair. 'I don't believe you can do it.'

Then I turned back to his mother and gave her a nod.

Stay calm. It's going to be okay.

Ignoring Max's protestations, I dragged him across the patio towards the terrace wall, hoping that Grigoris would no longer see any need to produce his weapon. If Max hadn't already cottoned-on that something was seriously wrong with the scene being played out before him, his catching sight of Grigoris's firearm would seal it. The chances of Amara making a break for it, let alone reaching safety with a hysterical five-year old in tow, would be zero.

'Look – there's one,' I whispered, letting go of Max and pointing to the corner of the patio, where a cascade of honeysuckle met the flagstones. 'What is that – a skink?'

At which point the throaty growl of a car engine, followed by a screech of brakes, silenced the chorus of cicadas in the surrounding pines.

'*Ti einai?*' asked Max, picking at his nose as he turned back to the pool.

'I'm not sure,' I said, throwing a look to Amara.

The slam of a car door was followed by a burst of raucous male laughter.

Moments later, as Grigoris backed away along the gravel path towards the sound, Ricky appeared around the corner of the villa, having changed out of his Bermudas into jeans, t-shirt and his trademark cowboy boots.

'Look lively, folks' he declared, pulling a cigarette out from behind his ear. 'We have a visitor.'

At which point, a second man stepped out from the shadows behind and drew up alongside Ricky under the hibiscus trellis; a swarthy wolf-of-a-man, with hollow cheekbones and greying slicked-back hair on his head.

'I believe no introductions are necessary,' continued Ricky, glancing first at Amara and then myself. 'Well – for two of you, at least.'

Catching my eye, the man gave a toothy grin and held up a hand in silent salute.

I froze, staring across the patio in disbelief.

Dressed in a light linen suit, stood a man whose acquaintance Amara and I had made on the island of Paros in '88. Sometime sous-chef at a local Parikia restaurant, he'd been Ricky's right-hand man, the villa's chief purveyor of alcohol and class-A drugs. The man responsible for ending the lives of numerous victims, executed on camera while engaging in the act of sex.

Ricky's Albanian assassin-for-hire.

Yannis.

'Oh, and the young lad is their son,' added Ricky brightly, turning to Yannis. 'Max.'

As Yannis licked his lips, Amara left the shade of the sun umbrella and crept across the terrace towards me and Max.

'Enough standing on ceremony, people!' concluded Ricky, throwing Grigoris a nod and clapping his hands together. 'Breakfast awaits.'

Under a triptych of Picassos, the antique oak table had been covered by a white tablecloth, along with a pair of candelabras and silver cutlery. An assortment of pastries, cheeses and cold meats was accompanied by various dishes of Greek salad, loukanika sausages and fried eggs, covering every inch of available space.

'Take a seat folks,' encouraged Ricky, with a sweep of his hand. 'Before Yannis scoffs the lot.'

Ricky had taken his place at the head, under the Picassos, with Kate on his right. She was now wearing a plain white t-shirt and jeans – the same clothes she'd worn when we left for the fishing trip on Zakynthos. Her new business partner had evidently stopped short of kitting her out with an entirely new wardrobe.

I took the empty seat to Kate's right – as directed by Ricky – a few feet away from Yannis, who had positioned himself at the opposite end of the table to Ricky. Amara was left no choice but to occupy the setting to the left of her ex-boyfriend, underneath a Grandfather clock that had apparently stopped working a minute before twelve.

Sitting Max down beside her, Amara quickly pulled in his chair so it touched hers.

'And here is coffee,' beamed Besnik proudly, sweeping into the room in a stained chef's pinafore before setting down a pot at each end of the table. 'Now you have everything, yes?'

Turning towards the French windows, I made a mental note of the geography of the furniture. I'd passed through the same room briefly the previous night, before moving to the balcony to talk with Ricky, but I had to remind myself of possible exit routes, as well as the position of the numerous CCTV cameras mounted on the wooden panelled walls ... where there might be a blind spot.

'You forgot the milk and sugar,' said Ricky, arching his eyebrows.

Besnik coughed. 'Ah yes – no problem. I fetch.'

As he walked the length of the table checking nothing else was amiss, my eyes lighted on his fellow countryman, arms behind his bony head, sucking on a cigarette.

Yannis should have served life several times over for his involvement in the horrors of '88, but his naming and shaming of the corrupt police officers within the Cyclades police force who'd colluded in the snuff film conspiracy had bought him a vastly reduced sentence.

'This should do the trick, eh?' Ricky continued, passing a plate of pastries to Kate. 'Can't have rumours spreading that I don't look after my guests.'

Kate nodded her appreciation, then twisted over her right shoulder and gave Besnik a smile. 'A wonderful spread. Thank you.'

'Is nothing,' he replied, blushing.

After pouring Kate a coffee, Besnik turned on his heels and made his way back to the door.

'And the rest of us, Bezza?' enquired Ricky.

'I get milk and sugar,' he answered, contrite.

'I'm sure we can help ourselves,' Kate offered, filling Ricky's cup as Besnik stalled in the doorway. 'Don't worry.'

Stepping to one side, Grigoris hustled Besnik through onto the landing before resuming his post as sentry.

'Think the old codger's got a soft spot for you,' said Ricky, tearing apart a croissant as he eyed Kate. 'But can you blame him?'

Kate flicked him a demure smile then glanced across the table at Max, who was helping himself to the loukanika sausages.

'I'm going to eat everything,' the boy announced with gusto, taking a bite of one of the sausages before scooping two fried eggs onto his plate.

His comment drew amused chuckles from Ricky and Yannis.

Distracted by the prospect of sustenance, Max had apparently forgotten his pressing desire to return to Athens. Not so, his mother: she was desperately trying to catch my eye, waiting for me to give her the nod – the command to flee the building.

She had every cause. We were rapidly running out of time.

I still hadn't the slightest clue what to do.

I'd wondered at first if we'd been brought to join in with breakfast merely to compound the narrative he was clearly spinning Kate – that we were merely houseguests until the kidnap ransom was paid – but I now understood it was out of practical necessity. It served to keep us contained in a controlled environment. Ricky also knew there was nothing I'd dare do, or say, in front of Max.

'Tuck in, everyone,' Ricky bellowed, helping himself to the cheese selection. 'Amara, don't hold back. Plenty to go around.'

Murmuring a muted 'thanks' – for Max's benefit – she eventually allowed herself a portion of Greek salad and a single slice of salami.

Only her son failed to notice her trembling hands.

'Not for me,' grumbled Yannis. 'Just coffee.'

He scraped his chair back from the table and twisted to his left, angling his sinewy torso towards the open French windows.

'And cigarettes, of course,' he added thoughtfully, reaching for his pack of Camels. 'This is my preferred breakfast.'

As Besnik re-entered the room with a jug of milk and a sugar bowl, Yannis reached out in front of Max and lifted up the plate of sausage and eggs.

'Come on, Mister Alistair,' he exclaimed, his tar-black eyes narrowing. 'We need to fatten you up. The food in England is terrible, yes?'

Ricky was leaning over his plate eagerly anticipating my come back, but I remained silent. Time for banter was over – I needed to think.

Better to play the defeated victim.

For now.

Yannis looked to Kate for corroboration, but she was concentrating on her plate.

Breaking the impasse, Ricky wished us all 'bon appetit' and began to regale Kate on the various tourist attractions that she should put on her 'to-do' list the next time she was in the country, including one of Cyprus's most famous landmarks – Aphrodite's rock.

'It's basically a sea-stack on a beach between Paphos and Limassol,' he explained, mopping up egg yolk with his thumb. 'The birthplace of the goddess Aphrodite – you know all about her, right, Haston? 'Course you do … Anyway, according to legend, Gaia – Mother Earth – asked one of her sons, Cronus, to mutilate his father, Uranus – who was God of the sky. Cronus was a shifty son-of-a-gun … cut off Uranus's nuts and threw 'em into the sea.'

He then went into further detail on how the locals believed the rock to be part of the lower body of Uranus; but I'd stopped listening.

I now knew exactly what kind of diversion I had to instigate:

A direct, physical attack.

Turning to my right, I glanced over at Grigoris by the door.

How, though?

And on whom?

Not Yannis. The brute would overpower me in a heartbeat.

If I attempted to tackle Ricky, Grigoris would almost certainly shoot me on the spot – to wound, if not to kill.

What about Grigoris, himself?

Say I went for his gun, it was likely Yannis would jump in to assist. Ricky, too – surely? Elias would be compelled to leave his monitors and come to Grigoris's defence – for his colleague's sake, if nothing else. And in the ensuing melee, Amara and Max would have the opportunity to make a break for freedom.

Yet there was still Besnik to factor in.

He'd stay downstairs, out of the way of any fracas . . . But that also meant he'd be on hand to intercept Amara and Max as they tried to leave the villa.

Then again, Besnik was an elderly man. They'd be able to outrun him.

Not if he were armed with his shotgun.

His shotgun . . .

'I don't understand the story, Uncle Ricky,' mumbled Max, his mouth full of sausage. 'What are Uranus's nuts?'

'His testicles,' clarified Ricky, with a spreading grin.

Max burst into laughter. 'You mustn't say "testicles" Uncle Ricky.'

'It's a perfectly decent word,' objected the latter. 'Right, Amara?'

Amara took advantage of the fact her mouth was full to avoid having to reply.

Ricky focussed back on Kate, in time to catch her checking her watch.

I'd forgotten to include her in my reckoning.

Instinct told me she'd probably hang back . . .

Although, as far as Kate was concerned, my instincts had let me down at every turn.

'Myth has it,' Ricky continued, wiping his mouth with a napkin, 'that anyone who swims around the Aphrodite Rock will be blessed with eternal beauty.'

Ricky cast a glance from Kate to Yannis and threw him a wink.

'But you have been there already, Kate?' said Yannis, tapping his ash into his coffee saucer. 'And you too, Amara.' He paused and grinned. 'Because you are both beautiful women . . .'

'Nope, never been,' said Kate, without looking at him.

Her dislike of our new visitor was becoming progressively more transparent.

Indeed, conversation had all but dried up between her and Ricky, the spark seemingly gone. Now her business meeting had been concluded, was she keen to get back on the road?

Back to Zakynthos, to tie up the loose ends; check that Xander's body had been properly disposed of . . .

Besnik arrived and suggested he clear away some plates so he could make room for the next course.

'There's more?' exclaimed Kate, puffing out her cheeks.

'*Dolmades*,' said Besnik. And then explained to her that they were vine leaves stuffed with rice.

Which Kate knew, of course – being half Greek.

'Sounds delicious – but I couldn't do any more,' she replied. 'In fact, I'll take another coffee, then get going.'

'Already?' exclaimed Ricky, unable to hide his disappointment.

'I imagine it'll take a while to get a taxi, up here,' she said brightly.

'Sod that,' Ricky replied. 'Bezza will give you a ride, once we've finished breakfast.'

Kate gave a dismissive wave of the hand. 'No need, seriously. Just call me a cab.'

'Bring up the next course and stick it on a side table, Bezza,' grunted Ricky, refilling Kate's cup. 'I'm sure she'll have room for a little something. We all will.'

As the old man shot back through the door and down to the kitchen, the penny dropped.

I knew exactly who my target would be.

Looking up across the table, I locked onto Amara.

'To be honest, I've got room for some dolmades,' I said, maintaining eye contact with her. 'When Besnik comes back, I say we get stuck in – don't you think, Max?'

The minute Besnik returned with the tray of food, I'd set on him.

'Huh?' said Max, wondering why I was talking to him, but looking at his mother.

I wouldn't hurt the old man, but I'd make it convincing. Enough to ensure the others dropped everything to assist him in his plight.

'We'll be ready, won't we?' I added, turning to Max. 'For Besnik and his dolmades?'

Being a soft target, I wouldn't have to fear physical harm from Besnik himself. As for Ricky's entourage, they'd hold off on using excess force on me unless directed to do so by Ricky himself – and of course, the latter was preserving me for his film. If Kate felt obliged to stick up for the kindly gentleman who had taken a shine to her, it would only add to the pandemonium, increasing Amara and Max's chances of making their getaway.

Max frowned and wrinkled his nose. 'I don't want dolmades. I want ice cream.'

When I cast my eyes back to Amara, she gave me an almost imperceptible nod.

We were on.

But then Max threw down his knife and fork:

'I need a pee pee, mommy,' he declared, clutching at his shorts. 'Can you come?'

For a moment, nobody moved.

Barely audible through the door came the slow ascent of weary steps.

Besnik was already on his way.

'You can wait, can't you, Max?' I said casually, taking a sip of coffee.

Next to me, Kate again checked her watch.

Ricky, meanwhile was eyeing me with an expression of amused curiosity.

'Don't stop the boy going for a piss, mate,' he objected, sweeping a hand through his hair before reaching for his cigarettes. 'When a man's gotta pee ... he's gotta pee.'

Max nodded vigorously and tugged on Amara's shoulder.

His mother was staring at me, transfixed.

'Maybe I should take him,' she offered, holding my gaze a beat longer, before turning to Ricky. 'Which is the best toilet to use?'

'Grigoris – you show 'em,' said Ricky, lighting up.

Through the door, Besnik's echoing footsteps grew louder.

'Well, off you go then,' said Ricky with a frown. 'Don't be pissing on the carpets.'

With a slow turn, Amara pulled Max to her side.

Steady ...

Not yet.

Wait for Besnik to enter the room.

But then Besnik's footsteps abruptly stopped.

He was on the landing below, taking a breather.

Kate drained her cup and stood up. 'Think I should probably make a move,' she announced casually, pushing back her chair and turning to an antique-looking telephone perched on a side table in the corner of the room. 'About that taxi ...'

'Seriously?' said Ricky, his voice plaintive.

Kate gave a rueful smile. 'If you don't mind.'

Ricky sighed and threw up his hands in mock indignation.

'Of course,' he conceded. 'But come and use the phone downstairs. We'll finish off our chat.'

As he rose from his chair, Besnik's footsteps resumed their ascent.

303

Amara clung tightly onto the wriggling Max's hand, her eyes locked on mine.

Any second now . . .

'*Ella,* mommy!' yelled Max, his free hand clutching at his crotch. 'I need to go.'

'Grigoris, take the boy for a piss, will ya,' snapped Ricky.

As the former set off towards Max and Amara, a noise outside the door heralded Besnik's arrival.

Ready to spring, I slowly eased myself out of my chair.

But then, as the door began to nose open, the telephone in the corner of the room burst into life.

For a moment, everything stopped.

As the phone continued to ring, the door eventually creaked to a close once more, followed by the sound of Besnik putting down a tray, or platter, on the landing floor.

'Shall I take it, Mister Ricky?' he called out, breathlessly.

'If you don't mind,' replied Ricky, throwing Kate a look of apology. Then added: 'Bloody phone doesn't ring for weeks, then I get two calls in one morning. Guess I'm Mister Popular, all of a sudden.'

When the ringing stopped, Ricky seized Max's free hand.

'Come with me, little one – I'll take you.'

'Thanks, Uncle Ricky,' said Max, beaming, one hand clasped to his crotch.

As Ricky led the boy across the carpet to the door, I hovered at the edge of my seat, one hand clutching the tablecloth, prevaricating as to what the fuck I should do next . . .

'Sit tight folks,' said Ricky, pulling open the heavy door and ushering Max through. 'I'll be right back.'

And with that, they were gone.

A silence descended upon the room.

Kate drifted over to the French windows and gazed out into the thickening heat haze building out over the valley plains, while Yannis helped himself to another cigarette and added yet more smoke to the billowing stratum being displaced by the slow-revolving fan overhead. Amara, meanwhile, had collapsed back into her chair and sat staring blankly at the plate of blackened sausages before her, her hands clasped tightly together on the table, as if in prayer.

As for myself, I stood, drained and defeated, one eye on the surly Grigoris, who had walked over to the door and planted himself before it.

Eventually, the sound of scampering feet from the landing was followed by the entrance of a grinning Max. When Amara leaped up from the table and rushed over to him, Ricky appeared in the doorway.

'Slight hitch in the proceedings, folks,' Ricky announced slowly, hands on hips. 'Grigoris – can I have a word?'

A hitch in the proceedings?

Jumping to attention, Grigoris followed Ricky out of the room and onto the landing.

'Can I play with my remote-control car now?' asked Max, pulling on Amara's dress and trying to head for the French windows. 'I don't want any more breakfast.'

'*Oxi, Maxi mou*,' said Amara, her voice breaking. 'Stay here. Please.'

Max frowned and looked up at his mother. 'Can I go and get it and bring it inside?' He whined, tugging once more on her dress. 'Mommy, what's wrong? It's just outside by the wall.'

Again, Amara shook her head.

'Mom?'

Kate backed away from the windows into the room and stood watching Grigoris at the door.

Now what?

'The boy wants to play – let him play,' growled Yannis, rising from his seat and stretching. 'He can't go far, no?'

'It's okay, Max,' said Amara, taking a deep breath. 'Everything is okay.'

And then Ricky re-entered the room.

'Sorry about that, Kate,' he muttered, as Grigoris followed him in. 'Come on downstairs – we'll get that cab booked. 'Oh, and Haston – Grigoris and Elias are going to take you guys on a quick guided tour while I finish up with Kate.'

Amara threw me a look of panic.

A guided tour?

Ricky nodded to Yannis. 'Chill out here – I'll be with you shortly.'

Yannis gave a puzzled frown, then nodded in consent.

What the fuck was going on?

'Kate – let's go,' said Ricky, beckoning her over. 'Got everything you need?'

Seemingly relieved to be leaving, Kate moved quickly across the carpet to the doorway.

For a split second, I considered taking on Grigoris, right then and there ... but I had no idea of Besnik's whereabouts. Or Elias's, for that matter.

I'd only get one chance ...

A better opportunity would present itself.

'Excellent,' said Ricky, rubbing at his neck as Kate passed by him and disappeared out onto the landing. 'Grigoris – I suggest you start with downstairs.'

A better opportunity was in no danger of presenting itself.

Escorted down three flights of stairs through the villa by Elias and Grigoris – both of whom were keeping a safe distance to allow the unhindered draw of a weapon – we were brought to the cast-iron door of the basement on the ground floor and instructed by the former to go on in and 'take a look around'.

'Come on, Mister Alistair,' said the oblivious Max, pushing

ahead once Grigoris had switched on the lights. 'I was here with Besnik, last night. We can play hide and seek.'

Knowing I was in no position to take on two armed men, I took hold of Amara by the arm and helped her down the crumbling stone steps into the increasingly cooler air, until we arrived at the bottom of a dank, low-ceilinged vault, where Max stood waiting, impatiently tapping his foot.

From behind us came the heavy thud of a closing door, followed by the metallic clang of a bolt being shot. A split-second later, Amara gave a muffled sob and collapsed onto the stone floor, pulling Max down on top of her as she burst into a fit of hysterics.

Terrified by his mother's cries, Max, in turn, began to howl, staring up at me with wide imploring eyes; one hand clutching at his matted hair as he struggled to free himself of Amara's desperate pawing.

But I'd been paralysed by the sight of what lay beyond them:

Further along the vault, on the edge of the pool of light cast from a single overhanging bulb, a pair of tall angle-poise lamps had been set up on either side of an old mattress lying on a bed of plastic sheeting. Off to one side, set back in the shadows of a crumbling brick-wall alcove, a camera tripod stood at the ready.

Ricky's film set.

22

A strangled cry shook me from my stupor.

Turning back to Amara and Max writhing on the floor, I dropped to my knees and thrust an arm into the tangle of limbs in an attempt to free the boy from his distraught mother's grasp.

Unleashing a volley of Greek profanities, Amara smashed an elbow into my face.

'Let him go!' I yelled, tucking my chin into my chest to avoid a further strike as blood gushed from my nostrils onto Max's t-shirt. 'You're choking him!'

In the confusion, Max sided with Amara, pummelling his balled fists down on my back.

'Both of you – STOP!'

With a backhand swipe of my right arm, I lifted the blood-spattered Max off the ground, separating him from his mother and sending him spinning across the concrete floor into the wall.

'Don't hurt him!' Amara screamed, swinging a kick at my jaw. 'Bastard!'

I ducked, seized her ankle and flipped her over, pinning her arms behind her back.

'For God's sake, Amara!' I panted, rearranging her dress which had hitched up around her waist. 'I'm on your side.'

Craning her neck up off the floor, she caught sight of her terrified son cowering against the brick wall and, after a guttural moan, went limp beneath me.

'Just breathe,' I continued, stemming the flow of blood from my nose as I rose to my feet and stepped off her. 'We're going to get out of here . . .'

'I want to go home,' whimpered Max, rushing forwards and clinging onto his mother's arm, as she too dragged herself up off the concrete. 'Please, mommy.'

Cradling Max into her bosom, Amara turned away from me. Which was when she saw the mattress.

'Don't,' I warned, lunging forward and taking her by the shoulder.

Shrugging me off, she took a step further down the vault.

'Why is there a bed on the floor,' sniffed Max, slipping from his mother's grasp. 'It wasn't there yesterday.'

Stifling a cry, Amara teetered back on her heels, fingers clawing at her hair.

'No, Alistair . . . no, no, no, no . . .' she whispered, staggering sideways and crashing into the camera tripod. 'Oh, God . . . please – no!'

'Mommy!' cried Max, choking back fresh tears. 'You're scaring me.'

'Shut up – both of you!' I snapped, rounding on Amara and seizing her by the wrist. 'We're going to get—'

The clamour of footsteps from above stopped me in my tracks.

Voices.

A muffled shout . . .

Followed by the sound of a car starting up and driving away from the villa.

Then silence.

Kate had left. Ricky would soon be on his way down.

'Back up the steps,' I hissed. 'Now!'

Seizing them both by the hand, I dragged them back up the stairwell towards the rusting iron door.

'Any moment,' I panted, 'that door's going to open. The second it does, I'm going to slam it into whoever's on the other side and throw myself at them. Soon as I do so, you and Max will run – as fast as you can – out the front door and into the forest.'

'You mean – like cops and robbers?' asked Max, wiping his snotty nose on his arm.

'Exactly like that.'

Hauling them onto the step below me, I pushed them back against the wall.

'They'll approach as a pair,' I continued, lowering my voice and twisting sideways on my haunches to maintain eye contact. 'One covering the other, at a safe distance. Being on this side of the door, here, where the hinge is, will give you more cover . . . when it opens.'

'Cover?' sniffed Max.

From gunfire.

I shot a look to Amara.

'It will hide you from the robbers.'

Initially, at least.

After that, they'd need a human shield.

'We'll hear them crossing the hallway,' I continued in a whisper. 'The second that bolt slides back, we go into action.'

As mother and son nodded in unison, there came a muffled thud from the landing above.

Footsteps, slowly descending the spiral stairs.

One person, or two . . .?

The echo made it hard to tell.

'Remember,' I murmured, reaching out an arm to steady the quivering Max. 'Go straight for the front door of the villa. Run. Don't look back.'

Behind him, Amara stifled a tiny sob.

Carefully placing both hands on the rusting door, I closed my eyes and tried to empty my brain ...

I could hear the rush of blood pounding in my ears; Amara and Max's erratic breathing reverberating in the stairwell behind me ...

Don't think.

Just react.

Then a faint creak off to the right.

A floorboard?

Not in the hallway – it was all stone paving.

'He's coming,' I murmured, eyes now open, watching the door. 'Any moment now ...'

Except, Ricky didn't come. No one came.

As we huddled together in the foetid stairwell, sweating, breathless and terrified, waiting for the bolt to be thrown, it became clear our malevolent host was biding his time.

Confined to two square metres – our only hope of survival being to remain right by the door where we retained a modicum of initiative – Amara and Max gradually succumbed first to listlessness and then exhaustion, drifting off into fitful slumber, slumped against the wall, limbs twitching from the spent adrenaline. The only time any of us shifted position was in order to relieve ourselves; pissing down the stone steps, our urine combining in a pool at the foot of the stairs.

Minutes turned into hours.

All the while, I strove to remain primed, willing away the searing cramps in my legs as I tried to second-guess what was happening on the other side of the steel partition, visualising how the scenario would play out when the moment came.

Grigoris or Elias would open the door ... I'd slam it into him ... catch him off guard and wind him. Then I'd go for his gun, turn it on him and pull the trigger ... Five shots left. Two

rounds to cover Amara and Max's flight to the front door . . .
Followed by two more – to allow them to get out and into the
forest. Then I'd make a run for the store room . . . Fetch Besnik's
shotgun . . .

Still Ricky didn't come.

Two hours turned into four.

Then six . . .

Finally, approaching 7.40 p.m., after nearly eight mind-
bending hours in the stinking stairwell, Amara announced she'd
had enough.

Staggering to her feet, she seized the wilting Max by the hand
and dragged him down the steps through the puddles of piss
and shit, declaring she was going to find another door in the
basement, or 'smash her way through the fucking wall.'

Caught unawares, I set off after her, barrelling down the
staircase as Max's cries ricocheted around the cavernous
cellar walls.

'Get back here!' I hissed, slipping in the congealed excrement.
'Our only chance is to stay by the door . . . Amara!'

Rounding the corner, I saw her and Max beyond the film
set – approaching a pile of packing boxes set into one of
the alcoves.

'There's no door, mommy!' cried Max, as Amara pushed him
back onto the mattress and ploughed into the stack, evidently
in a bid to search for a concealed entrance in the wall behind.
'Only bottles and boxes.'

'Amara!' I yelled, knocking over one of the lamps as I rushed
towards her. 'For Christ's sake get back to the steps—'

And then it came . . .

The unmistakeable sound of a bolt being shot.

The creak of steel.

'Get your arse up here, Haston,' came Ricky's voice, echoing
through the basement.

Amara froze, her arms wrapped around a cardboard box.

I reached out and grabbed hold of Max.

'Just you,' Ricky added, descending a couple of steps before stopping once more.

Both mother and son were now staring helplessly at me.

But what could I do? We'd lost the only initiative we'd had – the element of surprise.

'If I see a hair of Amara or the boy,' Ricky declared, clearing his throat, 'they'll get a bullet in the knee cap. Then I'll send down Yannis. You know what that fucker's like when he gets a whiff of blood. Just makes him hornier.'

Ascending the piss-soaked steps, I emerged at the top of the stairwell to find Ricky, cigarette in hand, stood ten feet back from the entrance of the basement, lit by a pool of orange light from the industrial lamp overhead.

Flanking him on his right, a few feet away from the front entrance to the villa was Grigoris; legs spread, pistol trained at my chest.

'Had a fight with the missus?' Ricky exclaimed admiring the blood on my shirt. 'Without waiting for us?'

Heart racing, I scanned the hallway, gauging the distance to the front door.

Where was Elias?

'So, yeah – the party's been pushed back,' Ricky continued, taking in a lungful of smoke. 'We got business to discuss.'

A scuffling noise from the stairwell caused Grigoris to drift wider, training his pistol at the opening behind my head.

'Get back!' I bellowed, calling out to Amara and Max. 'Stay down!'

'Wise words,' said Ricky, retreating a couple of paces. 'We don't want Yannis to get a head start on the festivities. There'll be nothing left for the rest of us.'

A flicker of light through the windows was followed seconds later by a distant rumble.

'Another storm on the way,' murmured Ricky, eyeballing me. 'Guess the last one didn't clear the air.'

Outside it was almost dark.

Ordinarily at this hour, even after sunset, there'd be an hour of residual daylight.

Not tonight. The sky had been blackened by gathering thunderheads.

'Business?' I exclaimed, scanning the dim hallway for a potential weapon. 'What kind of business?'

Then I lighted on the archway entrance to the storeroom.

Besnik's shotgun.

It had to be in there. Yesterday evening when Max and I arrived, our butler had disappeared through the front door and returned empty-handed almost instantaneously.

'You know damn well,' Ricky said, with a spreading grin.

Then he turned to his left and called out towards the kitchen.

'Get out here and lock the basement door, Bezza,' he instructed. 'And stay there until I tell you otherwise. *Endaxi?*'

'Yes, Mister Ricky,' grunted Besnik, emerging through the swing doors to the kitchen and hurrying over the flagstones.

'Haston,' snapped Ricky. 'Three steps forwards.'

As I put yet further distance between myself and Amara and Max, Besnik slid in silently behind me, slammed shut the steel door to the basement and slid the bolt back into place.

Through the windows, the forest was briefly illuminated by another burst of lightning.

For a moment, I caught the sound of muffled sobbing through the basement door, but it was quickly drowned out by a crackle of thunder.

'And the front door?' asked Besnik, casting a glance at Ricky before crossing over the flagstones to inspect the catch. 'I lock it?'

Ricky nodded. 'And keep it locked. When Elias is on his way back, he'll radio ahead.'

314

On his way back?

'He's a couple of clicks down the road,' said Ricky, clocking my confusion. 'Keeping an eye on things.'

What the hell did that mean?

To my left, Besnik produced a set of ancient keys, then locked and bolted the heavy oak door. 'Is done,' he said, standing to attention.

'Good job, Bezza,' said Ricky, sucking on his cigarette. 'Now stay here and don't fucking move, eh?'

Sidling back to the basement door, Besnik took up his post, his breathing shallow and erratic. Ricky then turned unsteadily on his heels, clicked his fingers in the direction of Grigoris and stumbled over to the spiral staircase.

'Go up to the second floor,' he muttered, drawing up short at the foot of the stairs. 'We'll be right behind ya.'

I hesitated a moment, wondering if I should make a run for the kitchen, find a knife – a frying pan – anything sturdy or sharp.

A split second later, I received a boot to my left hip and crumpled to the floor.

'*Tora!*' bellowed Grigoris,' springing backwards into a firing stance. 'Up the stairs!'

'Second floor,' repeated Ricky, casually leaning back on the wooden bannister. 'A door with a stained-glass window. Go straight on through.'

One hand clutching at my throbbing hip bone, I picked myself up off the floor, crossed the hallway and, passing Ricky to his right, slowly ascended the twisting staircase.

Behind me, Grigoris maintained his distance, the pistol pointed at my back.

But Ricky had disappeared.

Fearing I'd been duped – that he, Grigoris and Yannis were about to set upon Amara and Max in the basement – I spun on my heels, peering back down to the ground floor.

Which was when I heard the buzz and whine of an electric motor.

Ricky was taking the elevator.

Because of his back pain.

'*Ella!*' said Grigoris, cocking his pistol. 'Keep walking.'

I continued my climb, reaching the second floor at the same time as a mechanical clunk from the far end of the landing heralded Ricky's arrival.

Sliding open two sets of manual doors, he emerged from the elevator, walking stick in hand, and set off towards me, stubbing out his cigarette in an empty vase before reaching into his pocket and producing his bottle of tablets.

'It's that time of day,' he mumbled, leaning against the wooden panelling in order to pop a pill. 'Back starts to play up. But these little beauties sort it out. God bless fuckin' morphine, eh, Grigoris?'

Grigoris grunted his affirmation.

Ricky's walking stick was evidently to fill the gaps between doses of opiates.

'Well – what you waiting for?' said Ricky, setting off once more towards me as a bass thunderclap shook the villa. '*Mi casa, es su casa.*'

Turning over my right shoulder, I came face to face with an arched door fitted with a blue and red stained-glass window.

'Pretty, ain't it?' murmured Ricky, resting a moment against the wall. 'It's like they couldn't decide between building a hotel or a church.'

'Inside!' snapped Grigoris from behind.

'As the man says,' added Ricky, waving his cane.

Twisting the knob, I swung open the door.

The room was similar to the one above, where we'd had breakfast. But there was no large centrepiece table; just a series of leather chairs, surrounding an oversized TV set by the left-hand wall, bookended by a row of crammed bookshelves and a floor-to-ceiling rack of CDs and videocassettes.

Ricky's lair.

316

Off to my left was a second archway into a smaller room, separated not by a door, but an oriental-style bead curtain; Ricky's bedroom, I presumed. Directly opposite me, alongside the windows, a cuboid office had been constructed, made entirely of glass. Inside was a Formica desk, a pair of swivel chairs and a row of TV monitors. Elias and Grigoris's control centre.

My eye was caught by a movement over to my right.

A few feet away from an unlit open fireplace, Yannis was sat on the edge of a wicker chair, hunched forward over a low-slung coffee table; a foot-long hunting knife in his right hand.

'Is a nice place, no?' said Yannis with a leering grin. '*Very cosy* – is that how you say?'

But I'd stopped listening.

Opposite Yannis, pressed back into a high-backed leather armchair to the left of the fireplace, sat Kate; legs crossed, hands folded demurely in her lap.

I stared at her, dumbfounded, as a stab of lightning illuminated the lowering sky over the valley, followed moments later by a prolonged thunderclap.

'Kate has decided to stay for dinner,' Yannis growled, enjoying my confusion. 'Besnik is a fine chef. Almost as good as me – yes, Ricky?'

Lighting a fresh cigarette, Ricky grunted and, positioning himself on the arm of one of the leather armchairs, blew out a column of smoke.

'No need to stand on ceremony,' he declared, gesturing to a second wicker chair on Kate's left. 'Pull up a seat.'

Thoughts racing, I moved away from the gun-wielding Grigoris and sat down opposite.

All the while, Kate fixed me with a look of amused disdain.

'We felt this might be a good moment to clear the air,' Ricky continued, tapping his cigarette into an ashtray on the side table next to his chair. 'Straighten out a few facts.'

We?

I cast my eyes from Yannis to Kate, still utterly perplexed.

Relaxing into his seat with a chuckle, Yannis ran his forefinger up and down the blunt edge of his knife.

Grigoris, meanwhile, moved back to the doorway, gun at the ready.

Rising once more, Ricky drifted towards an opened window and began to toy with his Zippo lighter. 'Understandably, Kate's a little miffed at having been detained,' he announced, clearing his throat. 'So, the sooner we get this sorted, the sooner she can get back on the road.'

Kate threw him a smile. 'I'd appreciate that.'

Her delivery was measured, but the sweat beading below her peroxide fringe suggested otherwise.

Kate had been in the villa all this time?

Doing what?

Then Ricky reached into his pocket and, turning back to face me, produced a metallic object between his finger and thumb – about the size of a one pence piece.

'Know what this is?' he said, holding it up to the light.

I twisted further around in my chair.

'Are you asking me?'

'Yes, dickhead. I'm asking you.'

I frowned, cast a glance to Yannis.

'I have no idea.'

'Kate?'

Smoothing a hand down her jeans, Kate uncrossed her legs.

'You've never seen one before?' she murmured, her ice-blue eyes glinting in the lamplight.

Ricky grinned. 'Just tell me what you think this is.'

'It's a tracking device,' said Kate with a shrug.

'Bingo,' said Ricky. 'A tracking device.'

He tossed his packet of Marlboros onto the coffee table.

'Help yourself,' he continued, picking up his cane and tapping his way over to the rack of CDs on the left-hand wall.

Kate reached for the pack and took out a cigarette.

Producing a box of matches, Yannis leaned forwards over the table and lit it.

Was it my imagination, or were her fingers trembling?

'So, here's the thing, Haston . . .'

Ricky turned and rapped his cane on the floorboards.

'Early this morning,' he began, 'I get a phone call from Yiorgos to say the driver who picked you up at Larnaca airport found this little chappie under the back seat. Can you explain it?'

Baffled, I shook my head. 'Nothing to do with me.'

Ricky gave a thoughtful nod.

'That's what I told Yiorgos,' he continued. 'What the fuck would Haston be doing with a tracking device? He wouldn't know where to get one from, let alone how to use it. And more to the point, who's supposed to be monitoring the thing? Albertos got back on the plane and set off for Varaxos to pick up his next contingent – Amara and Kate.'

A sustained flicker of lightning was followed by a throaty growl of thunder; from behind the villa this time, up on the mountainside.

The storm was closing in.

'I didn't believe him, to be honest,' Ricky continued. 'But the driver dropped it off this morning when he brought Yannis. And sure enough, here it is.' He averted his eyes and turned to Kate. 'But then I realised – stupid me – that it was of course the same driver who picked up you and Amara from the airport. So, I'm thinking . . . I can't see Amara mucking around with gadgets like these, especially as she hadn't the slightest idea what the hell she'd got herself into – let alone the fact she'd making a trip to Cyprus. Which led me to wonder if this has anything to do with you?'

Kate smiled. 'Why would I need a tracking device?'

'Good question,' said Ricky, returning her smile. 'Let me answer that with another. Where is Albertos?'

Kate frowned and flicked her ash into the fire grate.

'I have absolutely no idea,' she replied. 'Why?'

'*Why?*' repeated Ricky, plucking a protruding CD from off the rack. 'Because at breakfast, I get another call from Yiorgos,' Ricky murmured, opening the case and wiping the disc on his t-shirt. 'This time, he tells me that when the plane touched down on Varaxos after having dropped you and Amara off in Cyprus, Albertos wasn't on it.'

Snapping the CD back into its cover, he slid it back into its position on the shelf.

'So, either Albertos jumped out of the plane, somewhere out in the middle of the Mediterranean,' Ricky mused, tapping his way back over to the ashtray on the side table, 'or he stayed here in Cyprus. Begging the question – why the fuck would he do that?'

'Is that why you locked me up in that fish tank for eight fucking hours?' Kate exclaimed, nodding in the direction of Elias and Grigoris's office. 'Why would I know Albertos's whereabouts?'

Ricky pursed his lips. 'You're his partner.'

'His job was done,' Kate retorted. 'After four consecutive flights, back and forth from Greece to Cyprus without a break, he probably checked into a hotel for a decent night's sleep.'

'Perhaps. But he should have told you.'

Kate gave a dismissive snort. 'Albertos is a grown man. He can do what he likes.'

'How will he get back to Greece?'

'I'm not his travel agent.'

Ricky suppressed a laugh. 'He didn't tell Yiorgos he was signing off?'

'Again – you're saying this like it's my responsibility.'

'You're a professional,' Ricky objected. 'You should have checked in with him.'

Dispensing with his walking stick, Ricky drifted over towards an open window overlooking the terrace.

The morphine had finally kicked in.

'You put the bug in the car,' Ricky intoned, staring out into the elements. 'So that Albertos could track you to the villa.'

A prolonged flash of lighting was followed by a resounding crack directly overhead.

'Are you serious?' objected Kate, raising her voice above the thunder.

Ricky snapped the window shut, muting the storm.

'Not sure why you're so affronted,' he added. 'You may have had good reason.'

'I had no reason,' Kate objected. 'Because it isn't true.'

Turning on his heels, Ricky approached the coffee table.

Re-crossing her legs, Kate studied him for a moment.

'First of all, I had no idea Albertos was going to be staying in Cyprus,' she eventually continued, running a hand through her hair. 'More to the point – why the hell would Albertos need to keep tabs on us? You think he was worried Amara might have been able to overpower me?'

Ricky puckered his lips. 'I'd say that's highly unlikely.'

'Exactly,' said Kate.

'But that wasn't my point,' he shot back. 'I said he wanted to know how to get to the villa.'

'Why?'

'You tell me.'

Kate gave him a puzzled frown. 'I'm not sure I like where this is going.'

'I didn't say it was going anywhere,' said Ricky. 'Methinks the lady doth protest too much.'

'You've lost me,' snorted Kate.

Ricky flicked Yannis a nod.

Jumping to attention, Yannis ceased his toying with the knife and sat up in his chair.

'I'll cut to the chase, shall I?'

Kate checked her watch. 'If you don't mind.'

Crossing to the side table, Ricky stubbed out his cigarette and, after a leisurely stretch, placed his hands on his hips and turned back to face us.

'I reckon that Haston, opportunistic little fucker that he is, persuaded Albertos to do a deal,' he intoned. 'For a fuck load of cash. Well – ten million dollars, to be precise.'

The first fat drops of rain smacked against the windowpanes.

'And you're in on it too,' Ricky added. 'To free Haston and the others in exchange for Amara's inheritance.'

Kate stared at him, her brow furrowed.

'You think I tried to ... turn Albertos?' I protested, jumping in. 'That's preposterous.'

But the penny had dropped.

Kate's comment at the poolside about my attempt to bribe Albertos – not only had it been out of character, she'd made the remark out of Ricky's earshot.

'Preposterous, indeed,' replied the latter, eyeballing me. 'But the truth.'

Her flirting with Ricky, the offer of a business partner-ship – it was a ruse to allow her time to scope the layout of the villa ...

'That's what you're thinking?' exclaimed Kate, bursting into laughter. 'You've got to be fucking kidding.'

Albertos had rejected my offer. Kate had changed his mind.

Ricky shook his head. 'You betrayed me.'

But they'd been rumbled.

Which is why Elias is stationed down the road ... to keep an eye out for Albertos.

'They told me you were paranoid,' Kate muttered, flicking her ash into the fireplace. 'But this is ridiculous.'

Ricky turned to me. 'Who else agreed to do this?'

Outside, the rain began to fall in earnest; a menacing hiss of static cutting through the now-constant rumble of thunder.

'Do what?' I protested, wiping away the sweat beading on

322

my forehead. 'I wasn't in a position to do any deal with anyone. This is bullshit.'

Ricky's eyes darted back to Kate. 'Just you and Albertos, eh?

'You on medication?' Kate added. 'For your back?'

'Nice try.'

She shook her head. 'And you wanted to go into business with me . . .'

'Enough foreplay,' snapped Ricky, stubbing out his cigarette. 'Let's move this to the floor above.'

Kate stood up and slowly backed up towards the fire grate.

'Thanks, but I've seen enough of your pad,' she said, smiling. 'I'm gonna get on my way. If you're lucky, I won't tell Yiorgos what a prick you've been.'

Yannis, too had backed off and was stood shoulder to shoulder with Grigoris, knife at the ready.

Ricky grinned. 'You think I give a fuck about Yiorgos?'

Yannis burst into laughter.

'No – we gotta be careful, Yannis,' jeered Ricky. 'French Foreign Legion material, this chick.'

Yannis cocked his head, studying Kate's legs. 'Yes, she's got a pair of balls on her. Maybe she should join the party?'

'That's not a bad idea,' murmured Ricky. 'But I say we give her the benefit of the doubt.'

Kate stepped around the table, her eyes darting between Ricky and the knife-wielding Yannis.

'You say you're on my side?' Ricky continued, smiling at Kate. 'I'm going to give you a chance to prove it.'

23

Marched at gunpoint up to the sitting room where we'd had breakfast, Kate and I were ordered out onto the terrace, into the storm.

'Sorry about the weather!' Ricky hollered, shielding his eyes from the gusting rain. 'But it's gonna look great on film.'

As Grigoris backed Kate past the table along to the east end of the patio, Ricky produced his video camera and wiped the lens, before taking up position at the French windows.

'A sweet little trailer,' he crowed. 'Before the main feature.'

Edging away from the knife-wielding Yannis behind me, I threw a glance along the terrace to Kate.

'For fuck's sake, Ricky!' I yelled. 'Let's sit down and talk.'

'No can do, mate,' said Ricky, twisting the lens. 'I'm just the camera man.'

Then he swung the video recorder towards Kate.

Soaked to the bone, Kate stood calmly with her hands limp at her side, peering through the rain at Yannis.

'So, you wanna prove your loyalty?' Ricky began, switching on the camera as a lightning bolt earthed itself up on the mountain behind the villa. 'Throw Haston over the wall.'

A split-second later, a thunderbolt let rip, shaking the flag-stones beneath our feet.

Kate didn't move a muscle.

Incredulous, I backed away from her, inadvertently kicking Max's remote-control car up against the wall.

Yannis seized me by the arm and threw me forwards.

'*Ella, malaka!*' he snarled. 'Englishman ... you can beat a woman.'

Taking a few steps to his right, Grigoris crossed behind Kate towards the wall and raised his pistol.

Over by the French windows, Ricky continued to train his lens on Kate.

Catching my eye, she began to advance on me.

Squinting into the sheeting rain, I wheeled slowly around to my left, inching past the terrace wall, eyes trained on Kate's hands, which were held out before her like a praying mantis.

Kate also began to circle, crossing with her back to the table, maintaining a steady distance of about six feet ...

Until we had swapped positions.

A few feet to my right, Grigoris stood with his back to the terrace wall, his gun pointed at my head.

Behind Kate, Yannis slowly tossed his knife from hand to hand.

'This isn't a disco, motherfuckers,' Ricky drawled. 'Action!'

Then came a blinding flash of lightning directly overhead.

A split-second later, the villa was plunged into darkness.

I caught the first syllables of Ricky's swearing, before thunder drowned out the rest.

Throwing myself to the ground, I rolled to my immediate right, hoping to knock Grigoris off his feet.

But he'd moved.

Suddenly, a brace of gunshots ripped through the night.

Deafened, I rolled back to my left and scrambled under the table.

Through the whistling of the wind, I detected a gurgling sound coming from the end of the terrace where Kate had been stood, just before the power had cut. As I raised my head from the waterlogged flagstones, I began to make out a figure lying prostrate in the shadows.

A sustained flicker of lightning revealed it wasn't Kate.

Clutching at his throat, Yannis lay convulsing. Squirting from his neck, a dark trail of liquid amassed in a thick pool in the guttering.

No sign of Kate.

Or Grigoris . . .

Or Ricky.

Ears still ringing from the percussion, I held my position as Yannis breathed his last; the spasmodic lightning display throwing his shadow in all directions about the terrace.

From inside the villa, two further shots rang out.

Then a third.

Recoiling further back under the table, I suddenly realised that they hadn't come from the sitting room . . . or the landing. They'd been fired at some distance.

Downstairs.

Squeezing out from under the table, I charged across the terrace, past the dying Yannis, and ducked through the French windows into the villa, twisting and turning my way through the clumps of furniture – my path intermittently illuminated by the lightning.

Reaching the door, I paused, waited for a thunderclap, then swung it open.

As I pushed out onto the landing, there came a clang of something metallic, followed by a high-pitched scream.

Amara . . .

Then a rapid exchange of male voices.

Another shriek – Max, this time.

'Let him go!' howled Amara, her voice faint, but clearly recognisable.

Her cry was abruptly cut off, followed by a dull thud.

'Mommy!' cried Max.

Then he too was silenced.

I had no weapon – nothing with which to arm myself . . .

But I went anyway, crashing down the stairs to the landing below, peering into the darkness for signs of Ricky or Grigoris.

As I approached the bannister to get a clearer view of the floor below, an arm shot out and clamped over my mouth.

'Don't make a sound!'

It was Kate.

'Ricky's downstairs,' she hissed. 'He's got the boy.'

Dropping her hand from my mouth, she beckoned me forwards to the railing.

A pulse of lightning flooded the hallway, revealing the front entrance to be open . . . and two bodies. One was lying twisted on the ground by the entrance to the basement, the other was slumped against the wall by the open front door to the villa.

'Albertos,' whispered Kate, pointing to the man by the door. 'Grigoris is by the basement.

'Are they dead?'

'Grigoris – yes,' she murmured. 'Albertos has a shoulder wound . . . and concussion from his fall.'

'Ricky?'

'In the kitchen with Max.' She leant in closer to my ear. 'Amara is in the cellar.'

I'd heard Amara scream . . . that thud.

'She's not . . .?'

'Ricky pushed her down the stairwell,' Kate said, drawing back from the railing and turning to face the stairs. 'That's all I saw.'

I peered down into the hallway, waiting for my eyes to adjust to the dark. The constant strobe of lightning made it impossible for my eyes to calibrate.

'Why didn't Ricky run out into the forest?' I whispered.

Kate leaned back in to me. 'Because Albertos has Grigoris's gun.'

Which was why Ricky had gone to the kitchen – to find a weapon.

'He's waiting for Albertos to pass out,' Kate added.

Twisting around, I craned my neck and gazed up into the shadows on the landing above.

'What do we do?' I muttered, wondering if Ricky kept a weapon of some kind in his bedroom.

'We wait for him to make the first move.'

Then she shuffled backwards and leaned her head against the wall, revealing Yannis's hunting knife clutched in her right hand.

I followed suit and sat back against the cool terracotta.

'How did Albertos get in?' I murmured. 'The door was locked.'

'He must have cut the power from the outside. Besnik will have opened the door to start the generator . . .'

'How did he get here?'

'On foot. Through the forest.'

A good job, too. Had he come by road, he'd have run into Elias.

'No other back up?'

Kate shook her head. 'Too dangerous – word might have got back to Ricky.'

'There's a shotgun down there somewhere,' I continued. 'In the storeroom, to the right of the main entrance. Besnik had it last night when we arrived.'

Kate turned to me, her drawn features briefly visible as another bolt of lightning struck the mountainside.

'You're sure of that?'

I nodded.

'Not in the kitchen?'

True – it could have been in the kitchen.

'Ricky may already have it,' Kate said dismissively, raking her fingers through her wet hair.

Unlikely, I thought. He would have used it by now.

'So, where's Besnik?' I added.

'Good question.' Kate sidled in closer; a faint scent of citrus hugging her t-shirt. 'Ricky ordered him to open up the basement and bring out Max. He could still be down there with Amara. Or maybe he's done a runner.'

Then came a shuffling sound from downstairs.

Moving as one, Kate and I shot over to the railing and peered down into the hallway.

Albertos had slid further down the wall; the pistol in his hand now momentarily visible.

'And if we make it out of here,' Kate began, without turning to me, 'you're good for the money? Amara's inheritance?'

'Of course.'

I hadn't spoken with Amara, but I couldn't see why she wouldn't be prepared to part with the money if it meant saving her son's life – not to mention her own.

'Because, if not – I'm walking out of that door,' Kate added.

All of a sudden, the power came back on and the hallway was flooded with light.

Kate and I shot back to the wall, squeezing ourselves out of sight from below.

There came a clanking sound from the kitchen . . . followed by a prolonged creak.

'Is there another door to the kitchen?' whispered Kate, knife at the ready.

I shook my head. 'No idea.'

A muffled groan drifted up from the hallway.

Albertos . . .

'Let's go,' Kate hissed. 'Stay behind me.'

As she began to descend the stairs, Besnik appeared, dripping wet, in the entrance of the front doorway.

Then a shout from beneath us.

'Is he breathing?' came Ricky's rasping voice. 'Besnik! Is the fucker alive?'

Kate and I froze.

Besnik hesitated, then bent down to Albertos and nudged him.

Pulling his gun hand away, Albertos rolled onto his left side and lashed out with a kick in Besnik's direction.

Which was when the old butler finally spotted us.

At the same moment, Albertos raised his gun in the direction of Ricky's voice.

'Take his fucking pistol!' roared the Australian, still out of view.

'Mommy!' screamed Max, before being muted yet again.

As Besnik tussled half-heartedly with Albertos, Kate shot down the stairs.

Following close on her heels, I saw Ricky begin to drag Max out across the hallway. But when he spied Kate and me descending the staircase, he turned and disappeared into the shadows once more.

'He's taking the elevator!' I yelled.

Sure enough, as we hit the last steps, there came a mechanical grinding noise.

Ricky was already on his way up with Max.

'Get back!' barked Kate, flying across the hallway and landing a kick in Besnik's groin. 'Haston – take the knife!'

As the old man doubled up and dropped to the floor, the basement door opened with a grating creak, revealing a bedraggled Amara, hovering uncertain on the top step.

Had Besnik left it open after bringing Max out for Ricky?

'Here – take it!' snapped Kate, thrusting Yannis's knife at me as she pulled the gun free of Albertos's grasp. 'Take care of Amara. I'll go after Ricky and Max.'

'No,' I shot back, closing in on Kate. 'He's my son.'

'You should stay here.'

330

'Give me the gun!' I snapped. 'I'd be useless with a fuck-ing knife.'

Emitting a cry, Amara hitched up her dress and lurched out of the basement entrance.

'Stay back!' bellowed Kate twisting round to her right.

Lunging forwards, I snatched the weapon out of Kate's hand and headed back to the staircase.

'Get back here!' yelled Kate.

'Max!' screamed Amara, setting off after me. 'My baby!'

Out of my peripheral vision I saw Kate grab her by the waist and pull her to the floor.

'Check the safety catch!' Kate called out after me, as she strove to pin down the struggling Amara.

'Find the shotgun!' I yelled back, leaping up the steps two at a time.

The elevator was still running.

Ricky was heading for the top floor . . .

Lungs burning, I continued my ascent up the twisting staircase.

'Kill the power!' I cried out, as I hit the second-floor landing.

Rounding the bend in the staircase, I looked down in time to see Kate release Amara before seizing Besnik by his shirt collar and thrusting him back in the direction of the front door. Besnik, however, threw a quick look back to Amara then veered off to his left, towards the storeroom.

'Is quicker – this way,' he yelled, arms flailing above his head as if expecting Kate to slash him at any moment. 'Come!'

Turning away, I continued up the stairs to the third floor.

A quick glance along the landing confirmed the elevator had already arrived.

Ricky must have gone into the sitting room.

To the terrace.

Seconds later, the power went off and darkness resumed.

Ignoring the scuffling sounds drifting up from the hallway,

I crept forwards, pushed open the sitting room door ... then froze.

Backlit by the moon, which had broken through the scudding clouds to the south, Ricky stood on the terrace, Max held tight in his grasp.

'Fancy a chat?' Ricky called out, backing away from the French windows. 'Come on over.'

Max stood rigid, hands clutching at the sides of his t-shirt, his head twisted towards where Yannis lay prone on the flagstones.

'Bring Amara too, why don't you,' Ricky added. 'Make it a family affair.'

Staying low, I weaved my way through the sitting room to the open French windows.

'Uh, uh ... that's close enough, matey,' Ricky snapped. 'Don't make me do anything stupid.'

Inching to my left, I moved into the gap between the open doors.

Slowly, I raised my pistol and aimed it at Ricky's head.

'You wouldn't dare,' Ricky jeered, dropping down to Max's height and clamping his hand over the boy's mouth.

He was right – it was too much of a risk.

'Now what?' I murmured, aiming off six inches to the right of Max's head.

'Dunno about you, matey,' he drawled, 'but I say we shoot the breeze and wait for Elias to show up with his AK-47. Like I told ya, he's been gagging to use it.'

'You think Elias heard the gunshots?' I countered. 'Not a chance, with all that thunder.'

'Sod the thunder,' Ricky exclaimed. 'I radioed the guy.'

Reaching into his pocket, he produced a walkie talkie.

'You're bluffing,' I said.

When had he had time to radio for help?

'Talk to him yourself,' Ricky replied, holding out the walkie talkie. 'Go ahead.'

I didn't move.

As he slipped the radio back in his pocket, I scanned the terrace, wondering if there was any other way up from the floor below.

Not without a ladder.

'Jump,' snarled Ricky, 'and the boy lives.'

'Not sure I believe you,' I murmured, creeping forwards over the sodden paving.

If Elias arrived by car, Kate would hear him ... she'd intercept him.

Although, what good would a hunting knife be against a semi-automatic rifle?

Ricky took a step to his right.

'Not a fucking millimetre closer,' he snapped, still keeping his head low. 'Jump. Save the kid ... And his mother.'

There came a scraping noise from the sitting room behind me.

Turning to my right, I saw a shadow slip past the table in between the leather chairs.

Ricky too had heard the sound, and promptly backed up closer to the wall.

In an instant, Kate was at my side, brandishing Yannis's knife.

Ricky grinned. 'Steady, bitch. One foot closer and the boy goes over the edge.'

'You wouldn't do that,' I said, stepping out onto the water-logged terrace. 'Not to your own son.'

Ricky's head popped up an inch higher behind the trembling boy.

'Funny, Haston.'

'Amara lied to you,' I continued, moving away from Kate and passing in front of the table. 'She lied to me too.' I stopped and lowered the pistol. 'Her father only put my name on the birth certificate because he didn't want the world to know the truth ... that Max had been sired by a murderer.'

Ricky stood still, unblinking.

'Max is your son,' I insisted, creeping forwards. 'You're prepared to kill your own flesh and blood?'

'Bullshit.'

Ricky took a step backwards, closer to the wall.

'I'm warning you, mate,' he snarled. 'Keep coming at me, and this nipper's going to learn how to fly.'

It was all bluster – he was hanging on for Elias.

'You're gonna kill your only legacy?' I murmured, eyeballing him.

Ricky grinned. 'If he's my legacy, why are you so keen to save the little runt?'

'Let him go!' I roared.

'Jump – and I will.'

Over by the French windows, Kate stepped out onto the terrace and began to inch around to her left in the direction of Yannis's corpse.

'Stay there!' Ricky yelled, twisting towards Kate.

'You won't do it,' I hissed. 'The minute you let go of Max, you know you're getting a bullet in the head.'

'Checked the safety's off?' Ricky scoffed. 'Won't work otherwise.'

I still couldn't get a clear shot.

Kate continued to advance, crossing behind Yannis's body towards the wall.

'You want me to prove he's your son?' I said, throwing a glance to Kate.

As Ricky's eyes darted over to Kate, I made a sudden lunge in his direction.

Recoiling involuntarily, he stepped on Max's remote-control car.

Before he could open his mouth, the toy skidded from under his feet, causing him to topple.

'Get down, Max! I screamed, as Ricky's hand slipped away from the boy's face.

334

As the terror-stricken Max ducked, Ricky regained his balance and stood upright ... his body now fully exposed.

I raised the gun and squeezed the trigger.

Click.

The chamber wasn't loaded.

Ramming back the slide, I took a second shot.

The air exploded.

Ricky jerked backwards ...

But the bullet had landed wide of the mark, passing through his collar bone.

As Max screamed and dropped to the flagstones, Ricky stared at me in disbelief, his hand clutching at the blood oozing through his t-shirt.

I raised the gun once more and fired.

But the magazine was empty.

With a puzzled frown stitched across his brow, Ricky prodded a finger at his wound.

For a split-second, it occurred to me that I should keep him alive – deliver him to the police. But then, out of the corner of my eye, I saw Max, curled up in a foetal position, clawing at his ears as he whimpered on the terrace floor.

Meeting Ricky's gaze, I advanced across the flagstones until I could feel his hot breath on my face.

He rocked back on his heels, one arm outstretched to maintain equilibrium, and broke into a twisted grin.

'Fuckin' pussy,' he croaked. 'Can't even shoot straight.'

Reaching out, I calmly placed my hand over his face and pushed.

Without a sound, he fell backwards onto the wall and flipped feet-first over the edge.

Seconds later, there came a distant crack as his body struck the rocks a hundred and fifty feet below.

As I stared, trembling, at the empty space where the man had stood, I caught a sudden movement to my left.

Elias.

Armed with an automatic rifle, he hovered at the French windows, scanning the terrace for Ricky. When he saw me, he raised his weapon to his shoulder.

'Get down, Kate!' I screamed, throwing myself to the ground behind the table.

Elias swung his rifle around and pointed it at the back of Kate's head.

The latter spun on her heels, then froze.

Too late.

A gunshot ripped the air apart.

Except, Kate remained standing.

As if in slow motion, Elias was jettisoned through the doorway, his chest exploding in a fine mist of blood, before collapsing on Yannis's corpse, where he began to twitch, his limbs intertwined with the dead Albanian.

Behind him, Amara stepped up to the French windows, Besnik's shotgun in her hands.

With a strangled cry, Max hauled himself off the sodden flagstones and staggered over to his mother, as Besnik appeared from the sitting room behind her.

Thrusting the still-smoking shotgun at the old man, Amara fell to her knees and gathered Max into her arms, while, after a quick check of Elias's pulse, Kate approached the terrace wall and gazed down into the abyss.

I lay the pistol on the table and stumbled over to Amara and Max.

Rising unsteadily to her feet, the former took my hand.

'Forgive me,' she croaked, her head falling against my chest. 'This is all my fault.'

Under my feet, Max pulled himself out of the rainwater and, encircling his mother's waist with his little arms, buried his face in her dress.

'How could this possibly be your fault?' I objected, tightening my grip around her quivering frame as the acrid smell of cordite drifted across the terrace.

How good it was finally to hold her.

To feel her.

'I should have told you right from the start,' she continued. 'None of this would have happened.'

Brushing her hair from her face, I placed a kiss on her cheek.

'You had your reasons – I understand.'

She gave a vigorous shake of her head. 'But you do not understand at all.'

Pushing herself off my chest, she glanced down at Max sobbing into her stomach.

'I was already pregnant,' she continued, stroking her son's matted hair. 'When we had our night on Naxos.'

I stared at her, dumbfounded.

Slowly, she lifted her chin and peered out into the abyss.

'Max's real father is down there,' she whispered. 'At the bottom of the cliffs.'

Epilogue

Kate and I spent the remainder of that night burying Ricky, along with Yannis, at the bottom of the rocky slope. Having fought our way down through the forest with a pickaxe and shovel, we had no choice but to carry the bodies away from the rock-fall to the more pliable sandstone further down the valley, where we eventually succeeded in digging a single grave for both. Back at the villa, meanwhile, Amara helped Besnik dress Albertos's wounds. Kate had been right – the bullet had gone straight through his shoulder; but there was considerable ligament damage, and he'd developed delayed concussion due to his fall. It was Max, however, who was suffering the most. Traumatised by his horrific ordeal, he had become mute. Communicating only with head and hand gestures, he remained glued to his mother's side.

The next morning, Amara made a phone call to Takis, who, without asking any questions, organised the transfer of a million dollars to an unnamed bank account of Kate's choice. The remaining part of her vastly reduced fee – thanks, primarily, to Amara saving her life – was drawn from Ricky's bank account, of which Takis was also executor: a further half-million dollars. For this payment, Kate agreed to dispose of the bodies of

Grigoris and Elias, which she bundled into the back of their own Mercedes van, the morning of their departure. When I asked how she'd get rid of the evidence, she suggested it was best I remain ignorant. As for Albertos's flesh wound, he assured me he knew people on the island who would be able to help, no questions asked.

After they had departed, Amara and I spent two days helping Besnik get the villa cleaned and back in order, and, in doing so, found over a hundred and fifty thousand dollars in cash under Ricky's mattress. We decided then and there that Besnik should retain it for his own use.

On the morning of the third day, I put in a call to Olympic airlines and booked Max, Amara and myself on a flight to Athens. A second phone call to Takis, before leaving, established that he would go to Zakynthos and clear up the villa. It was also decided, out of Max's earshot, that the line we would take on Xander – for everyone's benefit, including the boy – was that he jumped out of the car while on holiday in Zakynthos and simply never came back; his drink and drugs problem having finally got the better of him. Kate had assured us that Xander's body would have been properly disposed of by her colleagues who'd decided to take his life – a decision she had not been in agreement with at the time, she insisted.

Going through Ricky's drawers, Amara discovered numerous fake passports, along with the title deeds to the villa – in which it was revealed that the property had been bought under one of Ricky's pseudonyms and the ownership later transferred to Besnik. The old butler himself was oblivious of the fact; we explained that Ricky would have done it to ensure there was no paper trail that might one day come back to haunt him.

On the afternoon of the third day, a taxi came to collect us and take us to Larnaca airport. Shaking hands under the portico entrance to the ancient villa, we said goodbye to Besnik, now

339

the proud owner of the house his family had served in for over a century, and which I hope never to visit again.

I stayed ten days in Athens, during which time I helped Amara organise her affairs, as well as find a psychotherapist for Max, knowing it was possible our story might have to come to the attention of the authorities. The counsellor we chose assured us, on our initial introduction, that there was no legal requirement to inform the police of past crimes their client had been involved in – either as perpetrator, or victim. However, being a minor, they would have to make an evaluation as to whether or not Max had suffered abuse, or neglect, at our own hands. We agreed to start Max's course, accepting that there might come a point when we'd have to report what had happened to the police. I also re-took a paternity test, at Amara's insistence; the results of which confirmed that Max was indeed not my son.

On my return to the UK, I turned down the offer of teaching English in Japan for a year, choosing instead to work for a local painting and decorating firm. Six weeks later, in September, Amara decided that, with no ties in Greece other than her half-brother, Takis, she and Max needed a fresh start. In mid-October, they moved to England, renting a flat two streets away from where Vince and I lived in Putney.

Max's Greek therapist facilitated a handover with a colleague of his based in London, and Max continued with his course of psychotherapy – as did Amara and I, who were now also undergoing weekly counselling. By the beginning of November, Max was talking again and gradually returning to his former self. We hoped that by the autumn of the following year – assuming that, in the interim, we wouldn't be forced to report our experiences to the police and undergo investigations, possibly back in Greece – the boy might be well enough to enrol in the local junior school overlooking Putney Bridge and the Thames.

Amara employed a full-time nanny to help her in the house,

but held off looking for work until her son was back in school. She then hoped to rekindle her prospects of a career in acting. Amara and I also made the decision between us that Max would not need to learn of his father's true identity until he asked; most likely, after many more years of therapy.

Three months after their move to the UK, Amara and I started dating. Although we remained living in different houses, she and Max would frequently come over for Sunday dinner at the flat. I'd fed my flatmate Vince a heavily doctored version of the truth – that Amara had been left by her husband and was hoping to start afresh in a new country – and he honoured his word in never prying, no matter how much he'd had to drink. Indeed, he was instrumental in always brightening their day whenever they visited, and proved an excellent playfellow for Max.

In January 1995, while still working for the decorating firm in Putney, I began the application process for the Foreign Office. Amara, meanwhile, had started up with acting classes; now that Max was happy to be left alone for a couple of hours a day with the hired help – and sometimes even Vince.

One night in early February, Vince called me from work to say he was bringing a friend home for dinner. Would I be out? I had just had an argument with Amara, who was resisting taking up the offer of a front-of house job at the Lyceum Theatre in Piccadilly (she felt it was too early to be away from Max for so long at night) and I was in need of my old mate's company. Vince confessed he was in fact hoping I'd be home, as he had something to celebrate.

That evening, when I heard the keys turn in the lock, I uncorked a bottle of red wine and approached the front entrance to welcome him and his guest.

The door swung open to reveal Vince in his trench coat, a huge grin slapped across his face. 'Drumroll, please . . .' he

341

began, with a theatrical flourish, stepping off the path into the rose bushes.

A woman slipped out from behind him, hands clasped in front of her.

Sporting a Laura Ashley dress and fur coat, it took me a moment to recognise her.

Partly because her hair had grown and been dyed back to its original colour.

'Kate and I have decided to give it another go,' said Vince, with a self-satisfied smirk. 'Thought you'd approve.'

'I gather Greece was a success,' she purred, breaking into a smile. 'Can't wait to hear.'

I stared at her, thunderstruck, as Vince closed the door and ushered us back along the hallway.

'Don't look so surprised, mate,' he crowed, pulling off her fur coat. 'They always come back.'

'Don't make me change my mind,' said Kate, flicking Vince on the arm.

As Vince hurried off down the hallway, clutching Kate's fur coat and the bottle of wine, the latter turned back to me and held out her hand.

Speechless, I automatically reached out and shook it.

'Good to see you, Alistair,' she said, with a nod of the head.

Then she leaned in for the kiss.

After a brief hesitation, I too, leaned in and we air-kissed, cheek to cheek.

'That's more like it,' she said approvingly. 'A bit formal, the ol' handshake.'

Then she sashayed off into the flat to join Vince.

Which was when I realised she'd passed me a folded slip of paper.

Once she was out of sight, I opened it up. Scrawled across the scrap was a single line.

'I need a favour'.

Acknowledgements

I'm immensely grateful to Kate and Sarah Beal at Muswell Press for their continued belief in my writing, and also for their ceaseless encouragement, support and expertise in bringing *Second Skin* to fruition. I'd also like to thank Laura McFarlane for her laser-sharp editorial skills, and the phenomenal Fiona Brownlee, of Brownlee Donald Associates, for her belief and drive in marketing Second Skin. An enormous thank you also, to Charles Cumming and Helen Lederer, for their kind words of praise for the novel. Huge thanks also to Jo Stone-Fewings, Anna Montoro, Steven Arrell and Susan Washtell, who read early drafts of Second Skin, and whose observations helped shaped its outcome; and also to my chief champion, my wife Penny, for her boundless support, belief and patience along each step of the journey. Finally, I remain indebted to my mentor, friend, and agent Jeff Ourvan, of the Jennifer Lyons Literary Agency. Without Jeff's skill, tenacity and commitment, both *The Lizard* and *Second Skin* would have stayed locked away in a 'work-in-progress' file on my laptop.